Dearly Beloved

by

Peggy Jaeger

A Match Made in Heaven, Book 1

This is a work of fiction. Names, characters, places, and incidents are either the product of the author's imagination or are used fictitiously, and any resemblance to actual persons living or dead, business establishments, events, or locales, is entirely coincidental.

Dearly Beloved

Cover Art by *Diana Carlile*

The Wild Rose Press, Inc.
PO Box 708
Adams Basin, NY 14410-0708
Visit us at www.thewildrosepress.com

Publishing History
First Champagne Rose Edition, 2018
Print ISBN 978-1-5092-2362-6
Digital ISBN 978-1-5092-2366-4

A Match Made in Heaven, Book 1
Published in the United States of America

"Isabella has never referred to you that way." Good gracious, was that my voice? It sounded like an army of frogs had invaded the back of my throat. "But it's nice to meet you, Mr. Harrington."

"Slade is fine." He folded his hands into his trouser pockets.

If my voice mimicked web-toed croaking amphibians, his sounded like a lazy morning after a night packed with warm Irish whiskey and scorching sex.

Deep toned and low, with a scratch of gravel and a tiny smolder of smoke, those three words almost made me respond, "Slade is *way* more than fine," but I kept my thoughts to myself and indicated the chairs.

Dedication

For Shanel and Isaiah—
it was your beautiful wedding that sparked the idea
for me to write an out-of-town wedding series.
Blessings and Happiness on you both, for always.

Books from Peggy Jaeger

The MacQuire Women Series
The Voices of Angels
Passion's Palette
Skater's Waltz
There's No Place Like home
First Impressions

The San Valentino Family
3 Wishes (A Candy Hearts Romance)
A Kiss Under the Christmas Lights
Christmas and Cannolis (coming December 2018)

A Match Made in Heaven Series
Dearly Beloved, Book 1

The Deerbourne Inn Series
Hope's Dream (available November 2018)

Chapter One

"9-1-1! Colleen, I've got a 9-1-1 in the Bawl Room!"

I cringed at the crisis call blaring through my earpiece. I hated emergency calls, especially when everything was about to start. To pull off the perfect wedding, just like when invading an enemy country during wartime, you have to run on a strict, unbendable time schedule. There was no room for deviation. A 9-1-1 call was the equivalent of a ticking time bomb, set to blow up the whole operation.

"On my way," I said. "Any bloodshed?"

"None so far," my assistant Charity Quinlan replied, her small voice breathless with urgency. "But it's coming. Get here. I don't know how much longer I can keep them from killing one another."

I shot from my command post at the back of my hometown church in Heaven, New Hampshire, and sprinted down the long corridor toward the kid's section, affectionately known as the Bawl Room, which was the staging area for the soon-to-start wedding I was in charge of. The small space was given this moniker because it was where parents of unruly children shuttled their little miscreants when their behavior disrupted the congregation during Mass. My sisters and I had been banished to the room every Sunday of our childhood.

I took a calming breath in front of the closed

door—a door that did nothing to muffle shrill, raised, and angry voices—and ran a hand across my quaking abdominal muscles. They'd been throbbing and pulsing like a precision quartz timepiece from the confining, belly-flattening, spandex undergarment I wore to mask the extra eight pounds I'd recently packed on.

I said a silent prayer to St. Gabriel, the patron saint of strength. "Breathe," I whispered, making it a plea. "Just breathe."

Placing a broad smile across my face, I pushed through the door and entered into a tempest I regarded as the tenth circle of Hell: ex-wives.

Two lavishly dressed women—one in her fifties, the other ten years younger, and both trying desperately to look in their thirties—stood, dyed stiletto to dyed stiletto, glaring at one another. Both had fisted hands planted on their hips, shoulders hunched, perfectly coiffed heads bent, ready to do battle.

"Who do you think you are?" one screeched at the other. "You're not her mother. You're nobody in this wedding, just my ex's current squeeze of the second, so back the hell off. Now!"

The woman being shrilled at, all six foot of her in icepick heels, leaned forward and pulled her outlined, lipstick-enhanced mouth back into a perfect teeth-baring snarl. She jabbed one of her french-manicured tips at her aggressor and ground out, "I've been married to him longer than you were, bitch, and you know it, so who you calling squeeze of the second, because from where I'm standing, you were more like a mistake who got knocked up than a wife any day of the week."

The elder of the two was set to pounce, aiming for her rival's perfect camera-ready face so I did a quick little jog and insinuated myself between them.

"Ladies." My gaze ping-ponged from one to the other. "Please. The wedding is about to begin. We can't have this kind of behavior."

"She started it," the actual mother of the bride, Mary Ann Stively said, pointing at her ex-husband's current wife. "She says she should go down the aisle after me because she's married to my loser ex—"

"Who's the father of the bride," JoEllen, wife number two, said. She turned her back on wife one and faced me. "You're the wedding planner, Colleen. You know proper protocol says I should go down the aisle right before the party, since I'm married to the father of the bride. I looked it up, read all about wedding etiquette and procedures."

"In what? Your current edition from slut-of-the-month book club?" Mary Ann spat.

JoEllen's eyes slitted under penciled eyebrows standing stationary on her unlined and unmoving forehead, a paralytic effect—I surmised—from years of Botox injections.

"Why, you—" She inched forward and tried to reach by me, but eight years of track in school and four more in college gave me a decided advantage in swiftness. I blocked her, my arms splaying out at my sides so she couldn't go around me.

My left eye started to twitch—never a good sign—and I knew I had to set this situation to rights. *Now.* The wedding was scheduled to begin in less than ten minutes.

"Mrs. Stively." Both women stared at me. "Um, the current Mrs. Stively."

JoEllen pulled herself up to her towering height

and gave her paid-for breasts a good forward thrust. "What?"

"I know you feel you deserve to walk down right before the wedding party—"

"I do."

"—but I'm sorry. Whatever you've read stating that was the correct procession is incorrect. The actual mother of the bride is the one who immediately precedes the party. Unless, of course she's not present or deceased. Then it would be proper for a stepmother to be the last person down the aisle before the attendants and bride."

JoEllen slanted a deathly glare at Mary Ann. I swear I could hear her brain running through scenarios on how to commit murder in the next five minutes.

"Now, I need you both to take your places so we can get this wedding started. Stop arguing and let's go."

I'd dealt with these two overbearing women many times in the past few months and knew neither would give an inch, or relinquish control, of their own accord. Since they continued to stand rock-still, daggers zipping between them, I did what I always do in situations like this and got physical.

I grabbed the first Mrs. Stively firmly by the forearm and gave her a good yank while motioning to Charity, who'd been cowering behind a pew, to do the same to Stively spouse number two.

Charity, at a spit above five foot, was no match for the lengthy, stilettoed second wife, but what she lacked in height, she more than made up for in determination. With a firm hand draped along JoEllen's back, Charity began walking, propelling the woman forward.

"Can you believe that bitch?" Mary Ann asked as I

escorted her down the long hallway to the back of the church where the bridal party waited. I continued to hold her forearm in a grip of steel in the event she planned to escape and go back to punch her replacement.

"Forget JoEllen," I commanded. "It's your daughter's day. Focus on her. You don't want Annie to remember this day filled with problems or fights. You want her to have the most wonderful memories of her wedding, don't you?"

Before she could reply, I steamrolled right over her. "Of course you do. Fighting with JoEllen serves no purpose and will only upset Annie. Take a quick, deep breath if she annoys you again and ignore her. Believe me, you'll feel better for it."

I knew I was telling a bald-faced lie.

Mary Ann and JoEllen both wanted to scratch the other's eyes out, and today's incident was another in a long line of antagonistic outbreaks since Annie had retained me as her wedding planner. The two Stively wives despised one another for various and obvious reasons. Their only compatible redeeming value was their mutual unconditional love for the bride-to-be.

In the vestibule, the melodic strings of a Mozart concerto serenaded the waiting congregation.

Annie Stively's parents had spared no expense on their cherished only daughter. From a twenty-thousand-dollar, custom-made, hand-stitched, lace and satin gown complete with a five-thousand-dollar tiara and train, to the five-hundred-dollar-an-hour stretch limousine waiting outside the church entrance, prepared to whisk the happy couple off to their reception a mere five minutes away, Dr. and the two Mrs. Stivelys set out to give their little princess everything she desired in a wedding.

With my help, they had.

"Mom? JoEllen? What's going on?" The bride glanced from her mother to her stepmother, concern creasing her flawless brow.

"A few last-minute details we needed to go over," I answered before either woman could. "They wanted everything to be perfect for you. It's all settled now, correct, ladies?" With an arched and determined glare, I all but dared them to contradict me.

Both women, with uncharacteristic placidity, nodded.

"Good. Now, let's get you all lined up, and we can get this beautiful girl married."

I went into command mode, corralled the wedding party into their appropriate places, and gave the all-start command. "Let's roll."

Once the bridal party was in place around the altar and the two warring Mrs. Stivelys were seated, I gave the command for the violinists to start and Johann Pachelbel's *Canon in D* drifted through the air.

I stood behind one door, Charity the other. On my count, we threw open the doors wide at the same time. A collective wave of sighs blew through the church as the first view of the stunning bride broke through. While she floated up the aisle on her father's arm, my photographer darted ahead of them, filming, as they slowly made their way to the altar. Charity and I closed the doors behind us and slipped into the last pew to watch the wedding.

At the front of the church, Dr. Stively stopped, lifted his daughter's veil, and then kissed her cheek. I could hear dueling sniffling from the front pew, Mom and Stepmother each trying to outdo the other in the waterworks department. Once Dr. Stively took his seat between his first and second wives, the congregation sat as a unit.

"Did you check to make sure the best man has the rings?" I asked Charity, looking toward the stable of tuxedoed ushers at the altar. The groom's younger brother looked as if last night's bachelor party had been a rousing success, evidenced by the pasty tinge to his skin, the railroad track redness covering the whites of his eyes, and the none-too-subtle tremor in his hands.

"He does," Charity replied.

"Did Devon bring the basket with the bird seed?"

"He did."

Off to one side of the altar, I spied my trusty and talented photographer being as unobtrusive as possible while he captured the happy event through his lens.

"Kolby has everything he needs?"

"He does."

When I slanted her a look, Charity grinned. "And before you ask, I already called the inn. Everything is ready. The champagne is chilling, and the band is warming up. Maureen told me to tell you not to fret. She's got it all covered. No worries."

Two of the most overused and least accurate words in the English language, especially when speaking about a wedding.

With as deep a breath as I could manage (I really was going to throw in the towel with this pseudo-girdle and cut back on the carbs instead), I sat back and watched the ceremony I'd put together, and prayed the rest of the day would go on without any further problems or arguments between warring family factions.

What's that old saying? *Man makes plans and God laughs?*

Yeah…the story of my life.

****

Eons later, I collapsed onto one of the comfortable sofas in the inn's library.

"I think I've aged five years today." I kicked my shoes off and plopped my feet up on the ottoman. Flexing and extending my toes to get some circulation back into them, I glanced out the huge bay window across from me to view the inky darkness engulfing the inn.

"What time is it?" I asked Charity.

My assistant was supine on a neighboring couch, her tiny, shoeless feet elevated on the arm panel. "Almost midnight."

"I'm turning into a pumpkin right now. I'm beyond bushed."

"Breakfast is at eight," Charity reminded me. "Are you staying here tonight or going home?"

"She's staying here," Maureen announced from the doorway. My youngest sister leaned against the doorjamb, a dishtowel in her hands. "You're not driving home when you're this tired," she said to me. "You can crash here too, if you want," she offered Charity.

"I'm good, Mo, thanks. I've got a ride." The little pixie sat up, stretched her arms over her head, and yawned. "Devon's driving me home as soon as he's finished cleaning up the bar."

"He's done," Maureen said. She came into the room and sat down next to me. "He's saying good night to the crew."

"Kolby still here?" I hadn't seen my photographer since the wedding cake had been cut more than two hours ago.

Maureen grinned. "I just saw him in the kitchen, charming some leftovers from Sarah."

"He doesn't need to charm Sarah into anything," Charity said, her perfect little mouth turned down at the corners. "She'd lie down in the street and make like pavement for him if he asked."

One of my sister's delicate auburn eyebrows elevated a tad, but she kept silent. I was about to question the origin of Charity's snarkiness but stopped when my weekend helper slash part-time bartender came into the room.

"Hey, kid, ready to go?" Devon Church asked Charity.

She bounced off the couch and grabbed her shoes. "Do you want help in the morning?" she asked me while slipping into them.

"No. I'm good. Sleep in and enjoy your day off. Both of you. This is the last weekend we're not double booked until after the holidays. Get some rest now, because you're gonna need it."

Theatrical moans blew from them both.

When I was alone with my sister, she gave voice to the question that had been running through my mind for a while.

"What's going on with Charity and Kolby?"

"I don't know. They've been circling around one another for the past month or so. It's weird."

"Nothing happened between them? No fight or…something else?"

"Honestly, I don't want to ask. As long as they do their jobs, which they have been, I don't care if they've had a disagreement. I have enough to manage on a daily basis with running the business and looking after Nanny Fee. I don't want to add worrying about warring employees to the mix."

Maureen stayed silent, something she was good at. The old expression "still waters run deep" described the baby of my family to a T.

"Come on." She stood. "Let's get to bed. I've got to be up at five to start cooking for all these people, and I need at least three hours sleep so I don't fall into the oatmeal."

I lifted my arms, and she tugged me up.

"I can't feel my feet."

With a chuckle, she slipped her arm around my shoulders and walked me to the back staircase, toward her private apartment. "I have zero sympathy for you, sis. You know nothing good comes from wearing those ridiculous shoes."

"But they're so pretty," I said. Okay, I'll admit, it was more of a whine than an actual declaration. We'd had this discussion too many times before, and I wasn't in the mood to debate the value of heels with a woman who thought modern shoe design began and ended with flip-flops.

Washed and clad in an old, faded T-shirt I found in Maureen's dresser, I climbed into the bed in her guest room fifteen minutes later and sighed.

I'd moved my wedding planner business from Manhattan to my hometown a little over a year ago after the death of my younger sister Eileen, Maureen's twin, from breast cancer. I'd been based in New York, and when Eileen got sick, I'd shuttled back and forth to Heaven weekly to help my sisters in any way I could. With business obligations, employees to take care of, and a gone-south personal relationship, it had been a trying time.

Maureen and Eileen, identical twins, owned and operated Inn Heaven, a sprawling Victorian mansion they'd bought for a song and turned into a successful bed and breakfast three years ago, right before Eileen's diagnosis. My older sister Cathleen also resides in Heaven. She's a lawyer and the town's justice of the peace, a profession she inherited from our father, Judge Fintan O'Dowd, when he retired from the bench.

The loss of our sister from the devastating disease had torn my family apart. My parents, unable to stand living in the same town where their child had grown and then died, migrated to South Carolina to escape the heartache, leaving in their wake the anger and frustration of their remaining daughters, and Nanny Fee, my ninety-three-year-old grandmother.

When I'd decided to stay in Heaven, my sisters agreed to help me run my wedding business. I'd been worried moving it from Manhattan would signal its demise, but it had, in fact, not only thrived, but grown.

Out-of-town weddings where everything was provided in what we call "one-stop shopping" had become quite popular of late, as my full calendar of weekends proved.

I set the alarm on my phone to wake me so I could be present when the Stively-Matthers enjoyed a last breakfast together before the newlyweds left for their honeymoon.

With a heavy and weary sigh, I snuggled down

under the quilt and closed my eyes. A silent prayer for no breakfast bloodshed from the combatant ex-wives club played like a silent movie in my head.

Chapter Two

Monday morning came around again as it does every week, and I was at my desk when my intercom buzzed.

"Isabella Harrington is here for her appointment," Charity told me.

"Send her in."

I rose and crossed to the office door. When I opened it, one of my favorite new clients was smiling at me.

Isabella was a blonde-haired, green-eyed pixie of a girl who wore a perpetual smile on her lovely, rosy-cheeked face. She'd attended a friend's wedding in Heaven I'd organized a few months ago and had been so charmed with the whole package, she'd fired her then wedding planner with a text sent as the buttercream-frosted cake had been served and hired me before the end of the reception.

She was alone today, but I'd met her handsome fiancé, Jackson Rainier, previously.

"Jack's not with you?" I asked, accepting her fervent hug and returning it.

"He's been on duty since yesterday morning," she told me. "Another thirty-six-hour shift. But I'll see him later when he's off-call."

Rainier was a medical resident finishing up a fellowship in pediatrics at a Manhattan hospital. The two had met when Isabella, then a Barnard undergraduate, volunteered at a community fundraiser for pediatric AIDS relief where Jack had been the resident in charge of the event. To see the two of them together was to know what true love really looked like.

"I'm glad you're here," I said. "I received the pricing on those favors you liked, and before I ordered them, I wanted to make sure you were okay with the cost."

She waved her perfectly manicured hand in the air. "It doesn't matter what the cost is; I want them. Go ahead and place the order."

I'd found when dealing with Isabella Harrington, this was a common statement. At twenty-four, she had the world in front of her and an older brother behind her who was footing the bill for the entire wedding. I'd yet to meet the elusive Slade Harrington, but to hear Isabella talk about him, he was the most loving, adoring, generous—you get the picture—brother on the planet. The subject of Isabella's parents was a sore topic, and though ravenous curiosity swam through me like a hungry lion in search of plump gazelles, I never asked why it was her brother's signature on the payment checks.

We made ourselves comfortable in my seating area and got down to business.

"Your gown is in," I told her, referring to my laptop with her opened file on the display screen, "so we need to make an appointment for your first fitting."

"You're going with me, right?" she asked as she took a sip from the water bottle Charity had brought her. "I was still with my old planner when I ordered it, so you haven't seen it on me. I want an honest opinion, and I know you'll be truthful."

"Of course I'll go with you. Do you want to invite anyone else? Jack's mother? Any of the wedding party? Your mom?"

Her beautifully sculpted nose wrinkled at the mention of her mother.

Sore subject, remember? I didn't push.

"No," she said, with a determined shake of her head. "I just want you."

A speck of sadness shot through me.

The wedding party was small, made up of Jack's married sister as the matron of honor, her small daughter as flower girl, and Jack's childhood friend as best man.

This was such a different wedding from any other I'd planned for brides in the Harringtons' social set. Usually, the typical rich-girl society affair I'd put together consisted of scores of sorority sisters in the party paired with an equal amount of just-as-wealthy old-network-fraternity groomsmen. From gown fittings to seating arrangements, table settings, favors, and even bridal-registry gift shopping, brides were encircled by a gaggle of twittering attendants, all desiring exactly what the bride-to-be had—a rich, up and coming, politically connected groom-to-be. Those brides were my bread and butter when I'd first started out in New York, and my business had thrived financially, bringing with it more and more vapid, spoiled, and demanding young women with access to Daddy's bank accounts and Mommy's demands.

Isabella Harrington was the opposite of every upper-class bride I'd ever worked for.

"Okay, let's call and set something up. What's

your schedule like this week?"

While I was on the phone to the Manhattan bridal boutique, my office door opened. I had one eye on my computer date planner while the other spotted Charity escorting a figure into my office.

A very large, male figure.

Isabella put her finger across her lips to hush whatever he'd been about to say. At the same time, I got an available appointment.

"Wednesday at ten okay for you?" I asked Isabella.

She told me it was and I confirmed it. That done, I hung up and turned around.

The smile I'd automatically put on my face froze in place at my first glimpse of the man who'd entered the room. There was a subtle resemblance to Isabella in his coloring, but he was a number of years older. Both had the same ash-blond hair, cut through with swaths of wheat, honey, and flax. Isabella's hair had a natural curl to it, silk threads drifting over her shoulders in a tumbled mass. His hair was cut shorter on the sides, longer at the top, with the same thick, luxuriant layers arranged in a disarray of waves.

For a hot second, my hands vibrated with a desire to run through all that disorder and clutch on tight.

If the old saying "clothes make the man" was true, this guy had made it to the top of the stratosphere.

A deep pink candy-striped tailored shirt covered him from neck to waist, broad shoulders to wrists, the collar opened and popped, the cuffs perfectly aligned. I was one of those women who loved colors on a guy—even pastels—and knew it took a confident man to pull off anything other than somber and professional blues, grays, and blacks.

His dark trousers fit comfortably down his long, long legs, dropping from a trim waist in a straight line all the way to polished loafers I knew cost a month's rent on my previous Manhattan hovel. He carried a sports jacket over one arm, and if I had to guess, every stitch of clothing on him had been hand tailored.

Isabella's face broke into a wide, show-stopping smile that lit my office in all four corners.

"At last you two get to meet," she said. Slinking her arm through the crook of his elbow, she added, "Colleen, this is my big brother, Slade."

"Commonly referred to as 'the checkbook,' " he said, while he stretched a hand out to shake mine, a disarmingly wry grin pulling at his full lips.

His hand remained out, waiting for me to take it. For some wacky reason, my brain wouldn't send an order to my muscles to extend mine to his.

Isabella giggled and swatted his arm, all sisterly affection behind the hit. The sound was enough to propel me out of my paralysis. I leaned forward and gave his hand a firm, professional squeeze.

Immediate warmth spread through my fingers like I'd dropped them into heated bath water, seeped up my wrist, then slid the length of my arm in one solid, sizzling glide. My biceps contracted, vaulting the heat onto my shoulder, which stiffened in response, before relaxing enough to let it soak through my system.

St. Brigid preserve me.

Amber irises shot with tiny flecks of aged cognac narrowed as the inky black of his pupils expanded.

His hand remained in mine, his eyes focused on my own. I don't know what he saw in them, but on his ruggedly handsome, chiseled-from-stone face a

17

smidgen of confusion, a speck of bewilderment, and a splash of intrigue all mixed together while we stood there.

My abdominal muscles contracted, and I wasn't even wearing the dreaded spandex today.

This wouldn't do. I hadn't been this discombobulated by a man since…well…let's not even go there. Attempting to shove some professionalism back into my office, I pulled my hand from his and said, "Isabella has never referred to you that way." Good gracious, was that my voice? It sounded like an army of frogs had invaded the back of my throat. "But it's nice to meet you, Mr. Harrington."

"Slade is fine." He folded his hands into his trouser pockets.

If my voice mimicked web-toed croaking amphibians, his sounded like a lazy morning after a night packed with warm Irish whiskey and scorching sex.

Deep toned and low, with a scratch of gravel and a tiny smolder of smoke, those three words almost made me respond, "Slade is *way* more than fine," but I kept my thoughts to myself and indicated the chairs.

As we sat, I cleared the frogs and said, "I'm glad you could join us today. I have some questions about the guest list. The invitations need to go out soon, and I want to assure I have all the correct names and addresses."

With a nod to his sister, Slade said, "I'm sure the list is perfect. Izzy wants to keep the wedding small, and that's fine with me."

I handed each of them a set of printed sheets and then referred to my own papers. With a visual sweep of the list, I asked a question I'd been considering before Isabella arrived. "I don't seem to have your father's mailing information, Isabella."

There was a subtle but profound drop in the air temperature of my office. At the mention of their mutual father, brother and sister both took a swift, audible breath.

It was Slade Harrington who broke the silence. "He won't be coming."

There was frost in his voice, and his face had frozen into a mask of steely, hard-pressed resolve. From what Isabella had told me of her brother's profession, I knew he ran the family business, a venture capital and investment company. He had an MBA from Wharton and had graduated from Harvard, originally, with a law degree. Added in was a PhD in economics. Very authoritarian and forceful careers. I was happy I would never need to sit across from him at a negotiation table. This was what I imagined his corporate take-no-prisoners face looked like. It was a little scary and a whole lot of intimidating.

And it was very familiar. Uncomfortably so.

My former fiancé, commonly referred to by my sisters as *Vlad the soulsucker*—because that's what he did: suck your soul dry—had the same expression on his face most days.

Long story better left untold.

I had never wanted to ask my next question so much in my life—*why not?*—but I knew I was treading on some very slippery family-dynamic ice, so instead I said, "Then, I'm going to assume you or Isabella's stepfather will be walking her down the aisle."

"I will be." His tone left no doubt of it.

Isabella, silent up to now, glanced down to her lap at her folded hands, her bottom lip tucked under her top teeth at one corner of her mouth. Slade slid a look at his sister, and I was charmed at the way his face and body softened. He reached over and took one of her hands, giving it a gentle tug. When she lifted her gaze to his, he lowered his chin and asked in a voice devoid of all the chill it had possessed a moment before, "Unless you want Fred to walk you down. It's okay with me if you do."

She squeezed his hand, and a tremulous smile skidded over her face. "No. I want you to. But…"

"What, Izzy?"

She glanced over at me and then back to her brother. "Well…I got a call the other day. From Daddy."

Granite was softer than Slade Harrington's jaw right then.

Isabella licked her perfectly plump lips, darted a look at me again, then focused back on her brother. "Don't be mad at me. Please?"

"You're not the one I'm mad at." Slade pulled his hand from his sister's, folded his own together, and rested them in his lap as Isabella had. His poor knuckles blanched from the amount of pressure he was using to hold them still, and his body was as rigid as a carved marble statue.

I didn't know much about the Harrington family history, and from the way this conversation was progressing, I didn't want to.

"Let me guess why he called," Slade said to his sister. "He heard you were getting married, probably from one of his polo cronies who heard it from one of their trophy wives. He wants to be included. Wants to run the show. Maybe even wants to play dear-old-dad and walk you down the aisle. How am I doing?"

Isabella's delicate shoulders slumped, and she stared back down at her lap.

"Izzy, look at me." His words were a command, but he'd gentled the tone.

She did.

"We talked about this. About what would happen if he came to the wedding. About why he shouldn't."

"I know. It's just…" She shrugged and my heart went out to her.

Both Slade and I asked at the same time, "What?"

I physically felt the knife-like, antagonistic glare he shot me slice through my skin like a paper cut, swift and cutting and sharp.

I'd been put in my proverbial place, without a doubt.

Images of the last time I'd seen Vlad—I mean, Harry—sprang to the front of my mind. The way his dark eyes had cooled over and turned cruel while he accused me of being cold, career driven, and neglectful of his needs were a twin to Slade Harrington's hostile, hard, and flinty glower.

I clamped my lips together so hard they tingled and then leaned back in my chair, moving physically and emotionally away from their conversation.

Isabella's expressive eyes swam with moisture, her lashes barely holding back the tears from tripping down her cheeks. She looked at her brother and said, "He sounded so hurt because he hadn't known about the wedding. That we'd…that I'd never called to tell him."

"Sweetheart, we both know what a manipulator he

is when it comes to your feelings. And," he added when she started to speak, "how appearances mean everything to him. He wants to play father of the bride so everyone can see what a great dad he is, what a chip off the old block. You realize that, right?"

Isabella nodded, her eyes swimming. "I do." She lifted her gaze back to his, and my heart turned over a tad when a fat tear slid down her cheek. "But he *is* my father."

"Just because you have some of his DNA, it doesn't make him a father." His voice had turned to a distinctly disgusted timbre, and I couldn't help but wonder who was the real villain here? Old man Harrington, who probably wanted to walk his daughter down the aisle, or Junior who seemed to have more issues with Daddy than Isabella did?

This conversation was getting a bit too personal for me, and I did have other things I needed to do, not spend time on family drama I knew nothing about, so I decided to step back into the scene and get the planning conversation back on track. They could discuss their father's presence—or lack of it—on their own time and in private.

"Why don't we bookmark this discussion for now and talk about the rest of the list?" Before either of them could respond, I jumped right in. "Isabella, you and Jack decided at our last meeting you wanted no more than eight to a table, right?"

As I refocused their attention, Slade Harrington shifted a side-glance my way. From his expression, I wasn't sure if he was impressed with the way I'd barreled straight through their discussion and gone back into wedding-planner mode, or if he was plotting fifty ways to cause my demise.

It was a toss-up.

A half hour later, after a few witty exchanges between the siblings about which relatives and friends should be kept away from one another, and with Isabella back to her usual happy self, I suggested we take Slade on a tour of the inn.

Since it was ridiculous to all drive separately, Isabella and her brother hopped into my car.

"You're going to love the inn," Isabella told Slade from behind us. I was a little taken aback when he'd slid into the passenger seat next to me. Having all that long, lean male in my office, seated across from me with room to spare, had been one thing. Having him so close now within the confines of the car was quite another. And because of his proximity, I noticed a few things I hadn't in my office, like the subtle—yet totally enthralling—scent of his cologne. It reminded me of the deep woods after a rainfall, strong and earthy, as it drifted over to me while I maneuvered out of my parking lot and onto the county road, aiming for Inn Heaven. I'm a sucker for warm, masculine scents, and his was so appealing, I had a momentary flash of sliding my nose up his neck and sniffing to my heart's content.

I took a giant breath to get a grip on my thoughts when we stopped at a traffic light.

While Isabella went on about all the inn's attributes in gushing detail, my gaze slid to where Slade's hands rested on his thighs.

His thick, muscular, *hard* thighs.

A rush of what it would feel like to be tucked between those strong limbs galloped through my head.

Oh, my.

His long, straight fingers were ringless, the knuckles drizzled with sparse tufts of the same wheat color in his hair. Isabella had mentioned at one of our previous meetings her brother was unmarried, a state he had managed to retain despite the best efforts of the most vigorous Park Avenue mothers of marriageable girls.

Isabella maintained her brother was the quintessential confirmed bachelor and *playa.*

Playa was the appropriate term. A quick Google search had yielded thousands of photos of him attending everything from society events to the opening of new, trendy restaurants and nightclubs at home and oversees. And in every one of those photos, he had a different supermodel/actress/pop star at his side. The most recent ones I'd found showed supermodel Katya Yurlenko frequently on his arm.

"Colleen's sister manages the inn, plus she's a pastry chef. When Jack and I were at Maisy Dimple's reception here a few months ago, he said Maisy's wedding cake was the best thing he'd ever tasted. He snuck two pieces. Maureen made it."

Pride flowed through me because it was true. My youngest sister was without doubt one of the most imaginative and creative bakers I'd ever come in contact with in all my years working in the wedding industry. And I'd come in contact with a lot.

A whole lot.

She'd abandoned her dreams of opening her own bakery when her twin asked her to go into business together. When Eileen took sick, Maureen stayed by her side, promising she wouldn't let anything happen to her sister's dream of having one of the best bed and breakfasts in the state. In doing so, she'd given up her own dreams and desires.

My gaze flicked over to see Slade's attention focused on me as it had been in my office. While his sister spoke, his expression turned thoughtful and his gaze drifted down to my lips and then back up again, his brows lifting slightly.

"That's some praise," he said. "Think I can hope for a…taste of something?" His eyes shot down to my mouth again, and I swear he wasn't talking about vanilla layer cake with mascarpone filling and buttercream frosting.

When was the last time a guy had looked at me like he wanted to devour me like a confection?

Let's be real here: never.

I tried to swallow, but my mouth had gone desert-dry, all the moisture in my body dropping down to my lady parts.

This wouldn't do. Not at all. I prided myself on my polished professionalism and poise when dealing with clients, and to date, I'd never had my lust-ometer react to anyone connected with any of the weddings I'd planned.

Until now.

Remember Harry, I told myself. Slade and my ex could have been brothers from another mother. Arrogant. Conceited. Proud.

"Maureen is usually baking something," I said as I turned the car into the inn's lengthy driveway. "Cupcakes. Pastries. Scones. Her baking talents are famous in these parts. I'm sure if you ask nicely, she'd be happy to let you taste whatever she's got."

Isabella giggled again.

Her brother turned around in his seat to face her. "What's so funny?"

"*You*, Mr. I-won't-put-anything-in-my-body-that's-not-good-for-it. I haven't seen you eat a piece of cake since my sweet-sixteen birthday party."

"That's not true."

"Yes, it is. You shun sugar like vampires shun the sun."

When I laughed out loud at the description, Slade squinted even more, and I swear, the heat seeping from his steely glare sliced like a laser beam right through me. My hands suddenly turned to two sweaty claws as they gripped the steering wheel. My thighs pressed in close together, and I could feel a little tickle of pressure in the lower edge of my spine. This guy should bottle whatever it was swimming around in him that gave off such a hot alpha vibe. He could sell it on the open market and make himself even richer.

I threw the car into park as Isabella asked, "When was the last time you had a cookie? A slice of pie? Anything even hinting of butter or white flour?"

While she'd been speaking, Slade slid from the car, and opened her door.

I was already out and standing with my keys in my hand.

"Just because I don't make a daily habit of eating junk food doesn't mean I don't enjoy something sweet now and then, Isabella."

The tone in his voice reminded me more of a father than a big brother and gave me a whole lot more insight into their relationship.

"There's nothing wrong with eating well. Ask your

fiancé. He's a doctor. I'm sure he can tell you why you should eat healthy, nutritionally sound food."

Isabella alighted from the car, giggled again, and then rose up on her toes to kiss her brother's cheek. "How old are you?" she asked, cocking her head to one side and nailing him with a wide-eyed stare. "Because you sound more like my grandfather than my brother right now."

Slade shook his head and closed the car door behind her. He took her arm and said, "Come along now. *Child.*"

Isabella giggled again and wrapped her free hand around the one held in Slade's hand. When she leaned into him and he dropped a kiss on the top of her head, my brotherless little heart sighed with longing.

Awww. Maybe I was wrong about him being a jerk like Harry.

And when his gaze lit on mine, his perfectly arched eyebrows lifting just a fraction in a condescending manner, the longing fled, replaced by a dollop of pique.

No. It looked like I wasn't wrong at all.

I lifted my chin, planted a fake smile on my face as I regarded him, and said, "Shall we?"

Chapter Three

"See?" Isabella said as soon as we were through the front door. "Isn't it gorgeous?"

Slade glanced around the wide, open foyer. After they'd signed the ownership papers for the inn, my sisters had spent two solid weeks touring around New England, visiting antique and specialty antiquarian shops for period-perfect furnishings. The foyer was bifurcated by a wide, carpeted staircase (think *Gone with the Wind*) that stopped at a central landing and then split into two sides to lead up to the second floor. The carpeting covering the stairs and landing was a lush, plush, deep red Maureen referred to as *harlot scarlet*. But Eileen had loved it, so her twin gave the okay to have it installed despite thinking it made the foyer resemble what my grandmother calls a bawdy house.

"It smells great in here." Isabella lifted her chin and gave the air a decided sniff.

"That's Maureen's lemon curd. She must be doing a tasting today."

"A tasting?" Slade asked, sliding his gaze from the foyer table to me. He held one of the inn's promotional pamphlets Maureen kept displayed on the table.

"For wedding cake selections," I answered. "She gives the prospective bride and groom a few varied tastes of the flavors she can bake for their cake."

He turned to his sister. "Let me guess what you decided on. Some kind of chocolate-coconut combination, right?"

Isabella socked him in the upper arm. "I hate that you know my weaknesses so well."

"Not so much your weaknesses as your obsessions." He looked back at me, a grin just this side of heart-stopping tugging at the corners of his delectable mouth. "The very first time I took her trick-or-treating she fell in love with those little chocolate-covered coconut bars and ate them all. She didn't touch any of the other stuff. And her bag was filled to the top with all kinds of candy."

"I don't remember hearing you complain," Isabella said, "especially when you ate every piece I didn't want."

Before I could stop myself, I said, "I thought you didn't eat sweets?"

Those gorgeous eyes regarded me through his thick lashes. "I eat…all sorts of things."

Holy Mother of the Lord. Was it me, or was there a whole world of meaning in that little statement that went beyond just eating candy? The tiny hairs on the back of my neck stood straight up at attention as a shiver sluiced down my spine and slipped under my thong. Unable to stop them, my thighs pressed together as a little pulse of awareness shot between them.

"When I was a teenager, though," he continued easily while I stood there, practically hyperventilating with…something, "I didn't care too much what I ate, and anything sweet was appreciated."

"Now there's a customer after my own heart."

Maureen came from the direction of the kitchen

dressed as she usually was—opposite to me in every way.

Her thick, curly red hair was secured into a messy knot on the top of her head, a pencil sticking through it. Her freckled face had nothing on it but a generic, drugstore-brand moisturizer. She wore a pale sky-blue T-shirt under a flour-covered apron that covered her from torso to knees. Embroidered across the front flap was *Keep Calm and Add Butter.* Under it, old, faded jeans fit over her narrow hips and lanky legs like a second layer of skin. I didn't even need to look down to know her feet were shod in flip-flops.

Maureen valued comfort and ease in everything in life, including how she appeared to the world. Such a contrast to the way I presented myself to others. I couldn't imagine going out of the house without makeup, hair blown out and styled, my body covered in an outfit that screamed *successful businesswoman,* much less shod in shoes that cost ninety-nine cents at the local hardware store.

I introduced my sister to Slade, charmed when his eyes lit with mirth as his gaze dragged down to her apron and read the message.

"Your sister said you're doing a cake tasting today."

"I've got three couples coming in this afternoon, so I've been getting everything ready. Would you like a tour of the inn and the facilities? Get a feel for how Isabella's wedding will look? I can take a break while everything cools."

She looked over at me and cocked her head. I nodded.

For the next several minutes, the four of us made

our way through the inn. Slade asked dozens of questions about the operational side of the business— something probably near and dear to his entrepreneurial heart—and Maureen answered every one of them efficiently and with as few words as possible.

He seemed impressed at the size of the main ballroom, evidenced by the way his eyes took in every inch of the spacious area. The tables were already set for the next event, a luncheon meeting of the local Chamber of Commerce Maureen was hosting the next day. Slade asked about the menu, where she obtained her staff for events, the time devoted to setup and takedown. All topics I knew Maureen loved to talk about. She was a wealth of knowledge about her business, never shy when it came to discussing all aspects of it. It was her personal life she kept quiet from everyone, including her family.

Even though she'd been baking since before the sun rose, her commercial kitchen was its usual spotless and shining space, all the industrial appliances sparkling and clean. Maureen'd had a mild case of cleaning OCD when she was a kid, and it had followed her into adulthood. When our sister took ill, Maureen's obsessiveness about having her surroundings clean and germfree proved to be a good thing when Eileen's immune system had been compromised by chemotherapy.

After a quick trip up the main staircase to the guest rooms and then a view of the garden where Isabella and Jack would say their vows, we were back in the foyer.

"You've a charming place," Slade said. Glancing down at his sister, he added, "I can see why you wanted to be married here instead of at the Carlyle. It's perfect

31

for you and Jack."

With a fast grin, Isabella nodded. "It is, and I'm so glad you agree." She threw her arms around his chest and squeezed.

When he dropped his chin to the top of her head and hugged her back, my heart gave a little sigh. Growing up, I'd always dreamed about having a big brother. When I was old enough to realize I couldn't— Cathleen held the distinction of being the oldest, with me right behind her—I changed that to a younger one. After the birth of the twins, my mother had declared her baby-making machine was now and forever closed, and I had to deal with the fact I'd be growing up in a cloud of estrogen.

As I watched the Harrington siblings' show of affection toward one another, that old wish pushed to the front of my mind again.

In the next instant when Slade's gaze turned and he smiled that sexy smirk and winked at me, I forgot all about not having a brother and wanted nothing more than to have a man in my life.

Isabella pulled back and, after a glance at the diamond-encased watch on her wrist, said, "I need to get back. If I leave now, I'll miss most of the traffic."

She hugged Maureen, then Slade slid his hand into my sister's.

"The next time I visit," he told her, "I'll want to sample some of those cake choices."

Maureen smiled back at him. "Just have Colleen tell me when you'll be back with Isabella, and I'll have some ready."

In the car, he turned to me and said, "Your sister's inn is beautiful, quaint, and looks like she does a good business."

"She's usually booked every weekend with weddings and their guests plus the events she hosts during the week. And during peeping season she's booked solid."

"Peeping season?"

I flicked a quick look at him while I drove, then turned back to the road. "Autumn. It's called leaf-peeping season in these parts. From mid-September until early November, when the leaves change colors. New England autumns are famous worldwide for the tree color changes. Haven't you ever been up here during the fall?"

"Slade only goes places where there are beaches, warm water, and naked girls," Isabella piped up from the back seat. I caught her eye roll in my rearview mirror.

"Not true." He turned to her. "Sometimes the water is cold."

She burst out laughing, and I followed suit.

"Well, since the wedding is in October, you'll be getting a first-hand view of the natural beauty around here," I said. "In fact, Isabella, my photographer, Kolby, has already mentioned a few places he'd like to shoot you and Jack before and on your wedding day. I'll send you the link to his website so you can see what he means. You can let him know the spots you like."

A few minutes later, it was my turn for one of Isabella's vivacious hugs.

"I'll be down on Wednesday morning for your fitting," I told her.

"Can't wait," she said, then hugged her brother. "Drive safe."

"Yes, Mom. You, too. Text me when you get back."

She climbed into her fabulous car, called out, "Yes, *Dad*," then, with a final wave and a cheeky grin, sped out of my office parking lot, gravel and dust in her wake.

Slade let out a breath and shook his head, hands fisted on his hips.

The afternoon sun hit him from behind, haloing his head in a bright circle of light. With the sun shadowing his face, his eyes darkened to amber like a warmed, barrel-aged ale.

A girl could get drunk from those piercing eyes, from that penetrating stare, especially if it was zeroed in on her, like it was, right now, on me.

I remembered my previous thought that Slade was way more than fine. But *fine* didn't seem to do him any kind of justice. God must have been in a particularly good mood the morning He spliced Slade Harrington's genes together.

"Well," I said, internally wincing at how lame I sounded. I shifted my purse to the opposite shoulder, my car keys still dangling from my hand. "You probably want to head back, too. Beat the traffic. It gets a little rubber-necky this time of day in some spots."

"I'm not concerned. I cleared my schedule for the afternoon. I didn't know how long this was going to take, and I didn't want to run out on Izzy and race back to the city for a meeting. She's been begging me to drive up here and get a look at the inn, see the area, for a couple weeks. Today was the first day I could manage."

"I'm sure she appreciates your being here. You two

34

seem very close."

He nodded. "We are. She's a good kid. Sweet, unspoiled. Smart. She deserves a shot at happiness. If this is what she wants for her wedding, I'm going to do whatever I can to make it happen."

His love for her was, again, apparent. I was a wee bit envious of that kind of affection.

I stared at him for a moment, mulling over how I wanted to ask him what I'd been dying to ask since we'd been in my office.

Finally, because there was no other way to get around it but bluntly, I said, "I feel like we need to discuss your father. Come to a decision about where he fits in the wedding."

When the warmth in his expression shifted to ice, a weaker-willed person might have stopped there. Since I'm not weak and my parents have always told me I have a real problem with knowing when to quit, I pushed on. "It seems to me as if Isabella wants him to be included. Whether in a father-of-the-bride role, or simply as a guest, I really do think she'd like him to attend, but, for whatever reason, she's reluctant to press you on it."

Did I say ice? What's colder than ice? Because whatever it is, that was the expression floating in Slade's eyes right then as he glared at me.

Warning bells blared in my head, but that thing about me not knowing when to quit? Yeah, it's real.

"I think Isabella's afraid of upsetting you if she tells you how she feels or asks your permission. She loves you so much and respects your opinion."

"You don't know anything about my sister. Or me." He lowered his hands from his hips, kept them fisted at his sides. "Or our relationship with our father."

"True, but I get the sense—"

He barreled over me as if I hadn't said a word.

"You've been hired to do a job, Miss O'Dowd. I suggest you do it and keep your thoughts about my family to yourself. You're a wedding planner, not a family counselor." His voice dropped a level, deepening as it became softer. The cadence became clipped, the tone more…lethal.

If this was the way he acted in business, it was a wonder he hadn't been convicted of corporate homicide yet.

"Look, I'm not asking simply to be nosy," I said, my voice rising in opposition to his. "I really do have to plan all this out. There's still the rehearsal and the dinner after it left to deal with. Then there's the reception seating. Plus, if he is included, I'll need to make sure he has a room, a tuxedo, and find out if he's bringing a guest."

"What aren't you understanding about this, Miss O'Dowd?" Slade asked, taking a step toward me. If he'd thought to intimidate me with his height, he'd miscalculated. Retreat wasn't a word in my lexicon. I simply lifted my chin and stared right back at him.

"I understand a lot more than you think, *Mr. Harrington.* About all sorts of things. Arrogant and pigheaded men included."

When he continued to stand like a plank of wood in front of me, his mouth turning down and creasing the sides of his jaw, I knew—*knew*—I should stop.

But…

"This is your sister's wedding," I said, pulling deep for some form of professional calm. "Your only sister, and she loves you and wants you to be as happy on her big day as she is. If that means including a father she so obviously wants to include, then I think you should suck it up and let her, no matter what your daddy issues are."

"Daddy issues?"

I swear on Nanny Fee's 120-year-old Bible, he snarled the words. His face turned the color of hothouse tomatoes, and his eyes widened to the size of poker chips.

In the next instant, his face changed again. It was mesmerizing the way he was able to pull in whatever irritation he felt for me and slap it back down. In a heartbeat, he turned back into Mr. Cool Controlled Corporate Icon. The look he tossed me was one I imagined royalty gave to their servants. As if anything I said or did was so unworthy of his attention and time, that he couldn't be bothered acknowledging it.

His lids dropped, covering most of his eyes as if he was fighting to keep them open through a bout of boredom.

Why did that look, that totally derisive and insulting glare look so...hot?

When Vlad had looked at me like he wanted to squash me under his Italian designer loafers like an annoying ant, I'd gotten pissed and pissy. Slade Harrington's disdainful expression caused a little niggle of heat to slide down my spine. For a scorching second, I imagined how much fun it would be to wipe the look off his face.

And by fun, I mean it in a purely sexual sense.

Before either of us was able to say another word, the shrill blast of Pink's "Trouble" split the air.

I reached into my purse and grabbed my cellphone. *Nanny Fee* danced across the screen.

Uh-oh. A call from my grandmother during the middle of the day was never a good sign. She wasn't one given to chatting you up to shoot the breeze. No. A call from Fee usually meant trouble, hence the ringtone song I'd assigned to her.

I connected the call. "Nanny?"

"Number two. Good. I've got—"

"Hang on a sec, Nanny. I'm with a client."

I slid the phone down to my side as I heard my grandmother's voice continue speaking.

Slade had his car keys in his hand and was swiping his thumb along the fob, his gaze still zeroed in on me. Or more accurately, my mouth.

"Look," I said again and after taking in a deep breath. "It's not my intent to overstep. I have no desire to get into any family drama. That's not what I was doing. I just want Isabella to have the wedding she's envisioned. Like you said, it's what I was hired to do."

He waited a beat and then nodded.

"You don't have to decide anything right now concerning your father. Just think about Isabella. What she wants and what you want for her. You two can discuss this privately and when I see her on Wednesday, she can let me know if there are any changes to the guest list. I won't even ask her about it, I'll just let her take the reins. Okay?"

Again, he waited a moment before giving me his reply. "Yes."

When he said nothing further, the moment grew awkward, and I could still hear Nanny Fee's voice spilling from my phone.

"I'm sorry," I said. "I need to take this call." I held the phone up, Nanny's voice going nonstop on whatever topic she'd called me about, oblivious to the fact I wasn't listening to her.

He was staring at my mouth again, and the sensation of heat tickling at my core suddenly grew lava-hot under his scrutiny.

With one more curt nod, he turned and stalked to his car.

No "goodbye."

No "It was a pleasure meeting you."

No social nicety at all.

Just a dismissive, regal nod, and he was off.

He slid into his vehicle, and I swear I could actually feel the butter-soft leather of the seat slide across his slacks. With a quick, last glance at me, and as his sister had, he gunned the engine and sped out of the parking lot, a gravel dust storm gusting up behind him.

A hot guy in a fast car shouldn't have sent my thirty-five-year-old insides quivering with lust and possibilities. Especially when there was no chance those possibilities could ever be realized.

I shook out of my musings and lifted the phone to my ear to hear Nanny saying, "—so what was I supposed to do? You tell me."

Good Lord. Now what?

Heaving a huge sigh, I went back to my office to figure out what mayhem my grandmother had caused this time.

Chapter Four

"So you think I look good?" Isabella asked.

She stood on a riser, facing a three-sided mirror, her worried eyes staring back at me, filled with uncertainty.

"I think you look like you've stepped out of a fairy tale," I told her, meaning it.

The salon's soft and subtle overhead lighting bounced off her shimmering flaxen hair, which she'd pushed up into a messy bun.

"You're sure I made the right choice?"

"Isabella, this dress was handcrafted by the gods of bridal fashion for you. Trust me, I know what I'm talking about."

On her trim, lithe frame, the dress truly looked as if it had been constructed for her and her alone.

A simple blush color, the top was an intricate corset of hand-embroidered pale gold roses and vines fanning out into two tiny cap sleeves. A thin illusion layer dipped down into a demure scooped neckline— not too low to be considered vulgar but just enough to have a tiny line of cleavage swell above it.

Around Isabella's tiny waist was the slimmest of belts in the same hue as the embroidery. A skirt of incalculable yards and layers of blush-colored chiffon billowed about her, ending a smidge above the top of her shoes.

The dress had pockets—*pockets!*

Standing atop the riser, hands now secured into those pockets, she was simply the loveliest bride I'd ever seen. And that was saying something, since I'd been up close and personal with hundreds of them.

"White tends to wash me out, so I thought the blush color looked better. I tried on about a hundred dresses before I finally found the perfect one."

"It's gorgeous with your skin and hair."

"My other wedding planner kept steering me toward white and pale pink, but I felt like I was going to prom instead of getting married in the dresses she picked out in those colors."

"You were right to go with your gut instincts, Isabella. This neutral blush tone is going to photograph like a dream. And you with it."

She nodded, turned back to the mirror, and swirled her dress back and forth like a little girl admiring herself while she did. "I tried to tell her that, but…well. That was only one of the reasons I fired her."

Her eyes found mine in the mirror, and she grinned. "I'm so glad you like it."

"I love it, but what's more important is you do," I told her. "Jack's eyes are gonna pop out the minute he sees you in this."

She giggled and turned to and fro again, making the skirt float around her like she was moving on a cloud.

Twenty minutes later, she was redressed and we were headed to lunch.

"I've got a reservation for us at the Crystal Room," she said as we settled into her limo.

"Wow. Who do you know?" I asked, grinning. "I

lived in this city for over ten years and couldn't get in there. Heck, I couldn't even make a reservation, or get on a list to potentially make a reservation."

Isabella smiled. "It's not hard when you know the owner. Or your big brother does. I just called and said the magic words *Slade Harrington*, and poof. Table for two, no problem."

I'd been in such a good mood ever since I'd woken knowing I was meeting with my favorite client and was going to be able to steal a few hours to shop at my old haunts. But the mention of Isabella's brother shot a little black rain cloud over my head, and any minute I expected my hair to get soaked.

For the past few days, I'd been busy with client meetings, venue checks, emails. I'd returned countless phone calls and booked six more potential new client meets for the following weeks. I'd taken care of Nanny Fee's uber-emergencies, which weren't more than minor inconveniences for me, and started the quarterly business taxes.

All that took up my workday.

During the evenings, when my staff went home and my sisters were involved in their own lives, I'd wandered the house I grew up in, since I was now the keeper of the ancestral manse, and tried not to let my mind drift to whiskey-colored eyes lit with anger, subtle contempt, and…promise.

Slade Harrington, Wall Street titan and entrepreneur, was exactly the type of man I shouldn't be thinking of. Ever. But, unfortunately, I was.

While I brushed my teeth, I remembered the few times he'd smiled openly at his sister.

When I gave my hair its mandatory one hundred

vigorous brushstrokes every night before twisting it up in a bedtime knot, hair the color of golden wheat swaying in the late summer breeze shot to the front of my mind.

And while I plowed through my closet trying to decide what to wear for the day, the expert cut of a hand-stitched jacket over shoulders that went on for yards blinded me to my own choices, most of which were bought at upscale secondhand consignment shops.

I'd spent way too much time fantasizing over a guy who, A, didn't like me, B, reminded me a little too much of my former fiancé, and C, and worst of all, looked down his nose at me as just a hired hand and not the successful business owner I was.

"I took Jack there on our third date," Isabella said, immune to the thoughts running through my head. She giggled again. "He was so cute. He started sweating when he saw the prices, and I could see him mentally tallying in his head if his credit card was gonna cover it. He didn't have to worry, though, because Paolo Tricetti spotted me when he was making his table rounds and told the maître d' dinner was on him."

"You know Paolo Tricetti?" I almost spilled the bottle of water the limo driver had handed me.

Isabella lifted her shoulders. "He's my godfather. Or one of them, anyway."

I didn't remember seeing the name of one of the biggest box-office action stars of the day on her guest list and said as much.

"He can't come. He'll be in South America filming his next movie."

Personally, I was happy he wouldn't be attending the wedding. Not only would it have been a nightmare keeping the paparazzi who perpetually followed him everywhere away from the inn, I didn't relish having to book security and then worry about crazy fans jumping up everywhere, eager for a selfie with the actor.

Isabella and Jack wanted a quiet, peaceful, and memorable wedding day. No way was that going to be possible if her godfather made an appearance.

We'd arrived at our luncheon locale. I have to admit, having a uniformed chauffeur open my car door and help me out was something I could definitely get used to. Definitely. In an alternate universe where I was a high-powered and decadently rich society woman, I knew this would be my normal routine.

The minute we moved into the restaurant, we were escorted to an outside patio table. The maître d' fawned over Isabella, gracing her with a professionally whitened smile that had me squinting from its glare.

He pulled out her chair, handed her a menu, and then did the same for me.

"What can I get you lovely ladies as a beverage?" he asked.

Isabella ordered a mimosa, and I settled on water.

While he went to fetch our drinks, Isabella clasped her hands on the top of the table and said, "I'm so happy you like my dress."

"I don't just like it." I reached across and squeezed one of her hands. "I love it. It's perfect. Perfect for your wedding vision. Perfect for you."

A dreamy smile tugged at her mouth. "I can't wait to marry Jack. He's…everything."

My romantic little heart fluttered. She was so happy, so in love. I remembered exactly what it felt like to have the world in front of you and the man you wanted for eternity at your side.

Unfortunately, in my case, the man in question decided he didn't want to spend eternity at my side.

Here's the Cliff notes version of Vlad, um, Harry and me.

We met in college and were virtually joined at hip for those four years.

Flash forward to post-graduation. He got into law school; me, business school. To save money, we opted to live together. At the time, it was a pretty hard thing for my parents to accept I was "living in sin," but Nanny Fee convinced them times had changed since they'd been young, and with changing times came changes in social mores and economics.

It hadn't hurt that she was living with her soon-to-be husband number four at the time. I think my parents were actually more concerned and scandalized about her relationship than mine.

Anyway.

Harry passed the bar. I graduated from business school and then went to work full time at *BridalWear* magazine.

Harry was offered a position at a top law firm and was fast tracked for success. I never minded the long, long, ridiculously long hours he worked, knowing how much it meant to him to make partner. My hours weren't exactly nine to five either, but I was usually the one home first to cook dinner, the one tasked with the cleaning, laundry, grocery shopping, and all the chores of a wife without the benefit of the title.

More times than not, my parents commented on this fact to me. And more times than not, I brushed off their concern, knowing—*hoping*—once Harry made partner he would put a ring on my finger.

While Harry was working toward his professional goal, I was climbing the success ladder at the magazine. I'd been hired as an assistant (read *go-fer* into the job description) to one of the associate editors, but when she left to have a baby, I was given her job, and then moved into a junior editorship for the planning line, until finally I was named the senior editor of the bridal-planning division.

Coinciding with my promotion and a huge increase in salary, Harry found out he'd made partner. I'd celebrated his success by throwing a lavish party at his favorite restaurant. It didn't pass my family's notice Harry hadn't done the same for me. But he did do the one thing I'd been dreaming of since we'd sat together in freshman English: propose.

I'll admit the ring wasn't exactly what I'd had my heart set on (two-carat square cut, flawless in a platinum setting), but the one-carat pear shape nestled in a gold band was pretty.

I started planning the wedding, and Harry started an affair with one of my co-workers.

I probably would never have found out about it, but fate is a bitch. I'd planned on going home for the weekend to visit my parents, but my mother called me right before I boarded the train to tell me my father had the flu and not to bother because she was keeping him isolated. I turned around and headed home.

When I opened the door to our apartment, something was…off. The lights were all on, so I knew Harry was home. I spotted an opened bottle of his favorite wine on the kitchen counter, two glasses next to it. One of the glasses had a lipsticked kiss along the rim.

I remember thinking that seemed wrong. Following the lit hallway to our bedroom, I heard voices. Okay, not voices, but sounds more along the line of groans and moans.

When I peeked in the bedroom at the bed I'd been sharing with the man I'd loved for a decade, I found him sprawled on his back and my assistant on top of him riding him at a galloping pace.

The rest of the night is a blur, the one thing I do vividly remember, though, was screaming at the top of my lungs just as it looked like Harry was going to climax.

Let's fast forward another month and forget all the hurtful things he said to me, like how I didn't value how hard he worked for us, and never appreciated anything he did. Or that I was about as interesting to talk to as a can of tuna. And my favorite—sarcasm inserted here, folks—I didn't understand the amount of pressure he was under day after day at a job that actually meant something and wasn't as inconsequential as a glorified bridal catalog.

Oh, and let's not forget the girl he was doing the horizontal mambo with, my assistant, was pregnant. With his baby.

Yeah. I know. That's exactly how I felt, too.

I walked out the door that night and a month later left my job because it was too upsetting seeing the woman who'd destroyed my almost-marriage every day.

I sold my engagement ring and used the money to start my business. After running the bridal-planning division of the magazine, I knew everyone who was anyone in the industry and most of them liked me. Right around this time, my sister Eileen got sick.

I've said this before, but what's that expression? You make plans and God laughs?

I still believed in a happily ever after, so sitting across from Isabella Harrington and watching her eyes go all soft and dreamy when she said her fiancé's name gave me a warm feeling inside.

"You two are so good together. I can't wait for you to be married, either." I meant every word of it.

Whatever Isabella was about to reply was preempted when she looked over my shoulder and squealed in glee. Thinking the man she loved had walked into the restaurant to surprise her, I turned my head, a smile wide on my mouth, and looked up into the pair of eyes that had been haunting me for days.

Lord, the man was a magnet for every female's attention in the place as he strode out to the patio and straight to his sister, a wide, open grin on his face.

Dressed in what I assumed was his titan-of-the-financial-world attire, he simply took my breath away. The severe black suit jacket fit snugly against his expansive shoulders, tapering down in one smooth line to his waist. He'd worn a splash of color in my office and did the same today, pairing the conservative color of the suit with a pale green dress shirt and a tie filled with a riot of mosaics.

He'd gotten a haircut since Monday, proven by the telltale, but subtle, exposed tan line at the nape of his neck right above his shirt collar.

Isabella shot up from her chair and wrapped her arms around his neck at the same time his went around her waist.

"I can't believe you actually came," she said.

"I told you I'd try, and as luck would have it, I was able to shift a few things around."

"I'm gonna mark this on my calendar, so I can never forget the day Slade 'I live for my work' Harrington actually took a break from ruling the financial world and joined his little sister for lunch."

His mouth pulled into a disgruntled line as he looked sternly down at her.

"Ah, there's the big brother I know and love." Isabella squeezed one of his hands. "For a second, I thought I'd lost you."

He tapped his index finger to the tip of her nose. "Behave, or I'll go back to ruling the world and forget about lunch."

Her giggle pulled another bright smile from him at the exact moment he turned and found me staring up at them. Something changed in his expression while his gaze glided down my face, across my mouth, and then slipped to my torso, before sliding back up to my eyes.

It was difficult to read. Wariness, maybe? Resignation that he'd be forced to tolerate me, a lowly wedding planner, for lunch? I don't know what it was, but I was determined not to let it bother me, so I slapped my professional smile in place and shook his hand when he offered it.

"Mr. Harrington."

"Miss O'Dowd."

"Oh, just call her Colleen," Isabella instructed as she sat back down. "The way you say Miss O'Dowd makes her sound like somebody's maiden aunt who has sixteen cats."

I had a momentary flash *that* was exactly the

direction my personal life was going.

Perceptive, much, Isabella?

Our waiter magically appeared, beamed lovingly at Isabella first and then took Slade's drink order. He opted for a glass of sparkling water. I was a bit surprised he hadn't ordered anything stronger since it had been my experience with businessmen who lunch that a few cocktails were always on the menu.

"So, how'd the first fitting go?" Slade asked his sister.

While she told him about the morning's appointment, I took the time to surreptitiously study him while appearing not to—I hoped.

The first time we'd met, his long, lean fingers had intrigued me, prompting me to wonder if he played an instrument. Now, as he folded them together and placed them on the table in front of him, the image of those fingers, gliding along a set of polished piano keys, executing the notes with an instinctual musical interpretation and the finesse of a master, was vivid. Just as easily I imagined the touch of those fingers as they brushed against a lover's cheek or trailed along a naked arm. Cupped a chin in readiness for a kiss; plumped a breast and teased a nipple into a pebble.

I sat bolt upright in my chair.

Whoa. What the heck? Why had my little mind-play drifted into the fantasy zone? There was no way I should be thinking of Slade Harrington playing with anyone's body parts.

Forget he was drop-dead gorgeous.

Forget he was a gazillionaire.

Forget he was a single, heterosexual male who practically exhaled charm with every breath.

Better to remember he was the brother of a client and was the one who was writing the checks for her wedding. In the purest form, the one paying my salary. And there were rules of conduct about those kinds of relationships.

Plus, better to remember he was cut from the same bolt of jerk fabric as Harry.

And I really needed to remember the last time we'd been together and he'd glared at me like I was an annoying piece of bubblegum stuck to the bottom of his expensive shoe.

In my haste to pull out of my mental meanderings, I sat upright way too fast. My knees bumped under the tabletop, and a tsunami of liquid gushed from our water glasses, splashing and drenching the linen tablecloth and Slade, who'd been taking a sip when the table lurched. The water spilled all over his chin and down the top half of his shirt.

Four-thousand-dollar cut-on-the-bias silk doesn't look good wet.

Ever.

"Oh, my God! I'm so sorry." A wildfire blazed up my neck and cheeks. Jeez, if the guy didn't like me before, he was really going to hate me after I ruined his custom suit.

While I sputtered my lame apology and offered Slade my own napkin to sop his jacket, Isabella laughed. A full belly-shaker complete with tears springing into the corner of her eyes. She balled her napkin into her hands and then pulled it up to her lips to hide behind, but her amusement was loud as it echoed around us.

Slade, who'd been dabbing his wet suit with his

own napkin, glared at her across the table. "I don't see what's so amusing, Isabella."

"You are," she said. "You're rubbing your jacket like you have a huge blood stain on it that you'll never get out. It's water, for goodness sake. It'll dry."

"Spoken like someone who has never tried to remove a stain from something in her life," he said, his words cut and clipped. Isabella's besotted waiter sprinted across the room to us, more napkins in his hand, which he offered to Slade.

He took them and thanked the waiter. When Isabella smiled at the man, I swear he looked as happy as if someone had told him he'd won the lottery.

Isabella kept her smile in place as she turned her attention back to her brother. "Not true and you know it. Remember Pinky?" she asked.

His head cocked to one side, and suddenly it was as if dawn edged out an inky night. Slade's mouth went from a hard frown to a sweet grin, then to a full teeth-baring smile as he let loose with his own laugh.

The sound—a deep, full-bodied baritone—had me leaning forward in my chair so I wouldn't miss a note of it.

A woman would want to be wrapped in the richness of that sound, cocooned in its warmth like an electric blanket set on high.

"Okay, you've got me there."

"Pinky"—Isabella turned to me—"was my first dog. A purebred Pomeranian."

"Nastiest little mongrel to ever walk the Upper East Side," Slade added.

"Be nice. She was just a puppy and still finding her way. Her tummy was getting used to the new food our vet had recommended for her, and the maid was supposed to feed her and then watch how she reacted to it. Unfortunately, one day the maid had a family emergency and forgot about Pinky. I came home from the park with my nanny and Pinky had, well…" Isabella grinned at her brother.

"Mutt threw up all over the new white carpeting in my bedroom. Literally. All over the carpet in a trail from the doorway to the window. The greenest, most vile-looking stuff you ever saw. Why she zeroed in on my room was a mystery."

"No, it wasn't, and you know it." Isabella beamed at the waiter when he brought our lunch. "She knew you hated her."

"I didn't hate the dog. She was merely…ridiculous. And very spoiled."

We went silent until the waiter left us, after first asking if he could do or bring us anything else. I'll add he addressed Isabella only.

"So what happened with Pinky's present?" I asked.

It was Isabella who answered. "I'd remembered hearing the maids talking one day about how soda water helps get carpet stains out, so I got a bottle from the pantry and poured it all over the mess on Slade's carpet."

"Did it get the stain out?"

"Not exactly," she said.

"Not even a chance," Slade offered. "My darling sister didn't know the difference between soda water and plain soda. She dumped sixty-four ounces of cola on my carpet—and I'll repeat, my new *white* carpet."

"Oh no."

"Oh yes." Slade shook his head and then nailed his

sister with a vexed stare.

"What happened when your parents found out? Did you get into a ton of trouble?"

For a moment, I'd gotten lost in the story, forgetting the family drama swirling around these two and the fact they only shared a father. I waited, breath held, for Slade to give me a verbal slashing and was surprised—and a little thrilled—when it didn't come.

"They never did. Luckily, they were visiting a friend in the Berkshires for a few days," Isabella said. She reached across the table and grabbed her brother's hand, giving it a squeeze. "This is one of the blessings of having a big brother who's always looking out for you."

Slade executed a very theatrical eye roll.

"When he got home, I told him what happened, and he took care of getting the carpet cleaned before Mom and Daddy came back."

"That's a very shortened version of what actually happened, Isabella, and you know it."

She smiled serenely and took a sip of her drink. "My story. My telling."

"Now my interest is really piqued," I told her. Turning to her brother I asked, "Would you like to give me chapter, book, and verse?"

His gaze drifted down to my mouth then back up to my eyes, and for a hot second, his lips parted while he inhaled.

"Chapter, book, and verse?" he asked.

I shook my head. "Sorry. Biblical reference. My grandmother has been saying that my entire life, and it's the way I usually ask for someone to tell me the whole story."

"Don't apologize," he said. Or I should say "commanded."

"The full story," he continued after a moment, "is I hired a professional carpet cleaning service and paid them three times what it should have cost so they could get the job done before Janelle and my father got back from their little jaunt."

"And he paid for it himself," Isabella added. "Out of his own money. He didn't have them send the bill to Daddy, just so he'd never know. See? He's always looking out for me. The perks of having a big brother are endless."

Slade slanted her a speaking glance but topped it off with a crooked grin that was on the north side of town between Charming Street and Captivating Boulevard.

And despite the fact I didn't want to be, I was both: charmed and captivated.

The rest of lunch was spent with conversation bouncing between my telling Isabella a few minor wedding details and she and her brother talking about a dinner they'd attended a few nights ago.

After all three of us declined dessert, Slade glanced down at his cell phone and asked his sister, "What are your plans for the rest of the day?"

"Nothing much. I'm gonna cook dinner for Jack for when he gets off duty later. He texted me this morning that he's been so busy with emergencies, he missed lunch and dinner yesterday and grabbed a stale bagel for breakfast before starting rounds this morning. I think it'll be nice to come home to a hot cooked meal."

"Who are you, and what have you done with my baby sister?" Slade's eyes went theatrically wide.

Isabella and I both laughed.

"Truly," Slade said, signing for the bill, "when did you get so domestic? I didn't even know you could cook."

"What did you think they were teaching me at that fancy Swiss finishing school mother insisted on? Carpentry? Martial arts, maybe?"

Slade grinned at her.

"I'll have you know I can not only cook a delicious, nourishing meal, I can give you the names of all the ingredients in perfect, fluent French."

"Jack's a lucky guy," I said. "Beauty, brains, and bilingual."

"Trilingual," Slade said. "She also speaks Spanish like a native."

"Okay, so now I'm really impressed."

After a quick glance at her own phone, Isabella rose and smiled at the waiter who magically appeared at her side. He asked if she needed anything else and looked like he wished she'd reply, "Yeah. You. Naked and in my bed." She shook her head and then moved in to hug and kiss her brother.

"I'll see you Saturday night at the foundation dinner," he said after patting her back.

"Jack's allowed to come, right? He's not on call this weekend."

"Yeah. He's at our table, no worries."

We all began walking, and once again, several inquiring female stares trailed Slade as we moved across the room.

"Is Katya coming?" Isabella asked.

Slade nodded.

The name rang a bell in the back of my mind from

Isabella's guest list. Katya Yurlenko, supermodel, her face and body currently gracing the newest cover of the *Sports Illustrated* swimsuit edition. Six feet tall, waist-length natural white hair, and blue eyes said to rival the color of the Caspian Sea. I didn't know if this part was true since I'd never actually *seen* the Caspian Sea, but as far as models went, she was the It Girl of the moment.

And she was Slade's date for this upcoming event.

"I'm gonna dash in here for a sec." She pointed to the ladies' room. "I guess I'll see you at my next fitting?" she addressed me.

"Or at least hear from me before that if I have any updates."

We hugged, and she gave us both a little wave over her shoulder.

I was about to say goodbye to Slade when a familiar voice called my name. My face grew numb as all the blood drained down my neck. My lips started to tingle, and a spastic trembling overtook my hands the moment the voice's owner filtered through my memory banks.

It couldn't be. It simply couldn't.

Not here. Not now.

But it was.

In the next second Slade, who'd been watching his sister leave us, glanced at me, then grabbed my upper arm in a grip tinged with titanium. "What's wrong?"

Concern filled his eyes. His mouth, which moments before had been soft and smiling, was now drawn tight and thin, the corners edging toward his jaw. His fingers, warm and long and—oh baby!—strong, for some crazy reason eased a little of my panic.

"Colleen?"

I turned my gaze from Slade's warmed-whiskey eyes to the man addressing me. Eyes the color of dung, heavily lashed like some kind of natural mascara coated them, and lit with an annoyance I'd grown to hate, my ex-everything Harry Green sidled up to me.

And yeah. I totally know if I'd married him my name would have legally been Colleen Green. Don't think my sisters didn't think up every lousy nickname in the book for it, either.

Let me introduce you to my sister, the wedding planner, Collard Green.

You get the picture.

"I knew that was you," Harry said. "What are you doing here?"

Now here's the thing about Harry. Despite being a total shit and cheating on me, despite being an irresponsible asshole and getting the girl he cheated with pregnant in this day and age of free, you-can-get-it-anywhere-and-everywhere birth control, and even despite taking me for granted and using me as his personal indentured servant and life-runner for a decade, the guy was still seriously mouth-watering in a suit.

Hair the color of warmed caramel, which I personally knew he got trimmed and groomed every three weeks because I'd been the one to make his stylist appointments, looked *GQ* perfect today, as always. He'd lost some weight in his face, the angles of his cheeks and jaw harsh and hard in the glare of daylight, which didn't do a thing to mar his good looks.

One look at him and my knees went a little soft. In the next breath, I silently chastised myself to remember all the dumb crap he'd done to me and all the years I'd wasted on him. Good years. Probably—with my lousy luck—my best years.

As soon as I remembered all that, I couldn't stop the annoyed tone in my voice when I said, "Having lunch. Isn't it obvious? Even to you?"

I added the last part just to be bitchy.

With that said, I noticed the petite, wide-eyed blond clinging—and I mean really clinging—to his arm. I got the impression she was terrified if she let go she'd be whisked away on a breeze. This wasn't my former assistant, the girl Harry had knocked up and left me for. Even though the last time I'd seen her she'd been buck naked and riding Harry like he was a mechanical bull, I remember what she looked like clothed since she'd worked with me for two years.

No, this chick was someone else.

And wasn't that…interesting.

"Still the same Colleen," Harry said with a fake smile and in the superior tone I'd listened to him to use when he'd rehearsed his mock trial summations in the bathroom mirror.

I wanted so badly to say something witty and double edged, like, "Funny. I don't remember you at all," or "I see Antonio is starting to comb over your balding spots now." But nothing would come. I knew later while I was propped up in bed not able to sleep, I'd think of something cutting and sharp and Nanny Fee-worthy, but right now I had nothing.

"I'm surprised to see you here," Harry said. "I thought you'd moved back to New Hampshire. Back to your parents."

I folded my hands together so the shaking wouldn't

be so obvious. "I have a lot of clients based in New York."

"Clients? Oh, yeah. That's right. You started a business after you left *BridalWear*. Something to do with the industry, right?"

If I'd had a drink in my hand, he would have been wearing it after making that crack, his voice mocking and so filled with disdain.

"I'm a wedding planner, Harry, and you know it." Seething, I fisted my hands at my sides. They were no longer shaking with nerves, but with anger and I was seriously wondering how I could get in a quick punch to Harry's jawline without being arrested.

As I was considering this, his gaze edged to Slade, and I knew exactly what was running through my ex's head. *Money.*

Slade oozed old money and power from every pore and, like a bee attracted to its queen's pheromones, I could sense Harry's subtle behavioral shift. Before he could say anything else, I jumped right in.

"How's Diana?" My ex-assistant.

He shot his gaze back to me, the fake smile on his face disappearing. "I don't know. We're not together any more. We—I—broke it off."

"What about the baby?" I found myself asking before I could think not to.

"Miscarriage."

"When?" Really, I needed to stop saying and asking everything the moment it popped into my head, but I couldn't help it.

With a dramatic sigh, he looked down at me. "A little less than two years ago."

So. Not very long after I left. Left him. Left our

apartment. Left my life as I knew it.

I had a passel of questions run through my mind but before I could give voice to them, Harry, dismissing me without another word, extracted his arm from little Miss Cling-On and stuck it out to Slade. "Harland Green," he said with that fake aren't-I-the-greatest-thing smile I hated. "I'm with Solomon, Uriah, and Engersol," he added, naming his law firm.

I always wondered if the law partners knew their initials were S.U.E.

Slade looked down at the proffered hand and, for a hot second, seemed like he was debating whether or not to take it.

Generations of good breeding must have driven through him, though, because he did and, from the subtle wince on Harry's face, must have put some force behind the shake.

"Green," Slade said with a nod. The slightly superior lilt in his voice combined with the clipped cadence in his tone made the name sound like he had something dirty stuck to his shoe. It didn't escape anyone's attention, especially Harry's, that Slade hadn't given his own name.

Again, good breeding jumped from the man because he turned to Harry's, er, companion, and with the uber-charming smile I was growing to like seeing on his face, said, "Slade Harrington."

The Cling-On was either painfully shy or didn't speak English. For a moment, she said nothing, simply stared up at all Slade's maleness, as if taking it in and not knowing what to do with it.

I know how you feel, sistah.

The mute button in her brain unstuck, and she

piped up in a voice shaking with fear (or it could have been lust for all I know), "I know who you are. I went to school with your sister. I'm Bunny Howland."

Bunny? *Really?*

Slade didn't even miss a beat. Either good breeding, as I've mentioned, or just growing up in a social class filled with Bunnys, Buffys, Ceces and Poppys, he kept smiling that panty-dropping grin at her.

Harry zeroed in on the name though. It was obvious in the way his eyes went wide and his chin tilted down a little. He recognized it, knew what the Harrington moniker meant in the financial world, and he was trying to figure out how he could worm his way into Slade's sphere.

He was about to say something when Slade, ignoring him and earning my lifelong devotion, said to Bunny—*Jesus! Bunny*—"You're Carl Howland's daughter, aren't you? The youngest?"

She nodded and for a second looked so excited, I feared she was gonna hop and give credence to her name.

"I saw your parents at the Met dinner the other night. Your dad's looking well. Retirement agrees with him."

Bunny rolled her eyes and snorted. The sound was so incongruous to the way she looked—all ladylike and put together—for a second it didn't register with me that it had come from her.

It did with Harry, though. He shot her the same irritated glare he'd reserved for me during the bad days of our relationship. I almost felt sorry for her.

Almost.

He turned his attention back to Slade and smoothed

his features into that fake bonhomie he just couldn't pull off effectively.

"I believe you know one of the partners in my firm," he said. "Addison Uriah. I've heard him mention your name."

"It was most likely my father's name you overheard," Slade said. God, what I wouldn't give to be able to pull off that superior, my shit-doesn't-stink-and-yours-does tone. "They're old yachting buddies. Uriah's considered a bit of a dinosaur."

"Yes, well." Harry never was a quick-on-his-feet thinker.

"I didn't hear you were getting married," Bunny piped in, addressing Slade. Harry tossed her that pissy glare again, meant, I know, to quiet her since he was the one who was center stage right now. I'd had to lob it more than a few times during the time we were together.

"I'm not," Slade answered.

"Oh. I thought, since you're with her"—she chinned me—"you were. You said you're a wedding planner, right?"

"The best in the business," Isabella said from behind her.

With a smile as broad as her trust fund, she joined our group and slid a hand inside the crook of my arm. "I wouldn't trust anyone else with my big day."

Harry gaped. There's really no other word for it. Whether it was at Isabella's statement or her blessed-from-God looks, I don't know. But open-mouthed and pop-eyed he went.

"I thought you were using Calista Guggenheim," Bunny said. "At least, that's what I'd heard…around."

TMZ has nothing on New York society for gossip.

"I was," Isabella said. "But then I met Colleen." She squeezed my arm, and I had such an irresistible urge to kiss her on the cheek, I had to mentally slap myself to hold back.

"But Calista does everyone's wedding. Everyone's. She's famous. Everywhere. I've never heard of you," she said to me. "You don't have a name."

I knew right then she and Harry were perfect for one another. Neither one cared a whit about anyone else's feelings but their own. Whereas Harry was, I'm forced to admit it, smart, Bunny seemed...not to be. Stupidity and selfishness usually do go hand in hand, though, with inbreeding, don't they?

"Yes, she does, and it's Colleen O'Dowd," Isabella said, shades of her arrogant brother in her voice. Her smile turned a tad pitying. "I'm surprised you haven't heard of her, considering she did Maisy Dimple's wedding. Didn't your sister go to school with her?"

"That was you?" Bunny asked me. "But I heard that wedding was, was..."

Poor thing. She was so overcome, she'd lost her train of thought.

Isabella got her right back on the tracks. "Amazing?" she offered. "Visionary? Yes. It was."

Bunny considered this as her gaze bounced from Isabella to me and then settled on Slade. I wondered if she realized she'd just been put in her socialite place. And by someone who was such a sweetheart.

"Calista lacks vision," Isabella said, examining her perfect manicure as if she was bored. "All her weddings look the same. She uses the same florist and arrangements, dress designers, chefs. Even the same bands. All old and dated. If you've been to one of her weddings, you've been to them all. Yawns, every one of them."

"But she's doing my sister Poppy's!"

Remember what I said about the names of the rich, famous, and societal?

Isabella shook her head and patted the girl's hand sympathetically. "And I'm sure it'll be a lovely event. But I wanted something fresh and new for mine. Something, you know, that won't look like it was planned by a great aunt. Old and tacky."

Bunny's mouth formed an open O, her eyes mimicking its width.

The tiny frown of confusion bending between Harry's eyebrows made me smile on the inside. He had no idea what was going on and hated that he didn't.

In what I knew to be an effort to gain back control of the conversation and Slade's attention, he cleared his throat.

Slade slanted him a glance, grinned, and again dismissing Harry without being overtly rude about it, crooked one hand under my elbow and one onto his sister's and said, "Well, we were just on our way. My regards to your parents, Bunny."

Her bafflement eased, and she smiled at him as if he'd hung the moon for her.

Slade's mouth dropped back to a superior smirk when he looked at Harry. "Green." Harry automatically stuck out his hand for a shake, but Slade's hands were full, between his sister and me. Something I think he planned.

"Bye," Isabella said over her shoulder as her brother escorted us out the front doors.

"She hasn't changed much," Isabella said when we alighted on the street. "Still clueless and inconsiderate."

Slade shook his head at her, that wise-older-brother look in his eyes again. "Her mother's the same way." To me he asked, "Green an old friend of yours? You two seem to have some history."

I really didn't want to get into the whole cheating/getting a girl pregnant/me leaving scenario with him, so I gave him the abridged version. The very abridged version.

"We used to be engaged."

I'd hoped the words and the finality of my tone would have been the end of it.

No such luck.

His left eyebrow tipped up a fraction, but enough for me to wonder what he was thinking. Was he having a difficult time imagining anyone would want to marry me? Or was he thinking we'd deserved one another, Harry the self-absorbed brownnose, and me the nosy wedding planner? Maybe he was just wondering why we weren't together anymore.

Isabella's limo pulled up to the curb.

"Can I drop you anywhere?" she asked me after she kissed her brother's cheek and then got in.

"I'm good." I knew she was headed uptown, me down, so I didn't want to take her out of her way. I could just as easily hail a cab or save a few bucks and take the subway.

"I'll call you in a few days," I told her.

She waved, and then she was gone.

For the second time in a week, I found myself alone with her brother. This time, though, I knew better than to stand around and poke into his family business.

A second limo pulled up as I turned to him and automatically stuck out my hand and plastered a smile on my face. "I'm guessing this is you." I cocked my head toward the limo.

As he had with Harry, Slade glanced down at my extended hand and then back up to my face. "Where are you heading?"

Before I could think not to I said, "Downtown."

He nodded and then finally, instead of shaking my hand—which I'd still had stuck out in front of me—he slipped his own up to my elbow again and said, "Get in. I can drop you wherever you need to be."

"Oh, no, really. You don't—"

"Sir?"

Slade slanted a look at his driver, then to me. At the same time Harry and Bunny—I was never gonna get over that name—came out from the restaurant. Harry zeroed in on Slade and me, a question creasing his forehead. Without another thought about why I shouldn't, I slid into the limo. Once I was settled, Slade turned to slice the two of them with an inscrutable glare before gliding in next to me.

As we pulled away, Harry's gaze tracked us. Thankfully, the windows were tinted limo-dark, and he couldn't see me.

"Where downtown?" Slade asked.

"What? Oh, um. Anywhere within two avenues of Macy's is fine. Traffic is ridiculous this time of day, so I don't think you can get closer."

"Macy's, Killian."

"You got it, Mr. H."

Slade settled into the seat across from me and regarded me for moment, the intensity of his stare making me a little squirmy.

"I'm just going to ask this, and I'd like you to be honest, okay?"

My spine went a little straight at his implication, but I nodded and said, "I'm always honest."

"I tend to believe that's true."

Why did that sound like an insult?

"Did you only accept a ride because your ex was watching us?"

Crap.

Well, I'd said I'd be honest, so now wasn't the time to start fibbing.

"Yes," I said, with more reluctance than common decency dictated.

I winced when he replied, "I thought so."

"That was rude of me. I'm sorry. It's just—well." I let out a breath. "I haven't seen Harry for a while, and I didn't want to be stuck standing there again, listening to him rant and rail at me. Which he would have, believe me. We didn't part on the best of terms, so I used you as an easy escape. And I realize how horrible that sounds, so I'm sorry. Again."

"You don't need to be. I've been used for worse things than an escape from a former lover." His quick grin sent my full tummy into a Ferris-wheel spin.

"Well, thanks anyway." I sighed again and turned to glance out the window.

"Why don't you tell me about it."

"It?"

"You. Him. The breakup."

"You're kidding?"

"Not really.

"Oh, please. You can't possibly want to hear all the

sordid details. My own sisters didn't even want to know what happened with Vla—Harry."

His penetrating stare hit me hard again. Really, the guy must be a killer in the boardroom. One quirk of an eyebrow, a minute drop of his granite jaw, and I'm sure minions and adversaries alike all did exactly what he told them to.

"What did you call him? Val?"

I rolled my eyes. "Vlad. Like, you know, Dracula? His real name was supposedly Vlad the Impaler." Saying it out loud sounded so ridiculous, I wasn't surprised when his deliciously sexy mouth lifted at the corners. But I *was* surprised when my own did the same.

"So, he's what? A bloodsucker at heart?" Slade asked.

"More like a soul-sucker."

"Sounds about right for a lawyer."

My sigh was deep. "You have no idea."

"So, why don't you tell me about it?"

Chapter Five

I couldn't for the life of me figure out why he wanted to know about my former fiancé. A weird sense of paying him back for helping me escape from what I knew would have been an emotionally charged scene wafted through me.

"There's really not a lot to tell," I said. "We met in college, lived together after. Got engaged when our careers took off and then everything went south."

"In what way?"

I looked across the seat at him and debated about how much detail to go into. The story of our breakup was Harry's fault for sure, not mine. Still, I was concerned Slade would think I was a loser who couldn't keep a man.

"Harry cheated with someone I knew. I found them together and…well." I lifted my hands and shrugged. "That pretty much put the kibosh on our engagement and future together."

"Rightly so. Cheating should always be a deal-breaker. In business and in life."

My mouth fell open, and I gaped at him. Before he could see how astonished I was by his statement, I slammed my mouth closed again.

"You look surprised at my saying that."

"I hate to admit it, but I am. Most men I've come into contact with don't view cheating—either emotionally or physically—the same way women do. It's—well, *refreshing* to hear those words come out of a man's mouth."

"You've been around the wrong type of men if you truly believe that," he said. "Most men aren't cheaters. The ones who are have no respect for women."

Well. Who knew a billionaire *playa* could have morals and scruples?

"The girl he was with today?" I said. "Bunny? And I'm sorry, but that's the stupidest name. Ever."

He laughed. "I think she was christened Theodora—"

"Another ridiculous name." I rolled my eyes.

"—but her sisters called her Bunny before she had braces. It stuck and followed her into adulthood."

I shook my head. "Sisters are like elephants. They have long, annoying memories. Anyway. She wasn't the one Harry cheated with. That was someone else. Someone I worked with."

"You seemed surprised when he told you he wasn't still with her."

"I was."

When I didn't elaborate he asked, "Why?"

I swallowed. It was amazing I could still feel so hurt, so battered and wounded after all this time. My grandmother's voice popped into my head. "Suck it up, lass."

Easier said than done.

I looked across the limo at Slade. The calm acceptance in his gaze convinced me he wasn't judging me on any of this.

"After I discovered them together, I found out she was pregnant." I looked down at my clasped hands. My

71

knuckles were white.

"I can only imagine how devastating that must have been for you."

"Yeah, well. All said and done now, isn't it? Anyway." I unfolded my hands and flexed and extended them a few times. "I'll apologize again for using you as a getaway. The bigger, better, more adult thing to do would have been to just confront him. Escaping was the cowardly way to deal with the situation."

"I don't think you acted like a coward, and there's no need to apologize."

Morals, scruples, plus kind and gracious. Why had I ever compared him to Vlad?

"I'm glad I could be of some help. Plus, I wanted to get you alone, away from Izzy, so I could offer my own apology for how I left things between us on Monday. I didn't handle the news she gave me about our father very well. I was angry about it, and I took it out on you."

I stayed silent, which, believe me, was a struggle.

"My issues, for lack of a better word, with our father are my own. They don't involve Izzy. He was a different parent to her than he was to me, beginning with the fact he was much older when she was born than when I was. He wasn't as involved in building the business when she came along, like he was when I was a child. Because of that he could be more attentive. More willing to spend time with her, especially since he had more free time to spend. More…well, loving is the best word. I need to remember that and not shove all my childhood anger about his never being around onto her."

I studied him for a few moments, completely taken aback. And I'm going to admit this freely: I was seriously crushing on him right now.

"That's a fairly evolved sentiment."

His brows kissed in the midline of his forehead. "Are you laughing at me?"

"No. I'm impressed. Thoroughly," I added. "Whatever your issues with your father, it really shows how much you love your sister if you're willing to put aside your personal feelings for her happiness. That's huge."

His features relaxed. "I do love Izzy. With all my heart. I want her to be happy. She deserves it."

I nodded again. "You're a really great older brother."

His lips slid up at the corners, and I was hit with an intense, irrational, *insane* urge to jump across the space dividing us and into his lap. I wanted to press my mouth to his and devour him, slide my nose along his thick neck and nuzzle behind his ear, straddle him, and feel his hard, hard body against mine.

When I found myself leaning forward to give action to those thoughts, a giant wave of horror bolted through my mind.

I wasn't going to be kissing, nuzzling, or straddling *anyone* in this limousine. Slade Harrington was a client, and I never, ever crossed that professional line.

Never.

I gave myself a deep, internal shake and willed my racing heart to get back to normal.

In the next breath, I was all business again. "Have you two spoken about your father's potential role in the wedding, yet?" I asked him.

If Slade noticed the edge to my voice, he gave no indication. "No. We've both been busy."

"You should. Soon. Not only because I need to know so I can make any necessary arrangements, but more because it will be one less thing for Isabella to be thinking about and worrying over. The levels brides tend to obsess increase exponentially the closer they come to the big day. I like to keep my brides as stress-free and emotionally calm as I can. It makes everyone's lives better, the wedding runs more smoothly, and all involved have a better experience in the end."

He'd crossed one leg over the opposite thigh and spread his arms open over the seatback. "Isabella is usually calm. She rarely, if ever, lets stress get the better of her. She was the same way as a kid. Oh, her teen years were, well, *normal*, I guess. Emotional at times when something didn't go her way. But she never ran away or had any breakdowns. She was the only girl in her age-set growing up who wasn't seeing a shrink. Janelle was a lucky mother in that regard."

The mention of the second Mrs. Harrington opened up a door for me to walk through.

"Can I ask a question? One I've been a little hesitant to ask your sister?"

"Go ahead."

"Why isn't her mother more involved in the wedding? Every bride I've worked for has had a mother who, at equal times, was demanding, frustrating, and bordering on dictatorial, but who was totally involved in every decision. They've gone to dress fittings, planned the gift registry, helped with reception seating. I've never met your stepmother, which is highly unusual, especially since the wedding is getting close."

He blew out a breath and looked out the window. "For the record, she's not my current stepmother. She was the first."

"Of how many?"

"Five. Including my mother, my father has been married six times. There were no other kids with the subsequent marriages."

"Your father's been divorced five times?" *Good Lord.* "He must have divorce lawyers on speed dial." I regretted saying it the moment I put a period on the end of the sentence. My cheeks burned, and my lips started to tingle. "I'm…sorry."

"Don't be. And he's only been divorced four times. My mother died when I was twelve from ovarian cancer."

The embarrassment running through me gave way to sadness. Cancer sucks. Big time. I was reminded how the dreaded disease touched so many lives, my own included. If nothing else, Slade and I had the loss of someone we loved from it in common.

He cleared his throat. "Anyway. About Janelle. The reason she's not too involved in the wedding has to do with Jack."

"What? She doesn't like him? What's not to like? He's a pediatrician, for Pete's sake. He helps sick kids, which puts him right up there next to a hero on the what-you-want-in-a-guy list. And he loves Isabella. Completely. Anyone who spends five minutes in their company can see it."

"I know. Janelle doesn't see him as a suitable spouse for her daughter, though. You have to understand her skewed viewpoint on this. Izzy was born with every advantage under the sun. Wealth, an old, established family name, a spot in the elite social registry. Plus she's gorgeous, inside and out. Janelle was grooming her to be the wife of a politician, preferably one with Pennsylvania Avenue goals. Jack doesn't fall into the category of the husband material Janelle wanted. He's from a middle-class family, and Janelle wanted a son-in-law who could claim ancestors back to the Pilgrims. She feels he's marrying her so he can move up in the world."

"That's just sad and wrong on so many levels. Especially for Isabella." I glanced out the window and then back to him. "You don't think he's marrying her for what he can get out of it, do you?"

"No. I know for sure he isn't."

"How?"

"What do you mean, how?"

"How do you know for sure? Did you have him investigated or something?"

"Of course I did."

And I'd called him gracious and scrupulous.

Ha.

"Of course you did," I said, not even trying to keep the repugnance from my voice. "People like you always do. Why am I surprised?"

"People like me? You mean people who want to protect their loved ones from frauds and those out to harm them? People who want to ensure the ones closest to them aren't hurt emotionally, physically, even financially? Because if that's what you mean, then yes, I'm exactly like that. I look out for those I love, and I love Isabella more than anyone. So yes, I had Jack investigated. He's exactly what he presents to the world. A great guy, working toward being a great pediatrician. His family, though not millionaires, have worked hard to be debt free and live a very comfortable, stable life, and they are exceedingly proud of their son. I think Isabella is getting a great guy, and she's lucky."

His voice hadn't risen a notch, his eyes had stayed cool and calm throughout his speech. Even so, I'd been thoroughly and expertly schooled. Only one other person was ever able to make me feel this level of contrition for something I'd said, thought, or done: my grandmother. My face, already hot, scorched now with shame. With a downward glance at my lap, I bit the inside of my cheek.

"I'm sorry. That was a terrible thing to say. I understand what you did was for her protection. I do. So, I'm sorry for what I said. What I implied. It was…nasty and wrong."

We were both silent for a moment.

This time it was my turn to clear my throat. "About Isabella's mother?"

"Yes?"

"This is one of those times in a girl's life when she really needs the love and understanding of a mother by her side, guiding and helping her. She should be involved."

He shrugged. "From your viewpoint," he said, "I would think not having to deal with a domineering or indifferent mother of the bride would make your job easier."

I leaned back into the car seat, folding my hands in my lap as I had before. "I can deal perfectly well with any type of mother," I told him. "I've done it more times than I can remember. But it's sad Isabella doesn't have someone—a girlfriend, a sister, a cousin, *someone*—she can turn to for guidance and help. Is anyone even going to throw her a wedding shower?"

His face, calm before now, changed. He pulled his arms from the seatback, uncrossed his legs, and, leaning forward, rested his elbows on his knees. With his fingers steepled together, he looked across at me.

"Okay, wow," I said. "I can see *that* thought never occurred to you."

"It's customary, isn't it?" he asked. "To have a shower? And a bachelorette party, as well?"

"Personal choice more than customary. And usually the mother of the bride or the wedding party organize it."

"*Damn Janelle.* I'm going to call her as soon as I get a chance and tell her to step up and start acting like the mother of the bride for her daughter's sake."

"No," I said. "Don't worry about it. Don't rock the boat. Isabella doesn't seem too concerned her mother has been absent. Maybe it's better if things stay the way they are. I'll get in touch with Jack's sister. I'll see if she's got any ideas. Isabella might not want to be bothered with all the fuss of a shower."

"Knowing Izzy, it's probably more she doesn't want to put anyone out," he said. His speared me with that laser-like stare of his again. "You arrange a shower for her. You can do that, right?"

I nodded.

"Good. Someplace nice. Someplace she'll like. I want her to feel like she's the queen of the world. I don't care what it costs. Use the guest list she gave you for the invites."

"Okay. But I'll need to find out what dates she's

got available. I can't plan something without knowing if she has a conflict."

"Give me your phone."

"What?"

He shot out a hand, snapped his fingers, and waved them at me. "Your phone. Give it to me."

My back went ramrod straight in the seat. *Jesus*, he'd snapped his fingers at me like I was a minion. I huffed out a breath when I yanked my cell from my purse and handed it over.

"I'm adding my secretary's number. She coordinates Isabella's schedule with mine for foundation parties and events. You can text her and ask what's on the agenda for the next few weeks. She'll know what dates are open."

He added his own number to my contact list as well and told me so. "You can let me know when you've got a date decided, and I'll clear my schedule."

"You do know men don't usually attend wedding showers, right? Not unless they're couples' showers? Do you want this to be? Because if you do, I'll need to coordinate it with Jack's on-call schedule as well. It may limit the available dates even more."

"*Christ.*" His head shook from side to side. "Who knew planning a simple wedding shower needed preparation and organization comparable to a military strike?"

"That's actually a very good analogy."

"Do whatever you think is best," he said, frustration slipping through his tone. "Whatever Izzy would like most."

"We're here, Mr. H."

The limo slowed and pulled up to the Broadway

side of the department store. Before the driver even alighted from behind the wheel, horns were blasting from drivers irritated that we'd stopped at the curb line.

He offered my phone back. The moment the tips of my fingers brushed against his hand, my body stilled. My previous thoughts of jumping in his lap and running my fingers all over him blasted to the front of my mind again. His unsettling, penetrating gaze shot straight through me. I swear he knew what I was thinking because he let his hand stay still, mine pressing against it. Shifting in his seat, he leaned in closer to me. His nostrils flared, and his mouth parted just a whisper.

When I felt the soft breeze of his breath drift over me, I blinked a few times, snapped out of my sexual fugue, snatched my phone, and tossed it back into my purse.

Slade's driver opened the door. The avenue was wall-to-wall crowded with midday foot traffic. The aroma of hot dough and salt from the curbside pretzel booth on the corner wafted toward me. Slade got out first and extended a hand to help me from the car. There was no way I should touch him again. A simple flit of my fingers against his palm a moment ago had been enough to send my thighs shaking. Putting my entire hand into his might snap the tenuous thread I still held on my emotions.

With inevitable reluctance, I slipped my hand into his, and for a second time in as many minutes, my body turned to stone. Soothing warmth wrapped around me as he closed his fingers over mine. A gentle tug and I stood upright.

Grudgingly, I let go of his hand.

"Thanks for the ride," I said. Goodness, was that

voice mine? Marilyn Monroe had nothing on my breathy, bemused tone. "I'll let you know the particulars of a shower once I nail down dates."

He nodded. "Fine. Thanks."

The moment stretched in silence. We were surrounded by a moving wall of noise from taxis honking and swerving in and out of traffic, to pedestrians speeding by, chatting on cell phones. But we could have been all alone, just the two of us as we stood, staring at one another.

When it looked as if Slade had said all he was going to, I took the hint and plastered a smile on my face.

"Well, I'll be in touch," I told him. "Have a nice day."

I tossed my purse over my shoulder, stepped into the throng of walkers, and wove my way toward the store, never looking back at him. The craving to turn around and see if he followed me with his eyes was torture. I didn't have to give in to it, though, because right before I went through the revolving store doors, I caught his reflection in the sidewalk display window.

And he *was* watching me.

Chapter Six

"Get me a roast beef wrap. I'm gonna head out to the property in a few and make sure everything is set for Saturday's Gunderson/Schmidt wedding, and I'll take it with me," I told Charity when she asked if I wanted anything for lunch.

"Provolone and mayo?"

"Do you even need to ask after all this time? And use the business credit card."

While she went to order, I pulled my planning bible from my files for Kimmy Gunderson's wedding and then mentally checked off everything that still needed my attention before her big day, two days from now. My concentration strayed a few minutes into the task, though, as a pair of amber eyes kept pulling me from my work.

Over a week had passed since that limo ride. Eight days for me to decipher what it was about Slade Harrington that made me a little uneasy, a little worried, and a whole lot of sexually aware.

When he'd grabbed my arm in the restaurant, an immediate sensation of being protected shot straight through me from the top of my head all the way down to the tips of my toes. His hand was like one of those heated inserts you put in your gloves in winter. I'd had the same reaction in the limo when our fingers touched as he'd handed back my phone, and once again when he'd helped me from the car.

All the nervous tension I carried around inside me every day, weighing down my shoulders, pinching my neck, snaking between my shoulder blades, dissipated the moment I touched him.

Weird. Really weird. I'd never once had that reaction when Harry had touched me.

Harry. Jesus, what a pain in the neck he was. After leaving him standing on the sidewalk outside the Crystal Room, he'd somehow gotten my new cell phone number and had left me numerous messages claiming he needed to speak to me.

I'd deleted every single voice and text message without replying. I hoped he'd get the hint and save himself the out-of-network phone costs.

Anyway. Back to Slade. I figured if he was a superhero, his secret power would be his calming touch. Coupled with the way he loved his sister and made no pretense about it, my original opinion of him as an egotistical, condescending Harry-clone was shot down in flames.

Don't get me wrong. He was still annoyingly arrogant. He'd actually snapped his fingers at me when he demanded my phone. He had no idea how much I wanted to slap his hand away when he stuck it out to take the cell from me. And the high-handed way he'd dealt with Harry, all his innate elitist heritage fully on display had both incensed and turned me on at the same time.

All his superior, master-of-the-universe behavior aside, I was truly having a difficult time forgetting about the way his lips curved and his eyes softened whenever he looked at his sister. Or the way his fingers, long and lithe and strong, had felt against mine.

Oh, and let's not forget the way his mile-wide shoulders filled out a suit jacket.

I shook my head to clear it. This had to stop. Now. I had work to do, an imminent wedding to check on, and a to-do list with ten thousand items I needed to check off. Fantasizing about a man who was so far out of my league that Jupiter seemed closer was, frankly, stupid and a major time suck.

A few minutes later, Charity came back with my lunch. At the same time, my cell phone rang. When I saw Maureen's name across the screen, I swiped right and connected.

"Hey," I said. "What's up?"

"Are you sitting down?"

"Oh, *Jesus*, Mo, never start a conversation that way. What's wrong? Is it Nanny? What's she done now?"

"Cool your jets, Coll. Nothing's wrong, and as far as I know Nanny's fine. I just need to tell you something, and I want to make sure you don't drop when I do."

"What is it?"

"I just got a call for a room booking for the weekend."

"Okay. So…yay?"

"It was Vlad."

Mary, Mother of God, preserve me. "What?"

"He wanted to book a room for Friday and Saturday nights. I told him the inn was full, and we couldn't accommodate him. He wasn't happy with that news and got all pissy and told me he was your personal friend, that you'd recommended the inn to

84

him, blah blah blah, and I had to put him up."

"He actually said he was my friend?"

"Yup. He had, of course, no idea who I was. I never said my name when I answered. I wanted to give you a heads-up because he asked about other places in town and in the area where he could book."

"Did you tell him about any?"

Her soft chuckle blew through the connection. "I told him the closest hotel was twenty miles north of here, but they were probably full for the weekend since it's a college town and school is just getting back in session. Again, he wasn't happy with that news."

What the heck? What was Harry up to?

In all the time we'd been together, he'd come to Heaven only a handful of times. He'd been whiney, complaining, and just plain awful to be around whenever he had. When I confronted him on his behavior, he'd given me the excuse he was tired from work, had too much to do to be gallivanting (his word) around New England on a weekend, and we should leave to go back to the city ASAP.

And I still wanted to marry the jerk. Go figure.

"Anyway, I just wanted you to know," Maureen said. "It sounds like he's going to pay you a visit. You should be prepared. Maybe even go out of town."

"I can't. Kimmy Gunderson's wedding is Saturday, and the Baylock/Teenar one is Sunday."

"I know, sis. Why do you think I told Vlad I was booked solid? I am, and it's with one of your bridal parties. I was joking about the leaving town stuff. Listen, I've gotta go. Wedding cakes to bake, rooms to get ready."

"Okay. I'll see you later. Thanks for the call."

"No worries. Love you."

"Love you more."

I slumped in my chair and glanced down at the still-wrapped wrap on my desk. My appetite had gone the way of the dinosaur with Mo's news.

Harry.

In Heaven.

That's all I needed to really ruin my day. Hell, my entire year.

I tossed my lunch into my office fridge and gathered up everything I'd need for my site inspection.

"I'll be out at the lake," I told Charity, who obviously had no problems with her own appetite, as evidenced by the half-eaten sandwich on her desk and the opened bag of chips next to it. "I just want to do a quick run-through."

"The forecast is calling for rain later on, and I know Devon already set up all the chairs around the gazebo."

"Okay. I'll cover them when I get there. It doesn't make any sense taking them all down again just to put them back up. It's easier to remove the tarps once the rain stops. Call me if you need me. I'll have my cell."

"You always have your cell." Charity's eye roll was a thing of snarky beauty. "It's been rumored by those of us who love you that it sits on the pillow next to you at night."

"That's not a rumor," I said with a grin while I opened the door.

And ran slapdab into a solid wall of concrete covered in a tailored, custom-made shirt.

Two hands shot out and gripped my upper arms. The file I was holding headed to the floor, its contents floating like confetti at the end of a parade around a familiar pair of Italian loafers.

When I'm flustered—like I was at that moment—my brain tends to think of really weird things. What shot through it right then was I was so happy I hadn't been eating my roast beef wrap as I started out the door like I'd originally been planning to do, because if I had, the second I slammed into Slade Harrington's perfect torso he'd have been slathered in mayonnaise and I would have ruined not only a suit jacket, but an expensive shirt as well.

"Going somewhere?" he asked.

Those bedroom eyes I'd been daydreaming about a few minutes before stared down at me. A slight grin pulled at the corners of his lips.

Just when the thought to lean forward and nip at them burst through my mind, I blinked. Really hard. It took everything in me not to lean forward and give in to the urge.

"What are you doing here?" A heartbeat later I winced at how awful that sounded. "I'm sorry. That was way rude."

"Yes, it was."

Despite the steel in his voice, the way the skin at the corners of his eyes crinkled told me he was playing with me.

His hands were still circling my arms. I looked down when his fingers started kneading my skin. I don't think he knew he was doing it until he saw them moving.

He dropped them and took a step back.

"Is everything okay with Isabella?" I asked.

"Of course. Why wouldn't it be?"

"Then why are you here? We don't have an appointment, do we?" I turned to Charity, who'd been watching this entire scene sitting on the edge of her ergonomic office chair, for clarification. She shook her head from side to side in spastic little movements, her blue eyes flicking from me to Slade and back again.

"Were you about to go somewhere?" Slade repeated, as he bent to retrieve the papers I'd dropped.

"I need to go check on a venue for a wedding this weekend. Thanks." I tucked the papers back in their folder. "Why?"

His expression was indecipherable as he took my elbow and said, "Let's go. You can drive since you know where we're going."

"Where *we're* going? Like in, you and me?"

He started walking, tugging me along, and really, I had no choice but to follow.

Okay, full disclosure here: I wanted to follow. Daydreaming about a gorgeous man is one thing. Getting to experience all his holy hotness up close is a much more enjoyable pastime.

And if I'm being totally honest, Slade's little caveman-alpha-dominant side was a total turn on. Go figure.

He turned to me, his lips twitching with suppressed laughter. "That's usually the definition of we, yes."

Before I could form a thought, he'd handed me into the driver's seat of my car and sprinted around to the passenger side.

When he'd fastened his seat belt and settled in, he said, "Let's go."

"Why are you here?" I asked again.

Remember the impulse control issues and never

being able to let something go I've mentioned before? Yeah. I really needed to start working on correcting that.

"I need to talk to you about a few things and didn't want to do it over the phone."

"So you drove almost four hours just to talk to me?"

He twirled his fingers in my direction, indicating I should get going.

I put the car in gear and glided it out onto the road.

"I had a business meeting in Boston yesterday and drove up for the day," he said. "This morning I realized Heaven is only an hour and change outside of the city, so I thought I'd stop by on my way back to New York."

Okay, that seemed…plausible. But for some reason I wasn't buying it. "So, what's so important you needed to speak to me face to face and not over the phone?"

He sucked in a deep breath in preparation, his chest heaving out, the buttons on his shirt straining a little with the movement.

Oh my.

"Izzy and I had dinner the other night," he said. "We talked about our father. About whether or not he has a role in her wedding."

"And?"

"And it was a fairly emotional discussion."

"By emotional, do you mean you made your sister cry?"

"No!" The word exploded in the car. "I'd never do anything to upset Izzy. Not intentionally."

Good to know. "So, what happened?"

"After about an hour of me explaining why I didn't think he deserved to be included in her wedding, and then another hour of her explaining why she thought he should, I told Izzy whatever she decided to do, or whatever she wanted, I'd support her. In every way."

Wow. Talk about evolved. "What did she decide to do?"

He blew out another breath and crossed his arms over his chest. "She's going to discuss it with Jack. See what he thinks. What his feelings about it are."

"That's a good idea." I nodded.

"Yeah. I guess it is."

"You know…" I slanted him a look and then turned my attention back to the road. "Isabella is a lot more mature and wise than I think you give her credit for."

"I never said she wasn't mature. She is. Always has been." The haughty note was back in his voice again.

"I realize that, but you treat her more like a baby sister than a grown woman. You're a little overprotective where she's concerned."

"I won't deny that. But there are reasons I am. Valid reasons."

When he didn't elaborate, I went with my gut and filled in the blanks. "I get the sense you were, and apparently still are, the most stable person in her life. And she's lucky you love her so much," I added quickly when his head whipped around to look at me. "And I also get everything is going to change now that she's getting married. She'll be looking to another man to help her make decisions, to bounce ideas and stuff off. I'm going to guess you're the one she's always gone to when she's had a problem to figure out, or when she was scared of thunder when she was little, or even for advice and such. Am I right?"

He waited until I'd mentally counted to five before replying. "Perceptively so. And it was spiders, not thunder."

Did I say haughty? There has to be a more descriptive word for the tone that oozed from between his lips.

"It's tough to know you're not the be-all, end-all in her world anymore. That you're not the only champion she's going to have in her corner."

"Is there a point to this conversation?"

I pulled the car into the long, hidden driveway of my grandmother's property and stifled a grin at the exasperated lilt in his tone now. "My point is," I said as I navigated down the road to the lakeshore, "I know how hard it is to relinquish that kind of role. I lived through it first hand with my younger sisters, as my older one did with me. One day you're the smartest person they've ever known. You can solve any problem and will fight all their battles for them without even being asked, and then the next day they're making their own decisions and not looking to you for guidance. Or worse, thinking you don't know a damn thing about life or what they're going through. Or anything else, for that matter."

I parked the car and killed the engine.

Slade was half turned to me, his hands folded in his lap, a pensive look on his face. "Are you always this intense and..." He shrugged.

"If the word you're looking for is insightful, then, yes. I am."

I can't tell you what it did to my insides when both corners of his mouth pulled up.

"Look." I pulled the keys from the ignition and

twisted them between my fingers. "You're always going to be Isabella's big brother. Her rock. Nothing will change that just because she's getting married. You two share a history no one else does. A family history. And family is the most important thing in the world. So just know how happy you're making your sister by letting her decide about your father's presence or absence in her wedding. As I told you once before, the less a bride has to stress about, the better the wedding, the experience, and everything else will be for her and everyone involved."

A heartbeat passed.

Something changed in his eyes. One minute he was giving me the tolerant look I'd seen in my parents' eyes too many times to remember when I'd gone on and on about a topic without end. But then it changed to something thoughtful. Something deeper. Something (*gulp!*) hotter. So hot, in fact, stress-sweat formed in all different areas of my body.

The car grew quiet. The birds chirping outside the vehicle from the woods surrounding us was the only noise audible.

Slade noticed it, glanced out the front window, then turned around to look out the passenger side. "Where are we?"

"My grandmother's lake house."

"You said you were going to check on a wedding venue. I'd assumed we were going to a church."

I got out of the car and grabbed my purse and the Gunderson wedding file. Slade followed me.

When he came around to my side of the car, I said, "My grandmother is allowing me to use this property for a couple who don't want to get married in a church."

"They want to get married here, in the woods?"

I had to laugh at the snobbish pitch in his voice. "It's actually quite a beautiful place to have a ceremony, especially in the fall with the changing colors."

We'd walked around the tiny bungalow.

"My grandfather cleared an area by the water and built a gazebo for my grandmother to escape to when she wanted a little quiet time to read or reflect on life. He picked the perfect spot." I pointed to the area we were walking toward.

Slade stayed silent as we made our way past the rows of white folding chairs set up in a semicircle on opposites sides of a walkway facing the gazebo. Saturday morning, the florist I'd hired would be out here decorating the gazebo and the walkway and lining the aisle with buckets of blooming flowers.

My grandfather had designed, and then built, the gazebo himself. An octagon, it was single storied, with a formed double cupola on its top, much, I'd often thought, resembling a bridal cake. Shale-colored shingles covered the two roofs and the structure was painted a soft white. Wooden latticework ran like a picket fence around the central portion straight to the slate floor. Kimmy Gunderson had chosen blue forget-me-nots for her bridal flower, and Saturday morning the roof and side pillars would be draped with them, ivy and sage wrapped around each bouquet as the flowers floated around and down the sides of the structure's thin columns.

A continuous bench ran around the inside perimeter where my grandmother used to sit and read, nap, and just enjoy the long days of summer and fall.

"At this time of day, and if the lake is calm and the air is still," I told Slade, "this is the most peaceful, perfect place to relax and just…be."

His left eyebrow arched as he dropped his chin and regarded me. "Why do I find it hard to believe you ever just…be? Whenever I've been in your presence, you're in constant motion."

I wasn't pouty about the dig, mainly because it was true. "You'd be surprised what a sloth I turn into when the spirit moves me." I walked up to the gazebo and looked around. Mentally, I made a list of everything I still needed to do before the ceremony. With a glance up at the rapidly darkening sky, Charity's words about the threat of rain echoed in my head.

"I need to get the folding chairs covered," I said while I walked back to the house, "before it rains."

After a brief look at the sky, he followed me.

My grandmother's lake house had two main rooms with a small powder room and bedroom. The living area moved right into the small kitchen, complete with a picnic table and bench used for meal times.

Now, the furniture had all been removed, and we used the house more for storing all the necessary items—like the folding chairs I needed to cover—for a woodland wedding.

I tugged several tarps from the pantry closet, Slade helping.

"Your grandparents lived out here?" he asked, while we moved to opposite sides of a section of chairs. His voice held a note of doubt.

"Not *lived* lived. They used it as a little getaway. Granddad liked to fish, and Nanny liked to read, so it was really just an excuse for them to be together more. He died before any of us were born. When we were kids, Nanny would bring me and my sisters out here in the summer and early fall to swim, explore, and just…" I shrugged and shook out one end of the tarp while Slade held the other.

"Be?"

"Yeah."

With the tarp opened, we fluffed it like we were making a bed over the tops of the chairs.

"Why don't you put the chairs away and then set them out again before the ceremony?" he asked, moving to another section with me.

"Time and logistics. I have a ton of stuff to do between now and Saturday. That's why they were set up yesterday. Rain wasn't in the forecast for today. Unfortunately, one thing that's always dependable around here is the undependable weather."

"You've got about five minutes before everything gets soaked," Slade said, after another glance up at the darkening sky.

He was off by four minutes. The moment we opened the last tarp, the heavens broke apart and within seconds we were saturated.

"Leave it," Slade called over the roar of the rain pelting down on us. "You can wipe everything dry later." He turned and sprinted toward the bungalow.

I should have heeded his advice, but there's a reason my family calls me stubborn. It wouldn't have taken more than ten or fifteen minutes to dry the row of chairs after the rain stopped.

But…

Trying to arrange the now-soaked tarp was a whole

lot harder single-handed. Just when I was about to give up and follow Slade, my hand was yanked in a grip of steel.

"*Christ*. Do you ever listen? I said leave it." He dragged me along with him, never letting go of my hand, the rain sheeting down on us.

"Caveman, much?" I mumbled. It wouldn't have mattered if I'd shouted it. The raindrops pelting the tree canopy and the bowling alley rumbling of thunder was enough to drown out my words.

Running through the rain as it came down at us in walls—never mind sheets—was an experience I'd always loved, even as a child.

Nanny Fee had finally given up trying to convince me to come in out of the rain more times than I could count, and simply let me enjoy running through the downpours, jumping in the puddles, and lifting my face to let the clear, cold water fall into my mouth.

Since I was born under Pisces, it was understandable why I loved it so much.

Right now, though, the soaking deluge was a bit much even for me.

Still gripping my hand, Slade spun me around once we were under the protection of the cabin's roof and glared at me. Fat raindrops dripped from his saturated hair, the color of wild goldenrod now that it was wet, and cascaded across his cut cheekbones. His long and enviable eyelashes were stuck together in little water spikes, and his shirt—*Mother of God, his shirt*!—was plastered to every muscle, line, and crevice of his torso. He would have obliterated any competition in a wet shirt contest, hands down. The saturated material outlined the defined and chiseled mounds of his pecs and the indentations and grooves of a well-constructed six-pack. The man obviously spent some hours in a gym. Many hours, from the looks of it. Through the material, his nipples had hardened from the chilly rain to two dark, puckered peaks. I had the most irrational impulse to press my lips against his shirt and suck on them through it.

If I wasn't so annoyed by his Neanderthal actions, I might have done it, too.

"Seriously, would it have killed you to leave all that"—he swiped his hand out the door to indicate the chairs—"until this downpour is over with? To chance pneumonia or a drowning for a few folding chairs?"

"Don't be so dramatic."

"Me? I'm dramatic?" His voice rivaled the crash of the storm raging outside.

I shook my head, the wet ends of my hair sticking to my chin with the motion. Swiping away a chunk that had swished into my mouth, I said, "You simply don't understand the time crunch I'm on. I have two huge weddings this weekend, ten places my team and I have to be at the same time, and little things like adding time to take down then put back up those few folding chairs is time I don't have to spare. So, yes, if it came to that, I would be willing to chance pneumonia, or even the plague, to ensure everything goes according to plan. You've never been married—"

"And never will."

"—so you don't know what it's like when one simple thing goes awry or messes with a timed-down-to-the-second bridal schedule." I wound down and took a giant breath. The words he'd spewed, interrupting me, settled in for the first time.

He was never going to get married. Never? Wow. Someone or something had really made an impression on him. I silently thanked the gods of matrimony he hadn't inflicted that thought on his sister.

"You know, I can't figure out if you're obstinate by nature or you simply don't like listening to anyone else," Slade said. He fisted his hands on his trim hips and looked down his perfect nose at me. With his brows touching in the middle of his forehead, he shook his head in disgust. Rainwater flung from his hair with the motion, the cold droplets slapping me in the face.

I flicked a few off my cheek. "Both," I shot back, letting my own annoyance break through.

It didn't escape me that even drenched and aggravated the guy was something to look at. How was that fair? I knew—*knew*—I looked like a drowned poodle. I'd straightened my hair before leaving for the office, but I could hear it frizzing and recurling as I stood there, the humidity and moisture whipping it up into a waterspout of kink. I was sure my mascara had me mimicking a rabid raccoon and God knows what other harried feral creature.

But Slade Harrington looked like a model for a popular men's fragrance. Any second, I expected him to murmur something in French, like *oui* or *eau.*

What was it about this guy that pissed me off to no end but turned me on enough to consider licking him from head to toes at the same time?

"Why doesn't that surprise me?" He lowered his voice, dragged in a breath, and raked a hand through his hair from his temple to his neck, slicking it flat against his skull. Like a squeegee, water slid from the tips of his fingers with the movement. "*Jesus.* We're

98

drenched." He looked down at his shirt and pants, and then back to me. His gaze took a slow amble from my head down to my neck, over my breasts and nipples, which were—*gulp*—as hard and pointed as his were, then farther down. My thin, cotton-blend skirt was literally glued to me from waist to knees. I could only imagine the view he was getting.

Every inch of skin on my body went goose bump crazy under his inspection. Or maybe it was because the rain was so chilly and the day had been so warm.

Nah. The temperature outside had nothing to do with it. The temperature of Slade's expression though, did.

When he dragged his attention back to my face, the annoyed glare in his eyes changed. Irritation was gone and in its place, want.

Pure, bold, rain-soaked want.

I can't truthfully say who moved first, but with the next breath I took, his mouth was on mine.

And mine, blessedly, was on his.

During the moments I'd fantasized about what kissing him would be like this past week, I'd imagined all sort of things.

His lips would be firm and forceful or, conversely, tender and soothing.

He'd go slow, savoring the kiss, allowing each of us to get to know the other's taste, or he'd swoop in and take over, overpowering me—willingly, I'll add.

So many thoughts ran through my head and every single one of them proved true.

From the moment he put his mouth against mine, all annoyance fled and, with it, the cold. Where moments before I'd been chilled, now a furnace blasted all over me, heating me straight down to my marrow. I craved the warmth, clung to the heat.

Slade's full lips completely consumed mine. Owned them. Branded them. Never in my life had I been kissed with such…possession. There really was no other word for it.

The sexy mouth I'd daydreamed about was at equal times hard yet soft, insistent yet giving. A thoughtful sigh bounced around my ears, followed by an erotic growl when he parted my lips and plundered. His hands, warm and wet, lifted my jaw, tilted my head back, and changed the angle of the kiss to go deeper, further, to draw out every and any response he could.

And there were quite a few, believe me.

He tasted of the rain—woodsy-fresh like morning dew—and clean. When I snaked my hands up his drenched shirt, kneading all that muscle and strength as I glided upward and then wound my hands around his neck to hold on fast, it never occurred to me I shouldn't be doing this. I shouldn't be standing in a storm, drenched with rain and desire, kissing a man like I'd never kissed a man before. Kissing a man who'd made no secret of the fact I annoyed the crap out of him.

A man who, for all thoughts and speculations to the contrary, was now totally absorbed with kissing me as if I was the last woman he ever would.

I don't even remember moving, but I felt my back ram into the opened front door, slick with rain, my shoulders flattening against the wood. Slade's knee eased between my thighs and rubbed side to side along the front part of my lacy thong while his tongue wound with mine and sucked to the same rhythm as the movement of his knee.

This time the groan that echoed around us was mine. His hands moved from my face, up and through my temples to clutch my saturated hair. A gentle tug and he changed the angle of my head again, this time though, his lips left mine to skim across my jaw. The feel of his hot breath along my neck as he made his way to my ear sent tiny shocks and jolts of electricity all through my body. I started to shiver, and it wasn't because I was cold. About as far from *cold* as a girl could get, if truth be told.

When Slade let out a smooth chuckle against my neck and then pulled my earlobe between his lips and bit down, the shiver turned to a quake, then a little jump, and I simply lost the tiny bit of sanity I had left.

With more force and ardor than I think I'd ever invested with Vlad, I tugged on the ends of Slade's hair, still gripped tight in my hands, and yanked his head so his mouth settled against mine again.

I felt a grin split his lips right before I touched the tip of my tongue to his bottom lip. The grin died when he sucked my tongue back into his mouth. That feeling of total possession overtook me again, especially when he slid his hands from my hair all the way down my back to cup my butt. Just as a clap of thunder boomed directly above us, Slade lifted and pressed me into him, so close in fact, I couldn't tell where his wet clothes ended and mine began.

From shoulders to knees, in one fluid line of connection, our bodies molded together. I can't begin to imagine how it felt for him to hold me this way, but I can tell you point blank, pressed against all that hard and defined muscle, all that rigid and long length of him—and, oh baby, was there a lot of length!—I felt so desired, so wanted, so *bloody* turned on, I didn't care if a twister from Kansas whooshed around us and transported us to Oz as long as I could stand there, held in this man's arms, and be kissed as if my next breath depended on it.

Look, it had been a long time since I'd tasted desire for, and from, a man. Too long. I'd thought more than once over the past year that Vlad had killed my *on* button with his lies and meanness. Because of his betrayal, I'd almost forgotten what deep want, that aching, needing longing, I'll-die-if-I-don't-have-this-man feeling was like.

For some weird reason, Slade Harrington knew exactly how to turn my sex-switch back to the *on* position—from zero to eleven with a kiss that shot me out of my shoes.

Another clap of thunder, closer and much louder, boomed above us. This time when I jumped, Slade's arms tightened around me.

"I've got you," he whispered against my ear, then trailed his mouth down to my collarbone. His tongue lapped the rainwater from my skin. When his lips nuzzled against the spot and I felt the subtle tug of sucking, combined with the gentle pressure of his knee between my legs, I swear on all that's holy and blessed I was a heartbeat from shattering.

I truly think I would have come on the spot, standing up, my panties and the rest of me dripping with lust, if my cell phone hadn't screamed "Trouble" right at that moment.

The phone call accomplished what the thunder hadn't, namely, jolted us apart.

I snapped back too quickly, the back of my head

careening off the old wooden door, the *thwack* competing with the *crack* of the rolling thunder.

Slade's eyes went wide as soon as I yelled, "Ow!" and he slipped a hand behind my head.

"Are you okay?" He grabbed my shoulders and tried to force me forward while he dipped his head around to the back of me.

I slapped his hands away and gave him a non-too-gentle push. "I'm fine. I need to get this."

I reached for my purse, which I'd dropped on the kitchen counter, and pulled out my phone, Pink's voice loud and clear. I swiped the talk icon.

"Nanny?"

"Number Two! He won't let me leave. I've been screaming about me rights and such for an hour, but he won't listen. Ya need to get right on down here, lass, and make him lemme go. I've got to be at the home by three, I do. Tilly Carlisle's countin' on me playing for her during the weekly social. Lord above knows she'll have a conniption if I'm not there. I called Number One, but she's in court. The bailiff won't let me through to 'er. I need you, lass. Now."

My grandmother's voice, the Irish brogue uncharacteristically thick, was so loud I had to pull the phone away from my ear. So loud, in fact, every word was distinct and clear not only to me, but to Slade. Usually, Nanny Fee takes great pains to hide the speech patterns that mark her native tongue as foreign. She's been in this country for almost eighty years, a citizen for over fifty, and she still feels like the young, immigrant colleen she was when she hit the US shores at the age of fifteen. When she's upset, angry, or exasperated, her Irish comes out full force and unabashed.

My left eye started to twitch, and I pressed two fingers against the lid to quell the spasming. "Nanny. Slow down. Where are you? Who won't let you go?"

"Jaysus, child! I'm down at the police station, and it's himself, Police Chief Lucas Alexander, holding me prisoner. The boy seems to have forgotten every lesson I ever taught him in Communion class about respectin' his elders and such. Treating me like a criminal, he is."

"Why? What did you do?"

"Now, why would you be askin' me that, lass? Nothing. I did nothing, but Chief"—and she practically spat the word—"Alexander up and arrested me like I was Bobby Sands himself."

The reference to the dead IRA leader proved she was pissed. Royally pissed. Whenever she'd uttered his name in the past, she'd made the sign of the cross and then pressed her fingers to her mouth in a sign of verbal contrition. Don't ask…it'll take too long to explain.

My left eye was doing a rapid merengue under my fingertips now.

Nanny continued to spew about Lucas like a hell-bent speeding train, and I couldn't stop her. I let her rant on. While she did, I moved back to the pantry closet and pulled out two large industrial towels, handed one to Slade and then, with one in my free hand, started squeezing rainwater out of my hair.

I'd avoided looking directly at him since answering the call, but I slinked a side-eye his way when I gave him the towel. He was staring at me, hands rolled on top of his hips again, chin dropped and forehead creased.

Lord only knew what was running through his

head.

When Nanny stopped to take a much-needed breath, I pounced. "I'll be right down. Don't antagonize Lucas, okay? It'll only make things worse. Behave until I get there."

"I'm not antagonizin' anyone, lass. It's himself who's so belligerent and all."

My eye felt like it was going to jump off my face. "Just take a few breaths. I'm on my way. Okay?"

"Aye. Put the wind at ya back."

After I disconnected, I sucked in a huge breath and held it. Between the sexually charged kiss, the raging storm, and my grandmother's apparent incarceration for God only knew what offense, I needed a moment.

Several, if I'm being truthful.

I closed my eyes as mortification crept through me.

I opened them again when the towel was gently tugged from my hand. Slade rolled both his and mine together, then tossed them on the kitchen counter. He pulled two more from the closet and handed one to me. With his own, he dabbed at his shirt and neck.

"So. Your grandmother?"

I closed my eyes again and dragged in another deep breath.

"She sounds…interesting."

"That's one word for her," I said, without thinking. I took the towel and rubbed at my arms and blouse.

When I'd sopped up most of the water, I chanced a quick glance in Slade's direction. His hair was damp now, not soaked, and his shirt wasn't as see-through revealing as it had been. A tiny smile played at the corners of his mouth as he cocked his head and regarded me, and all I could think was how pitiful he must think I am. We'd met exactly three times, and each time the universe and the fates had conspired against me.

Slade Harrington, financier and playboy, who never put a wrong foot forward socially or in business, had been forced to deal with an unmarried wedding planner in her mid-thirties, blessed with a sharp and quick-to-ignite tongue and a slightly demented grandmother.

Yeah, pitiful was the correct word to describe me.

"Look," I said, tossing the second towel on top of the other two, "I need to go deal with this situation before it gets worse."

"Can that actually happen? She's already in police custody. What else do you expect?"

I shook my head. "The list is too long to even consider." I picked up my purse, rummaged around for my keys. "Come on." I grabbed two more towels and tossed one to him. "The umbrellas are in the car, so use this as a cover to run."

We bolted through the rain, which showed no signs of letting up, and were in the car within a few seconds. I cranked the heat on full blast over the windshield to defog the humidity and backed out of the drive. "I'll drop you off at your car before I head over to the police station."

"No, don't. Your grandmother sounded frantic. It's better if you go straight there."

"She always frantic when she's in a state. You don't have to come with me. Really. She can wait the extra few minutes."

"There's that stubbornness again."

"I'm not being stubborn. It just makes no sense for

you to come with me. I'm sure you'll want to avoid as much traffic as you can back to the city. If you leave soon, you'll get through the tough spots before they start. Any later and you'll be reduced to a crawl for most of the highway, especially with the rainfall."

I sounded more than a little aggressive with my insistence he leave. In all honesty, I wanted to get rid of him. I'd been embarrassed enough for the rest of my lifetime with this man and didn't want him to witness what I knew was going to be a highly charged scene between Nanny, the chief, and me. I just wasn't strong enough.

Slade wasn't having any of it. "Sense or not," he said. "I'm going with you."

"Why?"

Jesus, Colleen. Whine much?

Chapter Seven

Why?

Good question. One I hoped he'd answer, truthfully.

"For one thing, I still need to speak with you about something Isabella-and-Jack related. For another, I might be able to help."

"Doubtful. This isn't your problem."

"It may not be, but your grandmother may need a lawyer."

"She has my older sister for that. Besides, you're not a *practicing* lawyer. You have a PhD in economics." The minute the words left my mouth, I regretted them. I spun around to face the windshield again so he couldn't see my face in full.

"How do you know that?" he asked. "Isabella?"

I could have lied. Should have, in hindsight. Thirty-five years of a Catholic upbringing aside. But old, ingrained habits die hard.

"Google," I said, leaving it there. He didn't need to know I'd spent hours trolling through every website I could find with a link to his name or a photo of him in his captain-of-finance role, or billionaire-playboy one.

"What did anyone ever do before the internet?" It sounded like a rhetorical question so I stayed quiet. "In case you don't know this from your research, I had a double major," he said, with a casual shrug. "Corporate law was my first choice, but I knew I needed a business degree to run the family foundation one day. When my father's misguided marriages threatened to ruin the business, I put law on the back burner and took over sooner than I'd intended to. I don't broadcast the fact I'm licensed to practice law, especially when I'm negotiating contracts and business transactions. It intimidates some people."

"No help needed there," I mumbled. I took a deep breath and blinked a few times. If I hadn't been driving I probably would have closed my eyes to shut everything out.

"Your sister is a lawyer?"

"Yeah, but she's in court today. She usually takes care of Nanny's legal troubles."

"Troubles? Does she get arrested often?"

I don't know how it was possible I didn't burn to a crisp on the spot from the degree of heat rising up from my chest and neck. "Define often."

"Okay, I'm not touching that line," he said, shaking his head. I snuck a glance at him and saw his lips quivering. "It makes more sense than ever for me to accompany you. If there is a legal matter, I can handle it for your grandmother, in light of your sister's absence."

I had no response for that, so I simply nodded and turned the car into a small municipal parking lot.

A sign with City of Heaven Police Department stood over the front doorway of a single-story structure. After parking and killing the engine, I shifted and reached behind me. In the narrow confines of the car, I brushed against him as I contorted my body between the seats. A few minutes ago, his hands had cupped my butt while he'd kissed me senseless. Right now, that piece of my anatomy was staring him right in the face while I stretched to get us umbrellas.

"Here." I handed him one, pulled another from under the driver's seat, and then inched my way back to sit properly again.

The rain pelted straight down on the car, beating against the roof.

"Aren't we going in?" Slade asked.

I fingered the closure on the umbrella handle.

"Colleen?" Before I knew what he was doing, he reached across the gearshift and touched my forearm. I startled and stared over at him, bit my bottom lip so hard, I wondered why it wasn't bleeding. Slade's hand wormed around my forearm when I didn't say anything, slid down to my hand, and he linked our fingers together. It was then I noticed I was shaking.

Pulling my gaze up from our joined hands up to his eyes again, I swallowed, my throat tight, the up and down action causing a loud gulping sound in the car.

"You really don't have to go in with me," I told him.

"No, I don't. But I'm here, so I might as well, especially if I can help."

"Just…" My gaze drifted back down to my lap.

"What?"

I almost came undone when he squeezed my hand. The gesture was so tender, so comforting. "I don't want…I mean…just, don't…judge her, is all."

"Why would I?"

"Most people do. She's not a typical ninety-ish grandmother."

"I figured that out all by myself. Most ninety-ish

110

grandmothers don't call their grandchildren claiming they've been arrested, falsely or otherwise." His grin was bright and filled with kindness.

Truer words were never spoken.

"She's really a wonderful woman."

"Let's go see what we can do for her."

We sprinted through the rain into the building. The umbrellas did nothing to keep us from getting soaked again.

"This place looks nothing like a police station," Slade said.

I could understand his confusion. Most urban police departments, like the one in my old Manhattan neighborhood, looked like every bad television show ever depicted on film. A front desk in which an unshakable and middle-age-spread sergeant would, like Cerberus guarding the gates of Hell, keep watch over the comings and goings of the rabble; a cloistered, locked cell block where the felonious would wait, concocting alibis; a tall, severe captain overseeing it like the lord of the manor.

That was an urban setting. This was Heaven, New Hampshire, about as far from the definition of urban as you could get.

No front desk elevated on a podium stood in our police station, merely a simple plywood table painted black, an empty chair behind it, one generic desk phone atop it. Off to one side were two offices, their doors opened, the rooms vacant. An old leather couch that had seen better days when I was a kindergartener sagged against one wall, a table in front of it strewn with magazines five years or more outdated.

"Where is everyone?" Slade asked.

"Probably in the kitchen. Come on."

He followed me down a narrow hallway.

I heard my grandmother before we ever saw her.

"You didn't steep that long enough, young man. 'Tis obvious no one has ever taught ya da proper way to make a cuppa. Let the bag rest for at least t'ree minutes. Five would be preferable."

My back stiffened at her tone. Nanny's Irish was still flowing thickly—never a good sign.

"Sorry. We don't get too many tea drinkers around here. Gut-rot coffee swillers or drunks is what I'm used to serving." The voice was deep, calm, and filled with a hint of humor.

A resounding "hrumph" came back to him.

The hallway opened into a kitchen. The decor was circa nineteen sixties, the table an oval of solid oak surrounded by four chairs, one of which was occupied by a leprechaun. A flaming red-headed leprechaun with the bluest eyes ever produced. While the eyes were their birth color, the hair was not. The shade was simply one not found anywhere in nature. I knew it came out of a box—two different boxes, in fact—because Nanny had never been able to find the exact color she desired, so she created her own. All the O'Dowd women resembled our grandmother in coloring and facial structure. My sisters and I could still claim, truthfully, our red hair was from God.

"Nanny, I'm here."

"Praise the Lord." She jumped up from the chair and bolted across the room with more speed and vigor than a woman in her nineties should have. "Get me outta here, Number Two. Tilly's probably having a coronary wondering where I am. I need to get to the home."

As she spoke, her eyes grazed over Slade and narrowed thoughtfully. "And who might this be?" she asked, pointing her chin in his direction, but addressing me. "Got the look of a legal man about 'im."

Before Slade could introduce himself, I moved to the other man in the room, one I'd known since birth.

"Lucas, what's all this about? What's Nanny done?"

"I've done nothin', child. I'm falsely accused. Police brutality, 'tis. Pure and simple." Nanny did her best to pull herself up some in height, but even standing on the tops of her toes, she couldn't achieve more than four foot ten.

"Nanny, please." I turned back to the chief. "Lucas?"

"It's what she didn't do, Coll, that has her sitting here. Her driver's license expired."

"Oh, my God, is that all?" I relaxed for the first time since the phone call. "She can just retake the test, then. Her license isn't too far out of date, is it?"

Lucas looked at Nanny and said, "Do you want to tell her when it expired?"

Nanny's mouth clamped shut.

"Well?" My gaze bounced between them. "How long ago?"

"Ten years," Lucas said.

What? "Te-ten? Years?"

Lucas nodded, flicked his gaze to my grandmother and then back to me.

"Obviously, you didn't know. I wouldn't have either, but she ran through the stop sign—"

"I did no such t'ing!" Nanny shouted.

Lucas ignored her. "—on Purgatory Place. Pete Bergeron was sitting in the squad and saw her blast through it."

"Lies! All lies."

"Nanny, please." My hand flew to my left eye, bracing it when it started twitching like a meth addict in need of a fix. I turned back to Lucas. "Go on."

I had to give the man credit. He never lost his composure when Nanny yelled her accusations. He simply waited until she wound down. "Like I said, Pete saw her run the stop and then gave chase."

"Lights a-blaring, sirens a-blasting like he was chasing a notorious criminal." Nanny shook her bottle-dyed head, the corners of her lips pulling down to her chin, a click of her tongue echoing with disgust. "The whole of Glory Road saw him barreling down on me like I was Whitey Bulger himself, come back from the grave!"

I ignored her outburst, never correcting her that the famous mobster was still alive and well and living out his days incarcerated.

"When he finally got her to stop," Lucas continued, "he asked for her license and registration, and where she was speeding off to so fast she blew the stop sign."

Nanny made a rude noise, crossed her arms in front of her chest, and said, "The man's a complete askhole."

"Excuse me?" Lucas's voice dropped several notches. I imagined criminals wet their pants when he used it on them.

"It's what she calls people who ask—in her opinion—stupid and pointless questions," I explained quickly. "Askholes."

My pulse slowed a little when I saw the ghost of a

grin tug at his mouth. "The car's registered to your dad," he said after a moment.

I rubbed my eye, then batted it a few times to focus. "Daddy left it for her to use when he and Mom moved. Is the registration expired, too?"

"No. Just her license to operate a vehicle." He finally turned his full attention back to my grandmother. "What I can't understand is why you let it go so long, Fiona."

"Don't'cha be addressing me as anyt'ing other than Mrs. Scaloppini. You've lost the right to use me Christian name, treating me like a criminal as ya are. I used to wipe your snotty nose when your ma brought ya to catechism class. You've no cause to be calling me *Fiona* as if we were friends. We're not from this moment on and never shall be."

"Nanny, stop," I pleaded. I lifted one of her gnarled hands in mine. "Answer Lucas. Why did you let your license lapse for so long? It's not like you wouldn't have known it was expired."

Nanny Fee's tongue clicked again as she shook her head. "It's not me fault," she said, her tone softer since she was addressing me.

"Then whose is it?"

"Carson Harper's," she said after a few moments. Reluctance for giving voice to the name was evident in the way she hung her head and all but whispered it.

"Doc Harper? Why is it his fault? I can't even remember the last time you went to see him."

"Probably about ten years or so, I'd bet," Chief Alexander said.

"And aren't you just the smartest one in the room," Nanny spat. She glanced up at my face and all at once the fight seemed to drain from her. Her tiny shoulders slid down from their raised and locked position at her neck, her chest heaved once, deeply. "He told me I needed surgery."

"Su-surgery?" My lips started to tingle, and the tips of my fingers felt numb.

"Sit down, child before ya fall," Nanny commanded.

The next thing I knew Lucas shoved a chair at the back of my knees and gently pushed me into it. I hadn't stopped looking at Nanny's face the entire time. "Wh-what kind of surgery?"

"Cataract removal. Both eyes. The old fool said I'd be as blind as a dingbat by the end of the year if I didn't have it done. It's been ten years, and I can still see foine, I can."

"Did you see that stop sign?" Lucas asked.

She slanted him a chilly glare. As a child, when I'd been the subject of that squinty-eyed glower, I'd usually cried. Lucas was made of sterner stock. He kept talking, never once ducking the daggers zipping his way.

"Because Pete said you never even slowed down but kept right on going. Luckily, there were no cars coming along Eden Lane. Otherwise you would have T-barred."

The implication of that statement made me gasp.

"You're upsettin' the lass," Nanny admonished him. "Puttin' images in her head that have no place being there."

It was at this moment Slade made his presence known. "Is Mrs.—I'm sorry, but is it Scaloppini?" he asked, addressing her.

"Aye, lad." She nodded. "Like the dish, minus the veal."

From the way he attempted to control the grin threatening his lips, I knew he understood her meaning. "Is Mrs. Scaloppini being charged with anything criminal?" he asked the chief. "Or is she simply being ticketed with a moving violation?"

"There's nothing simple about a moving violation," the chief said. "She was doing about forty-five in a twenty-mile-an-hour zone, plus she blew the stop sign. If she had hit something or someone, we wouldn't be sitting here, but at the morgue."

"But she didn't, and we are here, safe, sound, the public the same," Slade said. "If you're not going to charge her with anything, I don't see the legal need to keep her here."

"And who are you, exactly?" Lucas asked, his head cocked to one side. His body remained in a relaxed stance, but experience had taught me he wasn't as calm as he appeared. Several times over the years, I'd witnessed Lucas bare-handedly subdue disorderly drunks bigger than him and never raise his voice or break a sweat.

Slade introduced himself and told Lucas he was a lawyer.

"There now, I'm never wrong," Nanny said. "I knew he had the look of a barrister."

Lucas turned his attention to me. "I can't write this off, Coll. If your father was still around, even he'd make me charge her with something."

"No. No, I don't expect you to." I took a deep breath, then stood. It was a little embarrassing my legs were still wobbly. "Tell me what the fine is, I'll pay it, and I'll make sure she doesn't drive anywhere."

"Now see here, child—"

"Nanny. Stop." I stared hard down at my grandmother. "I mean it," I added when the old woman opened her mouth again. To the chief I said, "Let's get this settled."

Twenty minutes later, with me three hundred dollars poorer, a promise Nanny's car would be picked up in the morning, and that she wouldn't be driving it any longer, we left the police station. The rain had finally stopped, leaving a bite to the air along with the smell of fresh, wet earth. Slade helped Nanny into the backseat of my car.

"I t'ank you, lad. It does me heart good to see that not all men are arrogant, mannerless clods these days."

"Lucas is none of those things, and you know it, Nanny," I said from the driver's seat as I looked over my shoulder at my grandmother. "You're just pissed you got caught and now you can't drive anymore."

"Mind your language, Number Two. We'll be discussing me driving when we've got the time. For now, move it along. I've got ten minutes to be at Angelica Arms or Tilly'll be having an attack of the vapors. 'Tis bad enough I haven't had a moment to warm up me fingers. Step on it."

"I need to drop Mr. Harrington off first."

"No, that's okay. I'm in no hurry," he told me. "Let's get your grandmother to where she needs to be."

"You're going to hit traffic if you wait any longer."

"Traffic doesn't concern me."

I shook my head and pulled the car out onto the main roadway.

A series of staccato pops blasted from the back

seat. I looked in the rearview mirror to glimpse Nanny with her hands linked in front of her, the fingers webbed together as she reached her arms forward, stretched, and cracked her gnarled knuckles.

"My sister does the same thing before she plays her piano," Slade said, tossing Nanny a smile. "Do you play?"

Her own grin was quick and bright. "Aye, lad. Ya could say I tickle the ol' ivories when the spirit moves me."

"Nanny was a concert pianist for almost thirty years," I told him. "She traveled all over the world, played some of the most famous concert halls. Even for royalty."

"I'm impressed," he said.

"Ach, don't be." She waved her hand in the air. "They put their trousers on one hairy leg at a time, as do we all."

"Still, it's not everyone who can say they played for royalty, Mrs. Scaloppini. That's pretty amazing."

She smiled at him, the twinkle in her eye turning flirty. "I t'ink you can be calling me Fiona, darlin', seeing as you've already defended me in a court of law today. Plus, you're a friend of me granddaughter's, so you're practically family."

"We're not friends," I said, instantly. "Slade is the brother of one of my brides. He came up here today to discuss the wedding plans." My gaze shot to the overhead mirror. "Not to bail you out of a jam."

"Seems 'twas you paying th' bail, Number Two, and not your boyo here."

"He's not my boyo, Nanny. And you owe me three hundred dollars."

If this kept up, I'd be the one needing eye surgery to quell this spastic tremor.

Chapter Eight

The headache that had started in the police station was pounding like a full percussion section of bongo players by the time we got to the retirement home. My day was officially and literally shot to hell now, because without the ability and legality to drive, my grandmother would need to be escorted home after the performance, and everywhere else for the foreseeable future. She, unlike most of her friends, still lived in her own home. Okay, it was my parents' home and I lived there, too, but still, I couldn't just drop her off and leave her at Angelica Arms, content in the knowledge she'd be cared for with three hots and a cot. I toyed with the idea of leaving her and coming back later to pick her up, but I knew in my heart she'd find some way to charm one of the staff members into letting her *borrow* a car. Cathleen was tied up in court, and Maureen had a full house she needed to cater to and cook for, so I was the lone sister who could be held responsible for our grandmother.

While Nanny was greeted enthusiastically by the staff and shuffled into the filled-to-the-rafters cafeteria with the residents awaiting her accompaniment of one of their own rank and file, I tried to figure a way to salvage the rest of my day.

The presence of the very large, very intimidating man standing next to me as Nanny Fee warmed up on the piano was proving to be a distraction I needed to deal with. Right now.

"Look," I said, turning to face him.

Jesus! Where is the justice in this world? The man had been caught in a rainstorm, drenched to within an inch of his magnificent skin, and then had to deal with an annoying legal issue that was none of his concern. Why, then, did he look like he'd just stepped off the cover of a current men's magazine? I'd been caught in the same storm and knew—*knew*—I looked like I'd survived the zombie apocalypse. Why didn't he?

I forgot what I wanted to say. The thought shot out of my head as if it had never been a shred of an idea. I stood, statue-still, just staring up at pair of sepia eyes that lit on me with expectation.

"Um."

The expectation turned to quiet laughter. "Yes?"

It was the tiny tinge of haughtiness in the tone that broke through my vocal paralysis.

I flattened my lips together to keep from saying something snarky, took a breath then replied, "I can drive you back to your car. We don't need to wait around for the program to be over. By the time I get you back to my office and then get back here, Nanny will be done and I can take her home. There's no reason for you to stick around. I can—"

Before I could finish, a hush fell over the room, which up until that moment had been filled with hearing-impaired voices screeching at one another in tones they thought were acceptable for indoors. The sudden quiet was as jarring as the noise had been.

Tilly Carlisle, all six feet, seventy-nine years of her, sashayed into the room, her age-spotted arms held out at her sides, the sleeves from her voluminous caftan swishing in the air as she moved. A black turban covered hair I knew was sparse and bone white. Her face was made up for the stage, much as I imagined it had been forty years ago when she'd been the belle of Broadway musical comedy. After forty years of sagging, age, and collagen loss, the makeup didn't have the same beautifying effect it had back then, though. I don't suppose during her show-stopping days she'd resembled something out of a tacky horror film when she entered a stage.

Under thick, flesh-colored pancake foundation, jet-black eyeliner extended from the tops of her lashes almost to her temples, two round dots of dusty-rose blush covered her once-high-now-sunken cheekbones, and crimson slashed across lips that looked like she'd outlined them in bold red magic marker, Tilly smiled, bowed, circling her hands like the Queen of England greeting her subjects.

The room broke into applause. Why I was surprised to see Slade Harrington joining in on the greeting I had no idea.

Tilly nodded to my grandmother the moment the applause subsided, and Nanny went to work. A few chords later and Tilly burst into a rousing rendition of "New York, New York." You would have thought she was playing to a packed house of paying patrons instead of a nursing home cafeteria filled with old folks. Her pitch was perfect, her reverberations classic, and she gave the audience all she had and more.

The residents and staff exploded into applause.

"She's amazing," Slade said, smiling and clapping along with the audience.

When he turned to me, I have to admit my heart shifted a smidge. The controlled, uber-arrogant financier was grinning from ear to ear, his eyes wrinkled at the corners, and for the first time I noticed two little indentations running down his cheeks to his jawline.

Slade Harrington had dimples. Adorable ones, too. Who could have possibly seen that coming?

It was difficult for me not to smile back at him, so I did. "Yeah," I said. "She is pretty great."

His gaze stayed locked on mine, and I swear I heard him suck in a breath even over the noise in the room.

I was mesmerized. Transfixed. My breathing went shallow, and my blood pounded through my head.

All I could see, hear, smell, was Slade.

With slow and steady deliberation, he turned his shoulders to face me, his gaze never straying from mine. Scalding heat steamed from his eyes, and I figured it wouldn't be a surprise if I self-immolated right then and there on the spot. Slade's hand rose from his side, lifted to my face. He was just about to touch me when Tilly broke out into a loud and throaty opening chorus of "Oklahoma." The sound jolted Slade's concentration. He blinked and shook his head a bit like a dog shucking water off its back. For a second there, it looked as if he was going to kiss me again, but the only thing that kissed were his eyebrows when they pulled into the middle of his brow.

His face was etched with…shock? Confusion? Maybe revulsion? I had no idea. But whatever he'd been planning to do was a memory now as he glanced down at my mouth and then turned his attention back to

Tilly's performance.

I stood, rooted, unable to move despite wanting to run from the room in frustration. What the heck was it about this man that turned me from a mature, smart, and savvy businesswoman, able to cope with a myriad of wedding disasters and problems with nerves forged in steel and without blinking an eye, into a mindless, emotional shell of a woman?

Yes, he was good-looking. But so were any number of men I saw every day, Lucas Alexander and Kolby among them.

Yes, he was successful, but I knew—intimately—professional work success many times equated with personal relationship failure. Harry and I were the poster children for that reality.

No. It was something more. Something deeper that caused me to be so discombobulated whenever we were together. One minute I thought he hated me, the next he'd kissed me like I'd never been kissed before—like he owned me, body, soul, heart, and mind.

He'd been gracious and kind with Nanny both at the police station and then in the car. My grandmother could charm the socks off Lucifer himself, and apparently, she'd done just that to Slade. For once, I didn't dismiss the gentlemanly way he helped her into and out of the car or the way he matched her stride while walking her into the home as due to years of inbred manners. He'd genuinely appeared to like Nanny.

And she him. But that wasn't a good yardstick to measure a man by, because I've found in my thirty-five years Nanny liked most men and couldn't help but flirt with anything with an X and a Y chromosome, Lucas

Alexander being the exception to the rule.

Tilly arrived at the part where she was spelling out Oklahoma, and her voice, pitch, and arms rose with each new letter until Nanny's fingers pounded out the last chord.

Once again, the applause was raucous. Slade had apparently pulled himself out of his deep, confused musings, because he turned to me while clapping and asked, "How many songs does she do?"

"Anywhere between five and ten, depending on the theme."

"Theme?"

I nodded. "Today's seems to be United States locales."

Right on cue Tilly eased into "I Left My Heart in San Francisco."

I lifted my brows and a hand toward her as if to say, "You see?"

Slade's laughter was as captivating as his dimples.

We listened for a few bars, then I leaned a little closer to him so I wouldn't have to compete with Tilly's bluesy tenor and said close to his ear, "If she runs true to form her next number will be 'Viva Las Vegas,' complete with full body shimmies and finger-snapping *à la* Elvis."

Slade shifted to face me again, those panty-dropping dimples on full display. It took every ounce of control I could muster not to stretch up and run my tongue through the hollows.

Because I found myself starting to lift up on my toes to give action to the thought, I shifted back away from him.

He noticed the move. Those perfect brows pulled

in a little more in the center of his forehead. Just like when we'd been at the lake house, confusion shifted across his features when his gaze dropped to my mouth and then flittered back up to my eyes. I got the distinct impression he wanted to kiss me, couldn't figure out why he wanted to, and was a little pissed off about why our lips weren't sealed together at the moment.

With a determined head cock to one side, he motioned for me to leave the room with him, while at the same time clasping his hand around my upper arm.

Once we were in the corridor, Tilly's song ended, and the applause erupted again. Even through the closed cafeteria doors, the sound was deafening.

Slade kept his hand around my arm. "Finish what you were saying before the singing started."

I wanted to ask, you mean when I was thinking about running my mouth and hands all over you? But I didn't think he was referring to that. "It's just that I know you'd rather be anywhere but here in a nursing home listening to a faded Broadway diva tripping down memory lane. You don't have to stick around. I can take you back to your car and still be back here before the show ends."

Slade opened his mouth but shut it again when Tilly started singing the opening verse to "Viva Las Vegas."

"I thought you were kidding," he said, shaking his head, a tiny grin dancing on his lips.

"If you're a rhythm and blues fan, you're in for a treat. 'Midnight Train to Georgia' is next."

His lips curled even more. "What's after that? 'Last Train to Clarksville'?"

"You can laugh," I said, shaking my head, "but

you're not far off the mark. Tilly was a big Monkees fan in addition to loving the Eagles."

His face went blank for a moment.

"Wait," he said. He turned back to the cafeteria doors, then to me again and hitched his thumb over his shoulder. " 'Hotel California'? You've got to be kidding me?"

"Nope. 'It could be heaven, or…' " I let the rest of the lyric go unsaid.

He stared at me for a beat, and then we both burst out laughing. In a matter of seconds, it was obvious we weren't going to stop—couldn't! The two of us probably looked like crazed hyenas, standing in the empty corridor while Tilly bumped and shimmied, the faint smell of nursing home antiseptic and incontinence drifting around us.

Oh God, when was the last time I'd laughed like this? It had been way too long. I felt giddy and lightheaded and, for a moment, happy.

Really happy.

Slade looked…hot. Ridiculously so. With his gorgeous eyes crinkling in the corners with mirth, his perfect mouth pulled back in a smile that had my thighs trembling and my abdominal muscles quaking (and I wasn't even wearing the dreaded belly slimmer), Slade Harrington was the embodiment of all things sexy and male.

When our laughter finally wound itself down, he was still staring at me with the remnants of a grin pulling up the corners of his mouth. All at once, though, mirth was abruptly replaced by scrutiny; laughter by longing.

At least, I thought it was longing. It could have

been annoyance for all I knew.

With a subtle shift, he leaned in closer. "Colleen?" he whispered, making my name a caress.

I swallowed. Hard. "Y-yes?"

Instead of replying, he brushed his lips gently across mine. Just a quick, simple buss, but on my insides it had the impact of a rocket launching.

Yup. Forget the annoyance, this was longing, for sure.

And it was mutual.

Since his hand was still wound around my arm, it didn't take any effort at all for him to pull me flat up against the long, hard length of his body. His free hand skimmed around my waist to settle on the small of my back. With his palm flattened against me, he pushed me closer, his other hand moving up to cup my chin. He tilted my head back a bit, all the while his focused, intense gaze still imprisoning my own.

It was no mystery why any woman with a pulse would be captivated and drawn to this man like a hummingbird to nectar—instinctively and completely.

The thrumming of my heart competed in volume with Tilly and Nanny's performance, my heart the winner by a few decibels. Slade skimmed his lips across my temple, slid down to my cheek.

"Your heart's pounding like a drum," he whispered into my ear and then sucked the lobe into his mouth.

Firecrackers exploded along my insides, remnants of their heat shooting straight to my lady parts, and setting me on fire.

I snaked my hand between our bodies, up the front of his shirt to rest on his pecs.

"So's yours." I arched to give him better access to

my neck—which he'd started nuzzling. I don't remember doing it, but somehow I found myself practically climbing him. One of my legs lifted and hooked around the outside of his thigh, one of his hands moving down to cup the underside of my knee and aid me in my quest.

His fingers drifted up my naked thigh as one of his knees quite expertly snaked between my legs.

Holy Mother.

"Your skin is like silk," he whispered against my jaw, his fingers stroking the back of my thigh, the thigh that was currently straddling him like I was riding a motorcycle. "So soft."

"M-moisturizer," I said. Or it might have been a gasp. For all I knew, I could have thought it instead of saying it aloud. The man had my brain twisted six ways from Sunday. "Buckets of it."

I felt his smile drift along my cheek before landing on my mouth again. If I died right here and now, I'd go with no regrets, happy in the knowledge I'd been kissed by a man who knew what he was doing better than any man I'd ever kissed before. He nibbled at the corners of my lips, glided back across my jaw to my neck, and…feasted. There really is no other word for it.

The notion drifted through my brain that vampires knew what they were doing when they decided the neck was the juiciest place to suck.

Something in the back of my mind tickled as his tongue grazed across my collarbone. Something was different all of a sudden…wrong.

Warning bells went off like an air raid siren when it came to me.

The music had stopped.

Nanny was no longer drumming out chords. With a mental clarity that had all but shattered the moment Slade's mouth took mine, it dawned on me we were standing in an open nursing home hallway—a thoroughfare for staff, visitors, and residents—in the middle of the day, dry humping one another like feral animals.

Good God. What the heck were we doing? I yanked my leg from its lifted position around his hip and slammed it back down to the floor. With a none-too-subtle jerk, I tore my hands from clutching the ends of his hair and pushed back, away from him.

Slade's eyes were wide and blank, his mouth wet from licking—*Jesus, licking!*—my neck. His vision took its time clearing, going from glassy-eyed to focused to intense.

"Colleen." This time, my name on his lips was part question, part uncertainty, and all kinds of sexy as he physically took a step back from me. He dragged in a jagged breath and flexed and extended his hands a few times, as he attempted to get a handle on his heavy and rapid breathing.

I was doing a little deep breathing of my own, but it wasn't because I was trying to calm myself down. No, my heavy breathing was an aftereffect of the monumental make-out session I'd just had, in almost-public, with a man I was so aroused by, it was painful.

In a good-pain kind of way.

A throat clearing echoed in the hallway.

My entire body froze to ice-sculpture status. I knew that sound. Had heard it hundreds of times while growing up. It was usually followed by a thorough verbal tongue-lashing the likes of which would send me to my room leaking buckets of shameful and penitent tears for some childhood infraction.

When I turned, my grandmother stood at the door to the cafeteria, Tilly Carlisle towering over her, and both of them smiling. Mortification jumped up from my soul.

"Nanny Fee," I said, lamely. "It's not...I mean...we weren't....*Jesus!*" That last word was mumbled.

My grandmother has the distinction of being ninety-three years old with hearing along par with a baby bat. "Don't be takin' the Lord's name in vain, Number Two. You weren't raised that way."

"Sorry," I mumbled again. Really. Is there anything worse than being scolded by your grandmother when you're a grown-ass woman? "Why are you done so early? Don't you usually do more songs?"

"Tilly's got a little niggle in the back of her t'roat today, and I don't want her straining her pipes."

While I was being chastised, Slade ran his hands through his temples to smooth the hair I'd been clutching, then smiled that lady killer smile of his, and moved to Tilly, his hand extended.

"Ms. Carlisle. It was a pleasure hearing you perform. My mother was a huge fan when she was alive."

"Oh, now, aren't you the sweetest thing." Tilly pulled herself to her full height, shimmied her shoulders, and actually batted her heavily lined eyes at him, her false eyelashes sweeping across her cheeks like a cluster of spiders scurrying across her skin. "And who are you, darling man?"

Slade introduced himself.

"He's a client of me gran'daughter's," Nanny added. She slid me a side glance and added, "If client is what they're callin' it these days."

"His sister is one of my brides," I clarified, my cheeks stinging with heat.

"Oh, I adore weddings." Tilly wrapped one of her bejeweled hands around Slade's upper arm. "I've had five of my own, you know. Each was more perfect than the last. Too bad I can't say the same for the husbands."

Slade snorted.

"Come and have some post-performance punch," Tilly said, tugging him back toward the cafeteria. She leaned in closer and stage-whispered, "I've made sure it has a little extra zing today, but don't tell the staff." She wagged a finger at him. "They get so disagreeable whenever I try to liven things up a little."

"We can't stay," I blurted. "It's late, and Mr. Harrington needs to get back to New York." I turned to Nanny. "And I need to get you home. I've got a ton of work still left to do. This afternoon's incident has put me way behind."

"What incident?" Tilly asked.

"Nothin' to concern yourself with, Tilly darlin'," Nanny was quick to say. "Just a bit o' car trouble disabling me for a while. Colleen's me ride for now, so I'll be off with her."

The fact Nanny referred to me by my given name instead of the hated number moniker bore witness to how embarrassed she was. She didn't want her friend to know the truth about her current driving status.

As a subtle form of emotional blackmail, it was a golden nugget for me to keep in the back of my mind if

I needed to use it.

And I realize how horrible that sounds, but...

Nanny stretched up to buss Tilly's cheek as the diva bent at the waist to receive it. If there were ever two mismatched friends, it was these two. In addition to their dramatic height difference and upbringings, Tilly was an avowed democrat, liberal on most of her choices be they political or personal. Nanny was as devout a Catholic conservative as you could find, never having missed a Sunday Mass since she was baptized at eight weeks old. They were as different as—and Nanny was the person I'm quoting here—chalk and cheese. But their mutual love of music and performing surpassed all their differences.

It was Nanny who'd been the one to convince the independent Tilly it was time to move into assisted care when the diva had fallen last year and suffered through two reconstructive hip surgeries. And it was Nanny who'd helped get the family-less woman's home sold at a profit and who'd volunteered my lawyer sister Cathleen to help settle and untangle the myriad of legal issues Tilly had worked herself into.

"It was a delight to hear you perform," Slade told Tilly as he squeezed the woman's gnarled hand.

"Oh, darling man," she said, and leaned in to kiss his cheek. "The pleasure was all mine. Any day I can serenade a hottie like you is good for my soul."

Slade laughed, I blushed, and Nanny chortled.

Settled back in the car, with Nanny in the seat behind me again, Slade turned to her. "You're remarkably versatile, Mrs. Scaloppini. Old standards, classical pieces, not to mention rock and roll. I'm impressed."

"Ach, go on with ya now." Nanny waved a hand at him, but I caught her pleased grin in the rearview mirror. "I've been around long enough to know all music is related in one way or the other. Being able to find the similarities is the fun part."

I listened to them chat while I drove back to my office. It seemed Slade Harrington wasn't only a cold, hard captain of business, an entrepreneurial mover and shaker, and a heck of a good kisser, but a fan of music as well. This little insight into him was eye opening. I'd imagined he worked hard and played harder, evidenced by my Google search and all the articles and pictures I'd found of him tripping around the world accompanied by a new fresh face each week. But when he confessed to Nanny he was a huge fan of Broadway musicals, a love instilled in him by his mother, my impressions shifted a tad.

The man loved his little sister to no end, was charming and kind to the elderly, and could belt out the lyrics from *Phantom* in a rich, deep baritone, which he did at Nanny's insistence.

I almost blew through the same stop sign Nanny had earlier in the day when the first notes slipped through his lips.

"Now, young man, tell me why you're not trippin' the light fantastic on Broadway with a voice such as that?"

While we waited for the traffic circle to clear, his cheeks reddened and his grin went a little lopsided.

My lady parts quivered right there and then, and my tummy muscles shook. All I could think about was bringing him back to the house, pushing him up against the foyer wall, and continuing where we'd left off at the nursing home. Only this time we'd get to be naked.

Good Lord, what was wrong with me? This was a guy who cavorted with anorexic supermodels and ate small-business owners like me for a snack before taking over a nation's banking system while eating fancy finger sandwiches.

The two times we'd kissed, I could seriously chalk up to heightened emotions. The first time he'd been royally pissed at me—I still didn't understand why—and the last time he'd been overcome with laughter at the incongruity of Tilly's song choices.

Yeah, those are two great reasons for a girl to be kissed: anger and humor. *Not.* I was about as far from his type of woman as I imagined I could be. Beautiful? No. Reed thin and model tall? No. Submissive and quiet, reserved and unopinionated? Hell to the no!

I mentally snorted as I turned into my office parking lot.

I didn't kill the engine, the impression given that I didn't want to linger on goodbyes. I wanted him to climb out of my car, dash into his own, and then zip back to his world.

When it appeared he wanted to finish his debate with Nanny about which actress played the best female lead in *Evita*, I cleared my throat in a Nanny-like fashion and plastered a smile on my face that I prayed didn't look as crazed as it felt.

"Well, here we are. If you leave now, you'll only hit a little traffic. You can still be back in the city by about eight thirty or nine. Not too late if you have plans."

"I don't have any plans." Slade tossed me a quizzical glare.

"Oh, well, then." I bit down on my bottom lip.

"Do you?" he asked.

"Wh-what?"

"Have plans."

"Um, why?"

He shrugged, the natural, erotic ripple of his shoulders sending my seated parts into a spasm. "You seem in an awful hurry for me to leave."

From the back seat, Nanny Fee stifled a laugh.

"I just…I know what it's like being stuck in traffic when you want to get somewhere or you want to be home by a certain time. I made the trek every week when my sister was sick. It can be soul-sucking, all that driving, all the crazy drivers. I don't want you to have to sit in it and be bored. Or anything. That's all."

Jesus, Colleen. Shut up now.

For the first time in my memory, I listened to my inner harpy, who surprisingly sounded like a combination of my parents and Nanny Fee.

"So you don't?" Slade asked.

I blinked. *What?*

"Have plans?" he clarified.

"Actually, I do," I managed to say. I omitted that it was work-related, not personal, and involved putting the final touches on the weekend weddings, ordering supplies, and making sure everything was lined up to proceed smoothly for my brides.

Slade tilted his head, as if trying to decide if I was telling the truth or not. I tried not to squirm, but since my seated parts were already throbbing with need for this guy, it was hard not to.

With a quick nod, he turned to Nanny and gave her a smile that actually lit up the cab in my car it was so bright. "Mrs. Scaloppini, it's been a delight."

"The pleasure was all mine, boyo. Worth the part about being held under false arrest. If ever I need a lawyer again and Number One is busy, you'll be hearing from me."

"It'll be my pleasure." He turned to me, dropped the smile to a smirk, and said, "Miss O'Dowd."

"Mr. Harrington," I replied. For some reason, I couldn't quite mimic the snootiness in his tone.

He unfurled himself from my car and, before shutting the door, leaned in and said, "I'll be in touch. We have some unfinished business, you and I."

Why did that sound like a threat?

Nanny Fee was, uncharacteristically, silent during the drive home, something I thanked heaven for.

"Are ya hungry, lass?" she asked the moment we got through the door.

"Starving, actually. I never got to eat lunch."

"Well, then, go do what you need to do. Supper'll be in about twenty minutes. Maybe thirty, but no longer."

One of the advantages of living with my grandmother was I didn't have to cook any of my own meals. Ever.

Not that I couldn't cook, because I could. I just couldn't do it as well as my grandmother, and I'm not complaining about that in the least.

"Nanny?"

She turned back to me on her way to the kitchen. "Aye, lass?"

"We need to talk."

Her head bobbed. "Aye, we do. But save it for when there's food on the table. I think we'll both be in

a better frame o' mind when we're eating."
   Since she was right, I couldn't disagree.
   But we were going to talk. About a lot of things.

Chapter Nine

"You look tired," Charity told me when I arrived at the office the next morning.

I was, there was no denying it. After a long, oftentimes frustrating talk with Nanny over a delicious dinner of biscuits, chicken, and gravy, about how we were all going to manage her inability to drive solo, especially since she had such an active social life, I'd called Cathleen, informed her of what had happened and got a promise she'd call Lucas Alexander. Since the two of them had such history—Cathleen's late husband was Lucas's best friend from birth to death—I knew she'd be able to calm the legal waters surrounding Nanny and help figure out a way we wouldn't all be inconvenienced with having to drive her hither and yon.

After that, I settled down in my home office—which used to be my father's legal lair—and spent the next several hours answering all the emails I hadn't been able to due to Nanny's incarceration issue, dealing with supply problems, and making sure everything was set for the pair of weekend weddings fast approaching.

By the time I crawled into bed a little after midnight, my body was drained and my head was spinning.

Why is it when you're exhausted and overtired you can never sleep soundly? I tossed and turned all night long. The moment I'd fall asleep, my eyes would pop back open because my subconscious had remembered a crucial item for the weekend, or a detail I'd overlooked or forgotten.

Today, I didn't have a moment that wasn't scheduled, and I wanted a nap before the morning had even started.

"I didn't sleep well," I told Charity. "Too much going on up here." I circled my hand around my head.

We spent a few minutes going over everything that needed my attention for the day, and then I headed for my office.

Two new client calls later—complete with bookings—and a morning spent putting out fires and getting ahead of any potential problems for my upcoming weekend weddings, I was finally able to get on my way to the inn.

"I want to make sure Maureen has everything she needs for Sunday," I told Charity.

"And the fact that today is a tasting day never entered your head, did it?" She smirked as she looked up from her desk.

"I think there's a clause in your contract about my being able to fire you on the spot for insubordination."

Her giggle came freely. "Yes, there is. Feel free to enforce it anytime. I could use a vacation." She glanced nonchalantly at her fingernails, her grin never leaving her mouth.

"Pain," I mumbled as I grabbed my briefcase. "Why I put up with you I have no idea."

"I tend to think it's because of my winning personality."

"Must be."

The drive to my sister's inn took a few minutes

longer than usual due to a high volume of tourist traffic along the main road, the extra early leaf peepers already present and…peeping.

Maureen's wide driveway was filled with out-of-state licenses.

I loved walking through the front door of the inn. A large, fall-themed floral wreath sat on each of the side-by-side doors, their vibrant autumnal colors standing out against the pale cream-colored wood. The moment I went through the doors, the warm, spicy aroma of apples and cinnamon welcomed me like an old friend. My sister was truly a genius at innkeeping. Her guests never felt like guests, but like treasured family members. She allowed anyone who had a mind to, to sit and chat with her in the kitchen while she cooked, offered up a cup of coffee or tea, or at times, a glass of wine. She'd made the bedrooms a personal project when she and Eileen had first purchased the place, turning each separate room and bath into a little bit of a homey paradise. The soaps were all organic, purchased from a local manufacturer who used only local ingredients. The sheets and towels were washed daily, the detergent aromas changing with the seasons. Apple scented for the fall, evergreen for winter, lemon for spring, and rose for summer. The carpets were plush, the rooms airy and light.

When I'd come home to roost from New York, Maureen offered me the use of one of the extra bedrooms in her little manager's apartment. At the time, I'd refused, thinking we both needed the personal space, me in our childhood home, Maureen at the inn. Cathleen had tried to convince me to stay with Mo, stating that with her twin's death, this was the first time in her life Maureen had ever been truly alone. For this very reason, I decided to stay at my parents' house. After thirty years of being the "other, quieter twin," Mo deserved the freedom to find out who she was on her own.

I was glad I'd stuck to my guns on that decision, too, because my little sister had, as I'd always known she could, broken out of her shell. She'd blossomed and grown in her adult role. Every time I walked into the inn, I was proud of her. Her individual stamp was everywhere, in every room, in every personal touch she'd given the place. Instead of falling apart after our sister's death, as most in my family thought she would, she'd actually done the exact opposite. She was still quiet, often to the point I worried something was weighing on her, but she led a productive, busy life and seemed fulfilled.

I made my way through the downstairs, past the ballroom—set for the prewedding dinner being held there that night—and toward the kitchen. Just as I knew she'd be, Maureen was standing at a counter, a piping bag in her hand, adding the finishing touches on a bridal cake. The apron covering her trim body from shoulders to knees was red in color and had black lettering that read *I bake. What's your superpower?*

Green flip-flops covered her feet. I knew if there were no such thing as health code violations and spot state inspections from the food police, she would have been barefoot. My littlest sister was born in the wrong era for sure. She would have thrived in the earth-mother centuries, or as a hippie.

An educated, high-functioning, business-savvy, and non-pot-smoking hippie, but one regardless.

"You just missed the tasting," she said without looking up from piping white buttercream around the perimeter of the five-tiered confection. "I saved you a piece of each." She lifted her head to look directly at me, then settled her attention back on her handiwork. "You're welcome."

I planted my butt in one of the raised metal chairs circling the kitchen table and lifted the plate filled with samples of her newest cake offerings.

At her kitchen door alone I could lay the reason I'd gained these dreaded eight pounds. If she kept tempting me with these delicious sweets and flavor profiles, I was going to need a new wardrobe sooner than later. Of course, I could always skip the tastings and save myself a few thousand extra calories.

Yeah, like that was ever gonna happen.

"What are these?" I reached over and grabbed a fork from the utensil drawer and stabbed at each small piece of cake.

"The white one is french vanilla buttercream on the outside, orange vanilla sponge on the inside, and orange coulis in between."

I tried a taste. "Oh, this is yummy. Tart and sweet at the same time."

A corner of my sister's mouth lifted. "Exactly." She switched piping tips and began twining a scallop shell around the outer perimeter of the bottom tier. "The dark one is chocolate ganache on top, covering a milk chocolate sponge with coffee liqueur, and hazelnut cream in the middle."

Since I'd already finished the first, I dove into the second. "Good God, woman. This is a sin."

The other side of her mouth quirked up to follow

suit. "Only a venial one. No need to go to Confession."

I licked the plate with my fingers so I wouldn't miss a smidge. "And this last one? It looks a little like coconut."

Maureen nodded. While she ran a critical eye over the creation she'd decorated from every angle, she swiped her hands on her apron. "That's Isabella Harrington's inspiration. I'm thinking of naming it after her."

"Why?"

"Because she was the inspiration for the flavors," she said, coming to take a chair next to mine. "Deep dark chocolate ganache on the outside, covering a coconut pound cake base, and then coconut, rum, and cream as the filling. I had to experiment with a few different cakes before I settled on the pound. A sponge was too soft for the heavy coconut. So was a standard genoise. The pound held up the best. Tell me what you think."

I took a forkful and rolled my eyes around a little, tipping my head back and forth a few times. Then I took another bite.

"Well?"

"I'm thinking."

"Since when can't you think and eat at the same time?"

"Since I've never tasted anything quite as amazing as this before."

"You think she'll like it?"

"If she's as big a coconut and chocolate bar fan as I've been led to believe, she's going to love it."

"She is," a voice said from behind me.

The fork stopped on its ascent to my mouth.

No. It couldn't be. He'd left the night before. I saw him get in his car and drive away, heading for the highway entrance. Maybe I'd hallucinated his voice because I was so exhausted. Yeah. That was probably it.

"Need another cup?" Maureen asked, rising and crossing to the coffeemaker.

Before turning around, I took a mental breath.

Nope. Hadn't hallucinated it. Right there in the doorway looking way too sexy and hot, stood Slade Harrington.

I placed Maureen's fragile china plate gingerly back down on the table because my hands had started to tremble. "What are you doing here?"

I winced at how rude that came out, but really, what *was* he doing here?

"Getting another cup of coffee," he said, holding out his cup for Maureen to fill. "And hello to you, too." A little smirk crossed his mouth before he lifted the cup and took a long draft.

"I need to know what brand this is," he said to my sister. "I want to order a case of it to keep in the office. And at my apartment." He laughed. "Hell, even the Aspen house. This is the best-tasting coffee I've ever had."

"It's not a brand you can buy," Maureen told him. The small smile on her face meant she was secretly pleased by the compliment. "It's a mixture of a few commercial brands with some flavors I throw in to give it a more robust blend."

"You make this?" He held up his cup, while his eyes went wide. "Well, not make, because I know coffee comes from beans, but...put together, I guess is the best term."

Before Maureen launched into a topic she could have spent hours on, I jumped in—*rudely*—again. "Answer me. Why are you here?"

I'd stood when he'd moved into the room so Mo could fill his cup. Standing across from him now, I noticed a few things I hadn't in those first shocked moments.

He wasn't dressed in his usual "he who rules the financial world" designer suit today. A pale blue long-sleeved Henley covered his buff torso, tucked into faded jeans that had seen quite a few years of washing. Black penny loafers covered his feet, and if I were a betting girl, I'd say he'd had them a while. They looked broken in, whisper-soft, and comfortable.

If I didn't know he was a successful businessman, I'd have guessed he was an architect, or a contractor, or some other form of manly-man worker bee. But even without his usual sartorial flawlessness, he was still the walking embodiment of sex-on-a-stick perfection. Damn him.

Slade took another hit of his coffee. After swallowing, during which he'd stared pointedly at me, he took a breath. "I'm here because I never had a chance to discuss with you what I originally came up here for yesterday. We got sidetracked. More than once, if you'll remember."

Embarrassed heat crept up my cheeks because one of those times was out at the lake. When he'd kissed me.

And I'd kissed him back.

Kissed him? Ha. I'd practically devoured him. Whole.

"It's so important you couldn't simply call me with the details? You had to drive all the way back up here again this morning?"

"He didn't," Maureen said while she washed her pastry bags.

"Didn't what?"

"Drive back up here this morning. He spent the night."

"*What?*"

She shrugged. "I had a last-minute vacancy."

I turned back to him. His left eyebrow cocked a bit as he regarded me over his cup.

"Did you have a good run?" Maureen asked him.

"Yes. Your directions were perfect, thank you."

"You stayed here last night, and you went for a run this morning?" My voice had risen, and a smidge of something bordering on irritation had crept into it.

Slade nodded. "Do you have a problem with me staying here?"

Yes, but was it because he'd spent the night in my sister's inn, or because I hadn't known about it? And why did it bother me so much?

That question could be answered easily. *He* bothered me.

Yesterday's events had been a nightmare in so many ways and the reason for my insomnia. The two bright spots in the day had been when he'd kissed me. Those little events shouldn't have ever been considered a good thing. But they had. Were. At least for me.

For a few minutes, I'd been kissed by a man who was a master at the task, and I'd been made to feel wanted and desirable, two things I hadn't felt or been in quite some time. Looking back on the time before

Harry's betrayal now that I had older, wiser eyes and some emotional and chronological distance, the reality of our relationship had been more one-sided than I'd ever let myself believe. And that side was mine.

I was the one who'd done everything for him, who made sure his life ran smoothly, who was willing to sacrifice so he could thrive. His selfishness had extended to all parts of our lives together, including our sex life. Or lack of it. I'd accepted excuses of work exhaustion in lieu of date night. I'd gone to bed alone and frustrated because of deadlines that needed to be met. I'd accepted being taken for granted in so many ways, I'd forgotten my own needs and subjugated my own desires. My lady parts had been banished to storage, and I despaired they'd become withered. What's that saying? Use it or lose it?

But when Slade Harrington had yanked me into his wet, sturdy, and wanting arms yesterday in the rain, my ovaries jumped back to the front of the line screaming, "Here we are! Here we are!"

They were roaring in my ears again at the nursing home. I can truthfully say if we'd been alone somewhere—anywhere—and he'd kissed me like he had then, I would have stripped naked and got busy in no time flat. Which, I'll admit, was wrong on so many levels it made my head spin. Hence, the sleepless night.

So yeah, I did have a problem with Slade. But it wasn't because he'd spent the night at my sister's inn. It was because I hadn't been with him.

There was no way I could admit that out loud, though.

I took a mental breath and tried to calm my insides. "Why would I have a problem with it?" There. Better.

My voice was almost back to normal.

"You seem a little…stressed, that I did."

"She's always stressed." Maureen laughed and looked over her shoulder at him. "Stress is her confirmation name."

"Ha-ha. You're definitely the comedienne in the family." I gave her the now empty plate and fork to wash. Ignoring Slade, I said to her, "I glanced at the ballroom. You set up early."

With a shrug, she said, "My mind wouldn't calm down last night, so I used the insomnia wisely."

"Everything okay?" I asked while I rubbed a hand down her shoulder.

"Everything is fine." She lifted her gaze to mine. "Really. Don't worry."

If we'd been alone and without Slade hovering, I would have pushed. We all suffered the loss of our sister differently. Mo tended to keep her feelings and thoughts to herself, something rare in a family steeped in dramatic and emotional upheavals and showdowns. Eileen was the only person she'd ever really shared her total self with, and now that she was gone, I feared Mo was becoming more introspective and introverted every day.

"Telling me not to worry is like telling me—"

"Not to breathe," she finished. "I know, Coll, but I'm okay. Just busy."

I shook my head. Maureen's quiet stubbornness is legendary in my family.

I grabbed my briefcase from the chair I'd tossed it on and gave her a quick kiss on the cheek. "I'll be out and about all day, but I'll be back later and I'm bringing Cathy with me. We need to have a confab about

150

Nanny."

"Yeah. I know all about the no-more-driving edict."

"Cathy called you?"

"No."

I watched as she rinsed the dish I'd handed her for the third time. "Mo? I think that dish is clean."

"What? Oh yeah. It is."

My baby sister definitely had something on her mind, because she was never scatterbrained. Quite the opposite, in fact.

"Who told you about Nanny?" I asked. In the next second, it dawned on me the man standing in the kitchen sipping coffee and watching us had. I whirled around and gave him what Charity calls my death stare. Slade raised his free hand and mouthed *not me*.

"Lucas did. He…he dropped by last evening and…mentioned it." She looked a little flushed when she turned from the sink to me.

"Lucas dropped by here last night?"

She nodded.

"Why?"

"He does sometimes on his way home if he's been working late. Usually charms a to-go bag from Sarah."

"Hmm. And from you, no doubt."

"I always have plenty of food, Coll. You know that."

"And God knows you can never stand to see someone miss a meal." I sighed, loud and long. "Well, I'll bring pizza or something with me tonight so you don't have to cook. And don't tell me you have to cook for the guests anyway," I added, putting up a hand to stop her when she started to speak again "It won't kill you for once to eat something someone else made."

Her grin returned. "Yes, Mom."

I shook my head and then kissed her cheek again. Over my shoulder, I tossed a "Mr. Harrington," before moving to leave.

"Just a second, Miss O'Dowd." He placed his cup down into the sink, mumbled a thanks for Mo, then caught up with me and wrapped a hand around my elbow. Tiny little heat-filled missiles shot up my arm. A girl could work up a serious sweat from all that hotness. He propelled me into the breezeway between the kitchen and the breakfast room. With a quick glance behind him, he walked me into the now-empty space.

I expected him to let go of my arm once we were alone, but he didn't. Instead, he turned to face me, keeping his hand in place. We couldn't have been more than half a foot apart from one another. I was wearing my usual three-inch heels, so I was almost at eye level with him. Almost. Since we were standing so close, I had to tip my chin up a little to maintain eye contact.

I waited for him to say something, all my senses standing at attention.

He'd showered recently, probably after his run, the hair on the back of his neck still shiny with moisture, and he hadn't used Maureen's room-stock of products, either. I knew every one of the floral scents in the shampoos and soaps she kept stocked for her guests because I'd been the one to pick them out with her. No, Slade Harrington hadn't used the oatmeal body wash or the pomegranate-infused shampoo. But he did smell delicious. It took every inch of resolve I could call up not to lean forward and run my nose along his neck. A hot spice mixed with something woodsy, fresh, and clean clung to him. He smelled the way a man should smell: manly. Unlike Harry, who'd daily doused himself in enough cologne to cause a small nation to have a collective asthma attack.

Since patience has never been one of my virtues, I finally broke the awkward silence by saying, "You needed to ask me something?"

He cocked his head and moved a little closer to me. Somewhere in the back of my head, my brain told me to take a step back, but that innate stubbornness infusing my system rebelled.

"You had a late night." He cupped my chin, his inspecting gaze ping-ponging between my eyes.

"Excuse me?"

"You look tired, like you didn't get enough sleep." His thumb worried the angle of my jaw.

My spine shot straight up, and this time I did take a step back. "Just what every woman wants to hear," I snapped. "She looks worn-out and weary. You must have women lining up to date you with such a smooth line like that."

"I don't think I said you looked worn out and weary." His brows knitted. "Just tired. I imagine yesterday's incident with your grandmother caused you a restless night from worrying."

"You can imagine anything you want. My sleeping habits are no concern of yours. Now, I've got a very busy schedule this afternoon, Mr. Harrington, so if you've got something to ask or tell me, please do so. Otherwise, I need to go."

He waited a beat. "What I need to discuss with you is going to take some time. Let me just get my jacket. We can talk in the car."

Before I could respond, he started walking toward the main staircase.

"Wait a minute." I followed him as he sprinted up to the second floor. "Ask me what you need to know now."

He moved into one of the guest bedrooms, and without even thinking, I followed. Slade had one of my favorite rooms. Done in early Americana design, the four poster bed and matching dresser were a light oak, shined with natural beeswax Mo bought from a local keeper. A hand-stitched quilt in a chaos of blues, one of a set of six she'd purchased at an auction, covered the bed. An armoire stood in one corner of the room, one of its doors ajar. Inside were several days' worth of shirts hanging from the rod. A closed suitcase sat on the interior shelf.

"How long are you planning to stay here?" I asked before I could think not to.

Heat danced up from my neck as Slade tossed a light tan sports jacket over his arm.

"You've got enough shirts for about a week." I pointed to the armoire.

The left eyebrow he'd so disdainfully lifted at me several times over the past weeks did so again. "I was in Boston before I came here. I like to have enough clothes with me when I travel so I won't worry if I need to stay an extra day or two somewhere."

"Oh," sounded so pathetic when it slipped through my lips.

He motioned for me to go, but I didn't move.

"Look." I took a breath. "I've got a ton of things to do and places to go this afternoon—"

"Then we should get going."

"—and I don't need to have someone following me around, so tell me what you want to tell me, and then you can go home."

"Actually, I was planning on staying through Sunday."

"What?"

"You sister had a room available for the weekend, so I booked it."

"Why?"

Jesus, was I ever going to think before I spoke? Let's be honest, probably not.

Slade took my elbow again in a gesture I was starting to really like and shouldn't and escorted me toward the staircase.

"Several reasons, actually," he said while we walked. "I wanted to get a feel for the town and the surroundings before the wedding, see for myself why Izzy and Jack are so sure this is the perfect venue for them."

"It is," I said as he held one of the front doors open for me.

With a nod, he followed me.

"You said several. What are the others?"

"We should take your car since you know where you want to go," he said, pointing to it. "Another reason is I wanted to see the amenities your sister provides. While the wedding is small, there are still several family members who will be staying here. I wanted to ensure they'd be comfortable."

"No worries about that," I said as I slipped into the driver's seat. "Maureen is all about customer satisfaction and catering to individual needs and requests. The inn is handicap accessible, the entire facility non-smoking."

"I've seen that for myself."

Before pulling out of the drive, I checked my phone to make sure there weren't any fires I needed to put out back at the office.

"What's our first stop?" Slade asked.

"*My* first stop is the town butcher," I said, snottily, enunciating the word for effect. "So, what was so vitally important you couldn't discuss it on the phone?"

"I need your help."

I waved my hand at him. "With?"

"An issue with Isabella. I need you to help me convince her Jack needs to sign a prenup agreement."

Chapter Ten

Okay, I didn't see that coming.

"*What?*" I slammed the brake so hard, both of us jerked forward, reminding me why seatbelts were invented.

"She refuses to listen to me or our family lawyers. She won't ask Jack to sign the document that's been drawn up, won't even talk to me about it. She's being very stubborn," he said, "and as we get closer to the wedding, I have a feeling she's going to be even more intractable on his signing it than she is now."

"Intractable? Good God, do you hear how pompous and ridiculous you sound?" I resumed driving.

His spine went ramrod straight in his seat. "I don't think I sound anything of the sort. The prenup is a legal way of ensuring my sister's considerable financial assets are protected in case she and Jack divorce."

"I bet a million bucks Isabella doesn't see it that way."

"She doesn't," he spat. "She's got it into her head there's no reason they need a prenup, that's what's hers is theirs and what's his is theirs as well. The fact she has considerably more assets than he does isn't even a consideration in her head. She refuses to ask Jack to sign, which I why I need your help convincing her he should."

"Not gonna happen." I shook my head violently.

"No way. No how."

He turned to stare at my profile. "Why not?"

"Because I don't believe in prenups. I deal in happily ever afters. When I plan a wedding, it's with the thought it's gonna last a lifetime. Asking for a prenup is just accepting the marriage will fail. That you know it will inevitably fall apart because it won't be strong enough to go the distance. You're putting an expiration date on something that should only end in death. That's what *until death us do part* means."

"You do know half of all marriages end in divorce, don't you? You must, considering the industry you're in."

"Of course I do, but you're *assuring* it will by drawing up a document that basically says, I know we're gonna muck it up and I want to walk away clear and free when we do. With what's mine, mine, what's yours, yours."

"Excellent advice, as any first-year business lawyer will tell you."

"Marriage isn't a business."

"Maybe not by your definition, but it is a contract. A legally binding one between two parties. You can't argue with that."

"Yes I can, because even though it's a contract, it's not based on a business merger—"

"You obviously haven't done as many society weddings as you claim."

"—it's founded on two people loving one another enough to want to spend the rest of their lives together."

"Partners think along the same lines when they go into business together, you know. No one ever thinks things are going to go south, but in the event the partnership doesn't work out, there are always dissolution clauses in contracts to assure each party comes away with their finances as intact as they can. That's all I'm thinking about in this case. I want to make sure Isabella is protected financially. It's my responsibility as her older brother, her financial advisor, and the executor of her trust."

I slammed the brakes again and threw the gear into park with such a jerk, I feared the shifter might break off. "Wrong." I pointed my index finger at him. My eyebrows were tugged so tight together in the middle of my forehead a headache was bound to break through any minute. "Your job as her brother is to love her unconditionally—"

"I do."

"—and support whatever decisions she makes—"

"Again, I do."

"—and not to make her ask the man she loves to sign something she doesn't want him to. Forcing her to do something she doesn't want to is by no definition loving her unconditionally."

Before he could reply, I barreled on without taking a breath. "I get this is something famous and ridiculously rich people like those in your world do, and I think it's a crying shame it's allowed, even encouraged. I totally believe more marriages would survive if they weren't so easy for people to simply walk away from when they wanted to."

"You've obviously never read a prenup or you'd know how wrong your statement is. Prenups are extremely intricate and thorough."

"Anything that makes it easier to leave a marriage is just plain wrong." I stared at him across the cab of my car.

Lord, he looked so pompous and pious sitting there, his face a mix of annoyance and condescension.

"Let me ask you a question." I folded my arms across my chest and for a hot second, lost my train of thought when his gaze shot to my breasts.

Whoa.

"Is there any way I can stop you?" He closed his eyes and pinched the bridge of his nose.

Well, we all know the answer to that question, don't we?

"I'm going to assume your father had prenups for all his assorted and sundry marriages. Anyone who can so quickly marry and then discard a spouse must have."

His eyes eased open, but his jaw clamped so tight it was a wonder he didn't ruin the results thousands in orthodontia had given him.

"Your assumption would be wrong," he said through barely parted lips.

"Shocking."

The sound of his breath inhaling filled the space around us. The sight of his hands fisted in his lap and his shoulders practically kissing his earlobes was a fairly good indication at his level of pissed-off-ness.

He exhaled and then nailed me with that piercing stare he was a master at.

"Your sarcasm is noted. For your information, it was when wife number three went after most of his real estate holdings and number four demanded a seat on the board of directors of the foundation that I learned the value of a good prenup. If my father had been smart enough to insist on them before he married his much younger, much greedier wives, instead of following every organ but his brain into those ill-advised marriages, I wouldn't have had to step in, wrest the company from him before it was ruined, and take over. He was set to give them whatever they wanted to make them leave."

"That's wrong on so many levels I can't even think straight. Plus, it's downright sad. But I'm still not helping you."

"A prenuptial agreement benefits Jack, as well, you know, not only Isabella."

"On what planet? You're basically telling the guy you don't believe he's going to honor his wedding vows."

"No, I'm not. I know Jack loves my sister. *Now.* In five years, or ten, after a few kids and a lifestyle he realizes he doesn't like or want, who's to say he won't walk away from her? Vows are easily made and just as easily broken. I want to assure if it happens, he gets nothing belonging to her."

"Do you hear yourself? Good gravy, where did you get such a skewed opinion of marriage and love? Oh wait. Don't answer that." The disdain in my voice was so sharp, it sliced the air around us. "From dear old Daddy for sure."

I grabbed my purse and bolted from the car before he could respond and slammed the door. I fished a coin from my pocket and, with a vicious twist of my hand, deposited it in the meter, turned the timer, and stormed away from the car without a backward glance at my passenger.

I hoped he'd stay in the car and not follow me into the shop.

If I had a nickel for every hope that didn't get

fulfilled, I could retire to Tahiti and bask in sunshine and mai tais all day long.

****

"The entire pig is going to be displayed out in the open while it cooks? Head and all?"

I slanted him a side eye. "Yes, that would be the definition of a pig roast. You've been to Hawaii."

"Of course I have. How do you know that?"

"Don't look at me all confused, with your forehead folding in the middle."

He immediately calmed his features, and I ignored his question. No way was I copping to Googling him again.

"If you've been to Hawaii, you must have been to a luau. Every tourist goes at least once."

"The only times I've been a tourist is when my mother was alive and we traveled together while my father stayed home and built his empire. Pig roasts and luaus were never on the menu then, just helicopter tours and yacht jaunts with my mother's friends. Since taking over the company, I've only been to Hawaii on business trips, none of which has boasted a luau."

Why did I feel sad for him about that? "Well, a pig roast is usually the star component of a luau."

"Yes, but at a wedding reception?"

I shrugged. "Kimmy Gunderson's reception is a little different from the norm, but it's not an unheard-of theme."

"Theme? What is it, a Polynesian tribal offering up to the island gods? With the bride the virgin sacrifice?"

I bit down on a corner of my mouth to contain a grin. "Since she's eight months pregnant, the whole virginal sacrifice thing won't fly. And no, it's not an island theme. Kimmy's kin are fourth-generation farmers. They've been supplying Heaven and the surrounding sister towns with fresh, organic vegetables, eggs, even honey from their own hives, for over a hundred years. The reception is being held on her grandparents' property, and a pig roast is a family tradition. Every bride and groom since her great-great-grandparents' time has had one, and each marriage has survived 'til the proverbial death do us part." I pointedly stared at him and added, "Without a prenup."

Slade chose to take no notice of my comment. "So why did she need a planner, then, if this is a family tradition?"

"Kimmy's mom was in Nanny Fee's religious ed classes, and when she asked if Kimmy could be married at the lake and in the gazebo, Nanny agreed, but only if I was hired to plan everything. Mrs. Gunderson jumped at the chance to let me take over the details so she wouldn't have to lose precious work time on the farm. She got the gazebo wedding of her dreams for her daughter, and I got a happy, willing client. Win/win all around."

"Your grandmother doesn't mind having non-family members use her property?"

"Not at all. If I wasn't working out of Heaven, she probably would have let the Gundersons use the gazebo anyway. But this was her way of driving up business for me, getting some use out of the lake property, and doing a good turn for a neighbor. Like I said, win/win all around."

I stopped the car and threw it into park with less vigor than I had at our previous stop, the town butcher, Celestial Charcuterie. I'd double checked the particulars of getting the full pig to the Gunderson's property the next morning, and was assured the "spit would be lit at four a.m." We'd gotten back into the car and then driven to the opposite side of town.

Slade was looking up at the street sign.

"Ascension Avenue. Do all the streets in this town have a biblical connotation?" he asked, alighting from the car.

"Well, the name of our dear town is Heaven, so yeah. The town founder, Josiah Heaven, was an architect and engineer by trade and a minister by avocation."

"He named all the streets?"

I nodded. "To this day, whenever a new business petitions from the City Council for a license to operate, the business owner has to agree to use a pre-approved biblical reference or name."

"Hence, Ascension Avenue." He pointed to the sign.

"And Glory Road, Eden Lane, Peace Place, yada yada yada."

"And we just left the Celestial Charcuterie."

"Which is a fancy name for heavenly meats."

"It's a wonder you don't call your own business the Love Shack."

"Already taken." I moved toward the building. "Anson Levertree named his bar the Love Shack when he opened it in 1952."

"That's the name of a bar? And it's still open sixty-five years later?"

I nodded again. "His grandson runs it now, and it's wall-to-wall packed every Friday and Saturday night. Wednesdays too, 'cause it's five wings for a dollar from four p.m. until closing."

His gaze lifted to the sign over the entranceway. "Blessed Be Beer, Wine, and Spirits."

"I make my case," I said as I reached for the door handle. Slade beat me to it.

It was difficult to stay annoyed at him when his good breeding showed. I hadn't had a man hold a door open or escort me anywhere in so long, I'd forgotten how nice it can be when a little well-placed and mannerly chauvinism rears its head. The bonus was getting to brush by his body and getting a whiff of his scent.

After ascertaining the five kegs I'd ordered would be delivered to the Gunderson property at the appointed time, we then moved on to the Sweet By and By Bakery to assure the wedding cake was ready.

"I don't think I've ever seen a three-dimensional cake in the shape of a farmhouse before," Slade said as he held the door to the bakery open for us to exit.

"Kimmy's family are farmers, remember?"

"So what is it? A carrot cake?"

If he was trying to be funny, the joke was on him.

"Kimmy's favorite."

Back in the car, he asked, "Where to next?"

I glanced down at my watch. "I've got a quick stop at the church and then back to the office for some conference calls. I'll drop you back at the inn first."

"No need. I can stick with you."

With a quick glance at him and then out the front window again before he could see how much that notion bothered me, I asked, "Don't you have your own work to do? Portfolios to expand? Companies to take over? You must be missing out on some major stock deals by following me aimlessly around all afternoon."

His lips split into a charming smirk, and damn it, I got all squirmy in my seat. "Actually, no. I knew I was going to be out of the office for a few days in Boston, so I was able to arrange for my assistants to take care of whatever comes up. If anything becomes problematic, they can get in touch with me. Your sister has an excellent business center at the inn."

I was silent for a few moments while I turned the car into an empty parking lot. The announcements sign on the lawn of my family church read *Heaven on Earth Church...Christ Died for You. What have you done for Him lately? Confession, Saturdays at 4. Mass Every Sunday, 8, 10, & 12.*

"Interesting question," Slade said, chinning toward the sign.

"Father Duncan is an interesting man. In another week or so, he'll change the sign to say something like *If you're a leaf peeper, remember who made the trees and thank Him here on Sunday.* He's known for his quirky sayings."

"You sound like you know him. Personally, I mean."

We walked up the stone steps to the ornate church entrance doors. "Father Duncan has been the parish priest for decades. He baptized, communed, and confirmed all my sisters and me, and officiated at my sister Cathleen's wedding. He's one of Nanny Fee's oldest friends and card buddies."

"Card buddies?"

I dipped two fingers into the holy water vessel sitting on a table in the entrance, faced the front of the church, did a little genuflection curtsy, and tapped my fingers to my forehead, belly button, then shoulders.

"Five card draw every Tuesday night since I can remember." I'd lowered my voice, but the empty church still echoed around us. A black cassocked figure moved from the altar. With a happy smile on my face, I greeted him halfway up the long center aisle. "Father."

"Now here's a sight that brightens even the darkest of days, and you're right on time as usual." Father Duncan clasped my hand in his own and then planted a kiss on my cheek. Ireland flowed between his lips, lyrical, lilting, and bright. Father Duncan is a good six inches shorter than me and rail thin with a shock of snowy hair domed around his head like a halo. "I could set a clock by you. You're looking as beautiful as always, darlin'."

Heat rushed up my cheeks. I swiped a hand in the air, waving the compliment off. "And you've got as much of the old blarney in you as ever."

"You never could take a truthful compliment, Colleen Sinead Maura O'Dowd."

"Now I'm in trouble for sure." I laughed. "You never use my full name."

"Not in trouble, no, darlin'. Never that. Now"—he took my hand in his old and arthritic ones—"Fiona's been bending my ear all day about what happened yesterday. She's already called me three times, planning on how to get her license back without having her eyes seen to." He turned, his own startling blue eyes, fierce in their scrutiny, sizing Slade up from head to toe and back again. "You must be the lawyer Fee mentioned. Her description was spot on, as it always is." He let go of my hand and offered one to Slade. "Father Duncan Brennan, son of Ireland and family friend." I knew from past experience the old man had a grip like granite.

"Slade Harrington, Father."

I asked if we could go to his office to discuss the planned Sunday wedding.

Father Duncan's priestly lair looked much the way my father's study had when I was a kid. Deep, dark wood-paneled walls and crown molding surrounded the office on two sides, one bay window planted on the third, and a brick fireplace taking up the remainder. Bookshelves lined an entire wall, with two leather couches sitting in front of it, separated by a glass table. A large crucifix was poised over the fireplace. Numerous framed religious portraits hopscotched across the paneled walls.

Father Duncan sat behind his massive desk, Slade and I in chairs in front of it. We discussed the time schedule of the wedding and the vows, both religious and those written by the bride and groom as well.

The entire meeting took less than ten minutes, and in truth, I could have handled it all over the phone. When we were back in the church vestibule, I broached the real reason for my visit.

I hugged the priest and said, "So you're all set for tonight? I can count on you?"

"Darlin' child." He took my hands again like he had when we'd first entered the church. "Have I ever failed you?"

"Never. You're the one man in my life I can always depend on," I told him with a self-conscious laugh.

When he cocked an eyebrow and said, "The only one?" I felt the heat rise up from my neck again.

"Well, except for, you know, *God*."

Duncan grinned. "That's better. Tell Fee I'll bring the snacks. I'm sure she's got a bottle ready to decant. Now, off with the both of ya. I've got places to go, congregants to see, the sick to heal."

When we were back in the car, Slade asked, "So, what's tonight?"

"An unscheduled poker night at my house. They usually play on Tuesdays, but I need to meet with my sisters, and I can't trust Nanny won't get into mischief if left alone for too long. I don't treasure another summons to the jailhouse from Lucas. I called Father Duncan last night to see if he was free to come and Nanny-sit. And I realize how horrible that sounds." I laid my head down on the steering wheel and sighed. "I've actually got a babysitter for my ninety-three-year-old grandmother because I'm afraid she'll get into trouble if I leave her alone. What's happened to my life?"

As soon as I said it out loud, complete embarrassment sliced through me. I shouldn't be discussing my grandmother with anyone who wasn't family, but especially not a man who continued to cause such conflicting emotions to leapfrog within me.

I know I have a serious problem keeping my thoughts from falling out of my mouth, but I'm usually able to contain my behavior around clients. Why, with this man, did I have such difficulty controlling my verbal quirk?

And more confusing, why did it seem so natural to confide my problems to him?

As those thoughts played through my mind, his hand pressed into my shoulder, then his fingers skimmed across the tension knots in my neck, tenderly, as if he did it every day.

"I'm going straight to Hell," I mumbled.

"Why?"

I flexed my neck a little, giving him free access to rub more knots—which he did.

"Because disrespecting your elders is a sin. I think it's a venial one, but a sin nonetheless."

His quiet chuckle was so reassuring, so comforting, devoid of any of his previous condescension. "Are you hungry?" he asked.

I turned my head so I could see him out of one eye but stayed in the same position, an unsaid plea for him to continue massaging.

He got the hint.

"I'm lamenting the fact I'm going to spend eternity burning in hellfire and brimstone—and I don't even know what that really is—and you ask me if I'm hungry?"

"Even if you're going to hell, which I doubt, you still have to eat. I'm hungry since I missed lunch to follow you all over town—"

"I told you not to."

"—and I could go for something light to hold me over until dinner."

I lifted my head and shoulders, forcing him to pull his hand away. I was suddenly ravenous myself.

"Do you have time to take a break and grab something quick?"

"How hungry are you?" I asked. "I'll-faint-if-I-don't-eat-something-right-now hungry, or I-just-need-a-little-nosh hungry?"

"I've never fainted in my life."

"Okay." I rolled my neck from side to side, the ever-present knots just a memory now, put the car in gear, and pulled out of the church parking lot.

Chapter Eleven

"Why am I not surprised the only pizza joint in town is called Paradise Pizza?" Slade said as we waited for our order.

We were seated across from one another at a sidewalk table, drinks in front of us, a diet soda for me (I needed the caffeine hit because no sleep, remember?) and bottled water for him. My gaze took a slow stroll over his face at the question.

I'd chosen to sit with my back to the sun, so Slade was engulfed in the midafternoon autumnal glare. He'd slid a pair of aviator sunglasses on against it, which made him look even hotter and sexier.

All afternoon, with him sitting next to me in the car, following me to each stop I needed to make, asking his questions about the town, the venues, the people, my awareness of him had been on hyperdrive. I knew what he was doing, of course. It didn't take a genius. He wanted the prenup signed and assumed I'd be his ally in the cause. This whole following-me-around, solicitous, attentive *thing* he had going on was his attempt to get me over to the dark side.

Not gonna happen.

"You're not fooling me, you know," I said as the waitress brought out our food.

"About what?" When he lifted the slice of vegetable- and cheese-laden pizza to his lips and took a bite, I lost my train of thought. When he licked his lips free of the delicious sauce, I lost my mind.

To calm the sexual tsunami undulating in my stomach, I took a breath then a sip of my soda. When I was fairly certain I could put an intelligent sentence together and not just say "gah" while staring at his uber-sexiness, I answered him.

"I know you're only being nice and charming and following me around trying to be helpful because you think I can influence your sister's decision about the prenup. I'm onto you." I sipped my soda and tossed him what I hoped was a condescending eye flick and pout.

He swallowed, and it took everything in me not to reach across the tiny *table pour deux* and yank his mouth to mine before he wiped his lips with his napkin. The lips I wanted to cleave to took their time inching up at the corners. "You think I'm charming?"

I gulped the soda instead of sipping and started wheezing like an asthmatic.

Slade watched me through his glasses, his grin growing. He knew, damn him, he was the reason I was choking.

When I was finally able to take a breath, I glared at him. "Oh, you're good, I'll give you that." His grin widened more. Now he looked not only hot, but seriously bad-boy hot. "But I'm immune," I lied. "And I'm not going to talk to Isabella for you."

I took a bite of my own pizza—a tiny one in case I started gagging again.

"I know you're not," he said, matter-of-factly. "You made your opinion clear, so I'm not going to ask for your help again."

Okay, that was entirely too easy. Capitulation

wasn't in this guy's DNA, so I knew he was up to something. I squinted across at him and asked, "Why don't I believe you?"

His truck-wide shoulders rippled under his jacket when he shrugged, and I was glad I hadn't taken another bite because I would have needed to be Heimliched for sure. The sudden picture crossing my mind of Slade standing behind me, his powerful hands fisted under my breasts as he thrust upward under my sternum to save my life sent a river of liquid heat down my pelvis.

Jesus, Colleen, get a grip.

"I know you're a lost cause, so I won't ask again."

"When did you decide I was a lost cause?"

"When you made yourself clear on the subject outside the butcher's."

So. The first stop of the day. "Why, then, if you'd already decided not to pursue it with me, did you stay glued to my hip all afternoon? I'm sure you would have been happier doing a thousand other things than wasting your time being dragged all over town."

Oh, to be the proverbial fly on the wall of his brain and know what he was thinking, because I couldn't read a single thing from the expression on his face.

Finally, with another of those incredible manly shrugs, he said, "It wasn't a waste of time. I actually got to know quite a few things."

"About?"

"The town. The intricacies of timing everything for a wedding. You."

His last word made me stop breathing. Before I could respond, he went on. "Please do me the favor of not mentioning I asked for your help when you speak with Isabella again."

"Okay. Why not?"

"Because she's already upset with me, and I don't want her more so. You're the one who told me emotional issues grow and expand exponentially the closer a bride gets to a wedding. I'd like this time to be as stress-free as possible for her, and if she knows I solicited your help in any way with the legal issues, she'll definitely be emotional."

Why did this guy have to be such an arrogant bear one minute and a dreamboat, ultra-caring brother the next? I wanted to punch him, then kiss him, and I was having the devil of a time reconciling both those feelings. There was nothing in my arsenal of emotional protection devices to help me fight against my attraction to him.

Slade interrupted my thoughts—and adroitly changed the subject—by saying, "Tell me what you've planned so far for the bridal shower. My secretary mentioned you'd called to get our schedules."

This topic I could deal with without any internal angst. As we ate our slices, I went over the details I'd already worked out in order for Isabella to have a lovely shower.

"Thank you for keeping it in the city," Slade said as we tossed our napkins and paper plates into the trash receptacle.

"In the long run, it was easier since everyone who is invited lives in, or closer to, Manhattan than Heaven. It made sense to have it there. I've done showers and parties before at Alice's, and when I mentioned it to Isabella, she was thrilled with the venue."

Slade slid into the car next to me, and as I had so

many times before, I became acutely aware of how close he was. Our elbows had knocked together on the central arm rest several times when I was driving, and it had taken all the will I could summon not to straighten my arm, reach across it, and grab his hand. I knew precisely how warm and gentle it would feel against my skin.

I snuck a quick look at him as I put the car into gear. "What are you thinking about with a smile like that?" Was it wrong of me to hope—*wish*—he'd say, "You?"

"I was remembering the first time I ever took Izzy to Alice's. It was for her tenth birthday, and I'd just gotten into Harvard Law." He settled his butt down into the seat (lucky cushion!) and stared out the windshield. "I told her we could go anywhere she wanted, just the two of us so it would be special, and she said she wanted tea and cupcakes at this place she'd heard some girls in school talking about."

"And you took her? On a brother/sister date?"

He nodded, the smile on his face so damn sweet, my heart sighed. "She had two cups of tea which she over-sugared and over-milked, and two cupcakes."

"Let me guess. Coconut flavored?"

He laughed, and the sound was so rich and filled with humor and love, I forgot to move through the stop sign I was waiting at and had to be reminded by the honk of the car behind me. My gaze shot to the rearview to spot a disgruntled Nanny Fee look-alike peering over the very tip of her steering wheel as she waved me impatiently on.

"Got it in one," Slade said.

As I started moving again, I told him, "I'm taking

you back to the inn. I've got a bunch of calls I need to make back at the office, and then I have to get home and make sure Nanny is okay."

I was prepared for another protest, but instead, he nodded. "I've got some calls I need to make as well. Can I ask you something? Something personal?"

"Sure."

"Why does your grandmother call you Number Two?"

Heat flew up my cheeks, and I bit down on the inside of my lip.

"I heard her say it to you on the phone when we were out at the lake, and I even remember the first time we met, she called while we were in the parking lot of your office."

When I didn't say anything, he turned in his seat so he was facing me. "Colleen?"

"It's embarrassing," I said. "And stupid."

"Most nicknames are." He had a smile in his voice and when I glanced over at him the kindness in his expression had me wanting to tell him. Harry had only asked me once, and when I didn't tell him the reason, he'd never asked again.

I dragged in a deep breath and checked both ways before moving through the roundabout.

"My mother and grandmother never got along well. Still don't. I don't know exactly why, but I've always thought it was because they're like two alpha dogs and neither ever wanted to give up control of the pack to the other. Anyway. You might have noticed my sisters and I all have pretty similar sounding names."

"Yes, I have. Cathleen, Colleen, and Maureen. And your sister who died was Eileen, right?"

177

I nodded.

"Cute."

"That's one word for it. Nanny Fee would give you a different one."

"She's not a fan of your names?"

"I don't think she would have been a fan of any names my mom picked out, but the alliterative ones she definitely hated. She called Cathleen Number One because she's the oldest. Eileen and Maureen she always referred to as Three and Four." I glanced over at him again in time to see the grin he was trying to hide. "I came along second in line, so…"

"Did you get teased a lot in school?"

"Mercilessly. Nanny forgot how cruel kids could be, which is hysterical since she taught communion prep class for years. And she taught in our church school, so whenever she would see one of us in the hallways, she called us by the number name. When kids, especially the boys in my class, heard her say it, well, let's say things would have been easier for me if I'd been homeschooled."

"Kids are brutal. At any age."

"Truth." I pulled into the inn driveway. "Even though we're adults, she still refers to us as numbers. When my parents moved away after my sister died I'd hoped she'd stop, since I figured she'd only done it all those years to annoy my mother. But she didn't, so that tells me it's ingrained and not going to change. To keep the peace, the three of us ignore it for the most part. Calling Cathy and Mo One and Four isn't so bad. I still get a little resentful every time she Number Twos me, though."

I stopped, abruptly. I had just divulged more to this

man about this subject than I had to Harry in our ten years together.

"Why did you parents move after your sister died?" Slade asked, oblivious to my thoughts.

I parked the car but left it running. "They couldn't emotionally handle living in the place one of their daughters had died. They kind of, well, ran away, leaving the house and Nanny to us to look after and care for."

His gaze studied me for a moment.

"What?"

"I can't decide if you're mad at them for leaving or not."

"I'm not mad. I was a little pissed off in the beginning, especially since they had three living daughters who needed them for emotional support and balance. But with distance, I've learned to understand their reasons. There are times, though, like today, I wished they'd taken Nanny with them. Life would have been a little less harried if they had."

Slade smiled. "But not as exciting, I'll bet."

"Excitement is overrated. Look, I don't want to seem rude, but I really need to get back."

Slade got the none-too-subtle hint. With a nod, he reached over and opened his door. "Thanks for the interesting tour. I'll see you later."

"Later?"

"When you come back for your sister meeting. Remember?"

"Of course I remember, but you'll have gone back to the city by then." As soon as I said it I remembered he wasn't going anyway. Not for the entire weekend.

He knew exactly when I realized it, too, because he

179

leaned into the car, one arm braced above him on the roof, the other holding the door, and grinned. I bit back the groan threatening to fly free.

"See you later," he repeated, then waltzed into the inn as if he owned it.

For the second time that day, I laid my head down on the steering wheel and sighed.

Maybe my parents had the right idea about running away.

Chapter Twelve

"What's tall, blond, and loaded doing here?" Charity asked me the next morning while we were helping the florist decorate Nanny's gazebo for Kimmy Gunderson's imminent wedding.

I glanced over to where she was pointing her chin to see Slade carrying boxes from Kolby's truck. The two were speaking as they hauled Kimmy's programs and packets of birdseed and rice, along with some of Kolby's photography equipment.

"I don't know." I climbed down from the ladder after I secured the final section of forget-me-nots and boxwood. "But I'm gonna find out."

The day was starting out bright and gorgeous. With nary a cloud in the sky, the sun sparkled off the lake water and trickled through the tree canopy, while shimmering shards of light danced along the water's edge. The temperature was rising, and by the time the ceremony began, it promised to be in the low seventies, the perfect day for an outdoor wedding. The air was cool and crisp, and I knew Kimmy, in all her eight-month girth and glory, would be comfortable. There's nothing a bride despises more than to be sweaty and disheveled in her photos.

Slade watched me approach the cabin, his now-empty hands shoved in his pants pockets as he leaned a shoulder against the door jamb. The man gave a whole new meaning to looking laid-back and relaxed, two things I wasn't during the best of times, but certainly not while this delicious man stood in front of me with all his intense manliness on display.

I hadn't seen him since dropping him off at the inn the afternoon before. Even when I'd gone back for the sister confab, he hadn't been lurking about, which I was thankful for. Maureen told me he'd taken his dinner in his room and had been tied up with faxes and calls since he'd come back.

I was hopeful something had rocked his financial world propelling him back to the city.

Apparently, no such luck.

"Good morning." A smile played on his mouth. "It's a beautiful day for a wedding."

"What are you doing here?" I internally winced at the accusatory tone in my voice. Just when I hope I've got the speak-before-I-think tic nailed down, it fails me yet again.

He glanced down at the boxes at his feet and then back up at me. "Helping your photographer unload his truck."

I waved an impatient hand at him. "I can see that for myself. I meant *why* are you here?"

He pushed off the doorframe and moved toward me, keeping his eyes locked on mine. If I ever wanted to know how a lion looks when it's stalking prey, I can imagine this would be it. Slade had a determined, steely glare in his eyes, his jaw tight, his lips pressed together in a hard line. The heat in his gaze was intense, focused, and blistering.

Holy Mary.

When our bodies were a whisper from touching, he

182

stopped. Did I say his gaze was intense? I should have called it penetrating, because standing across from him, so close I could make out the individual colors circling his pupils, it felt like he was invading my thoughts and my very soul with his stare.

"Another bad night?" he asked, one of his hands rising to cup my chin and hold me still under his scrutiny.

"You sure do know how to flatter a girl. *Not*." I slapped his hand away.

He slipped it back into his pocket and rocked back on his heels.

I fisted my own hands on my hips. "I don't need you to comment on my lack of sleep," I told him. "It's no concern of yours. But what is, is why you're out here."

He lifted one of his square shoulders. "I didn't mean to offend you—"

"Too late."

"—but after investing so much time with you yesterday, I'll admit, I wanted to see how it all came together, how all those details you were so obsessed about work out."

He had no idea the amount of obsession I put into every wedding. He'd only seen a minute snapshot.

"You couldn't have just asked me after the fact, how things went?"

"I could have. But I've always been a big believer in seeing things for myself. And since you're in charge of Isabella's wedding, I thought it might be a good idea to see you in action."

Okay, all that seemed plausible. But still. "So are you planning on staying for the actual ceremony, or just here to see how we set everything up?"

"I'd like to stick around, if it's okay with you."

It wasn't, but I wasn't going to admit it to him. Stubborn pride or something else I couldn't and didn't want to put a name to swirled around my insides. The last thing I needed was for a guy I'd been having serious dirty dreams and thoughts about, hovering around me while I did my job. Slade Harrington was a major-league distraction. And the sexiest part of that? He didn't even realize he was.

"I can help in any way you need," he said. "Carrying things." He thrusted his chin toward the gazebo. "Decorating."

Now I was torn. Seriously torn.

On one hand, he was an extra pair of able hands, and I could always use another set of those when I was setting up.

On the other, I had a difficult time concentrating when he was in the vicinity. My mind turned a little nonfunctional whenever he was around, and I needed to be on my toes to make sure every aspect of the wedding went off without a problem or a hiccup. I was nervous being around Slade in a simple setting. I wasn't sure I'd be able to contain my nerves if he was watching and evaluating everything I did and had to do for the ceremony itself.

"Why do you want to? Really? You're not the kind of guy who…schleps." I flapped my hand in the air. "You're the kind who orders things to be schlepped."

"You do realize how insulting that statement is, don't you?"

"Almost as insulting as telling me how haggard I look, maybe?"

"I'm fairly sure I never said you look haggard."

"The implication was loud and clear."

"You need your hearing checked."

"My hearing is fine. Don't change the subject. Why do you want to help?"

He stared at me, his hands on his own hips now, defiant and a little ticked off. Well, good. If I was mad, he deserved to be too.

"Every reason I gave you was the truth. I've never been involved in a wedding before. I had no idea there were so many details that needed attending to. I'd like to see how this one turns out."

Again, plausible.

"Hey, Coll?" Kolby called out to me from his truck. "I need some help with this new runner. It weighs a friggin' ton."

Slade lifted an eyebrow and cocked his head while his gaze stayed glued to mine.

"Since I'm here, let me help." He took a small step closer to me.

I should have taken a step backward because the moment the scent of fresh, clean, male wafted over me, I forgot why I was arguing with him.

"Okay. Make yourself useful," I said, flipping my hand in the air again. "But when the wedding starts, stick to the sidelines. I need to concentrate on everything happening plus the fifteen things that will be coming up. I don't want you looming around, asking questions and stuff. Deal?"

"I don't loom, but yes." He stuck out his hand, good manners forcing me to do the same. "Deal," he said when I slipped my fingers into his. I wasn't prepared for the shock of warmth that cradled around them, although past experience told me I should have been.

He let go and went to help Kolby, while I rubbed a hand over my shaking abdominal muscles.

****

"So, this is a pig roast."

I slanted a look at Slade. "Is that a question or a statement?"

He turned from where he'd been staring at the spit holding the two-hundred-pound wedding dinner for the fifty quests, a sheepish grin on his face.

"A little of both, maybe?"

I shook my head, realizing it was impossible to stay upset with him for very long. He'd been an absolute Godsend pre-ceremony, helping Kolby install the one-hundred-foot runner from the cabin to the gazebo. He'd wiped down the chairs that were still damp from the early morning lake-mist condensation and had even climbed up to the top of the gazebo to help drape the flowers for a suddenly height-frightened Charity. I knew what she was doing, of course. Charity has never been afraid of anything in her life, but seeing Slade climb his way up to, and then dangle from, the roof to hang the flowers was an eye-opener she couldn't miss.

Me, either.

He'd done as I'd asked and stayed on the sidelines during the ceremony, which my sister Cathleen officiated at, and then had helped round everyone up for pictures at the lake. He'd even been helpful corralling the guests into their cars and trucks to shuttle them back to the Gunderson's farm for the reception.

So far he'd stuck by my side as we watched the

bridal party dance their little hearts out in the barn, listened to the good-natured toasts and the ribald ones, too, of the best man and maid of honor, and had wheeled Kimmy's one-hundred-and-three-year-old great-grandmother to her place of honor at the head table.

If I didn't know he already ruled a financial empire, I'd be tempted to give him a second job on the weekends as an event assistant.

"Oh, Colleen, I can't thank you enough," Kimmy Schmidt, nee Gunderson, told me as she pulled me into a hug. She had always been an enthusiastic hugger, clamping her body fully against whomever she was wrapped around, but before the added eight-month pregnancy belly, it had been easier to hug her back. Now, I couldn't get my arms even halfway around her midsection and I was afraid all her vigorous body bumping was harmful to the baby.

Kimmy had no such concerns.

"Everything was perfect. Abso perfection. Your team is simply the ultimate best."

One of Kimmy's endearing traits? She loved to speak in absolutes.

"Uncle Pecker said the pig is almost ready. You're staying for supper, right?"

"I can't, Kimmy, I'm sorry. I've got a thousand things to do before tomorrow, but Charity and Kolby are staying. Kolby will keep taking pictures and candids until the end, and anything you need or want, or any problems that pop up, Charity can take care of. But don't worry, because there will be no problems."

Kimmy yanked me in for another squeeze. It was a good thing I hadn't drunk anything all afternoon, because I could feel my bladder knock against my intestines with the force of this one. "Of course there won't be any problems. Look who my wedding planner is."

Her father called her name from across the field and with one more hug and a quick kiss to my cheek, she waddled across the freshly mown cornfield to him.

"Uncle Pecker?" Slade said, dangerously close to my ear. So close, his breath warmed over my entire neck. Before I did something stupid like turn around and pull him into a Kimmy-worthy embrace, I took a few steps forward and away from him and his hot—and by hot, I mean *wowza!*—breath.

"His given name is Woodrow. It's his father's name as well, and one Woody in the family was, I guess, enough."

It took him a moment. I could see when the dawn broke by the way his sexy eyes widened and his mouth opened for a second.

"And you had the nerve to make fun of Bunny," he said. "Being nicknamed after a rabbit, I have to think, is much more preferable to being referred to as a woodpecker."

"Maybe. But both names are pretty awful."

"Yes, they are."

"I need a minute to let Charity and Kolby know I'm leaving, then we can go."

How he finagled it so he drove out to the farm in my car, I still didn't know. But I was, for all intents and purposes, his ride.

Once I'd made sure my two assistants were set, Slade and I headed back into town.

"I assumed you stayed for the entire reception,"

Slade said.

"I usually do, if for no other reason than to ensure if any problems arise I can be the fixer and not have to worry the bridal party or the parents."

"So how come we didn't stay?"

"First, trust me when I tell you there will be no problems. And if any arise, they're going to be family and alcohol-related, so Kimmy's parents will take care of it. And believe me, they will do a much better job than I would. Nobody messes with Grover Gunderson and walks away unscathed."

I slid a side glance to him. My heart sped up a little at the sight of his smile.

"Is he related to Uncle Woodrow?"

"Brothers."

"Their mother must have had a thing for presidents."

I nodded. "She did. You didn't meet uncles Calvin and Millard."

His free and easy laugh tickled all the way down my spine.

"What's the second reason?"

"I need to get to the church. I've got a rehearsal for tomorrow's wedding scheduled, and Maureen is doing the rehearsal dinner back at the inn."

The car grew quiet as I drove. I had fifteen things running through my head about tomorrow's nuptials, an equal number concerning Nanny Fee and the talk I'd had with my sisters the night before, and then even more thoughts revolving around my work schedule for the week.

"What are you doing after that?"

"Making sure everything is set for the wedding.

I've got a list of things to double check back at the house, and I need to make some calls to verify times. I should have done it all yesterday, but as you're well aware, time got away from me. Why?"

All those important thoughts flew out the car window when Slade said, "Have dinner with me."

"What?"

"You heard me." He turned his body a bit so he was almost facing me. The penetrating scrutiny of his gaze sliced right through me. "I've been with you all day, Colleen. You didn't stop once to eat or even have a drink of water. You've been in constant motion since I arrived at the lake, and that was at nine o'clock. Charity said you'd all been there since seven thirty, setting up. You've got to be hungry by now because I know I am. Starving, in fact."

The thought of sharing a meal alone with him was too intimate, too unsettling for me to consider. Yesterday's stop for a quick slice of pizza aside, the last time I'd dined with him I'd ruined his suit and he'd been privy to a scene with Vlad I didn't want to think about again. Ever.

"The rehearsal shouldn't take more than an hour, right?" He glanced down at a watch that cost more than my yearly car payments. "We can go somewhere and have a leisurely meal after. I'm assuming you're not invited to the dinner."

"Why do you assume that?"

I heard him shrug. "Are you?"

"No. The rehearsal dinner is strictly for the families and bridal party. The last time they can all be together alone before the ceremony." I bit my bottom lip, and realized too late I'd probably chewed off the little lipstick that still remained. "Wouldn't you rather go back to the inn, eat, and relax there? Even though Maureen is catering the dinner, she still feeds her other guests. I'm sure she can make you something you can take to your room."

When he didn't respond, I turned my head to him. He'd crossed his arms over his amazing chest, his brows were almost touching, and his mouth had twisted into a thoughtful yet wickedly sexy frown.

"Why are you looking at me like that?"

"I'm trying to figure out—again, I'll add—if you're just obstinate, clueless, or you seriously don't want to be in my presence because you loathe me."

Okay, obstinate and avoidance I got. But *clueless?* What the holy heck did that mean?

"Which is it?" he asked.

Well, the closest reason was the last—I didn't want to be in his presence, but it wasn't because of any animosity or because I didn't like him. Quite the opposite in fact. I was starting to like him a little too much for propriety. He was the brother of a client, the person writing the checks for her wedding. Not to mention so different from me in every single way I could fathom from education, to social connections, to financial status, that I had no business dreaming all those sexy little dreams I'd been having or remembering exactly what he tasted like when he'd kissed me. Or hoping he'd do it again.

"Well?"

"I'm trying to decide," I said without thinking—nasty habit, much? Flames shot up my neck and jaw.

"You don't know if you loathe me or not?"

When I turned to him, that bad-boy grin was in

place again.

I shook my head and concentrated on driving. "It's not that," I told him. "I don't loathe anyone. Well, maybe one person. But it's not you." I sighed and pulled up to a stop sign. "I have a ton of prep work I need to do for tomorrow's wedding, and I already feel behind."

"Your work ethic is commendable. It's no wonder your business is so successful, but you still need to eat and I don't want to go back to the inn yet. Pick someplace you're comfortable with and since time is such a factor, a place where we don't have to linger if you don't want to, so you can get back to work before it gets late. Okay? Does that meet with your approval?"

Why did he have to be so logical and accommodating? Why couldn't he be the selfish, self-absorbed elitist I wanted and needed him to be?

If Nanny were sitting behind me she'd answer those questions with some of her own, like, "Why do you have to question everything in life, Number Two? For once, can't ya simply go with the flow?"

Maybe she was right. It was, after all, just dinner. He wasn't asking me to commit to life together, or— God forbid—plan his own wedding.

"Okay," I said when the silence grew heavy. "I know just the place. But I've got to get through this rehearsal first."

I wasn't sure because I didn't look at him again, but I think his smile widened.

Or maybe that was wishful thinking.

Chapter Thirteen

"The food here is good, fast, and cheap," I said once we were seated.

"Something every man likes to hear on a date," he mumbled.

Date?

"What?"

"Nothing."

Okay, had he really said date, or had I misheard him? Probably the latter because there was no way on God's green earth this was in any way, shape, or desire (mine!) a date.

Maybe in a parallel universe, but certainly not in the tiny New England town of Heaven.

"Everything on the menu is good," I told him after taking a sip from my water glass. "Not as good as the Crystal Room, but not many places are."

Thinking about the last time we'd been in that gorgeous establishment had my pulse racing. Slade, all decked out in his ruler-of-his-financial-empire suit, looking like the hottest version of King Midas I'd ever seen, sitting next to me. He'd made me forget every rule Nanny had ever impressed on me about how impolite it was to stare.

I simply couldn't help myself, though. Slade Harrington was without a doubt the handsomest man I'd ever been around. This was saying a lot, too, because at the bridal magazine I'd been surrounded by models—male and female—many of whom had graced the covers of top fashion mags worldwide. I could never deny Harry was a huge gobble of eye candy on the outside because it was true. It was his insides that were unpalatable.

I was pulled out of my thoughts when he said, "You haven't looked at the menu."

"Don't need to. I know it by heart."

His lips lifted. "Come here often?"

It was on the tip of my tongue to tell him I'd worked my way through high school waitressing, and the menu hadn't changed in the forty years the restaurant had been in business, but before I could, our waitress appeared.

"Colleen." To the casual listener, she'd merely said my name as a greeting. If you knew what to listen for, though, you'd know it was synonymous with an oath when it spilled from her lips.

"Hey, Sally. Long time and all. Busy night?"

She slid her gaze to Slade, ignoring my question. It was fascinating to see his reaction on women. Her brown, heavily mascaraed, and black-lined eyes widened, and I swear her pupils dilated. She arched her back a little making her stand up taller and forcing her ample breasts to jut forward in a blatant invitation.

Sally smiled, and for a moment, I thought I was hallucinating. I'd known her for over thirty years, and I'd never seen her smile before. Truly. Even as a kid she'd been surly.

If Slade knew the impression he was making on her, he gave no indication of it.

So," she said, when he remained indifferent to her

four years of teeth-straightening brace work. She cocked her hip, pad and pencil poised. "The specials tonight are our king-cut prime rib served with roasted veggies, our peppercorn-crusted salmon with mashed sweet potatoes, and our pasta primavera with your choice of soup. What can I getcha?"

I refused any of the offerings, knowing what I'd wanted as soon as I'd driven here.

"Bacon cheeseburger with mozzarella, please. Side salad, undressed."

"I wrote that down the minute I saw it was you sitting here," she said, barely looking at me. "And for you, handsome?" she said to Slade.

"I'll have the same."

"You want it mooing like this one does?" she asked, lifting her chin to indicate me.

"Medium will be fine."

After she left, I placed my hands on the table and took a mental breath.

"You two seem to know one another."

I winced. "That's a mild way of putting it. Sally and I have a long history, starting when she had my grandmother for catechism classes, and, well, she's not a fan. Of either of us. Nanny Fee didn't tolerate certain behaviors from her pupils."

"Such as?"

"Smart aleckiness, calling out in class without raising a hand, laziness are just a few."

"Which was Sally?"

"All three." I rolled my eyes. "At varying times. Whenever Sally sees me, I'm a reminder of all the times Nanny sent her to Father Duncan's office."

"What else?"

"What do you mean?"

"You said it started with your grandmother. What other history do the two of you have?"

"You really don't want to hear about this. It's all small town, teenage-girl drama and way in the past."

Lord. What was it about his sharp, direct, and studly glare that got me every time? He'd lowered his head and stared at me so pointedly, I fidgeted in my seat.

"Tell me," he said softly. It wasn't a request.

Resigned—because *really,* what could I do?—I did. "Sally and I are the same age. We went all through school together, every grade until we graduated. We were…well, the best word is competitors. In everything. Scholastically, we were a tenth of a point apart in grades—"

"Who scored higher?"

"I did. Routinely. We both ran track and were pretty well matched in that as well. My times were all a few tenths of a second better than hers, and she hated me for it."

"That seemed like a great deal of animosity flowing your way for just grades and some running times."

It appeared he was as perceptive as his younger sister.

"No, you're right. It was more." I stopped and glanced down at my hands, then back up at him. "In our junior year, we both liked the same guy. Chris Powell. He was the captain of the varsity track team. God, he was fast. And cute." Heat rushed up from my neck and for the millionth time since I'd met Slade, I cursed my Irish skin.

"So what happened? He liked you more? Another thing you won, this guy's heart?"

"I wish it was that easy, but no. Chris liked Sally. So much so they started dating."

The look on his face did wonders for my fragile ego. "That's a surprising twist."

"In more ways than one," I mumbled.

He tossed me that severe glare again. It was a crying shame he didn't use his law degree. One probing, penetrative look from him and anyone in a witness box would admit to anything, whether they committed a crime or not.

"Sally got pregnant right before graduation. She dropped out to have the baby, and they got married."

"From the look on your face, this isn't one of your happily ever after stories."

"It's not. Chris hated being tied down at such a young age. He started drinking, doing drugs. He was hauled in front of my father, who was the town judge, a few times and threatened with incarceration if he didn't change."

"Did he?"

I shook my head. "One night, he mixed a bottle of whiskey with one too many joints and wound up falling asleep behind the wheel on his way home. The coroner said he died instantly." I sighed, hating I remembered it all detail for detail. "To this day, Sally blames me."

"Why? You didn't force him to drink. To use."

"No. Nanny has this theory. She thinks Sally hates me so much because the one thing she got over on me in all our years of competing was Chris. If I'd…well, won him, instead of her, I would have been the one to suffer through his death. I would have been the one left widowed at the age of twenty with a two-year-old toddler, a mountain of debt, and no high school diploma."

"From the brief glimpse I got of your grandmother, I think she's very wise."

I agreed. Still… "Growing up in a small community where everyone knows everyone else can be trying," I said. "It's so much easier to get lost in a city. You have no history waiting to hit you in the face like a wet noodle." I folded my hands down on the table in front of me.

Slade reached across the table and touched my hand. I didn't pull away or flinch. I didn't move at all. Couldn't. Warmth, like steam from a heated bath, seeped through my skin where his fingers lay, calming, soothing my sad memories.

The notion that his superpower was his comforting touch burst into my head again. I was beginning to like that touch a bit too much for propriety—and my sanity's—sake.

"And yet," he said, when I lifted my gaze to his, "you came back here and stayed."

"Because I was needed." I sat back up and pulled my hands from under his. "Believe me, if possible, I would have stayed in New York. I tried commuting when my sister got sick, but it was too much. Too much traveling, too much work to catch up on, too much…everything."

"But you stayed even after she died. You never considered moving back?"

"Considered it? About a million times. Actually did it? No. By then, my parents had bolted, and the business venture with my sisters was taking off. Plus, someone needed to be around for my grandmother. Maureen was grieving, and Cathleen, well…that's another story in itself."

He looked as if he were going to ask me more but was prevented when we both heard my name. Stunned, I sat bolt upright. My fingers and toes started to tingle, and my blood drummed through my temples.

"Finally," a voice said. An all too familiar voice cried, "I've been trying to get in touch with you for days. You haven't answered any of my texts."

"Harry." His name tasted like acid on my tongue. "What are you doing here?"

"Obviously, I'm looking for you. I can't believe I finally found you. I've been all over this dumb town today." From his expression, he hadn't been happy about his trek. His lips were pinched, and the annoyed way he looked down at me made me want to wipe the sour look off his face and send him on his way. His gaze went from me to Slade. At first, his eyes widened in surprise and his mouth fell open. Just as quick he closed it, then put a smile as fake as a three-dollar bill across it.

"Well, this is unexpected," my former fiancé said. He stuck out his hand and leaned down. "Harrington. How are you?"

Slade took his time raising his own hand. "I'm sorry," he said, a tinge of confusion coloring his voice. "Have we met?"

Harry's sycophantic smile dropped a tad. "Harland Green," he said, his chipper bonhomie slipping. "We met at the Crystal Room." He looked over at me. "You two were having lunch at the same time I was there with a client."

"Is that what you're calling them these days?" I asked, channeling my grandmother's words.

I caught the quick lift of Slade's lips at my question. Why it reassured me I have no idea.

"Oh, yes. I remember now. You and Miss O'Dowd are acquaintances." Harry turned his attention back to Slade and away from me, his brows almost cleaved together.

As I've mentioned before, Harry has never been quick on his feet.

"We're a lot more than acquaintances. Colleen and I were engaged."

"*Were engaged* are the operative words in that sentence," I said. "Past tense. Again, Harry, why are you here?"

He looked, furtively, from me, to Slade, and then back to me again. "Like I said, you haven't responded to any of my texts—"

"Most normal people would see that as a sign," I told him. "Obviously, you need it spelled out for you. I didn't respond because I was ignoring them. Ignoring you. I don't want to talk to you, Harry. Via text, in a voice mail, or in person. Get it, now?"

"Coll, I—"

"I can't make myself any clearer. Please go."

I had to give him credit for his determination. Instead of leaving with his dignity intact, he actually pulled out an empty chair and sat down a little too close for my liking. I shifted my chair away from him, closer to Slade, a movement that didn't go unnoticed by my former fiancé.

Harry reached out and tried to grasp my hand. I yanked it back. Where Slade's skin had felt warm and gentle against mine, Harry's fingers were ice cold and the furthest thing from comforting I could imagine.

"Colleen, please." He grazed a glance to Slade and then back to me. "I want to talk. I…" He lowered his voice. "I need to talk to you."

"There's nothing you can say I want to hear."

"Coll, please. I miss you. I—"

This time when he leaned in, I recoiled. Then, my back and shoulders snapped straight up as if I'd been hit from behind. I lifted my chin and glared at him down my nose. "You have no one to blame for that but yourself, Harry."

He had the grace to look ashamed. I wasn't buying it for a second.

"I know. I know," he said, hanging his head. "I made a mistake. A huge one."

"Ya think? Calling what you did a mistake is like calling the sinking of the *Titanic* a leaky boat accident."

He winced.

"You destroyed my life, ruined my career, and humiliated me in front of everyone I knew."

"What I did was inexcusable, Colleen, I know. But you never really gave me a chance to explain."

"Are you kidding?" Fury bubbled up from deep down in the depths of my soul. "Seeing my naked assistant riding you like a jockey speeding to cross a finish line needed no words of explanation. The visual told the story in full, disgusting detail." He reared back as if I'd slapped him. The thought had crossed my mind. "I'm not going to ask again, Harry. Leave. Now."

"Green." Harry's attention turned to Slade. "Miss O'Dowd has made her feelings clear. I think it would be prudent if you left, as she's requested."

The glare he tossed Slade this time wasn't as ingratiating as his previous one had been. "This really is no concern of yours, Harrington. Butt out."

"Harry." I imagined about now my cheeks resembled a boiled lobster shell.

"It isn't," Harry said, turning his attention to me and pouting the petulant pout that made him look like a stupider version of Derek Zoolander. "This is between you and me, no one else."

"Wrong," Slade said before I could. "Miss O'Dowd's feelings are of great importance to me, Green, and you're upsetting her so that makes this very much my concern."

Harry's head jerked back at Slade's slicing tone.

He'd placed his hands, palms down, his fingers extended, on the table and leaned toward my ex. "Now, before you make me remove you, which I will, have no doubt of it, I suggest you leave of your own accord."

It took a moment for the threat to register in both Harry and me. When the meaning thrilled through me, my body jolted with surprise, and I whipped my head around to look at Slade. His entire posture was calm, but a storm brewed in his eyes as he stared Harry down.

Harry's gaze dragged across Slade's face. The debate swirling inside him about what to do, how to respond, was finely etched across it. There was a tiny bit of fear in his eyes when he shook his head and then stood.

Ignoring Slade, he addressed me. "I can see this isn't the right time to discuss our personal matters—"

"We don't have any personal matters."

"So I'll leave you to your business dinner. You and I are going to speak, though, Colleen. You're going to listen to what I have to say. You owe me that much."

"No, I don't." I lifted my water glass, dismissing him.

This time he took the hint. With an audible breath and that stupid pout still on his face, he moved from the table.

"And just for the record." Slade waited until he turned back around. "This isn't a business dinner."

With hands fisted at his sides, his shoulders almost meeting his ears they were held so tightly, Harry told me, "I'll be in touch."

"Don't bother."

We were both silent as he weaved through the dining room, inquiring eyes of our fellow diners following his back as he exited.

My hands were shaking so much the water in my glass looked like waves at high tide. Slade reached over and took the glass from me and set it down on the table. Then, in a move that was so tender I wanted to cry, he slid his hand into mine and wove my fingers into his.

I couldn't speak. Shame turned me silent.

"Here you go." Sally sidled next to us, her arms laden with a tray she placed next to the table. Her gaze zeroed in on our joined hands. I tried to pull mine back, but Slade simply squeezed harder.

Once Sally moved our dinner plates and salads from the tray, she dropped her hands on her hips and asked, "Need anything else? More water? Something else to drink?"

In all honesty, I could have used a glass of wine. Oh, who am I kidding? An entire bottle wouldn't have been enough to eradicate the myriad of jumbled emotions seizing through me. Slade told her no, and she ambled off to check on her other tables.

"Colleen?"

Slowly, I lifted my head.

"You should go ahead and eat that"—he pointed to my burger—"because you ordered it barely cooked. It's gonna get cold fast if it isn't already."

A bubble of nausea swelled up from my empty stomach. I was terrified if I put anything in it, it might come back up immediately. "I'm not hungry."

"Yes, you are."

"No. I'm not. I've lost my appetite."

A line formed between his brows when I tried to tug my hand out of his. He held on tighter. "There's that stubbornness again. You know you're hungry."

"Don't tell me what I am. I know if I'm hungry or not."

A woman at the table next to ours turned as my voice rose. I recognized her as one of the town court clerks. That's all I needed to really cap this horrible dinner. Someone who knew my family, gossiping about my behavior.

I inhaled deeply.

"Don't let him do this to you, Colleen. He's not worth it."

Slade's words made me go still.

"He's not worth one moment of your time, one moment of your thoughts. You don't deserve to be upset by him. You deserve to be treated so much better than he's treated you, and you know it."

His eyes were so compassionate, so filled with kindness the urge to cry hit me again. This time when I shook my hand, he let it go free.

I sat there, mute and thoughtful. It was amazing

how similar two men could be in so many aspects, and yet how different they were at their respective cores. I'd compared the two of them when I'd first met Slade, thinking they were as alike as unrelated men could be. I'd been so wrong in that supposition.

So wrong.

"I'm sorry about all this," I said after a time. "You didn't come up here to be embroiled in my drama. I'm sorry."

"Don't ever apologize for something that's not your fault. You've done nothing wrong."

"Still. I pride myself on keeping things professional with clients, keeping my personal life and issues detached from my business life. Twice now, Harry's barged into my life when you're around. It's mortifying."

"It shouldn't be. Not for you, anyway. He's the one who should feel ashamed."

I shook my head. "Harry doesn't do shame."

"I've been around guys like Green my whole life," he said after taking a sip of water. "Entitled, narcissistic, and selfish. They're users, out for all they can get from people and the world in general. You shouldn't feel embarrassed by his behavior. It truly has nothing to do with you."

While he ate some more of his salad, I lifted my fork.

"He wasn't always that way," I said after a bite. "Not in college. Not when we first started living together. Back then he was, well, different. Kinder. Calmer. Loyal."

"I tend to think he was probably always the way I described him but was good at masking it. Or you ignored any signs of it because you were in love with him. Women, even extremely smart and savvy ones like yourself, have a tendency to disregard and ignore the warning signs. Guys like Green use that to their advantage."

"My sister Cathleen said the same thing. Nanny Fee, too."

"From what I've seen of your grandmother, she's got a good, well-defined bullshit-ometer. She'd know a person for a phony fairly quick after meeting them."

"Truth." I sighed.

He was being so kind, so understanding. I should have been grateful. Instead, I was worried. "I know you don't want me to say this," I started, "but I truly am sorry you've been caught in the crossfire of all my drama for the past few days. First with my grandmother and now Harry. I can't begin to fathom what you must think about me, how out of control things are around me, but please know nothing going on in my personal life affects my business. I'll make Isabella's wedding dreams come true no matter what's happening around me. You can depend on it."

"I've never thought otherwise. I've watched you for three days, Colleen, followed you around and seen for myself how dedicated, professional, and focused you are. I know Izzy is in good hands. Believe me, if I weren't convinced of that, I'd encourage her to drop her association with you."

That was the part worrying me.

"Besides, I'm the one who pushed myself into your life," he continued. "If I hadn't been following you around, you still would have had to deal with everything that's happened."

"True, but I would have been saved the humiliation of you seeing me going through it."

He cocked his head, looked down at my salad bowl, and then back to my face. His lips quirked in the corners when he found my bowl empty. "Weren't you the one who told me all families have issues?"

"Yes, but I was referring to *your* family drama, not mine."

"Well, it only seems fair since you know about my mine, I know about yours."

"No, it doesn't. It's different."

"How so?"

"Because you and your sister are clients. You shouldn't be involved in my personal craziness. It's not like we're friends or anything, and we share our problems, pour our hearts out to one another over a bottle of wine and a quart of Rocky Road. I'm the hired help."

That groove popped up between his eyes again. He took his napkin, swiped it across his mouth in one swift stroke, and then put it back on his lap. His movements were precise and clipped and robotic.

"Is that really how you think I see you?"

Well, yeah.

"It's the truth. I'm getting paid to do a job for your sister. We have a professional relationship."

"But friends have business relationships. All the time. I can name several people I'm friendly with who also do business with me, and vice versa."

"Again, that's different. You're not from the same…well, *world* I am. I'm willing to bet you see many of the people you do business with at events like charity functions, dinners, even the theater."

He shrugged, nodded.

"I don't. I don't run in the same social sets as my clients. Once the wedding is over, I never see them again. I get a heartfelt thank-you note from a client occasionally, but once the final check clears, we don't interact, meet for a glass of wine, take in a movie. Our relationship is, for lack of a better word, terminated. It has an end date."

"So, to prove this theory, you'll never see Kimmy or her parents again because you worked for them?"

Why did I forget he was a lawyer? Of course he was going to try and see all sides of anything I said. It was in his professional nature to dissect and analyze.

"Okay, well, that's not the same thing. Ninety-nine point nine percent of my clients don't live in Heaven. Kimmy's is the first wedding of a resident I've done. I can't say for sure it will be the last, but my base of clients is most exclusively non-residential." I took a sip of water. "So, you see, my personal and professional lives are separate."

"What if they weren't?"

"What do you mean?"

He sat back in his seat, one elbow settled on the table in a casual stance while he regarded me. "What if we were friends or colleagues, not—to use your word—clients? Would you feel differently about everything I've seen you go through, then?"

"I—I don't…know." I blew out a breath with enough force to make the candle on our table flicker. "I don't really have any close friends other than my sisters. Harry was, well, *my world* for so long. He didn't really like if I went out for drinks with the girls from the magazine, so I wound up sitting alone at home or masterdating."

Slade choked on his water. "Excuse me?"

"Sorry." I shook my head. "It's another Nanny word, like askhole. It means going out alone, like you're dating yourself."

"You grandmother is an interesting woman."

I dragged in a deep breath. "No lie. Anyway. Harry wanted me home, waiting for him." I looked down at my hands and shook my head.

"Kind of proves my calling him a selfish narcissist true, doesn't it?"

I shook my head again and lifted my burger. "Yeah. He was. Is. I can't believe I let him treat me that way for so long just because I—"

I slammed to a stop. There was no way I was going to give words to what had popped into my mind. Not to him, anyway.

"Yes?"

"What?"

"Finish your sentence. You can't believe you let him treat you that way just because…what?"

"I forget." I shoved the burger into my mouth to stifle the fib and said a quick, silent prayer of contrition for lying. "Anyway," I said after swallowing. "It doesn't matter. This conversation is fruitless. Please just accept my apology about Harry's behavior."

He didn't look as if he believed me, but before he could press the point, I changed the subject to the wedding I was doing the next day. Slade listened, asked appropriate questions, and generally let me lead the conversation.

Talking about my business eased some of the strain, and I relaxed as we finished our meal and then refused dessert.

I drove him back to the inn in silence. The quiet in the car was companionable and comfortable, two words I don't think I've ever considered before when around this man.

When I pulled up the drive and stopped outside the front entrance, I put the car in park but didn't shut it down.

"Thanks for making me eat," I said. "And again, for being so understanding and nice about the Harry situation."

"Being understanding and nice had nothing to do with it."

"Oh? Well, I meant...I was grateful you were there. With me. When he arrived. If I'd been alone, I don't know what I would have done. Probably thrown a glass at him and caused a huge scene. Then, I'd have wound up in Lucas Alexander's custody like Nanny." My laugh had a slightly hysterical, nervous edge to it. "Sally would have been thrilled to call him. Payback, you know? For all those times she spent in Father Duncan's office. And everything else. So..."

Slade turned in his seat to face me. "I don't want your gratitude, Colleen. That's not why I spoke to him like I did."

"Oh? No?"

"No. I did it for purely selfish reasons, not simply because he's a jerk and needed to be taken down a peg."

"Selfish reasons?"

It had come to this. I'd been reduced to monosyllabic answers and repetition. A moment before I'd been thinking how comfortable and relaxed I finally was around him. That feeling flew out the car window when I caught the heated look in his eyes. The heated, *determined* look.

"Yes."

I swallowed when he leaned in over the gearshift, which I was gripping like a lifeline.

"Purely selfish reasons," he whispered as he lifted a hand and slid it around the column of my throat, coming to rest on the back of my neck. He gave me a tug and pulled me closer. "I've been wanting to do this for hours."

His eyes were huge and dark as they gamboled across my face and then stopped at my mouth.

"Do what?"

I was recalling the taste of his lips when he'd kissed me in the cabin in the rain. I wondered what he was thinking about.

In the next second I found out when, without any hesitation, he kissed me.

His lips were as amazing as I'd remembered. And just as intoxicating.

With our mouths touching, a soft sound groaned from the back of my throat and my head fell backward, cradling in his hand. Slade took full advantage and deepened the kiss. Our tongues twined, mated, begged for more.

Had I called his mouth intoxicating? That was too bland a word for it. At equal times I felt heady and energized, mesmerized and focused. The urge to shimmy across the seat, plant myself on top of him, and give in to this unexpected desire burst inside my head.

His fingers kneaded the back of my neck, and for the first time in hours, I felt all the tension and stress leave my shoulders.

He really did have a superpower when it came to that soothing-touch thing.

I leaned in closer and slid one hand up his granite-hard chest, around his thick neck, and then settled on his jaw. His skin was warm, and the beginning of an early evening scruff bloomed on his jawline. With our lips still fused, he cuddled into my hand and brought his free one up to lie on top of it, holding it in place.

The thought we were parked outside a busy inn, behaving like randy teenagers, skimmed across my mind. This is my hometown, and most people know my family and recognize me. I have a reputation—personal and professional—to uphold and being seen flagrantly making out in a car wasn't going to help either of those.

This needed to stop. Forget the fact I had a professional relationship with him, because that was bad enough. I was unencumbered romantically with anyone at the moment, but Slade *was* involved. With a supermodel. Even if there was some intergalactic shift in the cosmos or a parallel universe existed where someone like him and someone like me could actually become a couple, there was no way I could compete with a six-foot, twenty-something beauty who made her living showing the world how gorgeous she was. Nope. Not gonna happen. Maybe in my dreams, but certainly not in my reality.

And why, just why, was he kissing me when he had her to go home to? I knew why I was kissing him. What red-blooded female of consenting age blessed with all her mental faculties and a romantic imagination wouldn't? My mama didn't raise no dummy.

A deep, erotic rumble rolled up from the back of

his throat and jarred me into action.

First, I slid my hand from his jaw and dropped it into my lap. Then I eased back, breaking the kiss.

Slowly, slowly, he opened his eyes. Drowsy desire mixed with a slice of sexual need stared back at me. It took him a moment to focus but when he did, a lazy, tummy-fluttering grin of satisfaction split his lips.

"Why did you do that?" I asked, my voice a mere whisper. "Why did you kiss me…like…like that?"

He dragged a fingertip across my cheek. "Like what?"

Like you wanted me; like I meant something to you; like you'd die if you didn't.

Giving a voice to those thoughts wasn't going to happen in my lifetime.

I batted his hand away. "Like…*You know*." I flapped a hand in the air.

It took a moment for him to answer. "Because I wanted to and I couldn't think of a reason why I shouldn't."

That tummy roll turned to nausea in a heartbeat. Talk about selfish. He'd taken something simply because he could? Because he couldn't see a reason not to?

The nausea gave way to anger.

"That's just this side of insulting."

"No, it's not."

"Really? You couldn't come up with a reason why you shouldn't kiss me, so you just went ahead and did it? Didn't that used to be called pillaging?"

The grin disappeared, replaced by the scowl I'd been so intimidated by at our previous encounters. Not anymore.

"Colleen, I don't think you understand what I meant—"

"I understand you fine, believe me. Well, how about this for a reason since you can't come up with one: did you ever think I didn't want you to? Did that ever cross your mind?"

The scowl deepened. "No, it didn't, because from where I'm sitting you seemed to be enjoying it as much I was. Just like you were at your grandmother's cabin and then the nursing home."

My mouth fell open.

He huffed out a breath and flexed and extended his fingers. "For whatever reason, Colleen, I'm drawn to you, for lack of a better word. I can't explain it. Believe me, I've tried to. You're not the type of woman I usually become involved with—"

"Did I say insulting? How about offensive?"

"—but ever since we met, I've felt myself pulled to you. From the first day when you called me on the carpet about my father. Driving back home, I was angry at what you'd said, but all I could think about was how you'd looked with a smile on your face. How the colors in your hair made you look like an untamed gypsy. How your eyes lit up when you spoke to Isabella about her wedding plans. Why do you think I came here, decided to spend a few days? I wanted to get to know you better. Find out if this…spark, this connection between us is something worth developing, worth investing time in."

"Insulting, offensive, and you're a liar. This gets better and better. You want to find out if I'm worth investing in? You do realize you make me sound like some sort of acquisition you want to add to your empire with that statement, don't you?"

"Now, wait a minute. What do you mean by calling me a liar? I've never lied to you about anything."

"Yes, you have. You told me you came to Heaven for my help in getting Isabella to agree to the prenup, not to see if I'm worth *developing*. And—*Jesus!*—do you not get how horrible that sounds?"

"Yes, okay. I did say that. But it's not the only reason. I really did want to see you again. I wanted to spend some time with you without any distractions or interruptions—"

"So you could figure out why you have this illogical desire for me."

"—I never said that. Stop putting words in my mouth."

"I'm not. You said yourself you can't explain why you feel the way you do. That I'm not the type of woman you usually get involved with. And boy, isn't that just what every woman wants to hear from a man."

A few minutes ago, my brain couldn't see fit to process a complete sentence. Now? No such problem. My old hated best friend—verbal diarrhea—roared back to life, and she wasn't about to stop her tirade.

"You're definitely misinterpreting what I said." He shook his head so violently I felt the car sway a little. "Did you not hear the part about me wanting to get to know you better? That I'm drawn to you? Attracted to you?"

"I heard it just fine. I simply don't believe it."

"Why not?"

"I have my reasons, and believe me, they're valid ones."

"Maybe in your mind."

"Guys like you are all the same. Always working an angle, always out for yourselves. Never caring about someone else's feelings. Take, don't ask. Use, then discard when done."

"What the hell does that mean?"

It was as if he hadn't spoken.

"And let's not forget the fact you have a *girlfriend.* How do you think she'd feel hearing you hand me a line like that?"

He blinked a few times, his mouth standing open like a barn door. He slammed it shut and then said, "I don't know what you think your Google research yielded, but I'm not seeing anyone."

"Oh, come on. Now you think I'm stupid and gullible, too. Does the name Katya ring any bells?"

"Kat? She's not my girlfriend. She's a girl, yes. And my friend. A good one. But she's nothing more. Nothing, certainly, romantic."

"Oh, *please*. Men don't usually invite friends to weddings, especially family weddings. This is a subject I happen to know a great deal about."

"Well, you're wrong about this."

He looked sincere, I'll give him that. Wide-eyed, open-faced, he looked directly at me while he made his declaration. I was almost tempted to believe him.

Suddenly, the scowl returned, and his chin dropped back down. "Exactly who are you referring to when you lump me with a statement like *guys like you*? Your loser ex? Because if so, I'm nothing like that jerk."

"You're more alike than you think. I knew it the first time I met you."

"Now who's being insulting?"

"*Honest*. I'm being honest, which is more than you

216

are. By your own admission, you came here to get me to do something for you. I refused. This whole being nice and charming, try a little seduction thing, is meant to change my mind about helping you—"

"No, it isn't."

"—but it isn't going to work."

This entire conversation was going around in circles. Anger and hurt fought against one another inside me. Why the hurt was taking a bigger hit was unsettling.

"You need to go," I said abruptly, turning to face the windshield again. "It's getting late, and I've got work to do."

"So now you're dismissing me?"

"Semantics. I've got work to do. You're keeping me from it." I refused to look at him while I spoke. After a brief moment when I was afraid he was going to say more, like "you're fired," I held my breath.

When he pushed open the door and alighted, I finally let it out.

He leaned into the car, one hand resting on the roof of the car, the other bracing against the door, and said, "I'm sorry you're upset or if I've offended you somehow. It was never my intent."

"The best-laid plans," I mumbled, never looking at him.

"Thank you for having dinner with me," said, his voice calmer and softer. "Good luck tomorrow."

With that, he shut the door and went into the inn. I wanted to peel out of the driveway, get away as fast as I could, and put some real distance between the two of us.

What I did didn't even come close. I simply laid

my head down on my hands where they gripped the steering wheel, closed my eyes, and sighed.

Chapter Fourteen

"You've lost weight," I told Isabella a week later. She was standing on the riser in the bridal boutique again, facing the tri-mirror, garbed in her beautiful gown. The seamstress was busy adjusting the waist, and it looked as if she'd pinned a good inch all around. "You're not dieting, are you? Because that's a no-no for my brides. I won't have you fainting on the altar."

"I don't have much of an appetite lately," Isabella said, her voice sad and quiet.

We'd met outside the salon at the appointed time, and from the first moment she wasn't behaving like her usually exuberant self. Her smile seemed forced, and shadows under her eyes peeked through her concealer.

"You have one more fitting after this," the seamstress told her, gathering all her supplies and pins up. "I can't take it in any more after that."

"I know. I'm sorry."

"Don't apologize," I said. The boutique was empty, and when we were alone, I slid my hands around her upper arms, arms that showed some weight loss as well.

"Sweetie, what's going on? Is everything okay with you and Jack?"

This was the time, the critical few weeks before a wedding, where a bride's nerves and a groom's anxiety would usually start to climb. When I'd told Slade I liked to keep drama around my brides down, it was because I'd lived through so many emotional breakdowns and issues during this time frame when I'd been at the magazine and then when I'd gone out on my own.

"No, Jack and I are good. Really good. I can't wait to marry him."

"Then why aren't you eating? It can't be because you're worried about what you'll look like on the big day. You've got to know, you *have* to know, you're going to be a vision."

Her smile was sweet but tinged with sadness.

"Isabella, what is it?" I tugged her into my arms. I was usually the one being pulled in for bridal hugs, but this time and with this bride, I felt I needed to be the initiator.

Her sigh sluiced over me. "It's Slade."

Of course it is.

"Oh?" I tried to infuse my tone with mild curiosity and not the anger I was still feeling about our last encounter.

No. Anger wasn't the right word. Disappointment and confusion were the more appropriate terms for what I'd been experiencing this past week. But I shoved those feelings aside. Isabella was my first priority.

"What's going on with him?"

She pulled out of my arms and reached for a tissue. "He wants Jack to sign a prenuptial agreement."

I didn't let on I already knew this.

"And Jack doesn't want to?"

"No, he says he will. No questions asked. He doesn't care about my trust fund."

"Oh. Wow."

"I know, right? He's the best guy in the world, and

I'm so lucky to be marrying him."

"He's pretty lucky too, you know. He's getting you."

She dabbed at her eyes and managed a real smile. "You're sweet."

"So, what's the problem then? If Jack wants to sign it and your brother wants him to, it seems like there shouldn't be an issue."

Her mouth grew tight and thin. "*I* don't want him to. I hate that Slade thinks my marriage won't last. Just because Daddy has been married a few times, and Mom is on her second go 'round, it doesn't mean my marriage is going to fail, too."

"Of course it doesn't."

"But Slade thinks it will. He doesn't believe Jack loves me enough to spend a lifetime with me. To weather any problems or issues that come along. Otherwise, he wouldn't be pestering me about Jack signing on the dotted line. It's so"—she fluttered her hands in the air—"calculated and coldhearted."

I agreed. One hundred percent.

"We had a huge blowout last week, and I haven't spoken to or seen my brother since." She sniffled and swiped the tissue under her nose. "This is the longest we've ever gone without speaking. I miss him, but I'm so angry at him, too."

Tears slipped down her cheeks. I pulled her into a hug again and held her tight.

Damn Slade Harrington for making his sister so troubled this close to the wedding. Isabella should have been walking around in a cloud of bridal bliss, not having a dark and stormy one looming over her head, raining sadness down on her.

I was conjuring all the ways I wanted to punish him for making her so upset when the demon in question walked into the salon. He entered, his gaze sweeping the spacious area until he lit on us. As he began stalking toward us, the manager greeted him. He waved her away and made a beeline for his sister.

"What are you doing here?" Isabella said. She pulled away from me, swiped her cheeks dry, and glared at him. "Go away. I'm not speaking to you." She turned and tossed her tissue in a small trash bin, then looked at herself in the mirror. Her face smoothed, and she adopted an air of careless boredom.

Good girl.

"Izzy, please. I need to talk to you." His gaze darted once to me, then settled on his sister.

Isabella caught my eye in the mirror while she flicked a finger across her cheek, and said, "Colleen, could you tell my brother he has nothing to say I could possibly want to hear."

Apparently, grade-school sibling behavior is the same in any social class. My sisters and I had practiced this same kind of warfare too many times to remember.

I glanced over at Slade and raised my eyebrows. He scowled at me.

"Izzy, come on. Don't be this way." He came up behind her and lifted a hand to stroke her hair. Before he could touch her, she sliced such a heated glare at him in the mirror, I was surprised the glass didn't shatter. His hand fell back to his side. "I hate the way we left things the other day. I hate that you're not speaking to me and ignoring my texts and voicemails."

She brushed an imaginary piece of lint from her skirt and continued to ignore him.

"I know you're upset about the prenup, but you ran out of the office before I ever got a chance to tell you why it's so important."

In a move that bespoke her privileged and spoiled upbringing to perfection, Isabella lifted her perfect nose in the air, gathered the hem of her gown in her hands, and said to me, "I'm going to change. Then you and I can have lunch. I'm suddenly starving."

She quit the room without a word to her brother, slamming the changing-room door behind her.

"*Christ*." Slade dragged a hand through the side of his hair.

"Could you help Miss Harrington with her dress, please?" I asked the modiste who came over to us. With a nod, she followed Isabella.

I turned back to Slade. He stood, staring at the floor, his hands in his trouser pockets, his shoulders slumped. Even dejected he was still swoon-worthy.

All week I'd replayed the hot and mind-blowing kiss we'd shared in my car and then the heated conversation afterward, over and over again. He'd kissed me three times—*three!*—and each of them had been different. The first at the cabin had been filled with lust and urgency, both of us confused and bewildered at the burning, scorching flames igniting between us. The second was filled with a deep longing and growing appreciation. But the kiss in my car had been unlike the others. The heat and desire was still there—God help me—but added in was a softness and underlying sense of contentment I'd never experienced before, even with Harry. It was as if we'd known each other a hundred years and recognized the other's touch, the other's taste. Which, of course, was ridiculous since we'd met only a few weeks ago.

With his hand cupping my neck and his fingers trailing along my jaw as his lips covered and seduced mine, I'd felt…cherished.

And then his words had sliced through my heart and brought me back to reality.

He looked over at me now and shook his head. "She's still angry."

"Ya think? Can you blame her? She feels you're betting her marriage will fail like all of your father's have. That you don't trust it will last, and Jack doesn't love her enough to stick around."

"She doesn't understand. I know Jack loves her. I told her that."

"Did you?"

"Of course I did. I'm not an idiot. Anyone can see how much he adores her."

His voice had risen to an angry pitch. With an oath splitting his lips, he looked around, then grabbed my hand and yanked me through an open door.

"What are you doing?" I cried when he closed the door behind him. He'd pulled me into another dressing room, opposite the one Isabella was in. He still held my arm when he spun around to face me.

"I don't treasure having this conversation out in public for all the world to see and hear."

"Paranoid, much? There's nobody else in the salon but your sister and me."

"You're forgetting about the staff present. Now listen…" He let go of my arm but didn't back up. He stood in front of me, so close I had to lift my head a bit to stare up at him. I said a silent prayer of thanks I'd worn heels today. "I need your help."

"Don't ask me to convince her about the prenup. I already told you I won't."

He waved a hand in the air and the force of the movement shot a breeze over me, a shiver going down my spine. "I get it. In spades. That wasn't what I was going to ask."

"What, then?"

He huffed out a breath. "I can't stand having Isabella mad at me."

"You have no one to blame but yourself."

"Don't you think I know that? Stop talking and just listen to me for a minute."

My back went so straight, my body elevated and I could actually look him straight in the eye now. "Is this your way of getting people on your side? By strong-arming and ordering them about? Because it's not effective."

I tried to shoot past him, but he was bigger and faster than me. He slid his hand up my arm again and turned me around.

"Colleen, please. Stop and let me talk."

"Haven't you talked enough? Your sister certainly thinks so."

He winced and let go of my arm. I took a good look at his face, and for the first time noticed he, too, had lost weight. The planes in his cheeks were etched and stark, a bleak pallor infused his skin, and purplish shadows lay under his eyes.

His hands did a quick swipe at both his temples, and then he folded them behind his neck, cradled together. When he settled on me again, he looked so sad, I had to fight the urge to reach out and hug him as I had his sister.

"I don't want Isabella upset," he said after a moment.

"Too late." I really needed to figure out a way to prevent my mouth from speaking my every thought.

"I know." His lips pressed together into a thin line. "We had a very loud argument in our family lawyer's office, and she hasn't spoken to me since. She wouldn't listen to either the lawyers, or me, about why this agreement is so important, so necessary for her future. She won't listen to reason."

"Did it ever occur to you by forcing her hand this way you're hurting her? You're ruining what's supposed to be one of the happiest times of her life with all this talk of money and finances?"

"Of course I know that. Izzy has never *not* spoken to me, though. She's never shut me out this way, and it's killing me."

His words were verified by how ravaged he looked. Again, a bolt of compassion shot through me at how much he loved her.

I took a breath and gentled my voice. "Then why are you pressuring her? Why hound her to do something she so obviously doesn't want to and doesn't think she needs to?"

His head shook so violently, the hair on top of his head waved across his forehead. "Because she isn't thinking rationally or logically. She stands to lose a great deal of money if this marriage goes south. Our grandmother settled a trust fund on her for over fifteen million dollars. She comes into it on her wedding day."

The amount made my stomach flip.

"As soon as she says her vows and files her marriage license, she can access the money. If she doesn't have a specified prenup in place, whoever she marries is entitled to half of it when they divorce. I can't let that happen."

"Did you just hear yourself? You said *when* she divorces, not if. You don't believe a word you've said about Jack. No wonder Isabella is mad at you, especially if you broached the subject to her that way. I'd be mad too. Hell, I'd be homicidal."

"You just don't understand. I'm only trying to protect her, protect her future. Why can't either of you see that?"

"Maybe because she, like me, values love above money. Did you ever think of that? Maybe because Isabella actually has a warm, beating heart inside her filled with love for Jack and not a cold, logical, fiscally responsible one. She actually believes in a happily ever after. All you seem to believe in is protecting the family finances."

"Someone has to," he spat.

It was my turn to shake my head. With my hands fisted on my hips, I shot him a disgusted look. "You know, right before you got here she was crying in my arms about how calculated and coldhearted this entire thing is. She's not far off the mark with those words. It describes you, as well."

His eyes slitted, and his chin dropped. A swift sense of panic shot through me. I'd overstepped before with him, but this, this was much worse.

Slade moved toward me slowly, his gaze glued to mine. The strength of it hypnotized me in place.

His warm breath washed over my face as he bumped right up against me, his hands lifting to circle around my upper arms. Paralyzed now—there was no other way to explain why I was rooted to the floor, my body stone still—I stood, helpless as he glowered above me.

His voice lowered, all the previous anger and raw frustration gone. In its place was something smooth and silken, deep and filled with intent. "You didn't think I was coldhearted when I had my tongue wrapped around yours. Cold was the opposite of what you were feeling."

Before I could form a response, his lips claimed mine.

Claimed? Owned is more accurate.

His mouth covered mine, hungrily lapping, probing, sampling.

I tasted annoyance and irritation on his tongue when it tugged at my own. In a whisper of time, that impatience changed to adoration and want.

My hands developed a life of their own as they slid up his jacket and crossed behind his neck. With one of his hands slipping behind my head to hold me in place, the other wound around my waist and tugged me in closer.

He felt…wonderful.

Perfect, in fact.

All my negative thoughts and responses about his behavior disappeared from my mind as if waved away by a magic wand. In their place all I could do was feel.

How could he do this to me so easily? One moment I was furious with him, the next my female organs were spontaneously combusting in an explosion of need igniting from his touch.

I gasped when his own desire became apparent as it rolled and grew against me. My thighs trembled apart when he snaked his knee between them, rubbing erotically against the front of my dress. Arrows of exquisite pleasure shot straight up my spine. The hand at my waist glided down over my hip and lower still. Slade kneaded my butt, his long, powerful fingers pulling me closer with each movement and driving me near the brink.

He groaned when his lips left mine to skim across my cheek and jaw. I jumped when he nibbled my earlobe and then sucked hard on it.

"You feel amazing," he whispered, both his hands now settled on my butt.

"So do you," I echoed before I could think to keep the words unspoken. My hands glided across his wide, hard shoulders, then moved down the front of his jacket. I snaked them inside and circled around his waist. The flesh under his designer shirt was toned and solid. Slade Harrington's body was perfect and as hard as granite.

I could stand here all day and just…feel him.

The moment I had that thought, a tornado of reality whirled up in me.

"Slade, what are we doing?" My hands pushed against his chest to move away.

He tightened his hold on me. With his lips pressed against my neck, he murmured, "Giving in?"

"What?"

His exhalation was thick and loud. He lifted his head and looked me straight in the eyes. "I've been thinking about you all week. Even with all this uproar between Izzy and me, you've been what's uppermost in my mind. I haven't been able to concentrate at work, and I've taken more cold showers this week than the entire time I was at boarding school." His mouth dipped in a crooked smirk. "All because I can't stop thinking about you."

"M-me?"

"Don't look so surprised, Colleen. I told you how I felt the last time we were together. I'm extremely attracted to you, and I know you feel the same way about me. You couldn't kiss me like you do if you didn't."

Truer words. But… "You also told me you couldn't understand why you felt the way you did."

"Yeah. About that." He hung his head and actually looked embarrassed. "With a little distance and time, I've realized how tactless I sounded. It took me a day or two, but I finally understood why you were so angry."

"Not angry," I confessed. "Hurt, I think, more than anything."

"I could see why you would be. But believe me, it wasn't my intention to hurt your feelings, just like it's not my intent to cause Izzy all this emotional pain right now with the wedding so close."

He pulled me to him again and rested his forehead along mine.

All I could think was *wow*. Had I misjudged him that much, thinking him elitist and spoiled? Exactly like Harry, in fact? Was I wrong?

Well, maybe not on the elitist part, because he couldn't help that. He was born to it.

But the rest, yeah. Maybe I was mistaken to have thought of him as selfish and cold.

Harry, for instance, would never have cared one whit if his words upset someone else or caused someone emotional pain. I was the proof of that. He'd discarded me like a piece of scrap paper and hadn't cared one way or the other how I felt about the dissolution of our engagement. Harry loved Harry. No one else.

Slade loved his sister. Dearly. He was in actual visible pain because they were fighting.

His warm, firm lips skimmed across my brow, bussed my closed eyes, and stopped to nuzzle on my neck. "What are your plans for the rest of the day?" he whispered against my skin.

"Lunch, and then some more bridal stuff. We're meeting Jack's sister and his niece for a fitting. Why?"

His wet lips pressed against the bottom notch at my neck. He opened his mouth and sucked at the thin skin there. I'm not lying when I say my knees buckled. It was a darn good thing he had his hands glued to my butt because his grip was the only thing keeping me upright.

"I want to spend some time with you, alone. Away from…everything and everyone. Just you and me."

The possibilities of why he wanted to and what we'd do together leapfrogged thought my head.

Oh, my.

This was moving a little too fast for me but before I could tell him that, I heard my name float through the closed door. My heart stopped.

"Colleen? Where are you?"

"Isabella," I whispered. "I need to go." I tried to pull out of his embrace.

Slade squeezed my arms and shook his head.

"Colleen—"

"Your sister is waiting for me, Slade. Please, let me go."

Reluctance smeared across his face when he dropped his hands. "Can you meet me? Later on when you're done with everything? We could get a drink or dinner before you go home."

The very fact I wanted to so badly was enough to make me think twice about saying yes. Meeting Slade for anything right now when my mind was in such a jumble and my emotions were so strained might not be the best thing to do.

"I'll text you when I come free one way or the other, okay?"

He nodded. "And about Izzy—"

"I'm not saying anything about the prenup to her, so don't ask me to."

"I wasn't going to. I know where you stand on it. Don't even mention it to her. Just tell her I miss her. Tell her...tell her I love her, and I want her to be happy. Please, try and get her to talk to me. I don't care what you say, just try. Please?"

In the end, despite hating being a go-between, I acquiesced.

He pulled me closer again and held a hand against my cheek. I nuzzled it and then placed a swift kiss to his palm before he'd let me go.

With one hand on the door handle, I placed another against my quaking, shaking abdominal muscles.

And I wasn't even wearing the dreaded spandex today.

In the end, after a long afternoon first listening to Isabella's ire at her brother's request, and then dress fittings with Jillian and her five-year-old daughter Bailey who badly needed a nap, a doozy of a headache started and built until my eyes started to water. I needed to get home and get to bed. I didn't need to meet a man who pulled me in so many emotional directions at one time I couldn't think straight when I was with him.

Right before I hopped on the Metro North train which would take me to New Haven where I'd parked my car for the day, I texted him I was going home and couldn't meet him.

His replay had been instantaneous. He texted back he was disappointed but understood. The travel time alone wouldn't put me back in Heaven until after ten p.m., he wrote, and he realized I hadn't planned on staying in the city later. He ended the text asking if he could call me tomorrow.

Thinking he wanted to discuss Isabella and what—if anything—I'd said to her about their argument, I agreed, citing a time I knew I'd be free.

His final text was an emoji of two wine glasses and the words *next time.*

On the drive home, my head was pounding and my neck badly needed a hot shower jet massage. By the time I pulled off the highway, the throbbing was so hard and loud, I could actually hear my blood pumping.

I did a quick check on Nanny, who was sound asleep in her bed, then got myself ready for the same. Right before I succumbed to total exhaustion my phone chirped with an incoming message.

Hope you got home safe and sound, Slade wrote.

Aww. He was worried about me.

Snuggling under the covers right now, I typed back.

The three little dots waving across the screen indicated he was typing something back, so I waited.

A GIF popped up of Grouch Marx wiggling his

eyebrows lasciviously up and down.

Slade Harrington flirting. What a rush.

Get some rest, he added.

You, too.

Was it any wonder my dreams were filled with whiskey-colored eyes and strong arms holding me…and doing all sorts of other, equally satisfying things?

Chapter Fifteen

"Everything looks perfect, Colleen," Jillian said, as she glanced around the room. "It's like something right out of a romance movie."

I was delighted because that had been my hope.

Alice's, the popular and exclusive upper West Side tearoom (yes, *that* Alice), had closed for the afternoon to accommodate Isabella's shower. The staff had done a terrific job of transforming the quirky establishment into an old-fashioned movie set. Isabella and Jack shared a love of classic black and white movies from the 1930s and 40s. Romantic comedies where the dialogue was quick, witty, and snappy, and always ended with the leads riding off into the sunset together, and the tragic dramas where the heroine and hero professed their undying love right before one of them did, actually, die. On screen that is.

I'd found vintage movie posters online of comedic classics like *His Girl Friday, The Thin Man* series, and *Philadelphia Story*, and dramas like *Dark Victory* and *Jezebel,* not to mention a dozen others, which I'd had framed. They were scattered on easels and displayed on some of the walls around the restaurant. I'd filled plastic popcorn containers with favors and gifts, all movie and wedding themed.

Tablecloths and linens adorned the tables in alternating patterns of black and white. A fabulous party store I found online carried streamers resembling individual filmstrips and everything old movie-worthy you could imagine. Paper invitations made to look like clapper chalkboards used in filming movie scenes had been sent out, tiny replicas now used as table seating markers with each guest's name written in white chalk.

Alice's was famous for its individually decorated cookies and cupcakes. I'd ordered an array of shortbreads and black and white sugar cookies, finely detailed in piped frosting with *I do, Mr. & Mrs.-to-be, Bride-to-be,* and many more little phrases, all bridal themed. Cake pops bedecked as tuxedos and wedding gown torsos, chocolate cupcakes with Jack and Isabella's engagement picture embossed in edible photo-frosting on top of them were displayed regally on trays around the serving station.

Lunch was going to be light fare, to leave more room for all the delicious desserts and sweets.

All in all, the room was exactly as I'd imagined and promised it would be to Isabella. Sometimes, I surprise myself with how quickly things can get done if you have a plan and stick to it. I've said many times throughout my career that planning a successful wedding is like putting together a military operation where every component has to run on a strict and unbending time schedule. I wasn't wrong when this came to planning wedding showers, either. I'd been able to put everything for Isabella's together in less than two weeks, courtesy of my exceptional team and Slade's open checkbook.

Slade.

I sighed just saying his name in my head. I hadn't seen him since Isabella's dress fitting, but we'd spoken almost every evening. He was in Europe for a few days on business, but even with the time difference, he'd made an effort to keep in touch. Each conversation left me feeling I knew him better and wanting to know him even more. It was a strange feeling being seduced via cell phone and text messages.

The one angsty spot in our budding relationship was Katya Yurlenko. A picture of her and Slade attending a fancy celebrity dinner had popped up on a celebrity gossip site I routinely scrolled through, taken when the two of them were in London, which coincided with the week he was gone. Her emaciated arm was wrapped around his waist, one of his draped across her shoulders. There wasn't a gasp of space between their bodies as they smiled for the paparazzi.

To the casual observer they looked more like a couple than the simple friends Slade had assured me they were. I was trying to keep an open mind about this and believe him, but shades of Harry kept drifting around my head.

Before Slade had left, he and Isabella had met for lunch where they'd hashed everything out. They were on speaking terms again, something Slade was thrilled about. It warmed my heart how much he loved his baby sister and how far he was willing to go to ensure her happiness. We hadn't discussed the prenup once in our conversations, and I hadn't asked if he'd broached it with his sister.

Whatever decision they'd come to, it didn't involve me. As long as the two of them were reconciled, I was happy because a happy bride made for a great wedding. A stressed, emotional one did not.

And I wanted Isabella to have a great wedding.

The guests began to arrive a few minutes later.

Jillian and I decided she should be the hostess and greet everyone so I could be available as the party gofer, put out any annoyance fires that developed, and generally make sure the event stayed on point. Because of Isabella's schedule and my work one, we'd decided to have the shower on a Thursday afternoon. An unconventional day, I know, but luckily it had worked well for all those who were invited. Except for Katya, who RSVP'd she'd be in Florida at a magazine shoot, everyone else invited was attending. Isabella wanted a simple ladies' lunch, not a couple's shower, so that's what I'd planned, and I'd arranged it so she would be the last one to arrive.

Jack's mother and his sister Jillian, her young daughter, and other family members plus a few of Isabella's female relatives were all present, chatting, and several had glasses of the signature drink Devon had concocted for their wedding toast. Isabella's autumn wedding in New England called for something original, and Devon had devised the perfect taste to meet the season: a sweet apple cider mimosa. I'd sampled it while setting up the room and it was delicious with just the right mix of sweet and tart, like the perfect fall apple should be. It also packed an unexpected punch from the amount of champagne in each drink.

There was one glaring absence from this party so far. Janelle Thorne, Isabella's mother, hadn't arrived yet. I'd hoped to meet the elusive mother of the bride before her daughter made her entrance, but when Isabella walked into the tearoom wearing a strained smile she was trying valiantly to hide, I knew that wasn't going to happen.

The bride-to-be was engulfed in hugs, kisses, and well wishes, and then led to her chair of honor at the head of the room. She caught my eye as she was escorted by her niece-to-be, threw me a kiss, and mouthed a "Thank you."

Bridal showers can go one of several ways, depending on the age group of the attendees, the amount of alcohol served, and even who is throwing the shower. Younger bridesmaids tend to approach a shower as a let's-get-drunk-and-give-her-sexy-lingerie-and-talk-about-sex event. Family-sponsored showers tend to be a tad more sedate, with the bride literally being showered with presents and good wishes. Friends envision the shower more like a get-together with gifts.

The most important goal in every bridal shower though, no matter who plans or attends it, is making the bride-to-be feel happy, special, and blessed. Looking at Isabella sitting in her bridal chair right now, the happiness factor was missing. It didn't take a rocket scientist to figure out it had something to do with her absent mother.

Just as I gave the okay to the wait staff to serve lunch, Jillian pulled me aside.

"Where's her mother?" she asked. "Didn't she RSVP she was coming?"

I nodded. "I have no idea where she is, but from the look on Isabella's face, something happened between the two of them. An argument, or something."

Jill's lips pursed in annoyance. "I know. The poor thing looks about ready to bawl her eyes out. The only reason she's not is because there's a room full of people around her and she's trying to keep face. Damn her mother."

I had to agree.

"You know, she never even reached out to my parents when Jack and Izzy got engaged? My mom called her, several times, to try and set up a meet and greet, but Janelle always had some function or other she and her husband had to attend so they couldn't. Mom finally gave up at about try number five."

"Jack has met her, though, hasn't he?"

"Yeah. He wasn't too mouthy with the details, but I don't think it went well."

I sighed. "Maybe it's a good thing she's not here, then."

The moment the words left my lips the door to the tearoom opened and the woman in question walked in. Even if I hadn't seen a picture of her during my Slade-stalking Google searches, I would have known she was related to Isabella in an instant. Their skin tone, the shape of their faces, even their eye color were identical.

"Speak of," I said, leaving out the words that should have ended the phrase.

Isabella's mother was the very definition of chic. Truly. Open the dictionary and her picture would be next to the word.

I approached Janelle Thorne with a smile and an outstretched hand and introduced myself.

She neither smiled back, nor shook my hand.

"Yes, I believe I've heard Isabella mention your name. You're the one responsible for this?" She flicked her perfectly manicured hand in the direction of the tearoom.

"Yes."

She ran her gaze from my face down to my shoes

in a thorough rake. I said a silent thank you to the gods of fashion for helping me choose one of the best suits in my closet for the day. Everything I was garbed in had a designer label. Janelle didn't need to know I'd found the suit in an upscale thrift store and bought the shoes on eBay for ten cents on the dollar of their original retail price.

"If I'd been consulted, I would have chosen a different venue," Janelle told me. "Some place less plebian."

Okay, what? I should have told her she hadn't been consulted because she'd shown zero interest in anything wedding related. She should have been the one to throw the shower or at least have a hand in planning it. Instead, I kept my tongue. This was Isabella's day, and I wasn't going to ruin it by having an argument with her mother in public.

"Mother." The bride-to-be wove through the tables, a wide-eyed look of surprise on her face. "You said you weren't coming."

"After giving it some consideration, I felt I should be here. Especially since family members were invited. I haven't seen some of them in quite some time and didn't want any discussion about why I was absent."

Isabella looked down her perfect pert nose and cocked her head. With a nod, she said, "Of course. Appearances are everything."

"Mind your tone, young lady. I'm your mother."

It took everything inside me not to spurt out, "Then start acting like it," but, again, I kept the thought silent.

Jack's mother, Vivienne Rainier, came up to us then, a wide, welcoming smile on her face. Vivienne "Call me Vivi" was Janelle's opposite in every way.

Where the mother of the bride was tall and looked as if she hadn't eaten in quite some time, the groom's mom was under five foot three and what Nanny Fee would describe as shaped like a ready-to-be-picked Macintosh apple. Janelle obviously spent a great deal of time with her hair colorist and stylist, her shoulder-length bob split-end-free and a perfect honey-blonde hue. Vivi's wiry short hair was threaded with alternating strands of salt and pepper. Even their expressions were at opposing ends of the spectrum. Vivi's smile was wide and open, free and welcoming, to Janelle's more sedate, bland lifting of the corners of her mouth.

"Well, you must be this lovely girl's mom," Vivi exclaimed. "I can see where she gets her beauty. I'm Jack's mother, Vivienne."

"Call her Vivi," Isabella said as she watched her mother and soon-to-be mother-in-law. Janelle lifted her hand to shake the other woman's. The way she held her fingers up, limp like a wet noodle, it looked as if she expected it to be kissed. Vivi glanced down at it, then, with a good-natured swat at the hand, pulled a stunned and open-mouthed Janelle into her arms.

"None of this stiff handshake stuff," Vivi said, patting Janelle's back. "We're gonna be family."

Isabella covered her mouth and looked away, her shoulders shaking. After a moment, she'd composed herself enough to look back at the two women with her features relaxed again.

Janelle took several steps backward once Vivi released her hold. Her suit jacket had ridden up past her minuscule waistline when she'd been held, so she grabbed the hem of it and, with a violent tug, pulled down, righting it once again.

"Come on." Vivi twined her arm into Janelle's. "We've got a seat all saved for you at the head table."

With effortless care Janelle unwove herself from Vivi's grasp. "In a moment. I need to discuss something with my daughter first."

When Vivi made no motion to move, Janelle's jaw tightened. "In private."

The Harrington/Thorne households must have dentists on call, I thought. All that jaw clenching and gnashing could pose quite a dental issue.

Once Vivi went back to her seat, Isabella turned to her mother.

"Well? What do you need to talk to me about that's so important you had to be blatantly rude to my future mother-in-law?"

"I was nothing of the sort, Isabella, and I'll remind you to watch your tone of voice when addressing me."

With an eye roll I'd seen many times on my assistant Charity's face, Isabella adopted a casual stance and said, "Yes, Mother? What would you like to discuss?"

Janelle grasped her daughter's arm and moved her behind the room divider separating the main room from a side one. Even though I wasn't asked to, I followed them.

"I just got off the phone with Button Valentine who said she heard from her husband that your *father* is attending the wedding. Is this true? Have you invited him?"

Okay, first, *Button*? Seriously? I'm assuming this was a grown-ass woman along the lines of Janelle's age. To know someone in that decade was called by such a ridiculous moniker almost made me regret ever being annoyed at Nanny for using my hated nickname.

Almost.

Isabella squared her shoulders and stared her mother down.

"Yes, I did. And he's coming."

"Have you completely lost your mind?" Janelle spat.

"No, Mother, I haven't. Daddy wants to be there on my wedding day, and I want him to. It's my decision who I invite. You haven't wanted to be included in any of the planning or decisions, so I get to say who I want and who I don't."

"Is he giving you away? Because he doesn't deserve to."

"No. Slade is still walking me down the aisle."

"Well, thank goodness for that small grace. Although I feel Fred would be the more appropriate choice. He's been more of a father to you than that man ever was."

"That man is my father, Mother. And despite whatever happened between the two of you, he still is and always will be."

"Is he bringing that woman with him?"

Isabella rolled her eyes again. "They're married, mother. Have been for over a year, and yes, Shirley is invited, too."

"This just gets worse by the minute." Janelle flapped her hands like an angry bird. "Now I not only have to endure the man who cheated on me with his secretary and broke my heart, but his newest chippy, as well. This is more than can be tolerated."

Janelle's face reddened under her foundation. For a moment, I feared she was going to explode, literally and figuratively, and that was the last thing I wanted for Isabella.

"Maybe you two should table this discussion until after the shower," I said. "The guests are all here and waiting to enjoy the afternoon with Isabella. I'm sure this conversation would be more appropriate in private."

Janelle turned and regarded me as if I was a piece of garbage stuck to the underside of her stilettos. In a voice filled with enough ice to chill all of lower Manhattan, she said, "This is none of your concern, young lady, so shut your mouth."

Her words had the sting of a slap.

"*Mother*."

Janelle ignored her daughter, focusing her fury—misplaced though it was—onto me. "If it had been up to me, I would never have allowed Isabella to retain you and plan this ridiculous, inconvenient wedding."

"It wouldn't have mattered who my planner was, Mother, because you're against the wedding anyway. No one I hired would have been good enough for you because Jack isn't good enough for you." Isabella's voice started to rise as she nervously twisted her hands in front of her.

"He's not good enough for *you*, Isabella. You're a Harrington and a Morgan. You're marrying someone with no name, no history, no connections."

"Do you hear yourself?" Isabella shook her head and fisted her hands on her hips. "Jack is a wonderful man, more than good enough for me, despite what you consider his failings. He loves me, and I love him." She burst into tears while her mother merely looked on.

What kind of a mother doesn't comfort their child

when they're crying?

Janelle didn't move, so I did. I gathered Isabella into my arms and tossed her mother a pleading look. "Mrs. Thorne, please. You're upsetting her."

"She's just being dramatic." She swiped a hand in the air with a dismissive flick of her wrist.

I bit my tongue to keep from calling her a bitch— again—and said, "I think it might be best if you leave."

If her words had felt like a slap, the glare she gave me now was strong enough to stab my flesh. "How dare you? This"—she pointed to her daughter—"is all your doing. Don't think I don't know that."

"I'm not the one upsetting Isabella. You are."

Her rose-colored lips pulled up into a very unbecoming sneer.

"What's going on here?"

Slade.

He was standing behind Janelle, a bouquet of roses in his hand. I don't think I'd ever been so happy to see someone in my life.

With an assessing sweep, his gaze traveled from his former stepmother, to me, and settled on a crying Isabella. "Izzy?"

She pulled herself from my arms and flung her body into his.

"Mother's being horrible," she wailed against his jacket, the sound, thankfully muffled from anyone but the three of us. We'd been missing from the main room for several minutes, and although the noise level was where I expected it to be with a gaggle of women at a bridal shower, I felt our absence wasn't going unnoticed.

"Janelle?"

Boy, what I wouldn't give to be able to sound like that. If her words had been a slap to me, just her name on his lips was hard enough to bruise.

"What did you say to make Isabella cry?"

"Nothing I haven't said before." She yanked down on the hem of her suit jacket again with a determined tug. She lifted her chin and, although Slade was a good six inches taller than she, stared down her sculpted nose at him. "This entire wedding is ridiculous. Out of state, no one of substance invited, not even held in a church. And now I hear your father is attending. This is too much for me. I have half a mind to leave town until the whole event is over."

Isabella sniffed. Loudly. In a parallel universe, where my actions wouldn't get me in trouble—or arrested—I would have clouted Janelle Thorne across her perfectly coiffed head.

"You'd boycott your only daughter's wedding?" Slade's voice was deathly soft.

Janelle lifted her chin higher, her lips pressed together in a flat line.

"You might want to think twice about that. Your actions will have far-reaching consequences."

"What do you mean?"

With one hand still around his sister and clutching the flowers he'd brought, Slade reached into his pants pocket, pulled out a handkerchief, and handed it to her. While Isabella dabbed at the corners of her eyes, Slade snuck a quick glance at me, then moved back to his sister's mother. "The tidy little financial package my father gave you in lieu of alimony all those years ago is managed by me, you know."

"So?"

"So, I've been reviewing many of the portfolios the company manages for some time now. Yours could do with a bit of…restructuring."

I was watching Janelle's face to see if she understood what he was saying, because I certainly didn't. With each word, I noticed the pulse at her temple drubbed a little harder.

"You wouldn't dare," she whispered, her voice trembling. With rage, I wondered, or fear? With Slade's next statement, I was pretty certain it was the latter.

"If you do anything to hurt Isabella, cause her any more strain or stress, or say anything to ruin her wedding, I will. That settlement won't be worth the price of the paper it's printed on."

"I don't believe you."

I did. Nothing I'd ever seen before looked as deadly as Slade Harrington's eyes at that moment.

"Try me."

The fear in her voice spread to her face and body. Her shoulders were pulled so tight under her jacket it was a miracle the material didn't snap at the seams. She'd fisted her hands at her sides and was blinking as if she had something in her eyes. Tiny beads of sweat spread across her upper lip.

I should have felt sorry for her but couldn't summon up even so much as a smidge of concern.

The air in the room was thick with tension, the only noise Isabella's tiny sniffles.

Slade rubbed a hand down his sister's arm and, addressing Janelle, told her, "If I were you, I'd plant a smile on my face and go take a seat. Start acting like a mother whose only daughter is marrying the man she loves in a few weeks."

"You're just like your father," she spat. "Cold, cruel, and callous."

"Don't forget manipulative and spiteful," he tossed back.

Without another word, she turned on her well-heeled foot and did as he'd suggested. Commanded, if truth be told.

"Are you okay?" He pulled his sister in front of him.

She gave him a tiny smile, accompanied by a final swipe of tissue under her eyes. "I am now." With the exuberance of a child given a new toy, she threw her arms around his neck and hugged him. Turning her face toward me, she said, "I told you big brothers are the best."

"Yes, you have. Multiple times." She laughed along with me. "I totally agree with you."

"Here, these are for you." He handed her the bouquet. "Now, go fix your face and get back to your party. I saw a boatload of pretty packages and boxes on a table when I came in and I know how much you love presents, especially when they're for you."

She grinned, sniffed, and then kissed his cheek.

"I'll be right out to check on things," I told her when she sent me a questioning look.

"Thank you," I told Slade when we were alone. "You saved your stepmother from a fat lip and me from potential incarceration."

He moved slowly toward me, the beginnings of a smile tipping at the corners of his lips. "I told you once before, she's not my stepmother. Not anymore."

When he was within a whisper of a breath from me, he stopped. Again, I said a silent thanks to the shoe gods. In my heels, I could look him in the eyes without tilting my head back. His gaze held a hint of humor as he stared at me. All I could think about was moving in and pressing my mouth against his. It was a testament to my professional self-control that I stayed rooted to my spot.

We must have looked a little goofy standing there staring at one another, silly besotted smiles on our faces. At least his smile was besotted. Mine could have looked like I had gas for all know.

After a few moments of this mutual admiration gaze-fest, Slade took one of my hands in his. The warmth spreading up my arm was a reminder of the first time we'd met.

"I'm surprised to see you," I said. "Happy you got here before any bloodshed, but surprised as well. When did you get back?"

He lifted his hand—the one he held mine in—and took a quick glance at his watch. "I cleared customs about fifty-five minutes ago. Then I broke a few land speed records to get here. I wanted to see Isabella before the party started."

Aww. That was just sweet. My heart sighed. "You got here right on time, believe me. And I know she's happy you're here."

He squeezed my hand. "I wanted to see you, too. I've missed you, Colleen."

My mouth went desert dry, and my heart sped to gallop mode. No one, aside from my family, had ever missed me before. The knowledge this gorgeous, powerful, and fascinating man had, was thrilling.

"Can you stay in the city after the party and have dinner with me?" he asked. "Please? You and Izzy don't have plans, do you?"

"No. I was going to help her cart everything back to her condo when we're through here, though."

"I'll help," he said, quickly. "That way we can get it done faster, and you and I can go somewhere to eat and…"

"Talk?"

A cheek-to-cheek, heart-stopping smile bloomed fast and knocked me back a few paces.

"Tell me you don't have any other plans. Please."

"I don't. When the shower is over, I was gonna head home. I've got two weddings this weekend."

"I won't keep you out late, I promise."

What would he have said—or done—if I'd admitted I wanted him to? That I wanted nothing more than for him to sweep me off my feet and fulfill all the promises his kisses had hinted at?

I nodded and, with another squeeze to my hand, this time he lifted it up to his lips and bussed my knuckles. My entire body relaxed, my eyelids growing heavy. Warmth steeped through me from head to three-inch heels. You know in those old Warner Brothers cartoons when a character gets a loopy, sappy smile on their face, their eyes morph into Valentine hearts, and little bows and arrows shoot above their head to indicate they've been hit by Cupid's arrow? I can imagine my face looked exactly the same the moment Slade's lips grazed across my skin.

"So," he said, "you'll stay and have dinner with me?"

I wanted to say *I'll stay and do anything you want me to do* but knew it didn't sound right. So I simply nodded. "Now, I've got to go help Isabella. Make sure everything is going as planned. With thirty women and free access to alcohol, someone needs to be on the lookout."

"I'm sticking around," he told me.

"Are you sure? There aren't any men in there"—I cocked me head toward the main room—"except for the waiters. Just a room full of women with love and marriage on their minds and booze in their champagne flutes. You might want to reconsider."

"None of that scares me. Besides, I think Janelle will behave better if she sees me keeping an eye on her."

"No arguments there."

And there weren't because it was true.

Chapter Sixteen

"So, how was Europe? Did you get to do any touristy stuff?"

Slade leaned back in his chair and blew out a breath. "I wish. I had meetings all day every day, and then I had to attend a few dinners in the evenings."

I didn't mention I knew of at least one dinner where Katya Yurlenko had been a guest, waiting to see if he would.

He didn't, and I didn't know whether to be concerned or not because of it.

After Isabella had been showered—literally—with presents and the afternoon drew to a close, Slade did as he'd promised and helped us lug all her loot back to her uptown condo. I'd never loaded a limousine with boxes of fine china and lingerie before, but I have to admit it made transport a whole lot easier and a whole lot more comfortable than Uber-ing would have. Isabella and I rode back to her place in her chauffeur-driven car, with Slade following.

The party had been a whopping success despite Janelle's initial behavior. Slade was proven correct when he'd stated staying would keep the woman in check, because it had. Her smile may have been forced and she hadn't said more than two words to any of Jack's family, but there were no further caustic remarks or little digs about the groom-to-be's lineage and lack of political potential.

Vivi, Jillian, and Jack's aunts and cousins lavished praise and sincere good wishes on the bride-to-be. I was so happy Isabella was marrying into a family who showed warmth and outward love and affection to one another. With such a hardhearted and critical role model as Janelle, it was a wonder Isabella had grown into the lovely woman she had. Of course with a brother who adored her, his influence and love must have been huge factors in keeping her from going to the dark side and turning out like her shrew of a mother.

"Have you ever been?" Slade asked, pulling me out of my thoughts.

"To Europe?" I shook my head. "Bucket list item for sure, but right now I'm too busy."

He looked across the table at me, a serious look of concentration on his face. We'd driven in his limo—and boy, could I get used to that form of transportation—to midtown after dropping Isabella and her load off, to a trendy restaurant I'd never been to before. Subtle lighting and quiet jazz filled the space, all the tables two-fers filled with couples. As far as romantic hideaways went, this place had it nailed.

The words *romantic* and *Slade* in the same thought sent all kinds of fluttering sensations through me.

"Do you ever get a break from it all?" Slade asked. "Take a few days or so of downtime?"

I shook my head. "Not since I started the business. When I worked for the magazine, I took my required three weeks every year because if I didn't, I'd lose it. No cash reimbursement, no time rollovers. I got paid to take the vacation, so I did. Now, if I take a weekend off, it equates to lost revenue because most weddings, as you know, take place on the weekends. The majority of my weekdays are filled with new client meetings, planning sessions, and everything else that goes into getting the day perfect."

"Perfection can be overrated," he said. Why did that sound so familiar? "Did you always want this for your career?"

"Initially, no. I wanted to rise to editorial management at the magazine. That dream went out the window when my personal life went up in flames. But because I knew so many people in the industry and I'd been planning weddings on paper for several years, I thought it would be a strategic career move. And it was."

He took a sip of his wine. "It's admirable, you know, how you've built such a success so quickly. All your hard work and missed vacations have paid off."

"Admirable, or necessary?" I shrugged. "I love what I do. My grandmother has this saying—one of thousands—that if you can turn what you love into what you do for a living, you'll be happy for the rest of your life. I think it's true, don't you?"

He was quiet for a moment, thoughtful. "I do," he said after at time. "You're lucky in that regard. You get to do what gives you pleasure every day."

"Don't you?"

This time I was able to read his expression perfectly. With his chin slightly tilted down, he caught a corner of his mouth between his teeth. The subtle shift in his mood told me all I needed to know. His answer confirmed my supposition.

"Not really, no. I fully intended to practice law. Growing up it was all I wanted to do. I only decided to get my master's in business because I knew it would be useful combined with a career in corporate law." He chewed on a scallop, and I stayed silent. His eyes seemed, I don't know. Haunted? Woeful?

"What changed?"

"The day after I graduated, my father left stepmother number two."

"The one who had a penchant for real estate?"

"You have a good memory. I'm surprised you recall that, since we were arguing at the time I told it to you."

"You were arguing," I teased. "I was trying to make a point."

"Oh, of course." He grinned back at me, the light coming back into his eyes. "When he turned over so much of his land holdings because he was in a hurry to divorce her—"

"Wait. Let me guess. Stepmother number three was in the wings already?"

"A good listener and perceptive." He tipped his wine glass to me. "It was then members of the board approached me to take on more corporate responsibility. I was already working toward my doctorate so I said no."

"But then wife number four wanted out?"

"No, my father did. After less than a year, and this one wanted a seat on the board of directors as a payout. He was going to give it to her, too, so that's when I stepped in and managed to strong-arm the company away from him."

"That must have been fun," I said. "*Not.*"

"It wasn't. My father relinquished control after a vote of no-confidence from the board. He, well, retired is the best word. It helped him save face to be the one to leave instead of being forced out. And of course he blames me for pushing him to it. He can't see it was his own ill-advised behavior that forced him out."

Which went a long way in explaining Slade's reluctance about his father's presence at the wedding.

"When was the last time you two spoke?"

"I saw him, briefly, at Izzy's college graduation. He came up for the day, saw her graduate, and then he went back to Charleston, where he lives now with wife number six, who, by the way, is the best of the exes. She's wealthy in her own right and wants none of my father's fortune."

"Sixth time's a charm?" I said. It sounded lame when it left my mouth.

"I'd like to think the first time with my mother was. But we'll never know."

"I'm sorry. That was a terrible attempt to lighten the mood."

His smile was warm and easy. "You do that just by being here with me."

Le sigh.

"Anyway. Back to my father. We didn't speak at Izzy's college commencement and hadn't at her high school graduation either."

"So when's the last time you had a conversation with him? A real one?"

"Ten years ago. The day he walked out of his office after the vote."

"*Holy moly.* That's a long time not to talk to a parent. Or any family member. I think the longest I've ever gone without talking to my parents was the two weeks after we buried my sister and they decided to move away from Heaven. And I speak with my sisters every day."

His casual shrug spoke volumes. What I couldn't decide was who was the more stubborn: him or his father.

"If you hadn't had to step in, where do you think you'd be today? Career-wise, I mean."

"I like to think I'd be practicing law. Corporate, or otherwise. Maybe even teaching the economics end of it at a law school. Put my doctorate to good use."

I could see him now, standing at a podium, lecturing. Every female in the class would be hanging on his every word, memorizing the way his lips moved when he discussed the concepts of procurement, third party payouts, torts, and tax liens. Fantasizing about the hot professor and the legal—and illegal—acts they could perform together under the guise of studying.

"I don't think he'll do anything to spoil the weekend. He loves Izzy."

"Are you okay with him coming to the wedding?" I asked.

"I have to be for my sister's sake. She wants him there, and it's her big day, her decision. I won't do to her what Janelle did today. And I'll do everything in my power to make sure there are no scenes between him and Janelle. He'll probably ignore me anyway."

I felt a little tug on my heartstrings with that statement. Slade was almost forty years old, a grown-ass man by anyone's definition. Yet his father's opinion still affected him.

"Speaking of the wedding." I ate another scallop, then brought him up to speed on the plans. "Jack and Isabella are coming up this weekend to meet with

Cathleen and do their marriage questionnaire."

"Their what?"

"Thirty questions she asks all the couples she's officiating for before she writes their vows. It's a pretty thorough document they each fill out separately and then give to her. She doesn't let them know what the other has written, but she incorporates their answers into the ceremony. The first time they hear it is during the wedding."

"This is the lawyer sister, right? The one who usually handles your grandmother's…situations?"

I winced. "That's a very polite way of saying what they really are, so thank you for that. But yeah. Cathy's a family lawyer and a JP. One of these days, she'll probably be the town judge like our father was before he and Mom decamped."

"I wish I could come up this weekend, too." He huffed a breath. "But I've got plans straight through until next Tuesday."

It took everything in me not to ask if any of those plans included a certain supermodel.

"I wish we lived closer to one another."

Okay, *what*? My face must have telegraphed the question swirling in my mind.

Slade reached across the table and took my free hand. With a grin as charming as it was wistful, he said, "Phone calls, texts, and on-the-fly dinners aren't the ideal way to date. I wish we were geographically closer, so we could spend more free time together."

I was so glad I'd swallowed before he started speaking because I was certain I'd have choked on my couscous. "Is that what we're doing?" I asked. "Dating?"

Good Lord, the frog brigade was back.

Slade cocked his head. His thumb was tracing little circles across my knuckles and every slide and glide of his finger shot an electrical spark straight down my spine. "What would you call what we've been doing these past few weeks? Or trying to, anyway?"

"I don't know, exactly. Getting to know one another on a personal level? Becoming…friends?"

His shoulders tightened up a little, and his smile lost a bit of its luster. "Is that what you think I want, Colleen? For us to be friends?"

For the first time in my life, I was speechless. No verbal diarrhea plaguing me, forcing me to spurt out words I'd regret the minute they were free.

I knew what I wanted but had no clue about him. To buy myself some time I took a sip of water. Okay, it was really a gulp, but I needed a few seconds to gather my thoughts. In the end, honesty was the easiest way to handle the question. A sudden bout of nerves rushed through me though, and I lowered my gaze to our joined hands. "I really don't know what you want," I admitted.

He tugged on the hand he still held, brought it to his lips, and kissed it as he had before. My little romantic girl's heart got all fluttery, and my entire body sighed.

"The answer to that question is very easy," he said, his voice soft and thick.

I swallowed. Then did it again.

"You," he whispered. "I want you."

Saint Brigid preserve me.

"I can't stop thinking about you," he said, shaking his head, a bemused grin on his face now. "From the first day when you sliced through me about my"—he made air quotes with his free hand—" 'daddy issues,' to the afternoon at your grandmother's cabin. In the rain…"

When he'd first kissed me.

"The entire time I was in Europe, I kept wishing you were with me. I wanted to show you how beautiful the London skyline is at night. I wanted to take you to the top of the Eiffel Tower. I missed you." The knuckle rubbing was driving me to distraction. I started to squirm from the movement and his words. "I came straight from the airport because I knew you'd be at the shower."

"I thought it was to see your sister."

"Knowing you were there was the added benefit."

"So would that make us…friends with benefits?"

Holy. Holy. Had I just said that?

A laugh swelled up from him and burst out loud and quick, like the blast of a cannon. The sound of it, so rich and free, shot right through my core and left me quaking.

He quieted his grin and squeezed my hand. Those amber eyes lit squarely on my face, a question crossing through them. "Tell me I'm not the only one feeling like this. You do too, don't you?"

Oh, baby, did I.

Knowing my feelings for him were growing with each moment we were together was the absolute truth. I couldn't and wouldn't deny it. "I do."

"Why don't you sound happy about it?"

I sighed, the air shoving from me in one long push. "The truth?"

"You told me once before you always tell the

truth."

I gathered my thoughts together in what I hoped was a coherent line. "You and I come from two different worlds. Different backgrounds, hell, even—as you said—different geographic locations."

"True. So?"

"I wonder if we give in to these…feelings…where this is gonna go. If it can truly build into something when we're so far apart all the time. For instance, you said you're tied up with business functions, dinners, and such every night until Tuesday. That includes the weekend, right?"

"Yes."

"I'm booked solid this weekend, and every weekend, most both days, so if there was an event you wanted me to attend with you, I couldn't. See what I'm saying?"

"I would think those details could be worked out, Colleen."

I'd like to think so as well, but I wasn't sure.

"Is that all? The fact that we live so far apart from one another?" He let go of my hand and leaned back in the chair. The waiter appeared at his side with the wine bottle, but Slade waved him off.

My shoulders slumped, and I immediately heard Nanny's voice in my head ordering me to sit up straight or I'd wind up with a hump when I hit fifty.

The things that run through my head when I'm nervous are wacky.

"Have you ever had a long-distance relationship?" I asked him.

"No."

"Neither have I. I don't know what's expected.

What's needed. I don't know how it works."

"The first step, I imagine, would be admitting you want it to and are willing to try."

He leaned forward and placed his elbows on the table, hands at the sides of his now-empty plate. "Are you?"

Was I? Was I willing to take a chance on a man so far out of my league in every way it was almost comical? And what if I did give in to these emotions galloping through me? What then? We'd actually be friends with benefits like I'd joked? Engage in a mutually satisfying affair until eventually one of us wanted more (me) or less (him)? Was I willing to give my heart to another man who would give it back to me in tatters when he was done with it?

Dramatic much, Colleen?

One thing I did know was there would be no long-term future in a relationship with Slade. He'd categorically said he was never getting married. I believed him. When people make such absolute statements and can back up their reasons for doing so, I tend to think they're being truthful. His father's disastrous marital history had scarred Slade, no doubt about it. So if I started something with him, I was going in fully aware there was an end point. An end point that wouldn't culminate in my dreamt-of happily ever after.

The problem was I wanted a life partner and a family of my own. At thirty-five, my ovaries were winding down the egg production line. I wanted kids before the machinery was retired, and I'd like to have them the old-fashioned way and not grow them in a petri dish. Not that there's anything wrong with that. I'd just envisioned a different kind of reproductive plan for myself.

"Colleen?"

The tiny flame flickering from the table tea light flittered across his handsome face, highlighting the shadows and planes of his carved cheeks and granite jaw. Forget he was as handsome as Adonis and as rich as a Silicon Valley titan. Forget he was a client. Forget everything but how wonderful it felt to be in his company, have his attention focused totally on me, and bask in the knowledge this man felt drawn to me.

Me.

How could I resist what he was asking?

My grandmother's voice shouted in my ear, her Irish thick and incredulous, *Why, in the name of all that's good and holy, Number Two, would ya?*

A valid question.

A quote I'd seen on a Pinterest board blew into my head: *Take a chance because you never know how perfect something might turn out to be.*

I stretched out my hands and placed them on top of his. With a smile I saw reflected back at me, I told him, "I'm willing to try if you are."

****

"Grand Central Station, Killian."

The chauffeur nodded and closed the door.

The privacy divider between the front and back seats had been raised while we were in the restaurant. Slade caught my glance and grinned.

"You must pay him well," I said.

With a chuckle that warmed my insides like a cup of hot chocolate on a chilly New England morning, Slade slipped an arm around my shoulders and pulled me close. With a kiss to my temple, he said, "Killian's nothing if not discreet. He knew I wanted some alone time before we said goodbye."

My reply died before it was ever given freedom. Slade shifted so he faced me. One hand snaked around my neck, the pad of his thumb caressing my jaw with a feather-wisp graze. His other hand slid to my back, then lower, drawing our bodies together.

"Do you know how much torture it's been to be around you today and not be able to do this?" The warmth of his breath as it fanned over my face was nothing compared to the cauldron in his eyes.

"Do what?" I asked, knowing perfectly well what he meant.

He knew I did, too. As he inched our bodies closer, our mouths a sigh apart, his lids dropped, drowsy with passion.

His mouth claimed mine as an answer.

From his words about the torment he'd been going through all afternoon, I expected the kiss to be urgent and demanding, racked with pent-up frustration and need. It wouldn't have surprised me one bit if he'd plundered my mouth and stolen my very breath.

I was about as wrong as a girl could be.

His kiss was slow, thoughtful, cherishing. *Persuasive*.

I fell into it, into him, all the strength in me dissolving like morning mist when the heat from the sun warms through it. My muscles yielded, my bones turned fluid, as his mouth brushed back and forth across my lips, nipped and licked at the corners.

Feasted.

From deep, deep down in my soul, a moan of sheer, absolute want floated up. When my lips parted, it burst through the air around us. Like any titan worth his mettle, Slade recognized his advantage and took it.

And I let him. Gladly.

Thankfully.

With a will of their own, my hands slid past his temples to the back of his neck and held on tight for the wild ride of emotions cycloning through me.

You know when you *know* something is right? When you realize a decision you've made is the correct one, no doubt about it?

Well, right then, with Slade Harrington's mouth pressed against mine, his tongue mating with my own, I knew—*knew*—I'd made the right decision in agreeing to give us a chance. All those thoughts about no future in our being together or the concerns we came from two different worlds faded away. Right now, we were simply two people who were attracted to one another— *baby, were we*—and were acting on that attraction.

"I'm so glad you said yes," he whispered.

Mind reader, much?

He pulled my earlobe into his mouth, bit down gently, and then sucked.

All the blood coursing through my body chuted to my pelvis like water cascading over a mile-high cliff face—fast, hard, and vibrating with power.

"*Slade.*"

I got no further because he dragged his lips back to mine, silencing what I'd been about to say. His mouth was wet and warm and infused my entire body with such a sensation of excitement I started to wriggle again, the action pushing me even further into his embrace.

I flattened my hand on his chest for purchase,

fearful I'd slide to the floor of the limo. If my bones were liquid a moment ago, they were now almost condensed.

Through his clothes, Slade's heart pounded like a tribal drum against my hands.

Good to know he was as affected as I was with all of this.

The moment I felt my toes start to curl and tingle inside my shoes, I was lifted in one swift movement and placed over his thighs.

I had a fleeting thought he must have done this a time or two before in a limo, evidenced by the fact he never broke contact with my mouth while he repositioned me.

I rested my hands on his massive shoulders, my fingers reflexively kneading the material. Straddling him, my skirt riding high up my thighs, I was brought into direct contact with exactly how much Slade was affected by what we were doing.

And it was *a lot*. A Whole lot.

The only barrier between us were his trousers and my thong. I couldn't even classify that little strip of material as much of a barrier because, saturated as it was, it did nothing to prevent me experiencing the long, thick line of him.

It was quite an experience, too.

"You feel so good," he ground out against my ear while his hands slid to my bare thighs and glided across them.

"I was just thinking the same thing about you. Great minds, and all…*oh*."

I jumped when he sucked the bare skin over my collarbone.

"You taste as good as you feel." He nuzzled my neck, and I tipped my head to the side to allow him greater access.

His tongue flicked over my skin, and a little niggle of realization that we'd stopped floated through me.

I sat upright, my hands still on his shoulders, and looked over my shoulder. Why? No clue? The privacy screen was still in place. The interior of the limo was illuminated by tiny track lights along the ceiling and the floor, so I could see inside without any problems.

"What's wrong?" Slade asked against my neck.

"We're not moving."

I bit back a giggle when I turned back to face him. His thick, wavy hair looked as if he'd been caught in a tornado. All that tugging and fisting I'd done to it had left it gorgeously disheveled, like he'd just woken after a fight with his pillow. His eyes were half open, his mouth wet and swollen. I must have tugged on his tie at one point because it was half done and askew.

His gaze was zeroed in on my torso, and a quick glance down told me why. While I'd been pulling him bald and tugging at his neckwear, he'd been unbuttoning my blouse. The sides were splayed open, my black lace bra pointing squarely at him. Even in the dim lighting I could see what he saw: my nipples were straining against the fabric, two hard points screaming to be set free.

"Nice bra," he said, a silly smile fanning his lips.

"Thanks."

"I think we're at the train station." He reached over and pressed a button on the side rest.

"Killian, are we here?"

"Yes, Mr. H."

"Okay. Give us a second."

Embarrassment shot through me. "Oh, Lord, he knows why we need the time." Flames burst up my neck while I bolted off him and tried to fix my blouse.

Slade's cavernous chuckle made me stop buttoning, my head snapping up to stare at him.

"It's not funny. He knows what we've been doing."

"I would assume so, yes."

"Well, it's mortifying that he knows we've been"—I waved a hand at him—"doing stuff back here. Private stuff."

He barked out a laugh, reached over, and kissed my nose. "You're adorable."

"No. What I am is a disheveled mess." I tried to tug my skirt back down, shove my blouse back into it. No matter how hard I tried, I still looked like I'd been ravished.

"A gorgeous disheveled mess, then."

I tossed him a speaking glance and went in search of my bag. I found it where it had dropped to the floor. Luckily, it was still clasped, so nothing had fallen out. I did a quick fluff of my hair while he redid his tie and swiped his hair back in place.

"Presentable now?" His devilish grin was on the south side of charming.

I planted a kiss on his cheek and stole his words. "Adorable."

With my hand in his, he knocked on the car window. Killian instantly opened it. "I'm gonna walk Miss O'Dowd to her train. I'll be back in about ten minutes."

Killian nodded and told me to have a safe trip home.

I couldn't quite look him in the eye when I thanked him.

Slade chuckled again and wove my hand into his as we walked into Grand Central Station.

"We're both adults, you know," he said while we walked past the grand staircase. "It's not illegal for us to engage in adult behavior if we want to. Killian knows that."

"I get that, but it's still embarrassing he knew what we were doing behind the glass. I mean, that's the reason for the privacy screen, isn't it? For privacy to"— I waved my hand again—"do stuff."

"First of all, he didn't know for a fact what we were doing."

"I don't believe that for a second," I mumbled. "What else would be we doing?"

"Talking comes to mind," he said, nailing me with his piercing glare.

I snorted. "If you believe that, I've got swamp land in Alaska to sell you. Cheap."

He shook his head, his mouth drawn into a tiny smirk. "Such a cynic." He yanked me to him, gave me a quick, hard kiss, and then stared up at the train schedule board. "There's a train leaving in eight minutes."

"I've already got my return ticket, so I can go straight to the track."

With another nod, Slade wound his hands around my waist and pressed his body against mine. I could get lost for days staring up at his chiseled face, losing myself in the soft moisture in his amber eyes. Heck, I could get lost for a lifetime.

Rein it in, girl. A lifetime isn't in the cards with this guy. You knew it going in.

"When am I going to see you again?"

I shook my head. "Maybe I can manage to come back down sometime next week. I'm not sure what my schedule is like. I know I'm booked solid from tomorrow on through the weekend."

"We'll work something out." He seemed a great deal more sure of that than me. "Colleen."

My entire body sighed. Slade laid his forehead against mine.

"Thank you for dinner," I said, breathing him in.

"I wish it included breakfast tomorrow morning."

Oh my. Can I just tell you how squishy my insides got at that statement? Seriously, this guy ticked every box on my lust-ometer checklist.

Every. Single. Box.

"Me, too," I admitted.

"I can't tell you how happy hearing you say that makes me."

His kiss was gentle and sweet, and so filled with expectation I had a doozy of a time moving when the announcement system called my train to board.

"Text me when you get home," Slade said.

"It'll be late. I still have a two-hour drive once the train arrives."

"Text me." My stomach got all fluttery again at the command. "I want to ensure you got home safe and sound."

I'd remembered hearing him say the same thing to his sister and knew it meant he cared about me. Those flutters turned to a gaggle of hula hoopers.

After another quick kiss, I began walking toward my track.

Curiosity got the better of me, and I gave in and

turned around. Slade was standing right where I'd left him, his hands folded in his trouser pockets, looking as sexy as any man had the right to look. His lips lifted at the corners when I threw him a wave.

He was still watching me as I descended the stairway to my awaiting train.

Chapter Seventeen

The next few weeks flew by. Each weekend I was double-booked with weddings, and every weekday was filled with wedding prep, final fittings, and generally making sure everything for every wedding was finalized, booked, paid for, and perfect.

The pace and workload were starting to affect my staff, Charity and Kolby especially. Things had been strained between them for a while, but with the added workloads and the glut of demanding and obnoxious bridezillas I was currently employed by, the two of them were forced to work closer together as I gave Charity more and more responsibility. I simply could not be in all places at all times, so I'd delegated some of the prep work and details to my assistant. Things came to an emotional head right before the ceremony of an exceptionally demanding bride started. I don't know what the inciting incident was, but raised voices in the back of the church pulled me from the Bawl Room.

My photographer and my assistant were glaring at one another, each talking over the other. I tried to discern what the argument was about. When they both began pleading their cases at the same time I clapped my hands, commanded them to stop speaking, and ordered them to get back to work and treat each other civilly.

I think my exact words were, "Whatever's going

on between you two, suck it up and act like professionals."

The wedding went off without a hitch.

One weekend, I'd had a bride pull a Julia Roberts and bolt two days before the nuptials. Half a bottle of wine and the reassurance everything would be perfect had calmed her and let her get some much needed sleep, which I was sure had been the impetus for her almost-flight.

I'd had runaway brides (and grooms) before, but so far had managed never to be compelled to cancel a ceremony. Nerves, jitters, stark raving terror all were common and expected emotions as the big day got closer and closer. Once I'd had a bride-to-be wake up the morning of the wedding to discover a zit the size of Rhode Island right on the tip of her nose. Her mother called me, hysterical, claiming her daughter had locked herself in the bathroom, shut off her cell phone, and was refusing to come out. There was no way she was going to get married looking like Witchipoo. I made frantic calls to a dermatologist and an aesthetician I knew, called in two favors, and four hours later, my bride walked down the aisle looking magazine ready, the professionals performing a modern day dermal miracle.

My busy schedule mirrored Slade's. The restructuring of his company chewed up most of his time, including evenings and weekends. I'd been back to the city twice for bridal fittings and a few client meetings, and we'd been able to squeeze in a quick lunch. Each time I saw him, my insides did a wild jig, my hands would start to shake, and I couldn't have wiped the smile off my face if I'd been compelled to.

The feel of his fingers, firm, strong, and possessive, across my lower back as he ushered me to a table, would spark tiny flares along my spine. He'd reach across the table at times and draw one of those fingers across my hand and I'd lose my train of thought. I'd been in a relationship for over a decade with someone I loved but had never felt the giddy, breathless, tingling sensations that bolted through me while in Slade's presence.

I could have stayed glued to my chair all day, speaking to him, listening to him tell me about his days, his plans, his life.

Lunch would end all too quickly, work demanding our time.

We spoke almost every night, sometimes late if Slade was at a business function. Once, from what he claimed was the most boring dinner of his life, he'd texted me right from the table, writing he wished I was next to him. I was already in bed with my laptop, ordering supplies for upcoming ceremonies. When Slade added what he was thinking of doing to me under the table and out of everyone's sight, I got so hot I had to toss my comforter off.

I'd never felt this way before. Not as a teenager, crushing on the unattainable quarterback of my high school. Not even as an engaged woman.

I had no romantic yardstick to measure Slade by. He simply was like no other man I'd ever known.

Before I knew it, Isabella and Jack's wedding weekend was upon me. I'd seen them, briefly, when they'd come up to meet with Cathleen and fill out their questionnaires, but I'd been involved with a wedding and hadn't been able to spend the time I wanted to with them. They'd arrived at the inn on Saturday morning, met with Cathy for about two hours, and then had driven around the area with Kolby, who took some prewedding candids of them.

Fall was in full brilliance in my little New England state, the robust reds and bright russet-orange leaves contrasting with the vibrant verdancy of the evergreens. Kolby brought them to Nanny's lake house and then to various spots around town. Afterward, the couple had driven to the next town over, enjoyed a meal, and then retired back to the inn. They'd left the next morning while I was setting up the church for my wedding-de-jour.

I opened a quick text from Isabella while I was with Maureen at the inn.

"She says she and Jack should be here in about an hour, give or take. Traffic is thick and slow going."

"Peepers are out in full," Maureen said, while she piped the final touches on Isabella's cake. It stood three tiers high, and each layer was a different-sized square. The bottom tier, the largest, was white, the middle a gorgeous fall pumpkin color, the top coated with a rich and glossy chocolate ganache. Cascading down the sides were waterfalls of leaves in every autumnal color and kind. Maureen made each of the individual leaves herself from modeling chocolate and had used her own personal mix of food dyes to create the most realistic colors I'd ever seen.

My sister's decorating skills were honed at our mother's knee. Mom never let a birthday, anniversary, or holiday go by without a homemade and personally decorated cake to celebrate. She even baked cakes for obscure days like Flag Day and National Hot Dog Day.

And yes, she did bake a cake in the shape of a hotdog, bun included. How she ever got the frosting to be the fleshy, sausage-y color of a hotdog, only the gods of baking know. She'd passed her superpower down to her youngest daughter.

Maureen stepped back and regarded her work. Today's apron was pale blue, had a mixing bowl imprinted across it, and the words *You only live once…lick the bowl.* That philosophy was why I was still carting around those eight extra pounds.

"It's one of your best creations ever, Mo," I told her. "Let me take a few pictures." I pulled my phone out of my bag.

"Let me do it, Coll," my photographer Kolby said from behind me. "It's what I get paid to do."

"And his pictures are better than yours," my sister said with a grin. When I tossed her the stink eye, she attempted to soften me up, knowing my kryptonite. She held the frosting bag up to me, cocked her head and grinned, a question in her laughing eyes.

Those darn eight pounds were screaming for me to resist, but I never could say no to Maureen. Pursing my lips in disgust—for my weak will—I stuck out my index finger. Mo piped a wallop of a dollop on it while Kolby snapped away. Right before I shoved my finger in my mouth, I said, "I hate you. Just saying," to my sister.

"Hate you more." She laughed. "And you're welcome."

"Wanna see?" Kolby held the camera up so we could view the LCD panel.

"That could grace the cover of *Baking* magazine," I said. Maureen's cake, viewed live, was mouthwatering.

Seen through the lens of my amazing and talented photographer, it looked like you could reach out and swipe your finger across the screen and came back with frosting on your finger.

"You take pretty pictures," Maureen told him as she started cleaning up.

He grabbed her around the shoulders and dropped a kiss on her temple. "You make pretty cakes," he said back.

This show of affection between the two was friendly, not sexual. Kolby was a bit of a man-whore, but I wasn't worried about him around my baby sister. He loved her like she was his own sibling, and she tended to fuss over him, as did her cook, Sarah. Both women routinely sent him home after he'd worked a wedding with left-over food, knowing he rarely kept anything in his apartment but beer.

It was almost too bad the two weren't attracted to one another. My beautiful red-haired sister looked like a lithe fairy and had the whole earth-mother thing down pat. Kolby, all six foot three, two hundred pounds of packed muscle and drop-dead sexiness gave new meaning to the phrase *bedroom eyes*. The two of them would have made beautiful babies.

But Maureen was married to her business, and I could never imagine Kolby tied to one female for eternity, so that blew the whole happily-ever-after dream for these two to smithereens.

While Maureen continued to clean her already immaculate kitchen, Kolby and I discussed a few things for the upcoming weekend weddings. Isabella Harrington's weren't the only nuptials I was in charge of.

After going over the time tables and locations for both shoots, Kolby accepted the bag of leftover morning scones Maureen had baked for her guests, kissed her again, this time on the cheek, and then told me he'd be back to film the wedding rehearsal and the following dinner for the Harrington-Rainier party.

"I'm gonna do a quick check on the pergola," I told my sister. "The florist will be here at six tomorrow morning, and I want to make sure everything is ready for her to decorate."

"It should be fine. I had one of the gardeners sweep and hose it down this morning. If it needs it, he'll do it again early tomorrow."

Isabella and Jack had opted not to say their vows in a church. Since he was—as his mother told me—a lapsed altar boy, and Isabella was raised outside of any organized religion, the two had decided to pledge themselves to one another in the garden of Inn Heaven.

When my sisters had purchased the inn, one of main deciding factors for Eileen had been the vast space cordoned off for a walking garden behind the main structure. The previous owners had been an elderly couple who hadn't been able to care for the surrounding land in many years. Eileen made it her job to get the magnificent plot back to its glory. She remembered visiting the inn once as a child when the summer flowers had all been in bloom, and she'd never forgotten how beautiful it had looked and smelled.

One of the main features she'd been able to see restored before falling ill was the six-sided columned pergola in the center of the garden. Nanny Fee called it a folly, an old-fashioned term that made no sense to anyone but her.

The pergola sat, elevated from the center of the garden walkway, on three marble steps surrounding it. Six Ionic columns set on white marble bases, circled the structure, and wherever someone sat or walked in the garden, they had a view of the interior, because it was open on all sides. Unlike Nanny's gazebo, which had a half wall and a built-in seat encircling the interior, this structure was topped with a galvanized steel dome in a Victorian curlicue design. On a sunny day, rays filtered through the dome, bathing the floor—and whoever stood on it—in curls and twists of light.

In the morning, a local florist and her crew would twine and affix white and deep orange roses down each column, their blooms cascading from dome to floor, and would line the steps up to the pergola and the path to it with a mix of fall blooms in ceramic vases.

It was the perfect setting for Isabella's autumn-themed wedding. The weather forecast, which I'd checked and rechecked through the days leading up to it, promised a clear, cloudless, sunny day with temperatures hovering in the low to mid-sixties.

I stepped up into the small building. The floor sparkled, nary a downed leaf or speck of dirt anywhere along the pathway or inside the structure. The midafternoon sunlight cracking through the dome's design threw shadows and shapes of soft swirls and waves around me. Since the pergola was in the center of the garden and situated in the back of the inn's property, it was surrounded on three sides by a forest of trees whose colors were a patchwork blanket of reds, yellows, golds, and umbers. I closed my eyes and imagined how beautifully Kolby's lenses would capture the private setting as the couple took their vows.

The air shifted slightly around me, and before I could open my eyes, strong and able hands pulled me against a solid wall of rock.

I knew this wall. Had dreamed about it many times lately. I slid my fingers along the hands now encircling my waist, leaned back, and sighed.

A soft, deep, and erotic chuckle filled my ear, warm breath flowing around it shooting little sparks of pleasure down my spinal column.

I must have shuddered, because Slade's arms tightened, and he whispered, "I've got you," right before he nipped down on the fleshy part of my earlobe.

I pressed further into him, my back aligned with his front from shoulders to the back of my knees. He was so solid, so strong. The notion I was safe and protected flew through me and settled deep in my soul.

"When did you get here?" I asked.

"Seconds ago. I wanted to arrive first so I could see you without sharing you with everyone else. Maureen told me where you were." I felt his head swerve. "It's beautiful out here. Is this where Jack and Izzy are saying their vows?"

I turned to face him. That familiar little jump in my stomach came and settled in like an old friend when I looked up into his smiling face.

Because I needed to touch him with the same need I had for my next breath, I traced a finger along his jaw then moved to outline his full lips. Slade sucked my finger into his mouth and bit down gently. Those sparks ignited along my spine again and flared straight down to my toes.

"It is. It'll be decorated tomorrow, but I wanted to make sure everything was okay now so we didn't have any problems in the morning."

"That's my girl," he said with a lopsided grin I swear no female with a pulse could resist. "Thorough and proactive, everything timed to precision, never missing a detail."

"God's in the details, as Nanny tells me often."

It hadn't escaped me he'd called me *his girl*. I didn't know how to respond to the declaration, so I glossed over it.

"Wise woman, your grandmother." Slade dropped a kiss on the tip of my nose.

We stood, arms around each other's waists, gazing into the other's eyes. He was making tiny circular motions with his fingers at the small of my back, much the way he'd done to my hand over the dinner table the last time we'd been together.

He took in a deep breath, his shoulders rising with the expansion of his chest. "I missed you," he whispered, pulling me so my head settled against his chest. The rapid thrumming of his heart mirrored the staccato beating of my own.

"Missed you, too."

"Talking on the phone is one thing. But this is so much better."

No lie, there.

"I know this is probably an idiotic question, but can you take some time? Go have lunch with me and relax for a bit?"

In truth, every minute of my afternoon was scheduled. I had a hundred things to check on for the weekend weddings, client calls to return, plus I'd finally convinced Nanny of the need to get her eyes examined, and her eye doctor had been able to squeeze her in for an appointment this afternoon. I was, as usual, her chauffeur since Maureen had to get the prep work done for the rehearsal dinner and tend to her guests, and Cathleen was tied up in court.

For the first time in more years than I could remember, I wanted to chuck my professional responsibilities, toss my event planner in the trash, and play hooky from my job. All because of the man holding me in his arms.

"I know you've probably got a million things that need attending to," Slade said, "but I'm not going to get a moment alone with you this weekend because we're both going to be so busy, and I'd like a chance for us to be together without anyone else around, even for a little while."

Phone calls could wait to be returned. Charity could deal with the laundry list of items that needed checking. She was, after all, my administrative assistant. And Nanny's appointment wasn't for two more hours.

In the end, the choice was an easy one.

I lifted up a little in my heels and pressed my lips against his. His grip tightened around my waist.

"Well," I told him with a grin, "a girl's gotta eat."

****

We wound up in Maureen's kitchen, and it was by no stretch of the imagination an *intimate* lunch. When I'd told her we were heading out to get something, she immediately made us sit down and served us hot sandwiches and soup, the same fare she was feeding her guests in the dining room.

Since, she said, I needed to be ready to take Nanny to her appointment and this was peeping season, we'd waste time trying to find a place where we'd be quickly seated. She wasn't wrong. I'd been so engrossed with seeing Slade in the flesh instead of on my smartphone screen, I'd forgotten how horrible it was trying to eat out during fall in New Hampshire. It's a blessing for much-needed tourism dollars, but a curse for the locals to go about their normal daily lives. Each year, dining out from September to November was becoming more difficult.

"This soup is delicious," Slade told my sister when she whizzed by, her arms laden with plates.

"Thanks. Plenty more," she said before slipping into the smaller dining room.

"This isn't exactly the quiet, romantic, catch-up lunch I had in mind," he told me, "but at least we get to spend some time together before everything starts."

"Isabella texted me right before you arrived and told me they were about an hour out. I'm surprised you all didn't come up together."

"I wanted to leave early this morning, and I knew Jack was on call last night. By the time he got home, showered, ate, and packed, I knew they weren't going to leave until late morning. I wanted to get on the road as soon as possible, like I said, to see you."

I couldn't help it. I sighed.

Loud.

Slade grinned at me.

With my elbow propped on the table, my chin cupped in my hand, I told him, "I'm so glad you did."

He finished his soup. "Promise me something." He reached across and ran his finger across my hand.

A kidney? A lung? My heart? Although he already owned that. I'd promise him anything he asked, no matter what. I had it bad, *bad*, for this guy. Why I wasn't terrified about this, I have no clue.

He took my hand and folded it into his own. Like the first time we'd met and shaken hands, the sensation of reclining in a warm, soothing bath seeped through me. There was no doubt about it now. His superpower truly was his soothing touch.

"I know you usually work at a wedding, running around, overseeing all the thousands of details, making sure everything is perfect. You don't get a chance to enjoy the moment, the party."

I shrugged because it was true. Part of the reason, though, was—as I've said so many times before—I'm the hired help. Dancing, chitchatting, drinking, none of those things are allowed from a professional standpoint.

"I'm not a guest, so I don't get to act like one," I told him. "But I do have a good time. Seeing how I've helped two people celebrate their love for one another is an amazing feeling. Knowing I played a role in helping them have a wonderful day full of memories is heady stuff. I don't need to be a guest to feel happy about that."

His fingers were doing that grazing, rubbing thing along my knuckles again, and I started to fidget in my seat as a delicious sense of pressure began building in my pelvis.

"Guest or not, however you define yourself, I want you to promise to do one thing."

"Okay."

"Dance with me at the reception," he said. "I want one dance, of my choice, with you. I want to whirl around the dance floor, hold you, and know every guy's eye in the room is on us and you're all mine."

Okay, so saying I had it bad for this guy really didn't do justice to the emotions swirling inside me like a category-five tornado across dry grassland. I was so head over heels in love with him I couldn't see straight. I'd tried to protect myself from it, had every intention of falling into bed—and every other place I could manage—with him at some point after the wedding, but I hadn't planned on losing my heart.

Yeah. I can hear it now: you make plans and God…well, you know how that ends.

All my life, my parents, my sisters, my grandmother have told me they can read any emotion I have clearly written across my face. Nanny always knew when I told a fib, claiming the gift of blarney skipped over me in the womb, making lying an impossibility for me. Like mini-Sherlock Holmeses, my sisters could detect when I liked a boy and would torture and tease me mercilessly about it, as is the privilege of sisters.

Knowing I wore my heart on my sleeve and my thoughts on my face, I tried to hide how his words quite literally destroyed me. If I couldn't protect myself from loving him, knowing in my soul there was no long-term future for us, at least I could protect my pride by never having him see the depth of my feelings.

I twisted my mouth at the corners and narrowed my eyes, digging deep for the snark.

"Is that all?" I asked. "You just want a dance? 'Cause I was fully vested in giving you a kidney or a lung if you asked." With a dramatic shrug, I added, "I'm getting off easy."

He tugged on my hand, brought it to his lips, and grazed his mouth across my knuckles.

Every ounce of blood in my body pooled below my waist. If the fire alarm sounded, I knew I'd probably burn to death because there was no way on God's green earth I could move from my seat. Lust is one thing. Being so turned on you were incapable of movement, speech, even a coherent thought, is quite another. Right at that moment, I fit into the latter category.

Slade cocked his head, his gaze locked on mine like a target. A smug, self-satisfied smirk danced up his face. "A lung, huh? Good to know."

Before I could respond or even form a thought, Maureen zipped back into the kitchen.

"Your sister and her fiancé are checking in," she told Slade while she spooned up another two bowls of soup. "I told her you'd already arrived." Her gaze lit on our joined hands before she went back to her task.

"So much for alone time," Slade murmured. He let go of my hand and swiped his lips with his napkin.

When he rose, I did as well.

"Leave all that." Maureen nodded toward our bowls and plates. "I'll get to it."

I ignored her and brought everything to the industrial sink.

"The least I can do is bus my own table," I told her. "You have enough to do," I added to her back when she sprinted back out to the dining room.

I turned and found myself drawn into Slade's arms. Looping his hands around my waist, he brought me close. "When will I get to see you again?"

"Later on when it's time for the rehearsal. The dinner is directly after, here, in the private dining room."

"How about after?"

"After?"

"When everything is rehearsed and everyone is fed and heads off for a good night's sleep. How about then? We can disappear somewhere, or better yet, you can come up to my room."

I knew what he was asking, what he wanted. I wanted it, too. But now wasn't the right time.

"I'm one of those people who needs that good night's sleep, Slade. As are you. You've got a big day tomorrow, and you want to be at your best, physically and mentally, for your sister, don't you?"

Disappointment crept up his face.

"And while I'd like nothing more than to disappear with you"—some of the disappointment fled—"I need to be at my physical and mental best tomorrow, too."

He tightened his hold on me. "After, then? After the wedding, the reception, everything, is done?"

I laid my hand across his cheek and smiled. "After."

"Promise?"

The need in his voice was powerful. It boosted my fragile ego into the stratosphere. The fact that this amazing, successful, and drop-dead gorgeous man wanted me—*me*—was too incredible for words to express.

With a swift kiss that had me wanting much, much more, I vowed, "Promise. Now, let's go greet your sister, and then I've got a million things to do."

Chapter Eighteen

Plans, as I've frequently avowed, are a comedic theme for God. The tight timetable I was on got tighter as Nanny took forever at the eye doctor, and I worried I'd either have to leave her there and try to find her another ride home or be late for the rehearsal, which was something I would not allow. Ever.

When I'd booked Nanny Fee's appointment, the receptionist had neglected to tell me my grandmother's eyes would be dilated. I'd assumed she'd have a simple vision check like I did at my yearly exams.

No such luck.

Due to the density of her cataracts, her age, and the necessity for surgery, the ophthalmologist insisted on dilating her so he could look at the back of her eyes, ensure no other ocular issues existed, and determine her eye health. Her twenty-minute appointment morphed into an hour and change, added to by Nanny's unending questions.

Finally, with only fifteen minutes to get back to the inn, the appointment ended. It would take too much time to drive Nanny back home and then head for the rehearsal, so I opted to bring her with me. I knew Maureen would feed her while Cathleen and I were busy. Cathleen could bring her home afterward since she didn't need to stay for the dinner.

The sun was three-quarters down in the autumn sky

as the bridal party assembled on the first floor. I palmed Nanny off on my sister and then made my way to the foyer.

Isabella and Jack were holding hands, nary enough space to slip a piece of paper between their cuddled bodies, giant smiles on their faces. Vivi was holding hands with a man I assumed was Jack's father. Put thirty years and an equal number of pounds on Jack, and you could predict what he'd look like in the future. The foursome stood together, smiling and chatting with Jack's sister, her husband, and their flower-girl daughter, and another man I assumed was Jack's best man, Gage.

Standing off to one side and not interacting with the party, were Janelle Thorne and her husband. If you opened a dictionary and looked up the word *tense*, I can guarantee you'd see a picture of Janelle. Her beautifully made-up face was pinched and her coral-colored lips clamped and pressed so close together her mouth looked like one continuous line across her chin. Her gaze darted around the spacious foyer from her daughter, to Jack, to Vivi, and then back again to Isabella, her expression cautious and guarded.

I'd had mothers of the bride who were on edge before, but Janelle looked like a too-tightly wound spring ready to uncoil at a finger snap.

Cathy came from the kitchen, gave me a wink as greeting, and moved to the happy couple. She accepted a warm hug from each of them. She'd sent me a quick email after their visit to tell me she'd met with them, fallen in love with both of them, and had gotten a great deal of material to write their ceremony from their questionnaires.

Just as I had in the pergola, I sensed a subtle shift in the air surrounding me. When I turned, Slade had materialized behind the Thornes. That scrutinizing, paralyzing gaze of his was centered directly on me, and I swear my body temperature shot up a good ten degrees from the searing heat zeroing in on me like a waiting-to-launch missile. My own vision narrowed, my hearing stilled, the chatting voices around me muffled as if they were all under water. All I could see was him.

I'd read a horribly written historical romance I'd found one summer in Nanny's lake house. I forget the title, but I remember one passage vividly. The heroine glanced across the room and saw the hero for the first time as he entered a ballroom. Resplendent in a finely cut tux and tails, he filled the room with his powerful air of mystery and hotness. In that moment, the heroine's body quieted, all the hullaballoo of the dance dissolving into thin air. She felt as if she and the hero were alone in the massive room. The chandelier lights dulled her vision, blurring the faces of family and friends surrounding her. The hero and heroine's gazes linked, their breaths mirrored each other, and she knew in her heart, this was the only man she would ever love.

A little purple prosy, I know, but I was thirteen, didn't know anything about real love, and this sounded like a perfect depiction. I felt the same way, right now, as that virginal Victorian heroine had, with Slade's eyes focused on me.

In the next instant, he blinked and turned to say something to Janelle.

I gave myself an internal shake and then corralled the bridal party outside to the pergola. Kolby was walking around, lining up shots and angles to film from. One of the extras of being one of my brides was Kolby photographed every aspect of the wedding. Some of the best pictures were often the candid ones he'd capture during the rehearsal, or the time before the ceremony. As usual, he was his unobtrusive self, meandering about, snapping away.

Throughout the rehearsal, I instructed everyone how to proceed up the path, where to stand or sit and repositioned the antsy flower girl a few times.

Cathleen took over and went over a cursory reading of their vows. She didn't do the JP spiel she'd written for them, keeping it a secret until the actual ceremony.

I've said this before, but to see Jack and Isabella together, staring into one another's eyes as they pledged their love and devotion, was to know what true love looked like.

At one point, I let my gaze drift over to Slade. After he'd escorted his sister up the aisle, he'd moved to where his seat would be the following day. He'd folded his hands in front of him and was listening to the vows. Visions of how his fingers had raked and teased my own that day appeared in my mind. My imagination ran to all the delicious ways his hands could torment and pleasure me while the rehearsal proceeded around us.

Cathleen said my name at least twice before it filtered through my daydreaming. Better to not fantasize about Slade and his hands when I had a wedding ceremony to get through.

When they were all seated in Maureen's private dining room being served dinner, I bundled Nanny into

Cathy's car, thanked my sister for bringing our grandmother home, and said I would be along shortly.

Back in the kitchen, I took the cup of decaf coffee my youngest sister handed me.

"Everything go okay with the rehearsal?"

"Time-wise, yeah. There are some undercurrents, though."

"Yeah, I got that feeling when I started service. The moms don't look like they're besties."

I snorted. "As far from it as can get." My little sister may be the quiet one, but her powers of perception and observation are strong. "Jack's mom is a bundle of happiness her boy is getting married. Isabella's mother isn't feeling the love. I'm hoping we don't have an emotional crisis before the ceremony."

Maureen arranged her signature autumn pork and apple recipe on the plates and shook her head. "Why do weddings bring out the worst in some people?"

I swiped an apple slice dripping with cinnamon and nutmeg off a tray and said, "Sixty-four-thousand-dollar question. I'm gonna take a peek inside and make sure they're behaving."

"They are. When I was in there, the conversation was flowing nicely. No raised voices. Just a little tension in the air."

Perceptive and correct. When I opened the connecting door a crack, I could see and hear everyone. Isabella was seated in the middle of the table between her brother and her husband-to-be. Flanking the men were the matriarchs. Jack's dad, Jerry, sat at the head of one side of the table, Fred Thorne the other. Jill and her family, and Jack's best man, Gage, rounded out the group.

Isabella was beaming, her attention flitting from her brother to her man. My eyes settled on Janelle. She was silent and tipping her wine glass up to her lips frequently. In front of her was a glass of toasting champagne, and I wondered if she'd down it before Slade got up to speak. He'd mentioned to me while we were having lunch that he'd finally written everything he wanted to say to his sister and Jack tonight, knowing tomorrow would be Gage's moment to toast his best friend. The rehearsal dinner was typically the bride's family's time to wish the couple happiness, and since Slade was the de facto man in charge, it was up to him to make a speech. Their father would be arriving in the morning before the ceremony, a subject I hadn't broached yet with Slade.

I also hadn't mentioned the prenup in the weeks leading up to the wedding, and neither had he. Isabella, after her tearful episode in the bridal salon, had gone silent on the topic as well. She sat between the two men she loved most in the world. None of her previous anger about the document was anywhere to be seen. My curiosity wanted to know how the situation had been resolved, but my professional judgment ordered me to forgo asking. Everything was calm and happy between the three of them, and I wanted those feelings to last through the ceremony and reception.

I'm sure I'd find out if Jack had signed it, or not, eventually. Tonight, though, I wasn't going to ask.

Back in the kitchen, I told Maureen, "Okay. Looks like you were right. No bloodshed. I think I'm gonna head on home. I've got a few last minute details to go over for tomorrow and then Sunday's affair."

"The Canterbury-Golman wedding, right?"

"Yeah. I'm surprised you know that since they're not staying or having the reception here."

"Kolby mentioned it when I gave him dinner. He told me the wedding's small and the reception's at Krinckles over in Haversham."

I nodded. "Since it's a second marriage for them both, they decided to keep it small. It should be an easy day for me, but I still have to go over the details."

She handed me a plastic container filled with food. "You haven't eaten since lunch. Take this for when you get home."

If there was anyone on the planet who deserved to be married with a passel of kids to take care of, it was Maureen. She was the natural nurturer of all those close to her. I wasn't a bit surprised when she said she'd fed my photographer dinner. If Charity had been there, instead of out on a date, she would have gotten something, too.

"Can you slip this into Isabella's room for me?" I asked, handing her an envelope.

"You can go do it before you leave. I've got her in the blue room."

Two minutes later, after sliding the letter I'd written her under her door, I headed home.

Nanny was already asleep in bed by the time I walked in. I did a quick check of the daily mail, then heated up Maureen's pork and apples. While I was eating, my phone pinged with a message.

You left without saying goodbye, Slade wrote.

I didn't want to disturb you.

Three little undulating dots crossed my screen.

You disturb me every minute of the day. More dots.
That didn't come out right.

With a laugh, I typed, *I knew what you meant. All good.* I added a laughing face emoji and hit send.

A few seconds later he wrote back. *Sitting here listening to Vivi talk about Jack's childhood. Janelle stone-faced and silent. And drinking.*

Exactly what worried me.

Did you make your toast yet? Did you make your sister cry?

All done. Izzy lost it, but in a happy-cry way...I miss you.

Those three words never failed to warm me inside and out.

Miss you, too. Get a good night's sleep. You want to look handsome for pictures.

A gagging face emoji shot across my screen.

Off to finish some work. See you in the a.m.

I debated about whether or not to add a kiss. I scrolled through my phone and found a crimson-mouthed kissing GIF, so I sent that.

You're killing me, you know that, right? I'm not gonna get any sleep now cuz I'll be thinking of kissing you. Thanks a heap.

For a reply, I sent him a string of emoji kisses, which he responded to with a series of dagger through the heart icons.

Who knew text-flirting could be so much fun?

An hour later, I'd finished all the prep work I needed for the weekend weddings to go off without an administrative hitch and was in the process of locking everything up for the night. I was at the back kitchen door when my phone pinged with an incoming text.

Slade.

What are you doing? he wrote.

Just about ready to get into bed.

Can I join you?

"If only," I said out loud. I typed, *Slade...stop. Is the dinner over?*

Yeah. Everyone's in bed for the night.

You should be, too.

Then let me in, and I will be. In your bed, I mean.

What? What was he talking about? A tiny tapping noise came from the back kitchen door I'd just locked. I looked up and saw him waving his phone through the door window, the light from the screen illuminating his face in the dark.

My feet sprouted wings, and I bolted across the room and shot open the lock. Slade slid inside while I asked in a hushed voice—Nanny has hearing like a bat, remember? "How did you know where I live?"

"Maureen." He grabbed me around my waist and yanked me up against him.

For a heartbeat, I had a thought to trounce my little sister for giving out that info. The second Slade's mouth covered mine, the thought died.

How is it possible for every nerve ending in your body to explode like a barrage of firecrackers and at the same time be filled with such an all-consuming and total tranquility?

I have no answer, but held in this man's strong arms, being kissed like I'd never been kissed before, that's exactly what I felt. Electrified and peaceful.

Crazy.

I pushed against his chest and pulled back from the kiss. "Slade, what are you doing here?"

"If you don't know, then I'm not doing it right." His mouth quirked in one corner and he kissed the tip

297

of my nose.

"You shouldn't be here," I told him. "You should be back at the inn, resting for tomorrow. It's going to be a long day."

"I've had long days before on little to no sleep," he told me while his hands drifted down my back to the dip in my spine, where they rested. He tilted his forehead against mine, and a thick sigh blew from between his lips. "I don't want to rest at the inn tonight, Colleen. I want to sleep in your bed."

"You want to…sleep in my bed?"

He lifted his head, the haughty and completely masculine grin I'd grown to love traipsing across his face. He tightened his hold around my waist. "Well, eventually. Sleep, I mean. I can think of other stuff to do in the interim."

When he kissed the corner of my mouth, my thighs vibrated against one another.

"O-other…stuff?"

His grin widened. "You're adorable when you're flustered."

Flustered? *Jesus.* I was ready to come apart at the seams.

"I want to sleep next to you, holding you all night. But first—" He slid his tongue down the side of my neck, his lips trailing after it. "—I want to make love to you. Several times, in fact." He settled on a spot behind my ear, nuzzled, then put his lips against my skin and sucked. "I want to make you come so hard you scream my name." He pulled back up and stared down at me, and I swear his eyes were on fire they burned so hot. "Then, after I do that, I'm gonna do it again."

The change in his tense didn't slip by me. He

wasn't making a request. Or even asking permission. If he had, I would have said *Yes.*

Said it? Hell, I'd have shouted it if I weren't so afraid of waking Nanny.

No, Slade wasn't really asking me if he could spend the night—and all that entailed—he was telling me he was going to. Commanding it, in fact, in that he-who-rules-the-world way of his.

I could have continued to put him off, pressing the point we all needed to be rested for the big day ahead of us. If I had, I know in my heart he would have acquiesced. I could have simply said no and shown him the door, but, really, have you met me?

After thinking, dreaming—hoping—for this for weeks, there was no way on God's green earth Fintan and Claire O'Dowd's middle girl was going to ask the best thing that had ever walked into her life to leave.

No. Way.

I stretched up on my toes and kissed him. His hands opened and then flexed against my back, his brow grooving a bit between his eyes. "Colleen?"

I touched his lips with my index finger and cocked my head. "There'll be no screaming," I said softly. "From either of us. Nanny's a ridiculously light sleeper."

I pulled his hands from around my waist and then, walking backward, tugged him from the kitchen to the hallway.

"The stairs squeak, so walk where I walk," I told him.

Gingerly, as I'd done for most of my teenaged, then adult life, I made my way up the main staircase, weaving and zigzagging around the spots I knew creaked as only they can in an old, weathered, much lived-in New England home.

When we got to the top of the landing, I guided him along the hallway to my room.

Once safely inside, the door closed and bolted behind us, Slade grinned and whispered, "You've done that a time or two."

"More than you know."

He glanced over my shoulder, his eyes widening. "Nice bed."

I nodded.

"Big."

"I move around a lot when I sleep."

I didn't want to discuss my bedroom furniture. Now that I had him here, I wanted to do every little dirty, nasty, bad-Catholic-schoolgirl thing I'd been fantasizing of doing to him since the first day he walked into my office.

Not gently, I pushed him up flat against the closed door, much the way he'd done to me out at the lake house that day in the rain. Then I snaked my hands up the solid wall of his pecs, silently sighing at how wonderful they felt under my fingers, to weave around his neck. With one hand cupping him above his collar and holding him prisoner, the other pressed flat against the door for purchase.

His grin was devilish, cocky, and so damn sexy my already-damp underwear got a little more so.

Taking another play from his, well, *playbook*, I slid my thigh between his legs, lifting it a little so my knee pressed against the very solid erection currently straining against his pants zipper.

His grin vanished. "Colleen—" He gulped.

"Shhh." I bussed his lips. "Remember Nanny."

I didn't give him time to say another word. My lips sought his as I pressed my body as close as I could. I covered his front, while his back was planted flat against the door. I hadn't changed out of my work clothes when I'd gotten home, simply shucked off my shoes and tossed off my jacket. Slade's hands dipped over my hip and down my thighs to bunch the hem of my dress. A swift movement and he tugged it up, his warm hands sliding under my thighs and lifting me up as well. He pushed off the door and with my legs wrapped around his waist, my ankles crossed at his back, he strode over to my bed.

When I'd left home at eighteen, rock star posters lined the walls and I'd kept the bed furnishings the same since I'd been ten and Mom had decorated my room in frilly, girly pink flounces and ruffles. When I'd moved back home after Eileen's death, I'd chucked the posters, got rid of the little girl linens and replaced them with a more muted, mature color scheme, complete with a four-poster king-size bed and canopy. No one aside from my sisters and grandmother had seen or been invited into my grown-up bedroom.

Until now.

Slade bumped the footboard with his knees, stopped, and let me slide back down to a standing position, our lips staying locked together.

While his tongue did wild and wonderful things to my own, he dragged my dress zipper all the way down my back. I dropped my arms from around his neck and let it fall straight to the floor. When his hands cupped the undersides of my breasts, then smoothed their way down to my waist, I sent a thank-you prayer to the saints above I hadn't put on the dreaded slimming spandex today. That thing was as far from sexy as you could get.

I think Slade was glad I hadn't either, (even though he didn't know I hadn't) because his fingers danced around the waistband of my thong before slipping down and squeezing my butt in his big, warm, and agile hands.

"You've got the greatest ass," he whispered into my ear before taking the lobe prisoner between his teeth. "I get hard every time I walk behind you."

Since the majority of those excess eight pounds Maureen's cooking had caused were settled in the area in question, I slapped myself an internal high five, for once not cursing them.

In the next breath, my bra met my dress. Before I could think not to, I gasped—loudly—when Slade pinched my nipples between his thumbs and index fingers. A self-satisfied, alpha-male chuckle bubbled up from deep inside him. "Quiet now," he whispered as he dropped a kiss to one breast then the other. "Remember Nanny."

Before I could form a response, he'd sucked one distended nipple through his wet lips while his fingers plumped and played with the other.

"All through dinner," he said as he trailed his way between then, licking one then the other, "whenever there was a lull in the conversation, all I could think about was being with you. Like this."

His lips took mine again in a kiss filled with intention, domination, and absolute want. "While Gage made his speech, I was fantasizing about doing this." He cuddled my breasts. "When Fred toasted Izzy and

Jack, I pictured myself doing this." He reached around me to squeeze my butt again. Hard. "And even when I was supposed to be giving my own speech, I couldn't concentrate, instead the image of you, under me with me pounding into you until we were both lost was all I could see."

He spread his fingers over my cheeks and kissed the tip of my nose. A long, deep sigh broke through his lips, its heat fanning over me. My heart turned over at the sound. For a moment, I had hope he felt something more for me than the attraction he'd admitted. Chemistry and lust are fine. I firmly and devoutly support both. But no matter how combustible we were together, there was an endpoint. I wouldn't be planning my own wedding any time soon to this man, despite the fact he now held my heart in his hands.

Even knowing it, I still wanted him. All of him that he'd give me. If I couldn't have his heart, I could have his attention, his thoughts, and his body. It was enough. It had to be.

"Something's wrong with this picture," I said, yanking myself out of my own head.

He pulled back and squinted down at me.

"I'm naked except for a tiny swatch of material that's really not covering anything, while you're standing here fully dressed. Why are you still dressed?"

His expression cleared. I don't think I've ever seen any other human move as fast as he did right then. I blinked twice, and he was as naked as I was. Well, *more*, since he wasn't wearing a red lace thong.

Oh my.

Fantasies of how someone looked under their clothes are one thing, and I'd been having an awful lot of them about this man for weeks. But actually seeing Slade in the flesh—all of his flesh—and every little fantasy I'd had proved once again real life is so much better than imagination.

He was, simply put, perfect in every way. From his broad, muscled, sculpted chest to the trenches and troughs cut through his abdomen, he was perfection. From the trail of goldenrod hair curling over his belly and covering his skin straight down to the tops of his thick, toned thighs, he was a masterpiece. But the part that made him a man was…well, there really aren't any descriptions that can do him justice.

As he stood in front of me, hard and swollen and divinely masculine, all I could think was how happy I was he was in my room. Naked.

Another eye blink and I was too. Slade lifted me and draped me across my bed, flat on my back, the thong a memory as he tossed it over his shoulder.

"There's something else I was thinking about all through dinner," he said as he stared down at me from the bottom of the bed.

"What?"

"This."

Before I could ask what "this" was, he tossed my legs over his shoulders, lifted and supported my butt in his hands, and dropped his head between my legs, his destination and intent clear as a crystal bell.

While his tongue drew a slow, mind-blowing trail along me from top to bottom, I shot my fisted hand to my mouth in a feeble attempt to hold back the scream volcanoing up from deep down inside me. Muted laughter made his shoulders shake at my dilemma, and when he curled his tongue and sucked what I've heard my grandmother refer to as a girl's "hot button," I grabbed my pillow and smothered it over my face.

In the next instant, I tossed it off because I didn't need it. I'd stopped breathing and making any kind of noise while Slade's long and strong fingers joined his fabulous tongue on its pillage and dipped inside me. My lower body spawned a life of its own as it rocked, circled, and tightened against those fingers, matching the rhythm he created as he slid them in and out of me.

A familiar tingling down my lower spine shot straight to my toes. They curled and flexed around his back and made my butt lift higher to him. Bless the man, he took every advantage of my body's instinctual moves. The tension coiling inside me sparked and shifted and grew.

"You're close," he whispered and dropped a quick kiss on my thigh while his fingers continued his erotic barrage.

I was about to confess how close I truly was, but the orgasm hit fast and furious, making speech a forgotten commodity. I'd had the forethought to grab the pillow again right before I was lost, because I knew Slade was going to deliver on his promise. He was gonna make me scream.

And he did. Thank God for the pillow.

My lungs began to function again after a time. Suddenly, the pillow was whipped from my face and tossed to the floor. Slade knelt in front of me with his hands on his thighs. His lids were heavy with arousal and heat, a smug and superior smirk twisted across his face, and his prominent erection proudly pulsated against his abdomen.

Oh, my.

"You screamed my name." Hubris danced in his quiet tone.

"You promised I would."

His slow nod had my toes curling again and my backside squirming against the tangled comforter.

"I never make a promise I don't keep."

If that was true, I could expect a few more pillow face-plants before this night was over. But first...

I pulled up to a kneeling position and pressed my body against his. The feel of his smooth skin was intoxicating and wickedly stirring. My thighs began to tingle again. As I'd done before, I cupped the back of his neck with one hand, but this time, instead of pressing against the door for support, I snaked my hand down between our bodies to grab the impressive, throbbing length of him. The tips of my fingers barely touched as they circled around his tumescent shaft.

His arrogant grin vanished. "Colleen—"

I almost came again from the burst of power I felt at all the emotion in his strangled tone.

"Shhh." I kissed his open mouth and squeezed and slid up, then down, his length. Slade sucked the very air from around me when he hissed in a breath.

"It's your turn to scream," I told him. "Lie back."

I didn't think he could move any faster than when he'd shucked his clothes. I was wrong. Flat on his back, he wiggled his butt into a comfortable position, then spread his legs wide, his gaze locked onto mine.

"You might want to have the pillow handy," I said in what I hoped was a saucy, sexy voice. Since I was whispering, I couldn't tell if it was or if I sounded like a demented Gollum.

That suggestive, arrogant grin returned when he

reached over and pulled it close to his side. His hand shook a bit in anticipation, the pillow fisted in his grip.

I couldn't help my own lips from mirroring his and pulling up at the corners.

With my next move, his mouth formed a solid, wide *O*.

I took him—all of him—into my mouth, slowly gliding and guiding him, my eyes staying trained on his. As he'd done to me, I then set out to drive him wild. Tiny, little pants every time I squeezed a bit tighter and stroked up, then down, whooshed from him. He'd thrown his head back on the support pillow, his neck working and bobbing rapidly.

When he shoved the pillow over his face and moaned, that sense of overwhelming power bolted through me again.

"Stop," he pleaded after a few moments, pushing up and halting my hand with his. "I'm gonna come."

I let him free from my lips. "Isn't that the point?"

The choked sound of his laugh echoed around us.

"Shhh." I went stone-still, my ears going on hyperalert for any indication Nanny had heard him.

After a moment of silence, I was assured we were safe.

Slade shifted, and before I knew it, I was the one flat on my back pinioned under him. He spread my thighs with his knees and nestled between them.

"It is," he said after a quick kiss, "but I want to be inside you when I do, not in your mouth, which"—his eyes went to half-mast as he peered down at me—"by the way, was amazing."

Power surge again.

Then it was forgotten as all my energy, my

thoughts, my very breath, centered on the sensations flowing inside me and all over my skin as Slade's hands and mouth branded me everywhere they touched. Muffled sighs and gasps filled my room.

A mounting wave of need churned deep in my belly. I wanted him inside me, needed it—him—as much as I needed my heart to beat. "Slade—"

"I know, baby." After a quick kiss to the notch between my breasts, he lifted and tugged his pants from the floor. From his wallet, he withdrew a condom and, with shaking hands, ripped the wrapper open.

The thought that I was making him tremble, *me,* shot that power surge off the scales.

"Look at me." Even though he'd whispered it, there was no doubt it was an order.

He twined his fingers in mine and then stretched our joined hands and arms over my head. Our knuckles grazed the headboard.

The pulse at his temple was pounding as he stared down at me, every emotion he possessed crossing his eyes.

And when he slid into me in one long, full, and complete glide, everything around me faded. I didn't care we both had to be up in a few hours for his sister's wedding. I didn't think about details or concerns that might come up and throw a wrench into all my well-thought-out plans. It didn't matter there were a thousand things to do before the ceremony which would need my attention. All that was important, all I could feel, see, think was Slade. Right now, in my bed, with this man, was everything.

He dragged in a breath as he settled inside me. "You feel...perfect," he ground out as he started to move his hips.

As his rhythm quickened and deepened with each thrust, mine following suit, the only word I could think was *home*. Being with him this way felt like I'd finally found the place I needed to be, had longed for a lifetime to be.

And I never wanted to leave.

The corded, defined muscles in Slade's back tightened beneath my hands as a heavy breath caught in the back of this throat. "Colleen—"

I lifted up and sealed my mouth across his. While I didn't think he'd actually scream, I absorbed the guttural groan swelling up from him.

Power is certainly an aphrodisiac because it rushed into my system again at the knowledge that I could make this man cry out my name as he came. With a primal, savage growl that barreled between his lips and straight through me, Slade pushed up and stared down into my eyes as he emptied into me.

Had I called it power? What's more intense, more potent, than the feeling of power? The answer came to me while Slade bent to kiss my lips again, the sweetest smile I'd ever seen on his face.

Love.

Love surpasses power any time, any day, and in every way.

Love.

Chapter Nineteen

Outdoor weddings are always a crapshoot, weather-wise. You want the day to be filled with sunshine—literally and figuratively—a gentle breeze, and calm temperatures. The old saying *Happy is the bride the sun shines upon* is true for a reason. Rain, wind, snow, and freezing temps never make for a happy bride.

Or a happy wedding planner.

When I opened my eyes at the crack of creation on the morning of Isabella's wedding, bright light was filtering through the slats of my bedroom venetian blinds and I was alone. After our first time together, Slade kissed me senseless, and in no time flat, he brought us both to the pinnacle of passion again. Spooning afterward, we both managed to fall asleep for an hour. I sensed him shift from the bed at one point to go into my connecting bathroom. When he emerged, he was dressed.

"Can I just tell you how much I want to stay here, all night, with you?" He sat next to me on the bed and lifted one of my hands to his mouth. "I don't want to leave."

"I don't want you to," I admitted. "But—"

He slid a finger across my lips. "I know. Your grandmother. Finding me here in the morning wouldn't exactly be respectful."

If I weren't in love with him already, that little statement would have cemented the feeling. "She'd probably be thrilled for me," I said, shaking my head.

His quiet laugh curled my toes. He leaned down and kissed me. "Colleen." His sigh warmed me all over.

"Come on." I threw on a robe and guided him back down the stairs so he wouldn't hit all the creaky spots. At the kitchen door, I melted into his arms. His goodbye kiss had me seriously reconsidering his departure and selfishly not caring about my aged grandmother.

"I'll see you in a few hours," he said with one last kiss and a smile.

After sneaking back up the stairs, I managed to get a full three hours of contented, sated sleep.

I tossed off my covers and whispered a big thank you to the gods of good weather, then jumped in the shower.

I dressed with a little more care than usual and tried to convince myself it wasn't because I wanted to look good for Slade. I knew I was telling myself a bold-faced lie and said a couple of Hail Marys in penance as I combed on mascara.

Nanny was still asleep when it was time for me to go, so I left her a note telling her Cathleen would be by to pick her up and bring her to the retirement home before coming to the inn to officiate the wedding.

When I turned into Maureen's driveway, I spotted a huge white box van with *Garden of Eden Nursery* stenciled across the side.

After I parked, I grabbed my wedding emergency shopping bag from my trunk. I'd done too many weddings not to know bobby pins, spare pantyhose, hair spray, even the garter, were often forgotten in the confusion of everything. My shopping bag was filled with a plethora of items including—but not limited to—cosmetic (water-proof mascara), medicinal (over-the-counter headache and pain capsules), and personal (tampons, stockings). It had saved many a bride from a meltdown.

Maureen was in the dining room getting everything set up for a buffet breakfast for her guests.

"It's gorgeous outside," she said after bussing my cheek. "The perfect day for a wedding."

"And thank you, Jesus, for that. Anybody up yet?"

"Jack's parents have been down searching for coffee. Your buddy Slade went for run. They're the only ones I've seen so far, but it's still super early." She slid a side glance at me, a small, knowing tug lifting one corner of her mouth.

Last night, I'd planned on berating her for giving Slade my address. After the way the night went, though, I couldn't summon up any recrimination. Instead, I wanted to send her flowers as a thank you.

I kept silent, stole a slice of bacon from the warming dish, and then went out to check on the garden. As I'd hoped and dreamed, the pergola looked amazing.

Martina Petal, the owner and florist of Garden of Eden—and yes, her surname really is Petal—was on a ladder draping rose vines from the dome downward. Streams of vibrant green pinnate leaves were woven around each column, with alternating white, deep pumpkin, and yellow roses twined within the vines. Around the circumference of the top, Martina had placed a continuous crown of white roses, mixed with saffron-gold camellias.

Along the walkway leading up to the pergola, the same runner I'd used for Kimmy's wedding was in place between rows of white folding chairs on both sides. Martina's crew was busy setting up and arranging the chairs and the huge urns of flowers lining the path and climbing the three marble steps.

By the time the ceremony began, the sun would be high and the light dancing through the dome.

"Everything looks great, Martina."

"Hey, Coll. Thanks. You lucked out with the weather, because these blooms will last well into late afternoon. Any hotter or colder and they might not look as pretty during the ceremony."

I agreed, on both parts.

Charity would be bringing the wedding programs and the confetti for the guests in a little while. Since all was going well here, I went back inside and to the main dining room, which Maureen and her staff had set last night.

For her color scheme, Isabella had chosen to stick with the hues of the season. Deep woodsy-green tablecloths were topped with individual placemats of russet. Maureen had a huge collection of dinnerware she'd bought at consignment stores and auctions, and Isabella's choice fit perfectly. Deep gold thirteen-inch chargers were topped with ten-inch ivory plates whose outer perimeters were etched with bronze. On top of each plate was a gold linen napkin with a calligraphy menu courtesy of Charity's skills, over it, and then both were tied together with a few sprigs of sage and eucalyptus leaves, secured with a deep orange ribbon. The flatware was sterling, etched with curlicues along the borders.

Amber wine glasses were set next to the plates, with matching salad and fruit bowls to the side. Champagne flutes and water glasses completed each setting.

Maureen knew how to set a table; that was God's truth. Each round table sat eight. In the center were contrasting heights of clear glass vases Eileen had bought at a consignment house right before she got sick. Some were filled with the same colored roses adorning the pergola, some with miniature pumpkins, apples, and pinecones. Thick, white candles fit others. A linen runner in a chaos of golds and russets ran through the center of each table and draped over the edges.

Putting her calligraphy talents to good use once again, Charity had written each guest's name and table number on a separate seating card which was now arranged on a table positioned next to the dining room entrance door. The cards were made of thick pale pumpkin cardstock, a hand-cut leaf affixed to one corner. We'd spent what seemed like a dozen hours over the past week cutting and pasting the leaves to the cards. When we were finished, my fingers ached and my eyes were bleeding with fatigue. God was certainly in the details, because the cards were unique, and I knew Isabella was going to love them.

At the back of the spacious room, a stage had been fashioned for the four-piece band due to start setting up in a few hours.

A quick check of the time on my phone told me Isabella had about a half hour before she was due at the local beauty salon/spa for her hair and makeup. I'd added appointments for Vivi, Jill, and Bailey as well. I hadn't for Janelle. When I'd originally emailed her about it, she'd responded not to bother. Even though she didn't want to take advantage of the service, I imagined she might want to at least accompany her daughter while she was made-up for her big day. Janelle's behavior of late made me not so certain of that any more.

"You're early," a familiar voice said from behind me.

How was it possible for anyone to look so damn good all the time? Slade was leaning against the doorjamb, arms crossed over his chest. He'd obviously just finished his run, evidenced by the steam gusting off his sweating body. His hair was plastered to his head, the ends spikey with perspiration. A saturated blue T-shirt molded and outlined every curve and bend of muscle in his torso and abdomen. Every. Single. One. The sweatpants dropping down his long, long legs rode low on his hips. Like the shirt, they clung to his thick, muscular thighs and did nothing to hide their power and bulging firmness.

Mother of God.

A ball of instant lust bounced through me, and I started to drool—*drool*! I swallowed, my neck muscles tight and rigid against the movement. "Game day," I managed to say. Okay, it was really more of a toad-like croak, but I couldn't help it. The man turned every fiber of my being, every system in my body, every nerve ending, to the *on* position.

He smiled and my toes curled up inside my pumps.

"So this is your, what?" He moved toward me, stealthily, predatory, his hands dropping to his sides, flexing and extending his fingers as he walked. His lips lifted a bit. "Game day uniform?"

He stopped right in front of me. The surrounding air went up a good ten degrees around me from the heat sluicing off him, but my body responded as if it had been slapped with an icepack. My nipples pulled to two painful points inside my lace bra, and my skin prickled with goosebumps, precisely the way it had when he'd kissed me right before leaving my house several hours before. My nostrils flared, filled with the fragrance of the autumn woods he'd run through, mixed together with his natural, earthy, *manly* scent. Desire drenched me.

Slade reached out and pinched the lapel of my suit jacket. "This color is gorgeous on you." His voice dropped to a sexy, just-out-of-bed timbre that made my knees wobble. "What's it called?"

"Aub-aubergine. You know? Like eggplant?"

His left eyebrow lifted, and his eyes twinkled with mirth.

"It's more like an autumn plum, and since Isabella wanted a fall color scheme, I thought this would be a good way to blend in when I'm running around and making sure things go as planned." I swallowed again. "I don't like standing out or drawing attention to myself when I'm working. I want people focused on the bride and the groom, so"—I shrugged—"this seemed like the ideal color for blending. So, yeah. Um…aubergine."

I really needed to get some kind of therapy to correct this nervous babbling Tourette's.

Slade's grin turned wicked, his eyes filling with heat. His fingers clenched my lapel and pulled me in closer with a simple tug. My senses were quite completely filled with the very essence of him. "Am I making you nervous?"

"You're making me insane," I blurted. Lowering my voice, I added, "Do you know how incredibly hot you are right now, all sweaty and perfect and—" I waved my hand in front of his body, in lieu of finding the right way to describe what he looked like.

Is *orgasmalicious* a word?

That wicked mouth widened, and I knew exactly how Red Riding Hood felt when the Wolf grinned at her—like she was about to be devoured. Whole.

A breath later, I was.

Slade's kiss sent an erotic shudder down my spine so powerful, my heart stopped then kicked back in at twice the normal rate. The only part of his body in contact with mine was his mouth, but he had me in a stronghold I couldn't move out of. Not that I wanted to. Ever.

With innate mastery, his tongue parted my lips and feasted. He cupped my chin to hold me in place and tilted my head back a bit. The angle allowed him full power over the kiss, which I willingly gave up. I couldn't have fought for control even if I wanted to, which—believe me—I didn't.

Did I call him a master at the art of the kiss? What's higher than a master? A prefect? A god? Whatever it was, Slade was so far up the scale, he made his own title.

He kept his body separated from mine, and I instinctively knew it was because I was dressed for the long day ahead of us while he was still in sweaty running clothes and needed a shower. I had an overpowering urge to step into him, wrap my arms around his trim waist, and forget everything. One of us needed to be the stronger person here, and I'm so glad it was Slade because if he'd even shifted a whisper closer to me, I would have put my yearning into action.

All too soon he pulled back. It took me a few moments to open my eyes and focus. When I did, he was grinning down at me again, his head tilted to one side and his fists back on his hips.

"Insane, huh?" He shook his head. "Now you know what I feel like every time we're in the same room and I can't touch you. Insane describes it perfectly."

A lump formed in the back of my throat. If I opened my mouth the frog brigade would croak again, so I took a few calming breaths instead.

"Colleen."

My name had never sounded so sweet. A million tiny fluttering butterflies beat against my spandex-free tummy muscles. There was something hidden in the way he said my name. Something…promising.

Slade shook his head and stared down at the floor for a second, before pulling his gaze back to mine. A long, deep exhale filled with resignation blew passed his crooked grin. "Not the right time," he murmured, almost more to himself, than to me. "I've gotta go grab a shower, get some breakfast. You'll be around?"

"I'm taking Isabella and the girls to the beauty salon in a bit. As soon as we get back, it'll be time for her to get dressed and ready."

Was that regret in his eyes?

"Charity and Kolby will be here, though, if you need anything. Maureen's available, too. Just ask."

Slade took a step closer to me again. "I wish this day was over already." His voice was soft and low, and a firestorm of need flamed low in my belly. "I wish I was back in your bed, this day behind us. I'd be able to take my time with you, knowing I had all the time in world. All the time to make you"—he leaned a little closer, dropped his voice to a caress—"scream my name over and over."

What would it have cost me to admit to him I wanted that, too? Too much, at the moment. "Don't say that." I took his hand in mine. "Don't wish your sister's day away. She deserves an entire day filled with wonderful, lifelong memories. Don't wish it away for her."

He covered my hand with his free one, sandwiching mine between them. "I'm not. I want Izzy to have her moment, I do. I just want you, too." A thin line spread between his brows. "I-it's just…"

"What?" I squeezed his hand. "Tell me.

His breath was deep and if I had to hazard a guess, troubled. With another shake of his head, he said, "Nothing. Sorry. I'm in a mood. I've been thinking about potential parental drama. Today is the first time Janelle and my father have seen one another in a while. I'm not anticipating a happy reunion. For me, either."

Why didn't I believe seeing his father was the root of his unease?

Before I could probe further, he stepped back. "Listen. I'm gonna go get cleaned up. I know you're going to be busy all day, but remember your promise." That penetrating gaze of his seared right thought me. "I'm collecting at the reception, and you're not gonna worm out of it."

Like I would? *Please*. My parents didn't raise an idiot, just a nervous twitterer. "I always keep my promises," I told him.

"I'm betting on it." He kissed my cheek and left me.

Something was up with him, weighing on his mind. While he might be a little anxious about how his father and ex-stepmom would behave, I'd wager the secret stash of chocolate-covered peppermint candies hidden in my office drawer for emotional emergencies, that wasn't all that was bothering him.

I'd heard no mention of the prenup agreement in the past few weeks. Could that be it? Was he still worried Jack wasn't going to sign it and now, at the eleventh hour when the vows were due to be said, he couldn't convince his sister to agree to it? Slade was in charge of the family trust and all the financial dealings concerning his sister. As soon as she was legally bound to Jack, everything would change and Isabella would come into her inheritance. While I knew in my soul Jack would never take advantage of his wealthy wife, in his mind, Slade had fifteen million reasons to be concerned he might. Carrying an emotional burden like that had to be taxing.

My phone pinged with a reminder about the beauty appointments.

I tucked Slade's mood into the back of my mind as I went in search of my bride.

Three hours later, I was kneeling in front of Isabella, sliding on the blue garter that had belonged to Jack's great-grandmother into position. Something old, borrowed, and blue all in the same package.

Score.

Once it was in place, my beautiful bride lowered her dress, and Charity and I fluffed it out around her.

My assistant's sigh was loud, long, and wistful. "You look amazeballs."

Isabella and I laughed.

Janelle, who was standing off to the side inspecting her daughter's reflection in the tri-fold mirror Maureen had provided, pursed her lips. "I'm not quite certain what that word means, but you do look lovely, Isabella. And, I'll admit, happy."

"I'm going to second your mother's words, Izzy baby."

"Daddy!"

As a unit, all heads turned to the doorway, which I hadn't heard open. An exceptionally good-looking and very tanned gentleman bedecked in a designer black tuxedo beamed at Isabella. Silver hair, perfectly styled and lustrous, covered his head in thick waves. His eyes were a bit richer in their amber color than his son's, but the gold flecks in the center of his irises were Slade's twin. Age crinkled at the corners of his eyes and fanned out to his temples when he smiled as his daughter threw her arms around him.

Facial features weren't the only thing the two Harrington men shared. Height, carriage, and charisma claimed them both, but on the elder, I sensed an easygoing contentment I hadn't gleaned from Slade.

"I'm so glad you got here in time," Isabella said.

"We checked in while you were off getting your hair done. Shirley's getting ready. She said to wish you good luck but knows you won't need it."

"You brought her with you?" Janelle's voice cut through the room like a sharpened razor. "It isn't enough you have to show your face, but to bring that...that...*woman* here is too much."

Peggy Jaeger

My stomach stopped, dropped, and rolled, but I didn't think that would extinguish this drama inferno. Isabella's bright smile disappeared, and a thin line etched between her brows. Before I could say a word— and the words on the tip of my tongue were *get out*— Slade's father moved from his daughter to his ex-wife.

I had a passing moment of irrational terror that he was going to strike her.

With his smile still in place, although not as bright as when it was aimed at his daughter, Edward Harrington bent and placed a chaste kiss on Janelle's cheek.

Who in the room was more surprised was debatable. Charity's loud gasp was drowned out by my swift and deep inhale, while Isabella stood rock still, staring at her parents with a strange mix of wonder and confusion.

I knew exactly how she felt.

"Beautiful as always, Janie. Right now, our daughter looks remarkably like you did on our wedding day."

Janelle seemed as confused as her daughter. A smidgen of pleasure broke through, though, at the statement, evidenced when her shrewish expression softened. Looking up at the man she'd been married to, she shook her head and said, "I'm surprised you even remember *what* I looked like on that day."

"Radiant," Harrington replied immediately, his smile widening. "Like the sun had come out after a rain storm. I remember you stole my breath away when I saw you gliding down the aisle on your father's arm."

Janelle's lips pulled up, and for the first time since I'd met her, she smiled. It transformed her face. The resemblance of daughter to mother was profound with that smile.

Janelle swatted her ex-husband's arm. "Don't try to charm me, Edward. I'm immune to you."

If possible, Harrington's smile got brighter. He reminded me a great deal of my father. The commanding presence, the air of inbred confidence. My father could be both charming and irritating at much the same times. Those qualities, mixed with a brilliant, logical mind made him a man to be respected and revered.

But he'd always been just Daddy to me, much the way I assumed Edward was to Isabella.

I snuck a quick look at Charity, and she at me. The slight elevation of her shoulders and look of bafflement on her face mimicked my own bewilderment.

Rich people are different. Enough said.

As long as they weren't upsetting their daughter, I didn't care if they started locking lips and reminiscing about old times on the family yacht.

And speaking of their daughter...

"Isabella," I said, morphing into professional planner again and not family-drama rubbernecker, "we need to finish getting you ready."

"I'll leave you ladies, then," Harrington said. He took his daughter's hands in his own and brought them to his lips. "I can't believe my baby is getting married."

"Believe it," she told him.

"He'd better be worthy of you, is all I can say."

"He is, Daddy. He is."

I tossed Janelle a look, one eyebrow raised as if daring her to contradict that statement. Her lips pressed together in a thin line, but she kept whatever she was thinking to herself.

"Knock. Knock. You decent?" Slade popped his head around the door, his gaze sweeping the room and finding Isabella.

The smiles on the male members of this family were lethal.

He pushed through the door, and I got my first look at Slade Harrington in a tuxedo.

He was orgasmalicious in sweaty running gear, but in formal wear?

There's this dessert called Death by Chocolate. It's a trifle made of individual layers of dark chocolate cake soaked with rum, whipped cream, chocolate pudding, and then chunks of either English toffee or any other milk-chocolate bar. It's layered cake, cream, pudding, and candy in a real trifle bowl, twice. If you've ever tasted it, you know your taste buds have never been the same since. With Slade's eyes on his sister, my gaze dragged over every inch of him, and it came to me in a nanosecond. Slade Harrington was my personal Death by Chocolate.

His gaze shifted to the man holding Isabella's hand and his devastating smile evaporated. Back stiffening, gaze hardening, Slade peered at the father he hadn't seen in years, and the savage look parading across his face had me thinking blood would be spilled before this day was done.

My own gaze ping-ponged from Slade to his father then back again. The elder Harrington's face betrayed none of the anger on his son's. In fact, he seemed pleased to be in the same room with him. He dropped his daughter's hands and then slid them into his tuxedo trouser pockets. Rocking back on his heels, he gave off a calm, non-threatening vibe as he stared across the room.

"Slade," he said by way of address.

I watched Slade's jaw clamp down, fearful his back molars would crack from the force.

"Dad." So much emotion was packed into that little word, it took me a moment to register he hadn't moved from inside the doorway. "I didn't know you'd arrived."

"About an hour ago. Shirley is upstairs getting ready."

Slade didn't reply.

"You're looking well son. Fit. Business is good?"

"Fine."

For a few tense moments, the air was thick with history, unasked questions, and a lifetime of suppressed emotions. I could only imagine what was flowing through Slade's mind as he stood in front of the father whose behavior had forced him to alter his life path to save the family company. I couldn't read the elder Harrington's mind at all. He could have been waiting to drag Slade into his arms like a prodigal or biding his time to lash out at him for usurping the company. Either way, both men were wary and cautious of one another.

I wanted to go to Slade, wrap my arms around him, and bring the light I was used to seeing back into his eyes. Then I wanted to smack him in the arm, scream, "Suck it up. This is your sister's day," and get the wedding started.

Isabella's nervous glance toward me is what prompted me into action.

"I'm going to have to ask you all to leave now," I said, firmly, my tone brooking no arguments. "We need to finish getting Isabella ready so the ceremony can start."

Janelle, either sensing something was going to happen she wanted no part of—like a blowup between father and son—or because she simply wanted no extended part in the wedding (which is what I really believed) was the first to move. With a perfunctory kiss to her daughter's cheek, Janelle told her, "I hope…"

"Yes, Mother?"

I held my breath for the reply, praying it would be something encouraging, or loving, or—damn it—maternal.

Janelle sighed. "I hope you know what you're doing, Isabella."

Not exactly what I would have said to a daughter about to marry the man she loved. The urge to slap this selfish, silly woman raged inside me. I caught Charity's gaze as she squinched her face into an angry scowl and shook my head. I wasn't going to allow either one of us to say what we really felt.

Isabella never even flinched at her mother's ill-meaning words. With a smile mimicking the most serene of princesses, she said, "More than you know, Mother."

With resignation on her face, Janelle nodded once to her daughter, then to her ex-husband. Slade, and the rest of us in the room, she ignored. The tension in the space, unfortunately, didn't exit with her.

"Your mother hasn't changed much," Edward told his daughter with a shake of his head and a rueful grin. "I'm sure she's happy for you. She just has a hard time expressing it."

Isabella's face gave no indication of what she

thought about that.

"I'll go get Shirley and find our seats." Edward took his daughter's hands and squeezed them again. With love shining through his eyes, he smiled down at her. "Your fiancé is a very lucky man, Izzy. I can't wait to meet him."

"I'm the lucky one, Daddy. And you're gonna love Jack."

He kissed her cheek. "Since you do, I'm sure I will. Well." He glanced around the room. "I guess I'll leave you all to it, then."

With one last kiss for his daughter, Edward moved to leave. As he brushed past his son, he stopped. Slade flinched when his father lifted a hand and squeezed his upper arm.

Edward disregarded the movement. "Thank you, Son, for giving her this. I'm so pleased you're walking her down the aisle. You've been a better father to her than I ever was."

I fell a little in love with Harrington Senior right then.

Slade's rigid posture stiffened even more, his shoulders squaring under this tuxedo with such a firm snap, I was worried the fabric would rip.

A quick, mechanical head bob was his only answer.

Isabella took a deep, barely audible breath when he left.

"Charity, go check on Jill and Bailey and let me know how they're doing, time-wise," I instructed.

Then, it was only the three of us left in the room.

Slade closed his eyes and rolled his neck. When he opened them again, he zeroed in on his sister and his eyes softened. "You look so beautiful, Izzy. Like the princess you are. That dress is perfect for you."

I could tell she was pleased from the way she grabbed onto the skirt, lifted it a bit, and then swayed right and left. "It is pretty, isn't it?"

"Pretty doesn't do it justice." He moved toward her, and the two of them embraced.

My heart stuttered a bit, and tears stung the back of my eyes. I blinked like a crazed hummingbird flapping at a bird feeder, to push them back.

Slade's gaze caught mine over his sister's head. He had a question in his eyes. About what, though?

A thought for later. Right now, I needed to go into command mode.

"Okay, you two. Enough for now. Slade, let her go. She just spent two hours in hair and makeup, and I don't want her smudged before Kolby gets some shots."

A knock on the door a half second later had me saying "Come in," and, as if I'd conjured him with my words, my fabulous photographer walked in. The next few minutes were spent in photo-mode as he posed brother and sister in a variety of stances and snapped away.

"Okay, bride-alone time," he announced, as Charity came in and said, "The girls are ready."

I spotted the quick glower she tossed Kolby and wondered for the thousandth time what had happened between the two of them. They used to be the best of friends, but lately they acted as if they couldn't stand to be in the same room with one another, much less work together. More thoughts left for later.

"We don't need you anymore for now," Kolby told Slade, "but I'll get a few pics of you two together right before you go down the aisle, okay?"

Slade nodded, tossed a quick glance at me, and then said to his sister, "I'll see you in a few minutes, Izzy."

"Wait." She stepped around Kolby and pulled something from her purse. "Here." She handed her brother an envelope, and I'll admit, my curiosity was piqued. "Signed, sealed, delivered. I don't want to hear you ever mention this again. Deal?"

Slade's beaming smile knocked me back a few paces so hard, I thought I was going to stumble and land on my ass. Whatever she'd handed him had completely erased the shadows I'd seen in his eyes when he'd come face to face with his father.

"Deal." He kissed her cheek. "It's for the best, Izzy. You know that."

"No, I don't, but I don't want to talk about it anymore. I've had enough talking about it to last me a lifetime."

The prenup.

It was the only thing that made sense. But why, and more importantly *how*, had he convinced her to let Jack sign it?

"So we won't." He bussed her cheek again and said, "I promise I'll never mention it again."

"Good."

With a fast, private wink at me, he left as Charity brought the rest of the bridal party in.

All thoughts of the legal document flew from my head. I had a ceremony about to start, and I needed to stay focused for my bride.

Chapter Twenty

What is it about two people pledging themselves to one another for all eternity that fills me with the sense all is right in the world? You'd think after all this time the wedding ritual would be old hat to me, but it was just the opposite. Every ceremony was fresh and new and filled with different levels and types of love.

Isabella and Jack's ceremony was one I will remember long after I take down my business shingle and retire my planner book.

As Slade held his sister's arm and walked her over the runner to meet her soon-to-be husband, my heart sighed loud and long. When they stopped at the pergola, Slade unwound her hand from his arm and slid it into Jack's waiting one—in essence—handing her over to her husband-to-be. He bent and gave her a kiss on each cheek, murmured something that had her laughing, and then went to take his seat. It didn't get past my notice that Katya Yurlenko was in the seat next to his. As soon as he moved to his spot, the model twined her arm in the crook of his elbow, leaned in, and kissed him. Granted, it was a quick, passionless little buss on the cheek, but still it caused a cauldron of jealousy to come to a rolling boil inside me.

True, I had no claim on Slade. He'd made it plain he wanted me in a purely physical sense while I was the one dumb enough to let my heart get involved. But it did sting to know he had other women, gorgeous women, *supermodels*, for pity's sake, who also wanted and who had, apparently, already had him.

When Jack walked Isabella up the steps to meet Cathleen, I snapped out of my thoughts, determined to concentrate on the event going on around me. An event depending on me to make it perfect.

The autumn afternoon sunshine shone down bright and luminous as the bride and her groom stood inside the pergola holding hands, the light billowing upon them through the design-cut dome and bathing them in warmth and joy.

After meeting with and then spending an afternoon with the happy couple, Cathy had gotten to know them. Once she'd read their questionnaires, she was able to write the perfect, individual ceremony to memorialize their day.

At one point, she mentioned their mutual love of old black and white movies. "Like one of their favorite films, *The Thin Man*," Cathy read from her prepared notes, "Jack describes Isabella as the perfect Nora to his Nick Charles. His partner in crime and his cohort for life. Together, Jack says, there's nothing he can't face if he has his dollface at his side, armed with a witty, deadpan comeback and dry martini in her hand."

The guests all laughed.

"Although Jack does admit Isabella will probably replace the martini with a pomegranate cosmo." More laughter. "It's more her style."

I did a quick pan of my staff. Kolby was on one side of the garden, his camera lifted to his face as he snapped away nonstop. Charity was on the opposite side, her eyes trained on Bailey who'd begun to grow antsy and fidgety while standing with her mother. Charity had already discussed with Jill in the event her daughter started to fuss, she'd take Bailey from the ceremony and bring her to the kitchen where Maureen would fill her with sweets and distract her until after the vows were said.

And when it came time for the vows, once again my sister wrote the perfect declarations for the couple.

"Isabella, will you promise to Jack, from this day forward, you will always know where your apartment keys, checkbook, and cell phone are, so you two can get out of the house on time?"

The bride laughed and tossed her groom a heavy-lidded glare. "Yes, I will."

"Jack, will you promise from this day forth to always make sure there is a spare milk bottle in the fridge before you drink the last drop of one, and when you eat the last of the leftover chicken, you tell Isabella before she plans on using it for the next night's dinner?"

With a good-natured eye roll, Jack said, "I promise. It'll be hard, but I promise."

When the guests stopped laughing, Cathleen continued.

"Do you two pledge to one another no matter what the reason, you will never, never go to bed angry with the other, always do your best to make the other person laugh and feel loved, and to listen to the other finish speaking no matter how much you want to interrupt?"

"We will," they said in unison.

"Do you promise to walk side by side, through whatever life brings you, good or bad, and always have each others' backs?"

"We do."

"And do you promise to encourage one another, trust each other, seek the other's council, ask for help when needed, and give it without question when it's asked for?"

"We do."

"And finally, Jackson and Isabella, do you promise to put the other's happiness and well-being above all else material and worldly, respect your differences, embrace your similarities, and love the other unconditionally and unequivocally, no matter what befalls you in life?"

They squeezed each other's hands, gazed into one another's eyes, and vowed, "We do."

Cathy closed her prayer book and smiled widely. "Then, by the power vested in me by the state of New Hampshire, I proudly, loudly, and joyously pronounce you...married."

A sea of clapping and crying filled the garden. Vivi and her husband were clapping *and* crying. Loudly.

"This is my favorite part," Cathy announced. She turned her attention to Jack. "Please seal your vows to one another with your first married kiss. And make it a good one."

With the sound of laughter ringing around them, Jack swooped Isabella into one arm, bent her backward over it, and with a grin as big as the garden surrounding them, planted a doozy on her. Isabella's entire body was shaking with laughter when their lips met. In the next instant, she dropped her flowers to the marble floor and twined her arms around his neck.

Even from where I was standing fifteen feet away, I heard Charity sigh. Hers started a wave of them through the aisles.

When they came up for air and Jack righted her again, Jill, crying and grinning, handed Isabella her flowers. Arm in arm, they faced their guests, and Cathy proclaimed, "It's my pleasure to present Dr. and the-very-well-kissed Mrs. Jackson Rainier, everyone."

Applause broke, loud and free, around the garden.

The couple made their way down the steps and then along the runner back to the inn to a chorus of clapping.

****

"Your bride's feet are gonna be sore tomorrow," Maureen announced as she glided past me, a bottle of champagne in each hand. She handed them off to Devon. "She hasn't sat down once since the reception started," she added when she went by again and back toward the kitchen.

From my vantage point in the back of the ballroom, the dance floor was filled while Maureen's servers bussed the tables from the first course, Isabella in the center of the dancing throng in her brother's arms. The band they'd chosen played all genres of music from pop to rock, swing to old standards. Currently, the lead singer was channeling Old Blue Eyes. Growing up with Nanny Fee, I'd had a fabulous education in music appreciation that served me well when helping couples decide on musical themes for their receptions.

So far, the reception had been stress and problem-free. Isabella had made the intelligent and tactful decision of dividing the parent tables into three camps. Janelle, her husband Fred, and their guests were seated at one; Edward Harrington and his new wife were seated at another with some of the Harrington extended family; and Jack's parents were with their immediate family members. Maureen had placed Jack and Isabella at their own table for two, their families flanking them. I'd done too many weddings where divorced parents were placed with their exes and new spouses and knew it was never a good arrangement. An open bar with easy access to alcohol, years of pent-up martial rage, and the heightened emotions of the day had caused many a reception yell-fest. Kolby and Devon had been forced to step in once or twice to pull back fists from flying. Charity had done due diligence once as well when she stopped a first wife from pulling out the extensions of a second wife as the wedding cake was being sliced.

Slade had elected to sit at his own table, surrounded by several of the Harrington board members and their wives. Oh, and of course, Katya. The six-foot beauty had changed after the ceremony from a flowy, calf-length deep green garden dress to a micro-mini jet-black backless little number that was almost frontless as well. I was betting there was a yard of double stick tape keeping the bodice (what there was of it) in place and not allowing the guests a view of her perfect twenty-something breasts.

I'd been told on several occasions that the supermodel was just a family friend, and I wanted to believe it. I really did. It was a little difficult though when every time I glanced over at their table she was touching Slade, leaning into him as he spoke, whispering into his ear. Her behavior was very friendly, but it wasn't the let's-go-grab-a-cup-of-coffee-and-catch-up friendly. It was more of an I've-seen-this-hunk-of-gorgeous-man-naked friendly. You know the kind of friend I mean. The one with *benefits.*

The dance floor started to clear as the servers began bringing out the main course. I caught the best man at the bar before he went back to his seat and reminded him now would be a good time to make his speech.

When he got back to his table, he lifted his champagne glass, clinked it a few times, and called for quiet. A quick toast to the happy couple and then he started. While he was speaking, I took a moment to slip out onto the terrace for some air.

Laughter and cheering followed me on the air as Gage told a funny story about how he and Jack had met and become instant friends.

Daylight Savings Time had come and settled in the week before so even though it was barely six p.m., it was full on dark outside. As I walked the length of the terrace, my thoughts were running with all the details left for this wedding and then the one I was in charge of for tomorrow. I was so engrossed in my thoughts, I never saw the person standing in front of me until I almost mowed him down.

"Oh." I sprang backward, and a hand came out to steady me. "Mr. Harrington, please forgive me. I didn't see you there."

He had one hand on my arm as an anchor, in the other a cigar. It goes to show you how engrossed in my thoughts I was that I never smelled the strong aroma of it burning.

"Miss…O'Dowd, is it?"

"Yes, sir."

He released my arm. "You're the wedding planner."

Since it wasn't a question, I simply nodded.

"It seems I owe you a huge debt of thanks."

"I'm sorry?"

"For my presence here today." He tilted his head to one side. "I understand you were instrumental in my being allowed to attend my daughter's wedding since my son was against it. When Izzy emailed me, she told me you were able to sway Slade's opinion on the matter."

"I didn't sway him, sir. I simply pointed out today should be all about Isabella's happiness, and if it made her happy to invite both her parents, then she should be allowed to do so without worrying about any—" I came to a halt, realizing I was about to say something I had no business saying.

"Any what? Shouting matches? Uncomfortable, emotional scenes? Bloodshed?" His lips lifted at the corners.

"I was going to say consequences."

He puffed on his cigar again, his expression unreadable. "Different word, same meaning," he told me. "Regardless, thank you for whatever you said to my son. Capitulation isn't a virtue of his."

I kept my mouth shut because, well, he was right. But I wasn't going to say that. It seemed a little traitorous to Slade.

"I don't know what I would have done if you hadn't been able to smooth the waters. Probably shown up anyway." He chuckled and shook his head before having another puff of his cigar. "Isabella is, after all, my little girl. My only daughter. And although I haven't been a presence in her day-to-day life, I've never missed a major event and wasn't going to this time. But there would have been a scene, words would have been spoken that should stay silent. I didn't want Izzy's day ruined if I showed up, uninvited and unannounced."

"I know she's glad you're here, sir."

"At least one of my children is," he answered.

Nope. Not touching that line either. "Well. I apologize again," I said, instead, "for bumping into you. I wasn't watching where I was going, and frankly, I didn't expect anyone to be out here. You might want to get back inside. The main course is being served now, and Isabella has mentioned how fond you are of fresh salmon."

In the darkness, his smile illuminated the space between us. "Izzy has a wonderful memory for stuff like that. Always remembers little things about people she uses to make them feel comfortable. She's a lot like her mother is. Well, used to be, anyway, when we were married. Izzy's going to be a wonderful asset to her husband's future."

I remembered what Slade had said about Janelle raising her daughter to be a politician's wife. To be an extension of her husband's career and life, in lieu of having one of her own. It appeared Daddy dearest thought along the same lines.

It was a bit disconcerting Isabella's parents didn't think she could be something worthy all by herself.

"Isabella is a lovely, warm-hearted, and extremely intelligent young woman," I said. "She'll be wonderful at anything she chooses to do."

Harrington silently appraised me through the smoke billowing up from his cigar. A flash of déjà vu sped through me. Slade had given me the same look the day we'd met.

"I get the impression you're very good at what you do, Miss O'Dowd. And very loyal to your clients."

Again, it wasn't a question, so I stayed silent.

"There you are."

Slade.

"I've been looking all over for you."

I turned and *Lord, help me.* The man looked like he'd just jumped off the screen from one of those 1930s rom-coms his sister and her new husband adored. Dashing, debonair, so damn self-assured, the man revved me up and made my legs go weak at the same time.

"What are you doing out here?"

The grin on his face died a quick death when he noticed who I was with.

"What's going on?" he asked. I wasn't sure the question was directed at me or his father, because though he'd stopped next to me, his heated stare lasered on the man standing in front of me.

"Dad?"

Harrington senior flicked a few ashes from his cigar, pulled it back toward his mouth, and puffed, twice, before replying. "Miss O'Dowd and I were just having a little chat, son. That's all."

Slade turned his attention to me. It didn't take a forensic facial profiler to decipher the look on his face. Slade was pissed. But at who? Me? His father? Both of us? "Colleen?"

I took a breath and measured my words. I didn't want to say anything to fuel the smoldering fire between these two.

"We were talking about Isabella and the wedding."

"What about it?" Slade slid his gaze to his father.

"Complaining it's not up to your usual standards? Not grand enough for you and your so-called status? You can save it." He shook his head, disgust competing with the anger on his face. "I already had this discussion with Janelle. I'm going to tell you what I told her. This is what Isabella and Jack wanted. Not some stuffy society shindig with people who only show their faces so they can gossip later on and deride everything they saw. It's their wedding. End of discussion." He turned to me and took my arm. "Come on, let's go back inside."

Before I could say a word or protest, Slade stopped in his tracks when his father said, "Son."

The word was said with such care and emotion, both our heads whipped to the man who'd uttered it.

Edward Harrington's eyes were glistening in the semi-dark, his bottom lip quivering. "Thank you," he said.

"For what?"

"For being the man you are. For being so loyal and loving to your sister. For stepping into the role of father and protector when I didn't. I'm proud of you, Slade. I'm proud of the man you've become."

I felt his body shake as he held my arm. I lifted my free hand and placed it over his. He flicked me a glance then turned back to his father.

"When Isabella told me how involved you were in her wedding, how you were the one paying for it, helping to plan it, and not Janelle, well, I have to admit I was a little taken aback."

"I'd do anything for my sister. You know that."

Edward's smile was sad as he nodded. "But I also know how you feel about marriage."

Slade's nostrils flared as he sucked in a breath. "And whose fault is that?"

"Mine. I take full responsibility for jading you. I let my heart rule my head too many times, I know, but I wanted to believe I could find happiness again after your mother died. And I finally have."

"Six is the lucky number?" Slade's cutting tone had me squeezing his arm.

"I know it's hard for you to believe this, son, but I loved each and every one of them—"

"Until you didn't."

"—but none of them was your mother."

Slade went rigid beneath my touch. He may have even stopped breathing for a few seconds.

"I loved your mother more than life itself. She was everything, *everything*, to me. After she died, I wanted to find that kind of love again. I needed to. I thought I had with Janelle." He shook his head again and dropped his gaze down. "But, through no fault of her own, she wasn't your mother. None of the other ones were, either. I admit, I made bad choices, impulsive ones. I acted irrationally, and because of it I almost lost the company." He lifted his head. "But you saved it. You stepped in when you didn't want to and did everything in your power to right my wrongs. I'm grateful in ways I can never express to you."

"You weren't grateful at the time," Slade said. Anger filled the words, but there was pain mixed in with them, too.

Edward lowered his head for a moment. "I know. I said some terrible things to you. Things that I can never take back and believe me, I would if possible. I know you and I have had our differences—"

Slade chortled.

"—and I know I've made mistakes." His eyes looked pleadingly at his son. "But can't you forgive an old man his mistakes? I love you, son. I miss you."

Slade said nothing. I squeezed his arm again, but he didn't respond. His attention was fully focused on his father, and I got the impression he was holding himself in check. "That's a lot to ask, considering."

With resignation on his face, Edward flicked burning ash from his cigar.

"Okay. I accept you can't forgive me. In truth, I didn't think you would. But I'd like to say something to you, now, since I probably won't get another chance to."

Slade's shrug mimicked his father's. "Go ahead."

Edward took a breath before he spoke. "Please don't let my actions, my mistakes, prevent you from finding love."

"*What?*"

"You know what I'm saying. I loved your mother. We would still be married if she hadn't died. But she did. And I found Janelle. I know how hard bringing her into our home was for you, but think about this, son. If I hadn't married her, we wouldn't have Isabella in our lives."

I thought that was a good point but kept my mouth shut. This discussion was one I shouldn't be privy to, and I was getting more uncomfortable by the moment being so. I'd started to move away a few times, but Slade's grip had tightened each time I had.

"I opened my heart to finding love again after your mother. You've closed yours off because of my actions. You've become a successful, formidable man, but I'd hate to see you go through the rest of your life alone, without a woman by your side, encouraging you, supporting you, loving you. You deserve that, son. Every man does."

With a practiced flick of his wrist, he dropped the cigar and then crushed it beneath his shoe.

"I hope when the right woman comes your way you let her into your heart. Now, if you'll both excuse me, I want to go dance with my daughter on her wedding day. Miss. O'Dowd, it's been a pleasure."

I nodded.

He strode back toward the ballroom.

Under my hand, Slade's entire body exhaled. I wanted to say something but didn't know what. Should I be encouraging? Comforting? Funny? That was the one I usually went with when emotional scenes developed. If I could make someone laugh, the situation didn't seem so horrible, then.

My relationship—if that's what it was—was still too new with Slade to know what would help him. If the situation were reversed, I would want to dissect the conversation I'd just had, go over it again and again, until it was emotionally picked clean like leftover carrion after vultures have swooped away.

But that was me, not Slade.

The decision on what, or what not, to say was taken from me when Slade closed his eyes and said, "I'm sorry."

"What for?"

He opened them again. Regret tinged with sadness stared back at me.

"That little father/son discussion you just had? Please." I swiped my hand in the air. If I knew how to pronounce *pshaw* correctly I would have added it. "That was tame compared to some family drama I've been stuck in the middle of at a wedding. Remind me to tell you sometime about the filet mignon that got tossed at the mother of the groom by the mother of the bride."

He cocked his head, his brows pulling together. Okay, so maybe funny was exactly the way to go in this situation.

"Or the time a best man gave a drunken toast detailing how he'd spent the night before in the then bride-to-be's bed. A very detailed story it was, too."

Slade's mouth flew open.

"I've even had a ceremony come to a screeching halt when the pastor asked does anyone have any reason this man and woman shouldn't be wed and a voice piped up from the back of the church. Seems the groom was already married to someone else, and she was due to pop out baby number two any second."

"Colleen."

I squeezed his hand. "Look. No punches were thrown. No blood was spilled. The police weren't called to the scene. I'd call that a win by anyone's standards."

I was thrilled when the sorrow lifted from his eyes. His gorgeous mouth pulled into a good-natured smirk that had those darling dimples popping up on both cheeks.

Without any kind of warning, he swept me into his arms and pulled me close. He nudged my head down onto his shoulder, and I complied. Willingly. He wound his hands around my waist, and I did the same to him.

"Thank you," he said.

"Not necessary."

We stood that way for a moment, just gently

holding one another.

When Slade pulled back a bit, I lifted my head.

"I came looking for you because I wanted to collect on your promise."

"My promise? Oh, you mean a dance."

"Mmm."

A subtle shift in his stance and we were swaying to and fro.

"Well, from the way my feet are moving, I'd say you'd accomplished your mission."

The devilish smile he tossed me kicked my already bounding pulse faster. He kissed the tip of my nose, and can I just tell you, I nearly swooned. It sounds better to describe it that way than to boldly say the crotch of my thong grew wet.

I laid my head back down on his shoulder as Slade pulled my body flat up against his. Each gentle shift and sway of our bodies against the other was like a thousand electrical charges all going off simultaneously. It was a wonder we didn't look like fireflies glowing in the darkness. His chest pressed against mine as he exhaled; his hips bumped against mine as his feet moved to the slow, dreamy beat of the song the band was performing.

All thoughts of the half dozen things I needed to see to for the reception were lost as I closed my eyes and danced with this beautiful, complicated man.

There was so much I wanted to ask him, tell him. So many feelings swirling around inside me I wanted to give a voice to. In the beginning, I'd seen him as an arrogant, elitist snob—Vlad's doppelganger. I hadn't known he was a boy who'd lost his mother and been abandoned emotionally by a grieving father. My heart ached for the little boy. As it did for the man he'd become.

So much of what made us the people we are is forged in our childhoods. The majority of my personal quirks, the nervous babbling among the worst, is due to never being able to get a word in after the twins were born. With an articulate older sister who was the apple of her parents' eye and a grandmother who could wax for hours on end about any and every subject, by the time the twins arrived and then started to speak, it was hard work to get anyone to notice or listen to me. I'd compensated by stretching one- or two-word answers to questions into soliloquies. I'd become the master at chapter, book, and verse, Nanny's version of telling a story. I'd talk for as long as I could just to ensure my point was gotten across, understood, and had made an impact on the listener.

Slade's aversion to marriage could be laid directly at the feet of his much-wedded father. And while my little romantic girl's heart applauded the senior Harrington's quest to find eternal love, I wish he could have done so without causing his son to be so cynical about the state of matrimony, because even though I knew marriage, Slade, and me were never going to all be said in the same sentence, a girl could still daydream about such things.

All too soon the music ended, and I was forced back to reality when Charity descended on us.

"Maureen needs you," she told me, her gaze shifting nervously from me to Slade.

I slipped out of his arms and tried not to whimper. It was tough.

"Go ahead," Slade told me as he folded his hands

into his tux trousers. His expression was again that unreadable calm he showed to the world. "I'll catch up with you later."

I took a breath, nodded, and then followed Charity to the kitchen.

Chapter Twenty-One

"Number Four, you've simply got to sell this commercially," Nanny told Maureen after finishing off her sample of Isabelle's coconut cake. "Tastes like sin, it does. Duncan'll make me say more than me usual Hail Marys tomorrow at Mass in repentance."

Maureen smiled while she cut a few more slices of the cake. Two servers immediately swept into the ballroom with them. "Say a few for me, too," she told our grandmother.

A tiny time hack had forced Charity to interrupt my dance with Slade to bring me back to the kitchen. Cathleen had been called to the local hospital by Lucas Alexander after one of her clients had been brought in suffering from a domestic abuse dispute. Cathleen had been guiding the woman through the system to get her untangled from her alcoholic husband, but unfortunately the man had confronted her about leaving him and then beat her.

Cathy had brought Nanny to the inn and was supposed to bring her home after the ceremony. It looked like that was going to be my job now.

I'd overseen the cutting of the wedding cake while Kolby took pictures of the couple from every conceivable angle. Isabella had been all giggles and smiles while she playfully pleaded for Jack to be gentle and kind when he fed her the first piece. The minute he'd placed the tiny bite in her mouth he'd leaned down and kissed her. The dining room exploded in applause while the bride blushed, giggled some more, and then ignored her own request as she stuffed a piece of the cake into her groom's mouth, frosting and chocolate smearing along his cheeks. Laughing, she licked the remnants off. I was standing close enough to them to see the heat flare in Jack's eyes and in his bride's. I knew these two would be exiting their own reception way ahead of schedule.

"I need a few more minutes before I can slip away, Nanny," I told her.

"Not a worry, lass. You've a job to do for that lovely young lady and her handsome man. Don't fret about me."

I snuck a peek into the ballroom. Most of the older guests were seated, enjoying their cake, champagne, and whatever else the open bar could provide. My eyes swept across the dining area to Slade's table. His seat was empty, as was Katya's.

I found them on the dance floor, slowly swaying to a Michael Bublé standard sung in a bluesy, smokey style by the band's lead singer. They weren't the only couple on the dance floor, but they could have been because my eyes only saw the two of them.

I tried to inspect them from an objective viewpoint. Okay, that was a lie. There was no way I could be objective about either one of them. Slade looked like Slade, a.k.a. raw sex in a tux. Katya was his female equivalent. If I ever wanted to experience a lady love connection, I'd probably want to do it with Katya. She was wrapped around Slade as they moved about the dance floor in perfect sync, as if they'd danced this way thousands of times before. Effortlessly. Eye to eye—because Katya stood six foot unshod and right now she was wearing four-inch heels—they were looking at one another with so much *intent* I was surprised smoke wasn't drifting around them. Slade was smiling while Katya went on endlessly about something. That smile hinted at late-night private dinners and lost nights in bed.

Damn.

They looked...perfect together. The striking model and the titan of finance. I knew Slade and I hadn't looked anything like this when we'd done our terrace shuffle.

A burning sensation sparked inside my chest when Katya said something, then leaned in and kissed Slade square on the smiling mouth. They were both laughing as she raised a finger to his lips and swiped away the splash of crimson lipstick she'd left behind. Spots jumped across my vision, and for a hot second, I couldn't see anything but red.

It was crazy to feel this way, crazy to be jealous of a man who didn't belong to me. What's worse than crazy? Delusional? Yeah, that's what it was. I was deluding myself into thinking I meant anything more to this man than a willing bedmate.

My vision cleared then clouded as tears threatened. I needed to get out of here, get my head on straight again and remember I had a job to do. Obsessing over a man I couldn't have a future with wasn't productive. Isabella deserved my full attention.

I did a quick swipe under my eyes, checked my finger to make sure no eyeliner or mascara was running—I didn't want to look like a raccoon at a wedding reception I was in charge of—then made my way over to the bridal table.

A half hour later, I settled Nanny in my car and drove us home.

"You don't usually leave a reception while it's still going on, lass," Nanny said. "It's sorry I am you had to leave on account o' me. Blasted driver's license."

"Don't be." I shot her a quick glance. "Jack and Isabella wanted to call it a night, and once the bride and groom leave the reception, it's really just a party for their guests. I don't need to be there. Charity, Devon, and Kolby can handle whatever comes up. Besides, it's way past your bedtime," I added when she yawned.

" 'Tis true. It's bushed, I am."

She was almost asleep by the time I parked at our house.

Once she was settled, I sent a quick text to Charity.

All's well, she texted back.

I wanted to ask if Slade and Katya were still dancing but thought better of it. It wasn't my business if they were.

My phone chirped with a text, and Charity's face popped across the screen. *Tall, rich and handsome just asked where u are. I told him you took Fee home. Was that okay?*

Fine, I replied. *What did he want? Did he need anything?*

I was secretly hoping she'd type back, *you,* but she didn't.

Everything's okay. He didn't say why.

I signed off telling her I'd see her in the morning at the church and to remember to bring the birdseed.

A chirping bird emoji was my answer.

I slid into bed, my planner for the next day's wedding opened for review. Everything was set and readied. All I needed was the bridal party and my sister to make it official. Easy peasy.

I snuggled down, tired. My last coherent thought before drifting off was about how Slade had looked as he walked his sister down the aisle.

Chapter Twenty-Two

The next morning I drove back to the inn. I typically arrived for the morning-after bridal breakfast to ensure everything was okay and to say goodbye to my couple.

All was quiet as I let myself in through the back door.

I found Cathleen in Maureen's kitchen, eating a bowl of oatmeal. She had dark purple splotches under her eyes, and before lifting her coffee mug to her lips, she yawned so widely, I could see her wisdom teeth.

"Long night?" I asked, accepting a cup of coffee from my baby sister.

"It hasn't ended yet."

"How's your client doing?"

Cathleen closed her eyes and took a long chug from her mug. "Battered and bruised," she said. "Two broken ribs and a possible retinal detachment. She's being life-flighted up to Lebanon today to see a retinal specialist."

"Please tell me Lucas arrested the husband."

She nodded.

"Thank God for small favors," I said, just as Isabella came into the kitchen.

"Oh, good, you're here," she said, coming up to me and giving me a big hug.

If she'd spent the night being a newlywed, you

would never know it from looking at her. She looked rested, relaxed, and her typical beautiful self. There were no sleepless smudges under her eyes, and her smile was radiant.

"I was hoping I'd see you before we had to leave for the airport." Isabella nodded at Maureen when my sister lifted the coffee pot up to her and held up two fingers.

"I checked with the limo service before I got here," I told her, "and they're all set to pick you up at eleven. It's a little under two hours to the airport, but you'll be there in plenty of time to check in and get comfortable before you leave for Bali."

"You are simply the best." I was grabbed in another hug. "Thank you for everything." She pulled back, and I really started to believe her smile was never going to leave her face. "Everything was wonderful. From the food," she said to Maureen, "to those fabulous vows." She beamed at Cathy. "And all the little extras I didn't even think about, like the champagne bottles in all the guest rooms and the goodie bags you left on all the beds. My mother even commented on what a nice touch it was."

"High praise," I said.

"Truth." Her laugh was infectious.

She let me go and took the coffee mugs from my sister. Turning to Cathleen, she said, "And thank you, again, for all your help and advice with the you-know-what." Her beautifully sculpted eyebrows rose ever so slightly.

Cathy raised her mug in salute. "You're more than welcome."

Isabella looked at the three of us. "Okay, so I'm

gonna go bring this upstairs to my husband. Husband," she repeated with wonder outlining the word. With a wistful expression, she left us.

"What was all that about helping her with the *you-know-what*?" I asked Cathleen when she stood and crossed to the sink, mug and now empty bowl in her hands.

"A little legal advice," she replied. "Her brother asked me to speak to her about something. Thanks for breakfast, Mo." She kissed our sister's cheek.

"Take this for later." Maureen shoved a paper bag into her hands. "It's two scones."

"You're the best."

"Wait."

Cathy stopped in her tracks when I all but shouted the word. Both my sisters stared at me, concern and confusion on their faces.

"What did Slade ask you to speak to Isabella about?"

"I don't feel comfortable talking about this with you, Coll. It doesn't concern you."

"Was it about the prenup he wanted Jack to sign?"

"You know about that?"

I nodded. "He asked me to convince her to have Jack sign it. I told him I wouldn't help him. You know how I feel about those things."

"I do, and we're gonna have to agree to disagree on this like we always do." Cathy crossed her arms in front of her and rooted her feet to the floor. This was her lawyer stance, the one she used in court. She was prepared to debate, question, and then argue her point despite her words.

I suddenly remembered the envelope Isabella

handed her brother before the ceremony.

"You convinced her to have Jack sign it, didn't you?"

"Well, I guess since you already know about it, there's no harm telling you." She uncrossed her arms and took a breath. "Yes. I did."

"How? She was dead set against it."

"I know you think having a prenuptial agreement puts some kind of voodoo hex on marriage, Coll, but it doesn't, and I told her that. You need a license to drive a car and then insurance in case there are any problems, right?"

"Well, yeah."

"You don't really want the hassle of having to get insurance and pay the premiums, but it's good to have in case there's a problem down the road. Having a prenup is similar. You need a license to marry, and you need a legal arrangement to divorce. You can equate the prenup to insurance. You don't want it, would rather not have it, but in case there are problems down that proverbial marital road, you're better off having it than not, especially if there's a great deal of money involved. Isabella Harrington is a very wealthy young woman, and from what I understand, she's richer today than yesterday because now she comes into her grandmother's trust. Her brother is doing his best to make sure her inheritance stays hers. He doesn't want to see her divorce any more than you do. But he's being practical and smart in thinking this way, while you're approaching it from a purely emotional viewpoint."

Everything she said made sense. Ridiculously so. But...

"You said Slade asked you for help. When?"

"Couple of weeks ago when Isabella and Jack came up for the weekend. He knew I was meeting them and he called me, asked me to talk to them." She yawned. "He didn't tell you?"

"No." And I was furious about it. He'd gone behind my back and elicited my sister's help without informing me. How dare he use her that way? Okay, what's worse than furious, because that's what I truly was.

"Well, sorry you didn't know, not that it makes any difference. Now, are we done? 'Cause I've gotta go," Cathy asked.

I nodded again, afraid to open my mouth. I was so angry, but she wasn't the person I wanted to spew at.

"You okay?" Maureen asked after Cathy left us.

I wasn't, but I didn't want to concern her.

"A lot on my mind," I told her, with a careless wave of my hand. "I've got to get going too. Get over to the church and make sure everything is set up."

I bussed her cheek. Maureen grabbed my hand to halt me. Her gaze dragged across my face, her brows knitting together above her eyes.

"I know you, Colleen Sinead. Everything over at the church is as perfect as it's going to get, and if it isn't, Charity is there, right?"

"Yeah, so?"

"That tone never worked when you used it on Mom and Dad, and it's not working on me, either."

Before I could ask *what tone,* she said, "You're upset about Slade asking Cathy for help, aren't you?"

Remember I said still waters run deep in my baby sister? She may not say much, but she sees and hears all. And understands a lot more than people give her credit for.

"Mad, more than upset," I admitted.

"Why?"

"Because he went behind my back to do it. I thought we were…well, I thought I could trust him."

Maureen stared at me for a few moments, the cogs and wheels in her brain turning as she processed my words. After a bit, she shook her head. "He's not Vlad, Coll."

Still waters, remember?

"Slade didn't lie to you," she added, "or cheat on you. Harry did."

I wanted to tell her my suspicions about Katya, but we were interrupted before I could by the man in question.

"Hey." Slade came into the kitchen and with a huge smile aimed right at me he said, "You're here.

"And I'm leaving," I said, sprinting by him to the breezeway. There was no way I wanted to speak to him right now.

"Wait a sec." He reached a hand to stop me.

I slapped it away.

Slade was nothing if not a determined man. "Colleen." This time he reached out both of his hands and caught my upper arms, propelling me to a stop.

"Let me go," I said, trying to pull out of his grip. Yanking out of a block of hardened cement would have been easier. "I've got a wedding. I need to get to the church."

"I know you do, which is why I'm surprised you're here." He tugged me closer. "Surprised and happy. I didn't think I'd get a chance to see you today," he added, lowering his voice to the pitch that turned my insides to mush.

As Nanny is fond of saying when she's about to do something difficult, I girded my loins. "Stop," I commanded. "I don't have time for this. For you."

His brow tilted, and he looked at me with equal parts confusion and uncertainty. "What's wrong? Why are you upset?"

"Upset isn't even close to what I feel right now."

He squeezed my arms, his intense, probing gaze consuming my face. "No, I can see that. You're angry, and I get the impression it's with me. Why?"

I didn't answer the question, saying instead, "I understand Jack signed the prenup."

"Y-yes," he replied, a mote of wariness in the word.

"How did you finally convince Isabella?"

For a brief second, something flashed in his eyes. As soon as I caught it, it was gone. But I'd seen it as sure as I'd seen Katya kissing him the night before.

The careless shrug he gave me was anything but. "I didn't."

"No?"

"No. I didn't have to. She, well, she came to her senses and realized why it was beneficial for both of them."

"She came to her senses?"

"Yes."

"Just like that? Out of the blue? One day she tears your head off calling you every name in the book and refuses to speak to you, and the next she's as right as rain with the decision?"

He gave me a perfunctory nod.

"That's a lie, Slade."

"No, it isn't." He continued to stare at me, his silence telling, and dropped his hands.

"I don't remember you mentioning the role my older sister played in helping Isabella come to—what was it you said? Her senses?"

He expression changed to one of sheepishness and regret.

"The older sister," I went on, "you went to behind my back to ask to do your dirty work. Which is despicable and underhanded in and of itself. But you just made it worse by lying to my face about it."

Okay, by now I have to admit my temper had gotten the better of me and my voice had risen to a shrill pitch resembling a handful of fingernails raking across a chalkboard. I'm even embarrassed to admit I stomped my well-shod foot like a two-year-old in the throes of a tantrum.

Slade said the worst thing he could possibly say to me—or to any toddler in the middle of a meltdown.

"Lower your voice. I never lied to you."

"Don't you dare tell me what to do. And you did so lie to me. Cathleen told me you called her and asked for help to get Isabella on your side of the prenup. Are you denying it?"

"Okay, yes. I'll admit it. I did ask her. But I never lied to you. I just didn't tell you."

"In my world, lies of omission carry the same weight as if you give a voice to the words."

"So because I didn't mention something, something of no concern to you, you brand me a liar?"

"If the shoe—and the lie—fits, then…" I swiped my hand in the air.

"You don't have a very trusting nature, Colleen."

"With good reason, obviously."

"Look." He dragged in a breath, and then scraped his hands along his temples. "I didn't tell you because I knew how you felt. If you'll remember, you made your opinion on prenups loud and clear on more than one occasion. I knew you were against it, against helping me convince Izzy the necessity of it, so I did the next best thing and spoke to your sister—"

"Behind my back."

He stopped short, the corners of his mouth pulling down. "What did you expect me to do, Colleen? Really? Ask for permission? What would you have said to me if I told you I wanted to ask Cathleen for help?"

"I would have said forget it."

He nodded. "Yes. And I knew that. Which is why I didn't ask you. I asked *her*. She's a lawyer. She's used to dealing with legal situations, so I knew she'd be open to the idea of a prenup more than your close-minded feelings were and that she might be able to help me. And she was, much more than you were, since you shut me down from the first moment I spoke to you about it."

"You used her."

"What? No, I—"

"Stop. No more lies."

"Damn it, Colleen, I've never lied to you or anyone else. Stop accusing me of something I didn't and don't do."

"You lied about Katya."

Crap. I hadn't meant to mention her, but once my mouth started it was hard to stop it.

"Now what are you talking about?"

"You told me you weren't involved with her—"

"I'm not."

"And there's the lie. I've seen the proof for myself."

"What proof?"

"She was practically wearing you last night when you were dancing. I can't tell you how many times I spotted her kissing you, whispering in your ear, holding onto you *intimately*. Lord…" I shook my head and closed my eyes for a second, disgusted with my naïveté. You'd think by thirty-five, I'd have a clue about men. I opened my eyes. "To think I trusted you, trusted your word. Well, fool me once."

He stared at me for a moment, his confusion morphing into anger when understanding hit him.

"Don't you dare compare me to your loser ex. I'm nothing like him."

"Then don't you dare stand there and tell me you're not sleeping with Katya, because I'm not an idiot."

"Then stop acting like one."

Like a slap, those words stopped me, cold.

"You're make presumptions and forming opinions without having facts, Colleen. You see a very good friend of mine kiss me, and you conclude I'm involved in a torrid affair with her."

"Actions speak volumes."

"Actions have reasons. Katya is a very physical person. With everyone, not only me."

"You were the only one I saw her dry humping on the dance floor."

My mouth slammed shut as soon as the words were given breath. I can't believe I said that out loud. Heat flamed my cheeks, and my stomach coiled into knots even a veteran sailor couldn't undue.

"Do you hear yourself?" Slade asked, hands now fisted on his hips. "You're acting like a teenaged girlfriend who discovers her boyfriend talking to another girl."

The jab hit—hard—because he was right. I did sound like an out-of-control girlfriend. Something I wasn't now, nor ever going to be to this man.

"Well, we both know I'm not your girlfriend, or anything even remotely resembling one. And according to you, I'll never be anything more, so let's just end this now and—"

"What the hell does that crack mean?" His own raised voice reverberated in the empty space above us. He felt the echo, glanced around us, and then heaved in another deep breath.

"You know what it means, Slade. It's the one thing you have been honest about."

When he shook his head and looked confused again, I said, "You and I have this, this, *chemical thing* going on between us, I won't deny that. After the other night, I can't. But you and I want different things in life. You're not a commitment guy. You're never getting married, and since I still harbor a slim hope of being so someday, we're wasting each other's time. Yes, I'm attracted to you, and yes, I've enjoyed the time we've had together, but it's not enough for me. I can't just be someone's"—I swiped my hand in the air trying to find the right word—"wedding hook-up. I deserve more. I want more."

"That's what you really think? That I've been, what? Toying with you? Playing you?"

"Maybe not intentionally, but the end result is the

same."

His lips were pressed so tightly together they blanched. His fisted hands dropped to his sides, and he started flexing and extending them as his jaw worked back and forth.

I said a silent prayer for the health of his molars.

I had plenty more I wanted to say but not the luxury of time to do it. I had to get to the church. I squared my shoulders and willed the threatening tears to plug up in my eyes. With my voice lowered, I tried to keep my tone flat and as unemotional and businesslike as possible. "I'm gonna be late. I need to go."

"Colleen—"

I steamrolled right over him. "Your sister is married. My job is done. There's no need for us to have any further contact. I'll send the final bill to your office when it's ready. Good-bye, Slade. Travel safe back home."

This time when I shot past him, he didn't bar my way.

Chapter Twenty-Three

Whoever said *time heals all wounds* must have said it and then died, because if there was ever an axiom that's been proven false *given time*, it's this little gem.

Two weeks after leaving Slade standing in my sister's breezeway with a scowl on his face, I was still in pain. Mental, physical, and emotional.

Swamped was too tame a word to describe what my weeks at work had been. After five weddings, two bachelorette parties, and one bridal shower combined with innumerable client meetings and the basic everyday planning/ordering/checking that needed to be done for the business, I was as cranky and tired as a three-year-old who'd missed her nap, her last feeding, and her pacifier.

Not a pretty sight, believe me.

I'd slapped on my professional happy wedding face for the events and client meets, but when I was alone in my office or at home, the smile vanished and sorrow set in.

In all reality, I should have been relieved about ending things with Slade. We had no future together and I was too old to be anyone's Miss Right Now, when all I wanted to be was someone's Mrs. Right. Add in the mistrust factor I'd felt after Isabella's wedding, and you'd think I'd be happy things were over. But I wasn't. That all too brief night we'd shared in my bed had proven to me how much I was in love with him. I didn't regret spending that time with him. I couldn't. But I did regret I hadn't been able to protect my heart.

No, it was better things ended when and how they had. Well, maybe not how they had. I still cringed every time I remembered what I said to him about Katya. Not my finest moment.

My cell phone buzzed, interrupting my pity party. My grandmother's number spread across the screen.

"Hey, Nanny. What's up?"

"Number Two! Thank the good Lord I got ya. Are ya at the office?"

"I am."

"Leave. Now. Doesn't matter where ya go. Hop in that car o' yours and punch the speed, just get out afore he gets himself there."

"Nanny, slow down. Before who gets here? What are you talking about?"

"Your ex, lass. Your ex. What's his name? Voldemort."

"It's Vlad, Nanny, not Voldemort. And that's not his name, anyway. It's just what Cathy and Mo call him."

"Whatever he's called, he's on his way to see ya. Right now."

"How do you know?"

"He stopped by the house, didn't he, just a few shakes ago? Demanding to know where ya were, all lord o' the manor and condescending he was. *Gobshite*. 'Twas all I could do not to call Lucas on him to get him off me porch, but I'm still not talking to that man."

"Did you tell Harry I was here?"

"What kind of fool do ya take me for, darlin' girl?

O' course I didn't tell him where ya were. But he's a crafty one, isn't he? He's on his way there sure as truth be told."

Crap.

Harry Green was the last person on earth I wanted to see on a Tuesday morning.

Or any morning.

Just as I ended the call with Nanny, my intercom buzzed. At the same time, my office door flew open, and Harry burst into the room before I could answer the phone.

Charity shot by him, pushing him out of the way. She's little, but she's feisty and fast.

Both of them started speaking at the same time. Charity's "I'm sorry, Coll, he wouldn't wait for me to let you know he was here," was drowned out by Harry's "Colleen, I need to speak with you, and I won't be turned away."

I told Charity it was fine and asked her to hold all calls. If eyes could spit, the glare she shot at him as she closed the door would have splattered his face with a humongous loogey.

"What's so urgent you had to barge in here on a day you should be working, Harry, after first tormenting my grandmother?"

"I took some personal time to come up here, and I did no such thing to your grandmother," he said, taking the chair in front of my desk. I'd opted to stay behind it to make sure there was a physical barrier between us. "I went to your house first, looking for you. I assumed your parents would be there. Instead, it was your grandmother who answered the door. She took one look at me and started screeching at me in Gaelic. I wouldn't be surprised if she put a hex on me."

Me neither. "She's very loyal to her granddaughters," I told him. "Now, why are you here?"

In all the years I'd known, lived with, and loved Harry, I'd never seen the expression on his face that met my question. He looked at me, then his eyes darted over my shoulder, back to me, and then down to his hands, which were clasped in his lap. His square shoulders slumped as he licked his bottom lip a few times, and then his top teeth bit down on a corner of his mouth. A thin shimmer of sweat glazed his forehead and upper lip.

If I didn't know this man as I did, simply by looking at him I would assume he was nervous or embarrassed about something. But I did know him—intimately. Harry's narcissism never allowed shame, humiliation, or any kind of embarrassment to worm its way into his soulless body.

"Ever since I saw you at the Crystal Room, I've been thinking about you. Thinking about us."

"There is no us."

He zeroed in on my face. "Not anymore, that's true." He paused, momentarily. He was organizing and planning out what he wanted to say and how he wanted to present it, just like he did when he was in court. "But there was. An us," he added. "We were together for a long time, Colleen. Over a decade."

"Ten years too many."

"Don't say that."

"It's true."

"Not all those years were bad. We had a lot of good times. A lot of fun together, Coll. You know we did."

He was right, of course. In the beginning, when we'd been young and naïve and I'd been stupid in love, things had been good with us. But it all changed around the time Harry made making partner his entire existence to the exclusion of everything else including me.

Well, *that,* and having an affair with my assistant.

"Until we didn't," I said.

His mouth turned down at the corners.

"At the risk of sounding repetitive, I'll ask you again, Harry. Why are you here? What do you want?"

He lifted his head, and a flicker of apprehension moved across his eyes. He drew in a deep breath and let it out by saying, "What do I want?" He shook his head and then said, "So many things, but uppermost to make amends. To tell you how sorry I am for what happened between us. And—" He swallowed. "—to ask for your forgiveness."

I was glad I was sitting down and there was a solid oak desk between us. If there hadn't been, I would have rocketed out of my chair and slapped the living crap out of him. Although I don't think crap is alive, but you know what I mean.

He wanted forgiveness? For destroying my life? Yeah, not gonna happen. Not today. Not ever.

I'm a horrible liar and secret keeper because, as my parents and grandmother have told me since I was a kid, I wear all my emotions and thoughts for all to see right on my face. I must have looked like I wanted to commit ex-fiancé-cide because Harry sat straight up in the chair and put his hands out in front of him as if to ward off an attack.

"Colleen, please. Let me explain. Please."

"No. That ship has sailed, Harry. How dare you

369

come here and ask for anything? You have no right."

"I know, but please. I need to do this. Please don't make me leave. Hear me out." His voice was etched with desperation, his entire body rigid with it. Harry had never pleaded for anything in his life. He'd never had to. Anything he'd wanted had been given, anything he'd requested, granted, without ever needing to ask twice.

For him to be in such a state had my radar pulsing and, I'm ashamed to admit, my natural nosiness standing upright at attention. With a quick flick at my watch to note the time—it was almost lunch and I was starving—I granted him his wish. "You have ten minutes. Then we're done. For good. Understand?"

With his head bouncing like a bobblehead, he sat forward and rested his elbows on his knees, hands clasped. "You never gave me a chance to explain what happened with Diana. Why I did what I did."

I put my hand up to silence him. "No explanation is necessary. I told you as much when you came up here last month. I caught you having monkey sex with another woman in our bed. There's nothing you can say to explain that."

"About that, you're right. There isn't. You saw what you saw. Then you packed and left that night without ever looking back."

"What would you have had me do, Harry? I see the man I love, the man I've devoted most of my adult life to, the man I was going to be marrying, having sex with another women. What did you expect me to say? Do? And I'll remind you, I didn't just leave. After you got her out of the apartment and while I was packing, you called me a cold and calculating career-driven bitch.

Accused me of neglecting your needs, being dismissive of how hard you'd worked, and not appreciating the life you were making for us. Which was all total bullshit, and you know it."

He flinched, his face screwing up as if I'd hit him. My voice had risen, and I'd come out of my chair, fisted my hands, and propped them on my desk so I could glower over him.

Harry swallowed, the sound loud in the quiet wake of my outburst. "Everything you say is true. I won't deny it," he said, quietly. "But I was under a lot of pressure at the firm to prove myself. I wanted to make partner before we got married so we'd have some financial stability."

"I'm calling bullshit on that statement, too." I'd lowered my voice after taking a deep, calming breath. "You wanted to make partner because, in your ego-obsessed brain, you thought you deserved it. From the moment you graduated law school, it was all you ever talked about, all you ever worked toward."

"Yes, but for us, Colleen. I didn't want us starting out in a marriage rife with debt and uncertainty."

"Everyone starts married life that way, Harry."

"Well, I didn't want to."

Not one word of what he'd said so far rang true. I knew Harry. In the biblical sense. I knew how his mind worked and how big his ego was. Something else was going on here, and it had nothing to do with forgiveness.

"None of this matters now. Even before I found the two of you together, there were deep cracks in our relationship. You were never home, our sex life was nonexistent when you were, and you treated me like an

371

unpaid servant. You never appreciated a thing I did. You looked down on my family, my career. I had no friends and no life outside of you and your needs. I had hoped once we got engaged things would change, but they got worse instead of better."

"Just for the record," he said, looking down at his hands, "I never intended to cheat on you."

Calling bullshit again was being a little redundant, so I said the word in my head, instead. "I didn't even realize you knew her until I caught you together."

"Really? You don't remember introducing us at the magazine Christmas party a few weeks before we got engaged?"

With a sigh, I sat back down. "No."

Harry nodded. "You were making the rounds of the higher ups, and she joined me at the bar for a drink. We got to talking. That was it. When I was getting our coats to leave, she came up to me and kissed me on the cheek. Only it wasn't on the cheek. I thought at the time I'd just moved awkwardly, but she'd done it intentionally and landed on my mouth. At the same time, she shoved a slip of paper into my hand. She giggled and said good night, and I slipped my hand into my coat. Later on when we got home, I pulled it out. It was her cell phone number with the words *call me* written next to it."

"How long did you wait until you did?"

A sheepish, regretful cast came over his face again. "Right after New Year's."

"And we got engaged on Valentine's Day."

Another nod. "When you went up to see your parents the weekend after, I, well...it was the first time we slept together."

"Why did you ask me to marry you?"

He didn't answer me, so, of course, I pressed.

"It wasn't because you loved me, that's for sure," I said. "You don't love someone and cheat on them. Tell me the truth, Harry. I deserve that much."

"Colleen—"

"The truth, Harry. Now."

The force of the breath he let out hit me all the way across the desk.

He raked his fingers down his face and then rubbed his eyes. When he was done, he spoke again. "The Christmas before we got engaged. Remember what I gave you?"

"A coffeemaker. I remember it vividly. I hated the damn thing."

"I know. You'd been hoping for an engagement ring. You'd been dropping hints about the new types and arrangements the magazine was profiling for the holidays. You even managed to work your ring size into a conversation one night. Every other sentence was about someone else you knew who'd gotten engaged, or married, or was having a baby. But I wasn't ready. Even after I made partner, I wasn't. At Christmas when we drove up here to visit your parents, your father cornered me in the den and asked when I was going to—and this is a quote—make an honest woman of you and stop using you."

"Oh, sweet Jesus." Flames shot up my neck. "I never knew he asked you that, I swear. I never said anything to him or my mother about our relationship."

"I know. I know how private you are. And just so you know, it wasn't the first time he'd said that to me. I thought if we got engaged, it would get you to stop dropping hints, your parents to leave me alone. So I bought the ring and gave it to you."

"And started sleeping with my assistant."

He winced. "Again, I never had any intention of cheating. But once you had the ring on your finger, I started to feel…" He shrugged.

"Trapped?"

He nodded.

"And cheating made you feel less so?"

"I know it's a shitty excuse, Coll. Believe me I know. I wanted to break it off with her almost immediately, but…well. I didn't. I have no explanation of why I didn't. And then she told me she was pregnant."

I had a million thoughts on that little occurrence but kept them to myself.

We stared at each other for a moment, each lost in memories and thoughts.

"Did you ever love me?" I finally asked. "Or was I merely"—I swiped my hand in the air—"convenient to have around?"

His eyes softened and swept over my face. "I loved you from the first moment you plopped down next to me in freshman English, late and out of breath, your hair a mess and your blouse buttoned wrong."

God. I was such a mess at eighteen.

Harry scooted forward on his chair, his eyes staying focused on mine. "And in all truth, I've never stopped loving you."

"Don't." I stabbed my index finger at him. "I don't believe you. Not after everything that's happened. Everything you've done."

He stood and walked around the desk. Squatting in

front of me, he took my hands. "It's true. I know I did something horrible, something that really should be unforgivable."

"It is."

"Maybe. These past two years without you have been…wrong somehow, though. Like something vital, like an arm, was missing from my life."

Okay, did he really think comparing me to an appendage was the way to gain forgiveness?

"It was almost serendipitous I saw you in the Crystal Room. Something…something had recently happened to me, and I'd been thinking a lot about things. People. What I want in life."

"Okay, so now we're getting to the real reason you're here," I said. "Finally."

Harry stood again, his gaze drifting around the room before coming to settle back on me. He leaned a hip against my desk and crossed his hands, settling them across his lap.

"A little over three months ago I was on the treadmill at the gym. Work was a shitshow, a case that was proving to be more than I could keep up with. I was working eighteen to twenty hours a day for weeks, not eating or sleeping well. I decided to go for a run in the company gym."

He stopped, blew out a breath. "Long story short, I passed out while I was running. Luckily, another of the partners was in the gym at the same time and called 9-1-1. I was brought to the nearest emergency room." When he stopped, he closed his eyes.

"And?" I asked.

"Condensed version." He opened his eyes and stared at me. "I had a blip on my electrocardiogram, so they sent me for some more tests. The cardiologist found I have a condition called atrial fibrillation—"

"A-fib," I said, nodding. "My father has the same thing."

"I didn't know that. Anyway, he put me on meds, told me to start taking it easy and even recommended I try and find some kind of passive stress relief. My father died at forty from a heart attack brought on by too much drinking and work-related stress. I didn't want to wind up like him, so I started seeing a therapist. He's been helping me…navigate through some personal stuff. One of the things we've talked about is making amends to the people in my life I have unresolved issues with."

"Like me."

"Yeah. You. My mother. Others."

I knew the list was a long one because Harry had always been a bit of dick to people. And even though I'd known it, I'd still wanted to marry him. "So this is why you've been so hell bent on speaking to me? To make amends for what you did? For what happened between us?"

He nodded. "But that's not all of it." He reached over and took one of my hands in his. I was surprised when I didn't flinch or pull my hand away at his touch. My hand in his felt familiar.

"I've taken a long hard look at myself since that morning on the treadmill, and I have to admit my life isn't anything like what I'd thought it would be at this age."

Mine wasn't either.

"I figured I'd be married—we'd be married—with a couple kids and a beautiful house in the suburbs.

Instead, I'm thirty-six years old, I have a job that's consumed my life, and I'm alone."

Pity Party, table for one.

"I don't buy the last part, Harry. You were with, what's-her-name, Bunny"—I was never gonna get used to that name—"at the Crystal Room, so I don't think you're hurting for female companionship."

"Bunny Howland is a client's daughter. I took her to lunch because her father wanted me to talk to her about her application to law school—"

"She's going to law school?" My shock made my voice rise again. "God help the judicial system."

For the first time since he'd come into my office, Harry smiled.

Lordy, I'd forgotten how handsome he could be when he did. For a hot second, I wanted to smile back at him, but common sense kept my mouth closed.

"She's not the smartest person I've ever known," he admitted. "But what I said was the truth, Colleen. I'm lonely. I miss being with someone. Having someone there at night. It sucks coming home to an empty, cold apartment."

"Get a dog."

He looked down at his hands, the ghost of a smile tugging at one corner of his mouth. "You're not the first person to tell me that."

This side of Harry, this calm, self-deprecating, *sharing* side was new to me. As appealing as it was, though, the past was still the past. So much had changed in my life the moment I caught Harry with Diana. My career, my future, even where I lived were all altered forever. I'd been able to survive it all by living on a diet of sheer will, anger, and a determination to never be hurt like that again.

And I *had* survived. My business was thriving; my living situation was stable. The one part I still needed to work on was my love life. Slade's face suddenly crossed in front of my eyes. What had I told him? Fool me once?

"Colleen?" Harry's voice interrupted my musings.

I took another deep, calming breath and stared up at him. "What do want me to say, Harry?"

A barrel of emotions filled his eyes. "That you can find it in your heart to forgive me. That we can move on from what happened and put it behind us. That maybe, just maybe, you're willing to give me another chance."

I stared at him for a few seconds, considering everything he'd asked. Forgiveness, Father Duncan had preached more times about than I cared to remember, was more beneficial to the person giving it than the one receiving it. I'd never believed that more than at this moment.

"Yes to the first two," I said. Harry's fast smile knocked me back a bit. Nanny's voice screeched in my ear, and I girded my loins again. "No way in hell to the last."

His smile lost some of the luster, but he nodded. "That was a long shot, I know. But I figured I'd try." He reached out and took my hand again. "Can we at least be friends? I do miss you, Coll. I mean it. I miss talking to you about things, running stuff by you. You're the best listener I've ever known. No one can pick apart a legal argument like you do."

"Comes from being the middle child," I said. "It's ingrained in the DNA."

His lips lifted again in a free and easy manner, and I was reminded of the nineteen-year-old boy I fell madly in love with.

"Can I ask, is there someone in your life now? Someone who treats you the way you should be treated? The way I should have treated you?"

My pride wouldn't let me tell him about Slade, so I opted for a half confession. "There was someone, but…"

"But?"

I shook my head. "We wanted different things. So."

"No compromise?"

"A word not really in his vocabulary."

Or in mine, if truth be told.

"I'm sorry it didn't work out. You deserve to be happy." He squeezed my hand. "Anyway, thank you for letting me stay and for listening. I know I barged in, probably disrupted your day, but thanks."

My hand was still in his. As he had to mine, I squeezed his. "I'm glad I did, too."

"So? Friends?"

"More like long-lost acquaintances."

His laugh jarred me—in a good way. "Well, *acquaintance,* will you let me buy you lunch?"

My stomach growled loudly, answering him.

"Ah, I recognize that sound," he said yanking me to a standing position. "Come along, woman, and I'll feed you."

With my hand wound around his arm, Harry opened my office door. I was about to tell Charity I was leaving when she stood upright behind her desk, the phone in her hand and look of nervous concern on her face.

"I was just about to buzz you," she said at the same time I saw Slade Harrington, a bouquet of white roses in his hand, standing in front of me.

Dearly Beloved

Chapter Twenty-Four

"Um." Charity's panicky gaze bounced back and forth between Slade and me. "Mr. Harrington is here to see you?" and yes, she did make it sound like a question. A highly concerned one. "He doesn't have an appointment."

He looked...amazing. I hadn't realized until that second how much I missed seeing him in the flesh these past two weeks. Dressed casually in a black leather bomber jacket over a white Henley and low-slung jeans, the man oozed sex appeal from every pore. I'd just spent a half hour in the company of a man I'd slept with for over a decade, but one moment in Slade's presence did more to tie me up in erotic knots than any memory I had of Harry did.

"Colleen." Slade's gaze drifted from me to Harry, and then down to where my arm was wound around his. Like I'd been speared with red hot poker, I dropped my hand and wound it with its twin in front of me.

"Slade. This is unexpected." The croaking frogs were back again. "Is everything okay? Isabella?"

"Is fine," he replied, looking back at my face. "Back from her honeymoon, tan and relaxed. She sends her love."

Another thing I'd missed was his searching, hyper-focused, penetrating glare. It was aimed straight at me, his head tilted to one side as if waiting for me to answer a question.

"You're looking well," I managed to say. I really wanted to tell him he looked good enough to devour and I was starving, but with the way things ended the last time we'd been together, prudence suffused within me and I kept my mouth shut.

Until this time Harry had been mute. He broke the awkward silence by putting out his hand, giving Slade a companionable grin, and saying, "Harrington, Harland Green. Good to see you again."

I could tell Slade was surprised at the pleasant gesture. It took him a moment before his good-mannered breeding took over and he shook Harry's hand.

The office phone rang, and Charity, who'd been watching this scene with as much intensity as any good little rubbernecker could, answered it.

"Colleen and I were about to go have lunch. Why don't you join us?" Harry offered.

Slade had been surprised by the offer of Harry's hand, but the suggestion to join us for lunch looked as if it—to use one of Nanny's favorite phrases—gobsmacked him. His eyebrows met his hairline and his mouth opened for a brief moment before he slammed it back shut.

"Colleen," Charity said, holding the phone out to me, "Chief Alexander needs to speak to you."

Okay, that wasn't a good sign. I took the phone from my assistant. "Lucas?"

"Colleen, I need you stay calm. I've got something I need to tell you."

"Oh, good God, Lucas, don't start a conversation that way. What is it?"

"Colleen, take a breath."

I tried to but my chest muscles were stricken with an instantaneous paralysis from fear—as was the rest of my body.

"Fiona was on her way to your office on her bicycle and she ran through the same stop sign she did before. She hit a stopped car, and she's on the way to the emergency room now."

I think I screamed. I don't really remember. I do remember someone trying to wrest the phone from my fingers, but I was holding it so tight, my grip wouldn't loosen.

I heard Harry say my name, place a hand across my back, and then felt Slade begin to pry my fingers apart. My vision started to narrow and tunnel, and I grew afraid I was going to pass out. To make sure I didn't I bit down—hard—on my bottom lip. The pain jarred the wooziness away, and I was able to clamp down a budding panic from being released.

Slade was speaking into the phone. "Yes. We'll get her right down. Okay. Thank you."

He gave the phone back to Charity. He still held the hand that had been gripping the phone when he turned to me.

"We need to get you to the hospital."

"Cathy and Mo—" My voice broke as tears neared.

"The chief is sending someone for them right now." He grabbed both my upper arms and turned me to face him fully. "Colleen, she's going to be okay. You need to stay focused on that. She's a tough lady." He flicked a quick glance at Harry. Something unspoken passed between them, some kind of silent male telepathy because Harry nodded.

Slade cupped my elbow and said, "Come on. I'll drive."

I let him lead me to the door before my brain kicked in. I stopped and turned back.

"Harry?"

"I'll follow in my car, Coll. I'll be right behind you, don't worry. Go now with Harrington."

"And don't worry about anything here," Charity piped up. "I'll take care of everything. You go to your granny."

"She hates being called granny," I told Slade as he secured my seatbelt around me.

"I don't doubt that."

"Do you know where you're going?" I asked when he pulled out of my office driveway.

"I've got an idea. I remember seeing the hospital when I followed you around the day before Kimmy Gulverson's wedding."

"Gunderson," I said. "Kimmy Gunderson, well, Schmidt now. The baby was due last week. She's late. First babies are sometimes."

God. I was babbling again. I hadn't been so mentally discombobulated since the last time I was with Slade.

He tossed me a quick glance then turned back to the road. "Are you okay?"

"No, I'm not okay." My lips started to tremble and my hands got fidgety. "Why would I be? My grandmother—my ninety-three-year-old, practically blind, frail grandmother—was hit by a car. Would you be okay if you heard that?"

The hysteria that threatened to be unleashed in my office had no reins now. I couldn't quell it, couldn't keep it in. I didn't even know how to.

Slade reached across the seat and grabbed my hand. My body calmed in a heartbeat. The heat of his skin, of his touch, spread throughout my body warming me as if I was standing in front of a roaring fire after coming in from an arctic storm. I was able to take a full breath again without sounding like I was having an asthma attack. I shifted in the seat so I could look at him.

"She's going to be fine, Colleen. Alexander said she was conscious when the ambulance arrived, barely two minutes after the accident, and she was shouting orders at the EMTs. She's a strong woman. Remember that."

"You're not just saying that so I don't go postal before you get me to the hospital? Lucas really said that?"

The corner of his mouth twitched upward. "No, I'm not, and yes, he did." He turned to me again and brought my hand up to his lips. "She'll be fine."

His face went all fuzzy as the tears I'd been holding back swelled, then let loose. He kissed my hand again and then, still holding it, concentrated on driving.

There are times I woefully lament living in a small town for several reasons. This wasn't one of them, because we arrived at Holy Mother of God Hospital (and yes, I know, the name is ridiculous) less than ten minutes after leaving the office.

The moment we shot through the emergency room doors, I spotted Lucas standing with Maureen.

"How is she?" I asked my baby sister as we hugged.

"Cathy's in with her and the doctor," Maureen

said. She must have come straight from her kitchen because she was still wearing her flour-dusted apron and flip-flops. Her hair was in its usual messy topknot, and her hands were shaking so violently, I pulled them into my own. None of us liked being in this hospital, Maureen most of all. There were too many painful memories of Eileen receiving chemo, being admitted for dehydration from the side effects, and ultimately, dying.

"Lucas, what happened?"

"Like I told Harrington"—he nodded at Slade— "Fiona wanted to get to your office, and she was hell bent on doing it fast. She blew the stop sign and barreled right into a car. Luckily, the car was stopped, so the impact was all from Fiona. She slammed pretty hard, though, into the front hood. Fell from the bike and landed hard."

"Oh, my God." I felt my vision tunneling again, a shrill ringing blast inside my head and then everything went black.

The next thing I knew, I was on the floor, with Slade's arms around me and him gently calling my name. I blinked a few times. "Did I fall?"

"No," Lucas said. "Harrington's fast. He caught you before you hit."

"Are you okay?" Slade asked.

I blinked again, bringing his face into focus. He was so close I could count every one of the eyelashes covering his concerned whiskey-colored eyes.

"Embarrassed more than anything. Let me up."

He eased back, stood, and then pulled me upright.

And kept holding me even when I was up, his arm wrapped around my waist.

"Here comes Cathy," Maureen said.

On any given day, my older sister is unflappable. As a lawyer—and a good one—she keeps her emotions and thoughts to herself. Even when she received the news her beloved husband had been killed by enemy fire in Afghanistan, she'd kept her composure in front of the grief officers who'd come to her door, and all through the wake, mass, and burial. She'd been the same when Eileen died. Our parents were emotional messes, so she'd been our family rock. I'm sure she'd cried her heart out when alone, but to the world, she kept herself in check. Which is why when she came through the ER doors biting her bottom lip, her smooth brow furrowed and her eyes misting, my heart stopped.

"Nanny?" Maureen's voice shook with terror.

With a heavy sigh, Cathleen opened her arms, and we both dissolved into them.

"She's okay. Battered, bruised, and pissed. But alive. Her wrist is broken and her hip hurts, so they're sending her for x-rays to see the extent of the damage. Thankfully, she had the foresight to put your helmet on, Coll. Otherwise, we'd be looking at possible head trauma as well."

She patted our backs and pulled back. When Maureen swiped her dripping nose and eyes with her sleeve, Lucas reached into his back pocket and handed her a handkerchief.

"Can we see her?" I asked.

"As soon as she's done in x-ray. They're going to admit her as a precaution," she added when Maureen gasped. "She's in pain, and they can control it better here than we can at home. If all is good, and it should be, she'll be released tomorrow."

"Back home?" I asked.

Cathy's eyes flicked once to Lucas and then back to me. "We'll need to talk about that. But not now. Let's focus on—"

She stopped so abruptly, I reached out and grabbed her arm. "Cath?"

"What's he doing here?" She was looking over my shoulder, her eyes narrowed. I turned to see what she was looking at as did everyone else. Maureen hissed in a breath.

Harry, who'd walked briskly through the ER door, slowed his steps when he caught the angry female glares coming his way. He stopped in front of me after a quick glance at the group. "Colleen?"

"What the hell are you doing here?" Maureen pushed in front of me, her face screwed into a tearstained scowl, her hands fisted on the sides of her apron.

To prevent her from punching him in the face, which is what I knew she was aiming to do—and being handcuffed and arrested by Lucas—I jumped in front of her and put my hands up in the air.

"Mo, it's okay. He's here with me. It's okay."

Surprised doesn't even begin to describe the look she gave me.

"What do you mean, he's with you?" Cathy asked, coming to stand with Mo, both of them looking from me to my ex-fiancé, anger and confusion on their faces.

"Harry was in my office when Lucas called."

"You were, too?" Cathy asked Slade. He nodded.

"Why?" she asked me.

Slade mumbled something that sounded like *the sixty-four-thousand-dollar question,* but I wasn't sure those were his exact words.

"I don't want to get into this right now," I said. "Just accept Harry is here, and I'm okay with it. Deal?"

From the hostile looks on their faces and in their body stances, I wasn't hopeful they'd agree. Fortune, for once, was on my side though. Cathy's name was called from the reception desk by a scrub-suited guy who looked like he hadn't slept in a week. I assumed he was the ER doctor who'd taken care of Nanny. When he told Cathy we could all see her now, I knew I was correct.

"Hold up a sec," Harry said, reaching for my hand. A noise remarkably similar to a growl came from Slade.

"Go on," I told my sisters. "I'll be right in." I turned my attention to him. "Make it fast, Harry. I want to see my grandmother."

He swung his gaze to Slade. "I just need her for a second," he said.

Slade's terse nod was his answer. Harry walked me back toward the entrance doors. "Look, Colleen, I'm gonna go. You need to be with your family, and I don't want to take any time away from that. Before I leave I wanted to thank you again for talking to me. I think, well, I think we both got a little closure today."

"Really, who are you and what have you done with Harry Patrick Green?" I was amazed I could joke at a time like this.

Harry grinned and pulled me into a hug. I didn't stiffen when he did. Like when he'd held my hand in my office, his touch was familiar. But that's all it was. No bells, no whistles, no fluttering in any of my girl parts. I was well and truly over this man romantically.

For a brief moment, though, Harry's body did go

still. Then, he bent and whispered in my ear, "Harrington deserves another chance. I'll bet he's willing to compromise rather than live without you."

I pulled away and gaped up at him. "What are you talking about? I never told you who I was seeing. You don't know it's Slade."

"The way he's looking at me right now—like he'd be happy if I fell off a cliff—is all the proof I need to know I'm right." He took my hands, squeezed. "Call me when you're in the city again. I owe you lunch."

He bussed my cheek and then left. No sooner was he through the revolving doors than the air shifted around me. I turned and there was Slade, right next to me.

"You going in to see your grandmother?" he asked.

I nodded.

"I'll wait out here."

"You don't have to stay. Thanks for bringing me, but now—"

"You'll need a ride home. We came in my car."

"I can catch a lift with my sisters."

"I'm staying, Colleen. Now, go see your grandmother."

It was on the tip of my tongue to say "Bossy, much?" but I didn't.

****

An hour later, with her left arm casted and an IV pumping pain meds and fluids into her system, Nanny was admitted to the hospital. Cathy drove back to the house to bring some of Nanny's things, like a clean nightgown, underwear, and her toothbrush to the hospital, while Mo and I stayed with her. Lucas came to Nanny's room under the guise of having to file an official accident report, but I think he just wanted to make sure she was okay. The man really did have a soft spot for my grandmother, and she for him, despite her saucy tone whenever she spoke to him.

Slade stayed in the background while Nanny was cared for, silently watching and assessing the situation. I have to admit, his presence was a soothing, calming balm for me.

In all, Nanny had fractured her left radius and ulna and was immobilized from her fingers up to her elbow. She'd requested—and been granted—a bright, neon-pink cast from the orthopedic doc who treated her. Her left hip was badly bruised, but, thank God, not broken. When Cathy and I helped her out of the hospital-issue nightgown and into one of her own Irish linen ones, we both gaped at the road map of bruises along her shoulder, back, and hip. She had several bad scrapes where the skin was avulsed and already scabbing over. Even though she'd been wearing my helmet, she'd still bruised her cheek and jaw when she'd careened off the bike.

"Nanny, what were you thinking?" I asked when she was finally settled in the bed, two pillows propped behind her head and shoulders.

"That I had to get to you, darlin' girl, afore Voldemort arrived at your office. The good Lord above only knows what that lowlife was gonna do to ya."

"Excuse me, Fiona, but who are you talking about?" Lucas asked, scratching his head with his pencil. "I mean, who are you referring to?"

"Harry, my ex," I said. "The guy who was in the ER with us."

"That gobshite is here? Lucas, arrest him. Right

now. The man's up to no good, he is."

"Calm done, Nanny," Cathy said. "He's gone." She turned her attention to me. "Right?"

"Yeah."

"Voldemort?" Lucas asked.

"It's really Vlad, but Nanny keeps forgetting that."

He dragged in a deep, heavy breath, his eyes finally resting on Maureen. She pushed off the wall she'd been leaning against and said, "Come on. I'll explain while you help me bring back drinks for everyone."

"I'll take a whiskey," Nanny piped from the bed. "Neat."

"You'll take ice chips like the doctor ordered," Cathy told her. "I need caffeine," she told Mo.

I dittoed the request.

"I'll see if Slade wants anything," she said before leaving the room, Lucas in tow.

"Me lawyer's here, too?" Nanny said to me. "Where's he hidin'? I need to discuss me lawsuit against the city with him."

"First of all," Cathy said as she straightened Nanny's covers, "I'm your lawyer, not Slade Harrington. Second"—she put up her index finger as Nanny started to speak—"you're not suing the city or anyone else. You were at fault. Totally and completely. You blew that stop sign, Nanny. For the second time. We're all hugely thankful the car you hit wasn't moving. Colleen's bike is destroyed, but she can replace it. What we can't replace is you."

I could count on the fingers of one hand the times in my life I'd seen my grandmother chagrined and be able to still use four of them.

"You need to get your eyes fixed, Nanny." Cathy

sat on the bed and held our grandmother's hand. "I think this little episode proves how necessary the cataract surgery is."

With a doleful downward cast of her lips, Nanny nodded. "Aye, child. It's true you are." She closed her eyes and sighed just as the nurse entered.

Cathy and I left the room while Nanny was tended to. I spotted Slade, slumped on a bench in the hallway, his long legs stretched out in front of him, his arms folded across his chest, eyes closed.

"You wanna explain to me what Harry was doing here? Because in case it escaped your hearing, he's the reason Nanny tore out of the house."

I winced. "Don't remind me. It makes me sick she thought I needed protecting."

"Why was he here, Coll? And please don't tell me it's because you're getting back together. I've had enough horrible news to last a lifetime lately."

"No, I'm not." I stole a quick look at Slade. His eyes were still closed, so I said a silent prayer he couldn't hear us. Quickly, I explained the reason for Harry's visit.

"Remember Father Duncan has always preached forgiveness is more important for the person doing the forgiving than for the person requesting it?"

"Yes."

"I realized how true that was today."

"Nanny always says 'let go and let God.' I think that fits here, too."

"It does. I'm truly over him, Cath. In every way. I don't even feel angry anymore. Or sad."

She pulled me into a hug, and whispered, "Now explain why Harrington is here."

"In all honesty"—I pulled back and frowned—"I don't know. He showed up as I was leaving to have lunch. He's the one who brought me here."

Cathy's gaze drifted over my shoulder, then back to me. Her brows pulled together, and she squinched up her mouth.

"What's that look for?"

"I'm trying to figure out what's going on between you and him, because I know something is. You didn't see him in the emergency room. He couldn't tear his eyes away from you."

"He was probably concerned. Before you came out to talk to us I, well, I fainted."

"You've never fainted in your life."

"I know. Harry, Nanny—it was all…" I shrugged. "Too much for me, I guess."

"But you're okay? Nothing's wrong?"

I knew where the concern was coming from. Eileen had fainted one day at the inn. After Maureen's incessant bullying to go to the doctor for a long overdue checkup, we'd found out Eileen had cancer.

"I'm fine, Cath. Over-worked and tired, but I'm okay, health-wise. Don't worry."

"The two stupidest words in the English language," she said. On a sigh, she nodded again. "Mo's back."

The next few hours were spent in sitting with Nanny, listening to her complain about being stuck in the hospital, and then deciding we didn't all need to be there at the same time.

"I'll stay for now," Cathy said. "My schedule is clear for the rest of the day, and if anything comes up, my secretary can take care of it. Mo, you've got a full load at the inn, and I'm sure you're overloaded with work as well, Coll. You guys go. I'll call if anything comes up."

We kissed her and Nanny goodbye. In truth, I don't even think Nanny knew we'd gone because the pain meds they'd given her through the IV had kicked in and she was in la-la land.

"I'll take you back to your office," Slade said.

The ten-minute car ride was a silent, awkward one. He still hadn't told me why he'd shown up at my office today, and for some weird reason, I felt uncomfortable and a little nervous about asking him. It had been two weeks since the wedding. Two weeks since our argument. We'd had no communication except for the final bill I'd sent via snail mail a few days ago. I had a million questions I wanted to ask, but no will to ask them.

He parked and came around to help me out, but I was already at my office door.

"Thanks for the ride," I said over my shoulder.

He stood there, hands in his jacket, silent, but I got the impression he wanted to say something.

"Well," I said. *Lame, I know.* "Thanks again."

I went through the door and was pounced upon by Charity asking fifty different questions about me, Nanny, and Harry. Before she could grill me about Slade, I put up my hand and told her I had work to catch up on since I'd spent the better part of the afternoon in the hospital. Charity's nothing if not a perfect assistant. Messages, she told me, she couldn't take care of, were on my desk.

The moment I walked into my office, I spotted the roses Slade had brought with him. Charity had placed them in a vase and centered them on my desk.

All my resolve about not asking why he'd arrived at my doorstep flew. I needed to know.

Now.

I shot back through the reception area, passed Charity's stunned face, threw open the front door and found an empty parking lot, save for my car and Charity's.

He'd gone, probably back to New York, without ever telling my why he'd come.

It would have been easy to just text him and ask. Or call. I did neither. Obviously, whatever had brought him back to Heaven hadn't been important enough for him to stick around.

With a heavy heart, I went back inside.

Chapter Twenty-Five

Sleep was a selfish bitch. I tossed, turned, sighed, and finally decided, since I wasn't getting any rest, I'd work. I had two weddings planned for the weekend, one at the inn and one at a hotel in Concord. I made multiple lists to ensure everything was ready and planned for, before crawling back into bed at about five.

When I opened my eyes again, my room was bathed in bright sunlight. I grabbed my phone but it was dead. I'd forgotten to plug it in to charge when I'd gotten home. The bedside clock I rarely glanced at was glowing, so I read the time across its face.

"Shit!" I was late.

I bolted up and started toward my bathroom when the aroma of fresh-brewed coffee drifted through my senses. Who was here?

Still in my sleep shirt and flannel Bugs Bunny pajama pants, I slipped down the back stairs to the kitchen, trying to be as quiet as when I used to sneak down in the middle of night as a child to get something to eat, when I heard two voices, Cathleen's and another's.

A man's voice.

A very familiar man's voice.

"Hey, you finally joined the living," Cathy said when I peeked around the corner at the bottom of the staircase.

Yup. The other voice *was* familiar, because it was Slade's. Had he gone back to New York and then driven back here this morning? He was dressed like he'd been yesterday. In fact, when I took a good look at him, the clothes he was wearing *were* yesterday's. So that was probably a no to the driving. I blinked and stared at him for a few seconds. For the first time ever, he wasn't clean shaven. A thin patch of stubble the color of dark honey mixed with flax covered his jaw and cheeks. I had to physically fist my fingers so I wouldn't reach out and run them along the spikey thatch.

"What are you doing here?"

I'd meant the question for him, but my sister answered. "I wanted to give you an update on Nanny. Charity called me a little while ago, by the way. Said you weren't answering your cell."

"Forgot to plug it in and it died," I said.

"Yeah, that's what I figured since you never miss a call. She said to tell you she's got everything under control for the morning, and whenever you get to the office is fine."

I tossed a quick glance at Slade and then moved to the coffee maker.

While I prepared my morning caffeine fix—and boy, did I need it today—I leaned a hip against the counter. Cathy told me she'd called the hospital earlier, spoken to the nurse in charge, and that Nanny was resting comfortably.

"She wants out, though." Cathy smiled and took a hit of her own coffee. "She's already called Doc Harper's office demanding to be released ASAP."

"Not surprising. She hates hospitals as much as Mo does."

"No lie. Look." She put her coffee mug into the sink. "I need to get to my office. I've got a meeting scheduled. We need to come up with some kind of game plan for Nanny before she'd officially discharged. Figure out how we're going to handle the next few weeks with her."

" 'K. What are you thinking?"

"Doc Harper suggested she could be admitted to Angelica Arms for a few weeks until she heals. That way the staff can keep an eye on her all day without us having to change all our schedules around. When she's healed, she can decide if she wants to stay there or come back home."

"She's never gonna want to stay there permanently."

Cathy nodded. "Maybe. But it's something to think about it. We'll talk more about it tonight. I'll call you and Mo as soon as I'm free." She bussed my cheek and turned to Slade.

"Thank you," he said to her and put out his hand to shake it.

For what?

Cathy swiped his hand away and pulled him into her arms. "In this family, we hug."

Up until now he'd been stoic and unreadable. But when he returned Cathy's hug, his face broke into the most charming, free, and easy grin I'd ever seen on him. His dimples looked like face craters. For a brief second, my heart went all fluttery.

With a final "Call ya" tossed over her shoulder, she grabbed her briefcase from one of the kitchen chairs and left.

As it had been the night before in the car, the silence surrounding us was loud and unnerving.

"Colleen, look at me."

Reluctantly, I turned, my coffee mug still in my hand. I did as he asked and stared across the expanse of the kitchen at him. Like me, he was leaning against a counter, his hands dropped into his pants pockets. Even with his clothes somewhat rumpled and unshaven, he was the most handsome man I'd ever laid eyes on.

"How are you holding up with all this?" he asked.

I shrugged and then took a long gulp of my coffee, my gaze never breaking from his. When I was done, I finally gave a voice to my thoughts. "Did you sleep in your car last night?"

"Excuse me, what?"

I pointed my chin at him. "You were wearing those clothes yesterday. I thought you might have spent the night in your car."

One side of his mouth pulled up, that damn dimple on the same side caving inward. "They *are* the same clothes. When I got here yesterday, I hadn't planned on staying over. I slept at Maureen's."

"She had a room available? I thought she was maxed out."

Now the other side of his grin lifted, and all I could do was stare mutely at his morning hotness.

"She had one empty for last night, so I took it."

"Oh. Okay. So, why are you here? I mean, it's obvious it was to see me for some reason. The fact you showed up at my office when all hell broke loose proves it. But why did you stay over?"

"I did come up here to speak to you, but with

everything going on yesterday with your grandmother and Green, I thought it might be better to wait."

"Okay. So. You're here. What did you need to tell me?"

He pushed off the counter. The kitchen is as wide as it is long, so it took him a few strides before he stood square in front of me. Every movement of his body as he walked—no, make that stalked—to me was precise, focused, intentional.

Sometimes at night when I'm driving home from my office along the county road, which has no street lights, I'll see deer attempting to cross from one thicket of trees to the other. When my high beams light on them they stop moving, their eyes glaze over, and their bodies paralyze from the glare. I have to slam the car horn with the heel of my hand to jolt them off the road before I hit them.

And like those damn deer, I was held captive, paralyzed and hypnotized, in the power of Slade's gaze as he came toward me.

He stopped far enough from me that I had to tilt my head back to keep looking at him, but not so close that our bodies touched. The clean, fresh scent of the soap he'd used in his morning shower drifted toward me. The heat his body naturally generated warmed over me. "Before I tell you, will you answer a question for me, first?"

Only if the question is *will you run away to a deserted island and spend the rest of your life there with me, having wild monkey sex and eating coconuts.*

Of course I didn't say that. But I sure did think it.

"O-okay."

"Are you back with your ex?"

Of all the things he could have asked, this was his question?

"What? Harry? Good God, no. Why do you ask that?"

"You mean apart from the fact the last two times I saw you together you looked as if you were planning his murder, but yesterday you came out of your office with your arm wrapped around his, smiling and looking happy, and then he followed you to the hospital?"

Well, okay. He had me there.

I dragged in a breath and told him the same thing I'd told Cathy.

I didn't mention the reason Nanny had been hell bent on getting to my office after Harry appeared at our front door, but otherwise I explained why he'd shown up.

Slade stood, listening silently to my entire explanation, nodding at times, looking pensive at others.

"We were on our way to lunch when you arrived and Lucas called." A flash jarred my memory, and I added, "Oh, Charity put the roses you brought in water while I was at the hospital. You can pick them up this morning, and they'll still be okay."

"Why would I be picking them up? They were for you."

"Me?"

"Of course. Who did you think I'd brought them for?"

Before I could tell myself not to, I said, "Cathy?"

Slade blinked a few times and shook his head, as if clearing it. "Why would I bring your sister a dozen white roses?"

"I don't know. You told her thank you a few minutes ago. I assumed she'd done something for you, and this was your way of repaying her."

If that excuse sounded lame to me, I can only imagine what it sounded like to him.

"She did do something for me. Two things, in fact. But the roses were for you."

"Oh. Well. Thanks."

I lifted my cup again for a sip, but it was empty. I wanted to refill it, but Slade was standing in my way. What to do? Say, excuse me, and move around him and hope—*pray*—I didn't bump into him? Because I knew if I did, I'd drop the cup to the floor to free up my arms and slide them around him. Or make like there was still something left in the cup and pretend to drink it.

Neither option was appealing so I simply stood there, the stupid cup in my hand, silent.

"Don't you want to know what your sister did for me?" Slade asked while I debated my choices.

I looked back up at him. Whoa...had he moved even closer?

With a careless—at least I hoped it was careless—shrug, I waved my hand as if to say, "Go ahead."

"Well, you already know I asked for her help with the prenup."

The mention of the word left a sour taste in my mouth. I narrowed my eyes at him and frowned.

"But there's something else she agreed to help me with."

Okay, he'd definitely moved closer. My chest bumped against his when I took in a breath. He took the mug from me, placed it on the counter, and then bracketed his hands on the countertop I was leaning against, imprisoning me. I arched back, but I couldn't go anywhere. He had me trapped, something I believe he'd planned.

"Aren't you curious what I asked her to help me with?" His warm breath drifted over my face as he glanced at my mouth and lingered there a moment before moving back to my eyes. I gulped in a deep breath and this time my braless breasts came in contact with his hard-as-concrete chest.

I wasn't wearing any underwear under my pj pants, but if I had been, they would have been damp.

I opened my mouth to say something, but my brain didn't send any speech signals to my throat.

Slade eased closer, his gaze glued to mine, his mouth hovering over my own. I swallowed the lump trapped in my throat.

He whispered my name, and it briefly crossed my mind if I hadn't been pressed against the counter I'd had fallen to the floor in a puddle of want. My name on his lips was heaven to hear. When he pressed his mouth against mine once, twice, barely even touching, his eyes still open and locked on mine, I knew in my heart I was still in love with him. I'd tried to quell the feelings I had for this man for two weeks, and it had been for naught.

"Colleen," he said again. On a huge sigh, he laid his forehead against mine. "I've missed you. So much." Another breath. "So much. These last two weeks have been miserable."

I knew the feeling. "It hasn't been great for me either," I admitted.

"You don't know how happy that makes me."

"You're happy I've been miserable?"

His quick grin had my knees shaking again. "Yeah, because it means you've missed me, too."

With another quick kiss, he grabbed my hand and said, "Let's sit down. We need to talk."

"About what? At the risk of sounding repetitive, I think we've said everything we could possibly say to one another already."

"You're so wrong about that. Please, just hear me out."

That was the second time in twenty-four hours a man I loved had asked me to do that. If I'd given consideration to one, I needed to give the same to the other.

He grabbed the coffeepot and refilled my mug and then his own while I sat at the butcher-block table my parents had bought the first year they were married.

When he was seated opposite me, he reached across the table and held one of my hands.

"You're doing that charming thing again," I said, shaking my head.

"How's it working?" With my hand in his, he worried my knuckles in that lazy way of his.

I wanted to tell him he was fogging my brain like he always did but thought better of saying it out loud. "So?" I said. "Talk."

After a few moments consideration, he did. "You said a lot of things the morning after the wedding I didn't understand. I've been thinking about them for the past two weeks, nonstop, and I finally realized something. Well, a few things, really."

"Like what?"

"First, I was wrong to go to Cathleen without telling you. My reasons were good ones, but I never took your feelings about it into mind. I'm sorry for that. And I'm sorry when you found out I dodged around the truth. Your point about lies of omission hit me hard."

"I was raised to believe they're just as bad as outright lying."

He nodded. "Obviously. So again, I'm sorry."

I believed him. "What else?" I asked. "You said you came to a few realizations, so what else?"

"That you'd misread my relationship with Katya."

"It's hard to misread someone's intent when they're wrapped around you like a cheap suit."

"I told you Katya's very physical. But there's something about her you don't know. Something I didn't think was my right to tell you." He stopped and pulled his cell phone from his pocket. "After we all got back to the city, I had lunch with her—"

"I know."

Crap. I was making an appointment with a behavioral therapist as soon as this conversation was done so I could learn some ways to keep myself from blurting out everything that shot into the front of my brain.

When he just gave me the signature Slade Harrington stare, heat shot up my neck and my cheeks burned. "There was a picture of you two. Online. On one of those celebrity gossip sites. I...I saw it."

His fingers squeezed mine. "Googling me, were you?"

"Don't let your ego get all swollen and pumped. I check those sites often to see which celebrities are getting married and what they're wearing for the big day. I consider it business research."

"Keep telling yourself that." He grinned. "Now, I

was saying Kat and I had lunch. When we were together, I related what you'd said to me and she told me, well, *ordered* is the better word, to tell you something about her which might change your mind about thinking we were having an affair."

"What?"

"Katya's gay."

"No, she isn't. She's been photographed with half a dozen of the sexiest-man-alive list."

He cocked his head to one side and smirked. "I told her you wouldn't believe me." He pushed a button on his phone and then hit the speaker icon. A second later we heard, "Slade?" The sexy, smoky voice with the thick middle-European accent was unmistakable.

"Yeah, Kat. I'm here with Colleen."

"Did you tell her?"

"I did. She doesn't believe me, just like I told you she wouldn't."

A string of foreign words spewed through the phone. I didn't need to speak Ukrainian to know the supermodel was annoyed.

"Colleen?" she said, only she pronounced the "O" phonetically, making it sound like she called me *Cole* with een put on the end.

"Hi." I squeaked the word, in a totally teenager fangirling way.

"What Slade told you, it is true. No big secret, but I do not publicize my sexuality to the world. Only to friends. Slade is very good friend. He has helped me make many—how to say? *Sound*?—investments with my modeling money. He is truthful. And good."

"Okay. Wow. Thanks for trusting me with your secret."

"No secret, just not for public, understand?"

"Perfectly."

"Good." Only is sounded like *goot*. "Now I'm hanging up. I am about to board a plane for Hawaiian photo shoot."

"Okay, Kat. Thanks," Slade said "I'll talk to you soon."

"Do what you promised, Slade."

When he pressed the end icon, he looked across the table at me.

"Okay, so that was…" I waved my hand in the air, unable to find the right word.

"The truth," he offered.

I looked down at the hand he still held. "It's my turn to apologize. I made an assumption, just like you said. It was wrong and, well, I'm sorry."

"Contrition looks good on you."

I lifted my gaze back to his grinning face and said, "Don't make me regret apologizing."

"I won't. Especially because I knew why you reacted the way you did." He pulled my hand to his lips and kissed the knuckles he'd been rubbing. Little sparks of lust flared along every nerve ending in my body.

"Oh?" I managed to say.

"You were jealous, weren't you?"

I tossed him a speaking glance. "What did I just say about your ego?"

"Is evasion a form of lying?" he asked. "Because if it is, I'm going to have to call you on it."

Is there anything as humbling as having your own words thrown back at you?

"You were, weren't you?" he pressed.

"Okay, yes. Yes, I was. Ridiculously so." I huffed

out an exasperated breath. "But so what? Like I said that morning, we want different things, Slade. Being jealous of something you can never have is infantile and unproductive, two things I don't want to be. You and I have no future together."

"You're so sure of that?"

"Well, yeah. You're the one who said he's never getting married because of your father's history, aren't you?"

"Yes. I did say that."

"Then there's nothing to discuss between us because I do want to get married. I want children and a future with someone who loves me enough to take a chance."

Suddenly, my night of no sleep hit me hard. Exhaustion seeped through my body straight to my bones. When I'm overtired, I tend to get weepy, and tears started swelling in my eyes. I'd already embarrassed myself more times than I cared to remember in front of this man, so I tugged my hand from his and stood. "Look, I need to get to work. Thanks for letting me know about Katya. Her secret is safe with me, but we're done here."

"Colleen, there's still something I need to tell you." He tugged on my arm and turned me to face him.

Lord, I could get lost in looking at him all day long if I let myself. "I don't think we have anything else to say to one another."

"You're wrong. So wrong." With his hands clasped around my upper arms, he dragged me closer. I didn't have the strength to stop him when he cradled my head and brought it to rest across his chest.

Okay, full disclosure. Even if I had the strength, I

wouldn't have moved away.

"When I figured out you were jealous of Katya, it gave me hope."

"What kind of hope?" My voice was muffled since I'd face-planted myself against his pecs.

"That you felt the same way I did about you."

I stopped breathing.

When Slade sucked in a deep breath, I did the same. I pulled away, still holding on to him. "What do you mean?"

With a touch so gentle those damn tears threatened even more, Slade ran a finger down my cheek. "I love you, Colleen. I think I fell in love with you that first day when you reamed me outside your office about my—to quote you—daddy issues."

I winced at the memory. "Not one of my finest moments," I said.

"No, you were right. I do have issues with my father's behavior, and it's affected me in ways I didn't even understand. That little talking smackdown of his you were witness to opened my eyes." He shook his head. "I've let his poor track record dictate my own behavior with women in so many ways. I've never let myself get close to a woman before, really love someone, afraid if I did, I'd be hurt, emotionally and financially, when it went south. Because I always expected it would, just like it had with my father."

"That kind of thinking is wrong on so many levels," I told him. "Everyone deserves to find love and be loved. Loving someone means taking a chance. The biggest one you'll ever take. But it's so worth it in the end."

"I understood that the moment you walked away

from me at the inn. I was terrified I'd never get a chance with you, to tell you and show you how I felt. How much I'd fallen in love with you and how I wanted—well, I wanted to be with you. Seeing you with your arm around Green yesterday almost did me in. I thought I'd lost that chance. That I'd never get another one to tell you how much"—he laid his forehead against mine—"how much I love you."

The truth was reflected in his eyes.

"I'm laying it on the line here, Colleen. Telling you something I've never told another woman and didn't think I'd ever say. You're such a big believer in the truth. Here's mine: I love you. Now, I need you to be truthful with me."

"About what?"

"Am I wrong to think you were jealous of Katya because you feel something for me?"

Nanny has about a thousand sayings she pulls out at opportune times. One of my favorites has always been *when given a choice, lead with your heart.*

So I did.

"I feel more for you, Slade Harrington, than I ever have for any other man."

He kissed the tip of my nose. "Any other man?"

I knew what he was asking, and I needed him to believe I loved him so much more than I'd ever really loved Harry. That little insight was driven home to me the day before, so I repeated myself. "Any. Other. Man. I love you, Slade. I love you. But I'm scared, too."

"Of what?"

"Where do we go from here? How do we make this work? Can we? We live hundreds of miles apart. We both have demanding, time-consuming careers. I don't want to make the same mistakes I made before, but I don't know how to prevent them."

A slow, tantalizing, wickedly erotic grin pulled at his lips. "About that," he said. "You never asked me about the second favor your sister did for me."

In truth, I'd forgotten all about it.

"Do you remember when you asked what I'd be doing if I didn't have to manage the company?"

I thought back to that conversation. "You said you'd like to practice law. Maybe teach it, right? Or teach economics?"

"Yes. And do you also remember when I told Janelle I'd been restructuring the company?"

"What I remember most is the terrified look on her face when she thought you were going to leave her without funds."

"One of my favorite moments this year," he said, with a grin. "Okay, well the restructuring is almost complete. Within the next month, the board of directors will be voting on a new plan for operation I've developed. If it's approved—and believe me, I'm going to do everything in my power to ensure it is—I won't be the one making all the decisions any more. The day-to-day operations will be divided up among different divisions, and my role will be mainly an advisory one."

"What does all that mean? And what does it have to do with the favor you asked Cathy for?"

"For one thing, I won't have to be based in New York anymore. Since I won't be running the business, I'm won't be chained to the city."

"And that means?"

He tightened his grip on my waist. "I can work—and live—anywhere I want to. Boston. London.

Heaven."

Okay, *what?*

I never got a chance to say it out loud because Slade rode right over my thoughts.

"And the favor I asked your sister was to speak to her old law-school advisor at UNH to see if they're looking for any law professors, either in a teaching capacity or on a visiting professor basis."

Oh. My. God.

"You should see the shocked look on your face. I can only hope it means you're pleased by this."

"Pleased doesn't even come close, Slade."

And it was true. No man had ever changed his lifestyle—heck, his whole life—for me before. I'd always been the one to change. With Harry, with my career, with my family. All the proof I needed that Slade truly loved me was in those actions.

"And who knows," he said, his eyes crinkling as he looked down at me. "If the position doesn't pan out, maybe I can hire out as muscle for a wedding planner. I had a kick doing it before. I think it would be fun again. And I personally know one who could use the added help."

"No lie, there," I said, grinning back at him. A moment later, reality burned through me.

"What does this all mean for us, Slade? What about marriage? Kids? I'm thirty-five years old. I can't wait around too much longer before motherhood's ruled out as an option. And I want kids. I always have."

"First of all, thirty-five isn't old by any standard."

"You're not the one with the aging and time-stamped eggs."

Again, rapid mouth syndrome takes over.

He laughed and hugged me. "I know I told you I was never getting married," he said. "But for the first time in my adult life, I'm going to admit my father was right when he said I deserved to have a woman by my side who I loved. I'd let myself forget how much he loved my mother when she was alive. I chose only to remember the times after she was gone. The quick marriages. The even quicker and more damaging divorces. It jaded me against marriage. Made me believe it was something I didn't want or need. But I also believe what my father said was true and if my mother hadn't died, they'd have lived a long happy life together. I want that, Colleen. And I want it with you."

"Slade." The tears finally swelled to a level that my lids couldn't contain them any longer.

He swiped his thumbs over my wet cheeks. "Happy tears?"

What's happier than happy? Joyous? Ecstatic? Whatever it was, that's what I was feeling.

I slid my arms up his amazing chest and wound them around his neck. "I love you," I told him right before I sealed it with a kiss.

"Please don't ever stop," he said against my mouth.

Chapter Twenty-Six

One month later

"She really wants to stay there?" I had to stop chopping carrots because I was so distracted with what I'd just been told I was afraid I'd chop something vital—like a finger.

Slade's eyebrows rose.

"Yup." Cathy's voice rang through the speaker on my cell phone. "She said living at the home was nothing like she thought it'd be. Twenty-four hour room service is what she likened it to, with people who got paid to make sure she was happy. She's in her glory. Plus she gets to see all her friends whenever she wants. No waiting for a ride from one of us."

"I thought for sure, once she was all done with her eye surgeries, she'd be chomping at the bit to come back home."

"You can confirm it for yourself when you see her tomorrow, but she's already asked me to start having you pack up her belongings. They're going to let her stay in the room she has now, right next to Tilly's."

"Wow."

"Look I've gotta go. I've got a meeting."

" 'K. Love you."

"Love you more. Bye, Slade."

"Bye."

Since my hands were occupied, he ended the call.

"I can't believe Nanny decided to stay at the nursing home."

Strong, warm, and loving arms wound around my waist. I leaned back into him, reveling in the soothing, yet arousing feel of our bodies touching. His hands knotted together over my belly button, corralling me.

"Maybe she thought it was time," Slade said against my ear right before he pulled it between his lips and nipped.

"Stop that. I've got a knife in my hand, and you're distracting me."

Full disclosure: I wasn't protesting very hard.

The warmth of his breath drifted over me as he chuckled. "Good. That was my intent." He lifted the knife from my hand, placed it on the cutting board, and then spun me around.

"I thought you were hungry?" I said.

He nuzzled my nose and grinned. "I am. For you."

And then he kissed me. I couldn't have stopped the contented sigh that pushed up from deep within me if I'd tried.

The past month had been…heaven. Heaven in Heaven, in fact.

Cathleen's law-school advisor had come through once he heard it was Slade Harrington who was looking for a position. He'd called immediately, offered him a teaching position, and Slade started next week. The drive to UNH was less than forty minutes from Heaven, and he'd be teaching two days a week. Slade's corporate restructuring had been given approval by the board of directors. He still owned the company, but it was going to be managed by other people who reported directly to him now. The dinner I was currently trying to make for us was a little celebratory one.

Last week, he'd moved most of his things into my house while he looked for his own place to stay. Since Nanny was still at the nursing home, I thought it would be nicer to have him around than staying at the inn during his search.

Since now I knew Nanny wasn't coming back, the thought to make Slade's stay a more permanent one blew through me. He hadn't mentioned marriage or anything else since that morning in my kitchen, and in all honesty, I hadn't given it a thought, either. I'd been crazy busy, as had he. Just having him stay with me, being able to come home to him every evening and spend time together was enough.

"Something's burning," I said, pulling away from him. Slade didn't let me go.

"Baby, that's me."

"Ha-ha. Let go. The chicken needs to be turned."

Instead of doing as I asked, Slade leaned over to the stove, turned the range top flame off, and moved the pan to a cool jet.

"What are you doing? That's not done."

"Don't worry about. We can go out to eat after if you want."

"After what?"

He didn't immediately answer me. Instead, he pushed me an arm's length away and held on to my forearms.

"Slade? What's wrong?"

"Nothing's wrong. I just need a moment."

His gaze dropped to the floor, and for an insane second, I got a strange feeling, almost a warning. He was going to call it quits between us. After spending so much time together lately, he'd realized he really didn't love me; he didn't want to waste any more time with me.

As if I'd been doused with a bucket of cold water, I went numb from head to toe.

Slade lifted his head back to me. That signature, penetrating stare was back in place as he regarded me.

I swallowed when he took a breath.

Here it comes. The brush-off. I willed myself to stay calm, to keep my mouth—for once—shut. I wouldn't fall apart. I wouldn't.

"Colleen—"

"Oh, sweet Jesus, you're breaking up with me, aren't you?"

So much for staying calm and silent.

"*What?* No. God, no. What put that into your head?"

"You're as serious as a heart attack, and you tell me you need a moment. I thought you were preparing what you needed to say to let me down gently."

With his head cocked and his hands now fisted on his hips, the line between his eyes turned into a crater. "Stop. Just stop thinking for one second, will you?"

I batted my lids to try and chase the looming tears back.

Slade watched me for a second, then nodded. With another deep breath, he took my hands in his and dropped to one knee.

"Oh. My. God!"

"Stop talking, too," he commanded.

For once in my life, I did as I was told without arguing.

"That's better. I'm only going to do this once in my life, and I'd like to get it right."

"Okay."

"What did I say about talking?"

If I'd had a needle and thread, I'd have sewn my mouth closed.

Again, he waited a moment to see if I'd keep my word.

"Colleen, I never thought I'd be lucky enough to be in this position. And before you say something, no, I don't mean kneeling in your kitchen."

Okay, forget sewing. Glue. Glue was better.

"I never thought I'd be so crazy in love with anyone that I'd want to spend a lifetime with them. These last few weeks together have been the happiest I can remember. I've never felt so—well, *blessed* sounds corny, but that describes it just right. From the first day we met, you stirred up so many emotions inside me I couldn't think straight. And when I was thinking, it was about you."

Those tears? Yeah, they were waterfalling down my cheeks now, and there was nothing I could do to stop them. I couldn't even swipe at them because Slade was holding my hands.

"You're an amazing woman in so many ways. You're savvy in business, you love your family unconditionally, you're strong and funny and as exasperating as hell at times."

It really said a lot about me that I was able to keep my mouth shut with that line.

"You're all that and so much more." He stood, let go of one of my hands, and reached around to his back pocket. "But there's one more thing I want you to be."

He pulled back his hand. An iconic blue box sat in it. "I want you to be mine. Forever." With a flick of his thumb, he opened the box.

I had to squint against the brilliant light bursting forth from inside it. Even through the haze of tears, I was blinded.

"Will you marry me?" Slade asked as he dropped my hand and pulled the ring from its resting place.

I squealed when he held it up to me.

"*Slade*. How did you know?" I asked, because the ring? It was the one I always dreamed about having. Two brilliant carats, square cut, set in platinum. Perfection.

"I have my ways, but I didn't hear an answer, Colleen."

"Yes," I said. Okay, it was more along the lines of a scream if truth be told. I threw my arms around his neck and rained kisses all over his face. "Yes. Yes. Yes. Ten million times, yes."

"Okay." He laughed and hugged me close. "I believe you. Here." He slipped the ring on my finger.

"How did you know my size? Or that this is the ring I've always wanted?"

"Like I said, I have my ways. So, you like it?"

"No. I love it." I held out my hand in front of us, admiring it from every angle. "And I love you. Now. Forever, and whatever comes after that. I love you, Slade Harrington."

His smile took up most of his face. "Love you more," he said back.

A word about the author…

Peggy Jaeger writes about strong women, the families who support them, and the men who can't live without them. When she isn't writing, you can find her cooking, painting, or reading. She loves to hear from readers on her website:

PeggyJaeger.com

and on her Facebook page:

https://www.facebook.com/PeggyJaeger.Author